"SO THAT'S YOUR GAME, IS IT, CHRISTIANNE?"

James laughed, his fists on his hips, his green eyes merry.

"Game?" she echoed weakly, her heart suddenly racing.

"I would wager a hundred crowns that you intended my attempting to ravish you, so that you—with a clear conscience—could break your sworn promise not to escape."

He was a devil, in truth, Christianne thought, numb with disbelief. He had plucked her very thoughts from her mind!

James noticed her deflated expression and the unshed tears that swam in her long-lashed, deep blue eyes and felt a stirring for the little wench. With a smile, he leaned over and pressed his lips to hers, intending but a brief, teasing kiss to restore her pride. But her response took him completely by surprise as her slender arms instinctively rose to clasp about his neck.

Christianne quickly realized that a kiss was not, as she had always supposed, a thing of lips alone. Hardly! It did strange things to the breathing, made her blood course through her veins—like a racing river of fire . . . .

EXCITING BESTSELLERS FROM ZEBRA

STORM TIDE   (1230, $3.75)
by Patricia Rae
In a time when it was unladylike to desire one man, defiant, flame-haired Elizabeth desired two! And while she longed to be held in the strong arms of a handsome sea captain, she yearned for the status and wealth that only the genteel doctor could provide — leaving her hopelessly torn amidst passion's raging STORM TIDE . . . .

PASSION'S REIGN   (1177, $3.95)
by Karen Harper
Golden-haired Mary Bullen was wealthy, lovely and refined — and lusty King Henry VIII's prize gem! But her passion for the handsome Lord William Stafford put her at odds with the Royal Court. Mary and Stafford lived by a lovers' vow: one day they would be ruled by only the crown of PASSION'S REIGN.

HEIRLOOM   (1200, $3.95)
by Eleanora Brownleigh
The surge of desire Thea felt for Charles was powerful enough to convince her that, even though they were strangers and their marriage was a fake, fate was playing a most subtle trick on them both: Were they on a mission for President Teddy Roosevelt — or on a crusade to realize their own passionate desire?

LOVESTONE   (1202, $3.50)
by Deanna James
After just one night of torrid passion and tender need, the dark-haired, rugged lord could not deny that Moira, with her precious beauty, was born to be a princess. But how could he grant her freedom when he himself was a prisoner of her love?

Available wherever paperbacks are sold, or order direct from the Publisher. Send cover price plus 50¢ per copy for mailing and handling to Zebra Books, 475 Park Avenue South, New York, N.Y. 10016. DO NOT SEND CASH.

BELOVED SCOUNDREL

BY PENELOPE NERI

ZEBRA BOOKS
KENSINGTON PUBLISHING CORP.

ZEBRA BOOKS

are published by

KENSINGTON PUBLISHING CORP.
475 Park Avenue South
New York, N.Y. 10016

Good luck she is never a lady
But the cursedest queen alive!
Tricksey, wincing and jady,
Kittle to lead or drive.
Greet her—she's hailing a stranger!
Meet her—she's busking to leave.
Let her alone for a Shrew to the bone,
And the hussy comes plucking your sleeve!

—Rudyard Kipling.

Prologue

Capt. James Mallory tilted back his tricorn and whistled through his teeth. By the gods, he thought, grinning, Lady Luck has indeed smiled on you, Mistress Nellie Flagg!

Before him rose the white-columned facade and polished wood portals of the fanciest bordello he had ever seen—and he had seen many. Yet a discreet, red-shaded lantern of highly polished brass was the only outward sign of the ancient profession pursued within. The many carriages drawn up to the stairs could have indicated merely an innocent ball or a pleasant musical evening inside, rather than numerous, hot-blooded young rakes in their pursuit of lusty pleasures. He rapped loudly with the brass knocker. The door swung smoothly inwards as if on oiled hinges. A gold-and-white-liveried footman barred his entrance.

"I would speak with your mistress," the captain said in a voice which brooked no refusal, one which his men knew well and obeyed without question.

But the mulatto footman was either dull-witted, or made of far sterner stuff than the crew of the *Fair Amanda*. He looked disdainfully down his nose at the tall, young captain, as if he found something amiss with his impeccably tailored coat and breeches of dark green, or liked not the high polish to his knee-high black boots.

"My apologies, sir, but the hour is late. Mistress Flagg has already retired—sir!" He hurried after the captain as James thrust impatiently past him and strode to stand at the foot of the curving staircase.

7

James Mallory, his booted feet planted firmly apart, his fists aggressively on his hips, threw back his russet head and roared, "Come out wherever you are, Nellie Flagg!"

Several heads, some male and others female, poked out of various doors leading off the hallway to peer at the cause of the disturbance. A bevy of scantily dressed lovelies, blonde, red-headed and brunette, all clad similarly in sheer, frivolous undergarments, came scurrying from all directions to gape at the dashing captain with speculation in their eyes. At last, a door was flung open above. It crashed back loudly on its hinges. All heads were upturned expectantly as a tattoo of heels clicked furiously along the landing.

"Oh, gawd!" muttered one young lady, "he's been an' gorn an' done it now, he has, mark my words!"

A red-headed whirlwind rushed down the stairs, a whirlwind who sported a cerise-pink wrapper hoisted up about her calves, revealing a neatly-turned pair of ankles.

"A pox on ye, ye scurvy, loud-mouthed swab!" the whirlwind shrieked. "Wot the bloody hell is all o' this ruckus down here? Can't a body get no sleep?"

James Mallory grinned, his sea-green eyes twinkling in the light from the chandelier. "The mouth of a sailor and the legs of a goddess! You've changed not a whit, Nellie, my sweet!"

The madam blinked. She gaped. Then she flew into the captain's arms with an earsplitting whoop of delight and a gaudy flurry of bright pink ruffles. "Glory be!" she exclaimed. " 'Tis the king of England hisself!"

"Aye, Nell, 'tis me!" James agreed with a smile. He set her down. "I came the minute I got word that you needed me."

"Aye, ducks, I knowed you would," Nellie said with a fond smile. "That loverly lad, says I, would never let Nellie down. He's too much of a proper gentleman for that, I says!" She grinned, then noticed the circle of amused

8

onlookers and bristled. "Wot?" she snapped, glaring at her girls, "Ain't you lot got work ter do?"

They turned away, hiding smiles. Many of them had felt the lash of Nellie Flagg's tongue, but she hadn't a cruel bone in her body, they knew well. One of the girls, a saucy, auburn-haired wench with an ample bosom, winked boldly and blew the captain a kiss over her shoulder as she flounced off.

Nell caught the roguish gleam of interest in James' eyes and grasped him firmly by the elbow. "We'll have none o' that yet! Let's go upstairs to me boodwar. We can talk there, private like."

The captain's eyes widened at the opulently — if somewhat flamboyantly — appointed room she led him into. Claret-colored velvet draperies fell in elaborate swags, fastened by gold-tasselled ropes over lacy, white under-draperies, A secretary and an armoire, both of heavy oak, flanked one wall; a long, curved chaise of French origins, upholstered in vivid crimson, flanked yet another. An erotic statue of the goddess, Aphrodite, draped strategically with a red-feather boa, winked knowingly in one corner. Nell waved the captain towards the brocaded chaise with a heavily bejeweled hand and jangled a bell-rope to summon a servant.

"We'll have a spot o' porter first, and then t' business," she declared, smacking her lips. "Aye, 'tis grand to see you again, Jamie, love!"

The decanter and crystal goblets were soon brought and Nell poured them both a hefty measure. They toasted their reunion.

"Well, ducks, what do yer think o' my place?" Nell asked, beaming expectantly as she came to perch beside him on the chaise.

He grinned, the grin spreading merrily from his lips to his eyes and crinkling the laughter lines there. "I would never have recognized it, Nell, not in a hundred years!" he said sincerely. "It is now the most elegant . . . establishment of its kind that I have ever seen."

"Ain't it just!" Nell chortled, enormously pleased. "I bet the old madam, that Yvette, do be turning cartwheels in hell, if'n she can see it! Aye, business do be right good, and Nellie Flagg do be getting rich as Midas, like wot I always said I would," she added proudly. "We got the prettiest doxies here in all o' New Orleans—an' the most expensive. The beds is well sprung, the piss pots emptied regular, an' the young ladies do love their work, they do! But—there's a little matter wot's botherin' me something fierce, love," she continued, a trifle sadly, James thought, "and it is on account of it I sent for ye."

James nodded gravely. "If I can be of help to you in any way, you know that I will, Nell," he promised, unusually serious.

"Aye, lad," Nellie nodded, "I know ye will, so I'll tell ye right now, an' get it off me chest.

"Well, as yer know, when I was forced to leave England, sudden like, nigh three years ago, I did so thinkin' all that were kin to me were dead and buried. Then about a month back, a letter arrived from London, addressed to me, care o' New Orleans. It were from me sister, Jenny, who I thought long gone from this world, not having had word on her in *eighteen* years! Fair blowed me away it did!" Nell took a long draft of her porter before continuing. "Now, our Jenny were a lovely lass, but a right hellion. When Pa died an' me mother kicked the bucket soon after, she used her looks to get into a fancy sporting house what catered to the gentry, not tryin' to make an honest livin' at first, as did I," Nell said with a little sniff. "I heard she took the eye of a nobleman, Lord Christopher Alexander, his name was, and that he'd set her up in a fancy house somewheres like a bleedin' princess. Word had it that she were in the family way, an' so I went looking for her, but it were as if she'd vanished off the face o' the earth. It bothered me something

10

bad, for a lass needs her family an' friends at such a time, as I know well, having once been in a like predicament myself," she murmured darkly. "But I never did find her, nor hear any more word o' her 'til this came." She withdrew a much-handled, yellowed sheet of vellum from her cleavage and held it out to the captain. "Read it, love," she urged.

James took the letter from her and unfolded it. It read:

November 7th, 1763

My Dear Sister Nell,

No doubt this letter will come as a shock to you, for I am sure you must have long thought me dead, not having heard from me these many years. I beseech your forgiveness, dear Nell, for not having written before, and knowing you were always of a generous heart, I am persuaded that you will give it, and answer my plea.

I lie at death's door, little sister, consumed, the physicians say, by a lingering fever of the lungs but I fancy 'tis not this, but a broken heart that ails me! I have vowed to cling to life until I have word from you, for you see, I have a child, yet young and full of vigor, who upon my death will be left alone and penniless amidst the vice and wickedness of London Town that you and I fell prey to. I beg you, Nell, if you are in any way able to do so, to come and fetch my little Chris and to take the sweet child away to raise as your own! I beg you to grant me this one, last wish, so that I may, with an easy mind, join my beloved Christopher in heaven. I await your reply with a hopeful heart and with much love,

Your fond sister,
Jenny (Flagg) Alexander
10 Darling Lane, London.

The writing was spidery and splattered with inkblots, but the anguish and fear behind the words was tangible. James looked up and was felled by what he saw. Nell, brave, feisty little Nell, was dabbing a lacy kerchief to her eyes and appeared to be crying. And little wonder, he thought heavily. The letter was dated four years past. The writer of that sad little missive would no doubt have succumbed to her affliction long since. "Now, don't, Nell," he said uncomfortably, at a loss for how to comfort her in her grief. "We sail on the morrow, and there is none whom I'd rather have aboard the *Fair Amanda* than yourself. I'll see you safely to England, never fear."

Fresh, loud wails resulted from these words. "Oh, no, lad, it ain't a berth I do be wantin', don't yer see? There's a price on me head in London Town, and I've no inclination t' be wearing a hangman's noose for a necklace, gawd no!" She doubled over with wracking sobs again.

"Then what do you want of me, Nell?" he queried, at a loss as to what she expected of him. "Name it and I'll do it, my word on it!" he vowed rashly. Anything to stop her tears!

Nell brightened miraculously, her tears wonderfully dispersed. She cocked her head on one side and eyed him craftily. "I just knowed ye would!" she crowed, clasping his handsome face between her palms and planting a smacking kiss full on his mouth. "Now, you fetch the lad t' me, and here's a purse with which t' see him outfitted proper afore ye return." She withdrew a velvet purse from somewhere, her garter, he fancied, and lumped it in his lap. "Now, I was thinkin' that if—"

"No!" James exploded, "Anything *but* that! I will give passage to you, or another of your choosing, but I will not play nursemaid to a snivelling babe, not long out of swaddling!" He paced angrily back and forth, his green eyes sparking, all but knocking the statue of Aphrodite flying with the ferocity of his movements. He realized suddenly that Nell's eyes had been quite dry when she'd looked up at

12

him. He had more than a suspicion that he had been set up by that wily little madam, be damned if he didn't!

Nellie sighed, deeply and mournfully. "Oh, well, if yer dead set against it, I 'spose there ain't nothing more t' be said, though t' tell the truth, I'm a wee bit disappointed in ye, Jamie, an' that's a fact! You gave yer word you'd do anything in yer power t' help me, and Amanda was always after saying wot a brave ye were, and how ye always honored yer word." She side-eyed him expectantly.

James scowled. Guilt elbowed its way into his anger. That crafty, red-haired baggage! She knew that name and the memories it recalled would squeeze his conscience! He and Amanda Sommers and Nell had gone through much together in New Orleans three years ago, and he had thought he loved Amanda before she'd married her Spanish Don, Miguel de Villarin, and returned to Spain with their infant son, Michael. Still, Nell had a point, be damned if she didn't. He'd told her to ask anything of him, and she had, and moreover, on second thoughts, it would not prove too difficult an errand. How much trouble could the little lad be?

He sighed resignedly. "Very well, Nellie you sly baggage. I'll fetch your nephew for you—or live to regret it!"

Nellie beamed broadly from ear to ear. "Gawd bless ye, love. I always knew ye were a man of yer word!" She stood. "And now, what say ye to sampling the fine fare my house do have ter offer? Will it be a dainty golden angel t' warm yer sheet, or a fiery señority with coal-black eyes t' fire your blood? Name yer choice, love, an' she's yours, compliments of Nellie Flagg!"

"Ah, no golden-haired angels nor fiery señoritas for me this night, Nell," he declared, his green eyes gleaming wickedly. "I've a mind to tame me a red-haired vixen this night. There was one below that caught the . . . eye!" He winked lustfully.

Nellie laughed and elbowed him in the ribs. "Men! Bless

13

your hearts, you do be all the same, no matter captain or king, lawyer or locksmith, an' that's the truth! A juicy pair o' teats and a fine broad rump, that's all ye ask—an' our Sylvie's bodice do be fair overflowin' with her treasures! Come along then, Jamie, love, I'll see ye bedded right well afore the morning tide, or my name ain't Nell Flagg!"

One

A light flurry of snow swirled over the London wharves as James strode down the gangplank of the *Fair Amanda*. He looked about him. His cargo had been signed over and unloaded, his crew released for a few days liberty with their pay jingling in their pockets. Now he was free to hire a carriage and go in seach of Nell's nephew—if he could find a hack, that was, for though it was but a little after noonday, the wharves were all but deserted, and few masts forested the Pool. A bleary white sky hung over the old city, promising that the light snow flurry they were now being blessed with intended to continue and worsen. His fur-lined cloak pulled warmly about him, the captain set off across the cobbles in search of a hack.

A roasted-chestnut seller, an old man with a bluish, pinched face, tended a brazier on a nearby corner, and James slipped him a farthing in return for some of his piping hot fare. He juggled the chestnuts from hand to hand in a vain attempt to warm his fingers as he strode along. The backstreets here were lined with taverns and grogshops, counting houses, warehouses and money-lenders' places of business. From the taverns that he passed, warm air billowed out, welcoming and scented with pork pies and draft ale. He looked up and down the street. There was still no sign of a coach for hire. Muttering a curse on the weather, he turned into one of the taverns, the Golden Goose, the swinging sign above it said. A few minutes to warm himself and a tankard or two would hurt no one and

15

perhaps serve to take the chill from his bones as even the fur-lined cloak could not.

The buxom wench that brought the ale was a saucy one named Lucy, with inviting blue eyes and a merry laugh and a full-lipped rosy mouth. She put him in mind of Sylvie. Ah, Sylvie! He grinned over his tankard. That night three months ago at Nell's bordello had been a night to remember; in truth, the memory of it alone warmed him more thoroughly than the mulled ale! Still grinning, he perched his tricorn, still wet from the snow, atop his head, and looked about him. The tavern was crowded, the smell of ale and the fresh sawdust sprinkled on the bare wood floor mingled not unpleasantly with the odor of horses, human sweat and the pork and beefsteak-and-kidney pies the proprietor, a Mister Waller, had to offer his patrons. The wide hearth was crowded about by a few toothless old men and women puffing on clay pipes and gossiping noisily as they warmed their old bones, while a great, black kettle spat and sizzled on the hob.

The mulled ale spread its heat through him. With a regretful wink at the saucy tavern wench, he got to his feet, picked up his cloak, and headed for the door. First, he'd find himself a hack, and off to Darling Lane in search of Nellie's nephew. Then, all being well, it would be a fine inn like this for them both and a hot supper, by God, he vowed! This weather could freeze over the fires of Hades, that it—

"Rogue!" he roared suddenly, leaping after the slippery urchin who'd snatched his cloak. "Come back, lad, or 'twill be the worse for you!"

He dived through the door in the nick of time to see the lad disappear around the next street corner. The frigid air took his breath away as he rushed down the narrow, cobbled streets, his booted feet slithering and sliding on the hidden, icy spots beneath the fresh snow, still falling heavily and blanketing everything in soft, white flakes. He hurried around the corner. The lad was gone—and so, perforce,

16

was his cloak!

He stormed up and down, combing the nearby streets that riddled the wharf area like wriggling maggots, in and out, back and forth, to no avail. He hugged himself, shivering with cold in his coat and breeches and leather jerkin, while cursing the thief in every language and with every rich and colorful curse he could recall, which, being a seafaring man, was many. He might as well give the cloak up for lost, he realized, tight-lipped and furious, and go back to his ship for another. Yet as he made to cross the street, a coach came barrelling down it, the horses' hooves ringing sparks on the cobbles. James leaped back out of its way. He looked up to see, clinging cockily to the rear of the elegant vehicle while sporting his cloak, the very lad who'd made off with it! Furthermore, as they passed, the boy cheekily thumbed his nose at James! His blood boiled. Rage tightened his jaw and gave a fiery emerald glint to his sea-green eyes. "By God," he growled, gritting his teeth," I'll catch you, you little knave, if it takes 'til doomsday morn!" He looked hurriedly about him. Dame Fortune be praised! A hack was coming down the street, the driver dozing on the perch.

James sprinted towards it and rapped on the cab, waking the man as he swung himself inside. "Lay on, driver! Follow that coach and quickly! There's a sixpence in it for you if you catch him, man!" he roared, slamming the dilapidated door shut.

The driver jerked to life at the mention of the sixpence. He cracked his whip across the old horse's back. "Geet up there, Sal!" he bellowed, "geet on up, gal!"

The coach careened down the street in pursuit of the other vehicle. Houses and bay-windowed shops flashed by. The quiet streets now echoed the furious ring of twin sets of hooves on the snowy cobbles, the shrill, protesting whinnying of the horse, old Sal, and the thunder-like rumbling of the coach's wheels. James craned his neck out

17

of the window to see as the hack jolted violently around one corner, drew it in the nick of time as the vehicle cut savagely close around another, throwing him clear across the shabby interior. The jolting continued for several hundred yards more, then the hack slowed and finally halted.

James leaped down to the cobbles and strode angrily to the driver. He glowered up at the man. "Why, in God's name, have we stopped?" he snapped curtly.

The driver shook his head apologetically. "The—the other carriage, I done gone and lost it, fine sir," he stammered, "and old Sal is all but winded."

"The lad, the lad in the blue cloak—what of him?" James queried hurriedly.

The red-faced driver chuckled. "Ah, that 'un! He jumped off, he did, little blighter! If it were him you was after, sir, you shoulda told me," he reproved.

James nodded gloomily. "Yes, my friend, I'm afraid you're right. Tell me, do you know Darling Lane? Is it close to these parts?"

"Aye," the driver nodded, " 'tis not far, sir. A few minutes and I'll have ye there, right as ninepence."

"Good!" James declared. "Do so, and the sixpence will yet be yours for your trouble."

He sat back as the coach rumbled on at a more sedate pace. The snow was falling heavily now, blanketing the rooftops and chimneys, and the old vehicle was drafty. James pulled up his shirt collar and slumped down in his seat, his arms wrapped around him and tucked under his armpits in a vain attempt to get warm.

Pedestrians, muffled to the earlobes in greatcoats and gloves, beaver hats, fur-lined hoods, muffs, boots and scarves, hurried along, heads down against the weather. Small children, equally bundled up, their cheeks apple-red with cold, their button noses like cherries, tugged toboggans through the streets, headed for some nearby hill.

A group of carollers had congregated on one street corner, he observed, and the hearty rendering of "Good King Wenceslaus" rang out as the carriage rumbled past those hardy souls braving the snow. The houses in this area were much grander, James noticed, than those closer to the wharves, and candles lit their diamond-paned windows with welcoming light. The white sky was now an amethyst hue as night began to fall, for all that it was but three o' the clock or thereabouts, he judged.

"Darlin' Lane, sir!" the cabbie sang out. James swung down from the hack, fumbling in his pockets with numbed fingers for the silver sixpence he'd promised the driver. It was only then that he discovered that his pocket had been picked, too, along with the stealing of his cloak.

"My good fellow," he told the driver through narrow, furious lips, "the lad that stole my cloak made off with my coin, too boot! If you will wait here while I conclude my business, I will see you paid when we reach my ship."

"You've no coin t' pay?" growled the driver, an ugly, mottled look on his ruddy face. "Arter I all but burst ole Sal's heart in chasin' arter that bloody coach?" He lumbered down from his perch, wheezing heavily, his meaty fists balled. He swung a punch the very second his feet touched the crisp snow.

James ducked smartly and the blow sailed over his head. He was loath to fight the fellow, for he greatly sympathized with his anger. "Look, cabbie," he began, dodging blows, "go down to the wharves, seek out the *Fair Amanda* there and her first officer, Mister Wright. Tell him Captain Mallory sent you. He'll see you paid for your trouble. Come on, man, be reasonable!" James urged as the fist whistled across his jaw. The glancing blow reeled him sideways.

"Aye," the irate cabbie snarled," and meanwhiles, you'll scarper, and there'll be no bloody ship when I gets there! Captain, my arse!" he laughed nastily. "You don't look like no bloody captain ter me!"

"Come on, man, don't force me to fight you! You are in the right, and I'll see you paid, my word on it," James vowed, but the cabbie swung at him again nevertheless, and James, murmuring an apology, hooked him back with a fist of oak. The cabbie grunted, an astonished expression on his ruddy face, and folded to the snow. James hefted him into his hack and took off down Darling Lane without a backwards glance, sucking his stinging knuckles.

The townhouses in this quiet lane had once been fashionable places of residence, he saw, the type of discreet, secluded area where married gentleman set up their light-o'-loves and spent a night or two or a week's end here and there in a semblance of connubial bliss. But now the area had gone to seed and the houses bore an air of genteel neglect, as witnessed by a broken shutter here and there, or a roof sadly in need of repair. The address that he sought, number ten, was the last in the row, and the most sadly neglected. The gardens, though devoid of leaves and grasses in this month of December, appeared jumbled and overgrown despite their covering of snow. The walls themselves were in need of replastering and the leaded casements were cracked and missing several diamond-shaped panes. The rusty wrought-iron gate groaned fiercely as he swung it open and strode up the front pathway.

He frowned when faced by the front door, his hand poised to knock. Surely no one lived here? Yet if not, what had happened to Nell's nephew, and how, in God's name, was he to find the lad in a rabbit-warren city such as London? Shrugging, he hammered on the peeling door. He would face that problem when he came to it. He had promised Nell he would find the boy and he would, one way or another, he vowed. He was a man of his word, and honor was at stake here. Yet no one answered his knock.

He went back down the path and looked up at the house. Ah, yes, he had thought so! A thin spiral of smoke curled

20

up from one of the chimnies, barely discernible against the darkening sky but there, nevertheless. Someone was inside, of that much he was now certain. He retraced his steps and hammered again at the door. Again receiving no answer to his knock, he turned the iron ring doorhandle and stepped inside, his hand clasped loosely over the hilt of his sword.

He stood in a spacious hallway. Beyond, leading off it, were several doors, all closed. A graceful staircase swept in a wide curve to the upper story, its once-lovely, ornately carved balustrade now chipped and sagging. The window sills were coated with a heavy layer of grime, and cobwebs festooned every alcove. The worn carpet beneath his boots was threadbare to the point of having sprouted numerous holes. And yet the customary feeling he associated with empty houses was not there; that feeling of loneliness within, that indescribable but palpable air of bereavement a house bore when deserted, was absent in this house. He cocked his russet head on one side and listened intently, the cold forgotten for the moment. Yes! There it was again, that faint, persistent scratching! He started down the hallway, headed towards that sound. If he was not mistaken, the noise seemed to be coming from the room with the chimney from which he had spied the smoke rising. He pressed his ear to the door. Aye, there it was again! It sounded as if someone were raking coals into a coal shuttle. He drew himself up to his full height, turned the doorknob and flung open the door.

He caught a glimpse of a pair of astonished faces before a blow felled him. He crumpled to the floor with a slight, bewildered grunt.

Two

James came to with a groan. The back of his head felt like it was afire, and twin devils hammered anvils in his skull. "Confound it!" he grumbled, opening his eyes. The sight he saw made him gape.

Two faces loomed over him, faces straight from the gates of purgatory itself! One was sooty black, with a wide slack grin, few teeth and red-rimmed, bloodshot eyes of indeterminate color that leered at him evilly. The second face, no less horrific, was wide and pasty white, with enormous lumps and hairy warts sprouting in all directions, surmounted by straggly mouse-brown hair! James shuddered and blinked, trying to rid his vision of the horrible pair. Yet, they lingered. He gingerly turned his head. An old crone, clad in an assortment of rags of varying and vivid colors, crouched by the grate, feeding the meager fire with small pieces of kindling. A collection of broken furniture limbs — legs, arms and a seat or two — was piled to one side of the hearth, and as he watched, the crone extended a claw-like hand and set a splintered leg upon the glowing red coals. Her hair was white, streaked with gray, and fell down past her shoulders. A grimy mobcap topped it. A long clay pipe jutted from between her pursed lips.

"Who are you people?" James managed finally, struggling to sit and clutching his head.

"He! He!" the sooty one chortled, nudging the warted one, "who are we, the fine gennelman arsks!" He slapped his thigh and hooted.

"Oo are we, indeed!" grimaced the warted one, winking horribly. "Why, we do be the residents o' this fine house, we do! What's it ter you, Master Long-Nose?" He glared threateningly.

James scowled. "If you are the residents, then I'm the king!" he growled. "Let me up, damn you!"

"Nay, not yet, fine sir," the old crone cackled, coming to join the other two. "First, we'll have yer word you mean us no harm, see, and then, yer sword! Unbuckle it slow, lad, an' no tricks, else I'll be forced ter brain ye!" She brandished a wicked-looking poker to add further weight to her words.

James snorted in disgust. "No man—or woman—takes my sword unless by force. I mean you no harm. Now, let me up!"

The trio exchanged looks, then stepped back. James lumbered to his feet, his sea-green eyes crackling with anger, his reddish-brown hair dishevelled. He retrieved his tricorn from the bare boards and dusted it off. Three pairs of eyes followed his every move.

He glanced quickly about him. The room had apparently once been a withdrawing room. Tattered remnants of velvet draperies still clung to the dusty windows, the broken panes of which had been stuffed with rags to keep out the wind. An overstuffed chaise, bursting in places, had been set before the mantelpiece and some filthy blankets had been strewn across it. A table that sagged drunkenly with a broken leg was lodged against one wall, a stub of tallow set in a hardened puddle of wax directly on its scarred surface. A long-haired gray mongrel cowered in one corner, yapping fiercely as James turned his furious glare upon it.

"I ask you again," he said, gritting his teeth to assuage the pain in his head, "who are you people and what do you here? I am looking for Mistress Jenny Alexander or Flagg, whichever name she used, and her child. Do you know aught of them?" He towered over the trio.

The old crone looked shifty-eyed across at the other pair. She opened her mouth to speak, yet before she could, James heard the door slam loudly behind him.

"I'll answer him, Gran," said a young voice. "Jenny Alexander was my mother. This house is mine, and I'll thank you to leave it!"

James spun around to face the newcomer. His jaw dropped at the same time as the lad's, for he sported a fur-lined dark blue cloak that James knew well! "Thief!" he roared, diving for his cloak.

"Nay, not on your life!" the lad disclaimed, backing away. "You couldn't catch me fair, tho' I gave you the chance! 'Tis my cloak now, and I'll kill before I hand it over to you!"

Somewhat mystified by the boy's peculiar logic, the captain shook his head. "Nay, lad, not so. 'Tis my cloak and you stole it, as you did my coin." He said softly, "Give up the cloak, and there's an end to the matter. You may keep the silver." The lad, he'd realized, was a pale, fragile-looking creature, bony even, and the harsh winter winds would find easy passage through the threadbare knee breeches and short coat he wore. Yet to permit him to keep the garment would be to condone its theft.

"I'll not give it up!" the lad insisted, eyeing him sullenly. "And I give ye fair warning, sir, I've a dagger beneath its folds. If ye try to take it from me, I'll slice you from gullet to bowels!"

James smothered a grin. "You will, will you, lad? I think not! I've bested bigger fellows than you, aye, and with one hand tied behind my back! I have no cause to fight a babe, and I will not fight you. Hand over the cloak!"

The bright flash of a blade whistled past James' shoulder as the boy lunged forwards, flailing his dagger. James neatly sidestepped, grasped the boy's upraised wrist and squeezed. The dagger clattered harmlessly to the floor. Still maintaining his grip on that bony wrist, James bent down, picked up the dagger and tucked it into his belt. He grinned. "Now, what was it you were saying, lad?" he asked amusedly.

"You whoreson! You misbegotten, scurvy toad! Let me go!" the lad spat, writhing to free himself.

James held him easily. "Ah, lad, 'tis plain you are Nellie's nephew! I would recognize the family talent for conversation anywhere!" he laughed. His laughter changed to a groan as the lad cracked him heartily in the shins. "Blast you, boy!" he roared. "You've gone too far now, by God!" In a single move, he gripped the boy by the shoulders and turned him over his knee. Deaf to the lad's loud, indignant wails and curses, he warmed the seat of his worn breeches with a few well-placed, stinging swats with his strong right hand. At length, he stood the boy upright.

Tears ran down the urchin's grubby face, making clean rivulets in the grime, which he tried bravely to wipe away with a dirty hand. Stringy, mouse-colored hair fell past his shoulders. He glared at the captain, fury burning in his dark blue eyes. "I hate you!" he hissed, before turning on his heels and racing away down the hall and out of the house. The long-haired mongrel, still yapping, raced after him.

James stood, glaring after them with his hands on his hips. He had won, but the victory was a hollow one. He'd forced a mere child back out into the cold, December night with scant protection against the weather. Damn, he'd handled it all wrong! But the sight of that defiant, cocky young stripling thumbing his nose at him from the back of the coach had been just too recent in his memory for rational thought to take precedence!

"Well, what are you gaping at?" he growled at the odd trio.

The old woman coughed nervously. "Well, fine sir, you was after asking fer the Alexanders, were you not? Well, that young 'un do be Mistress Alexander's—"

"Son!" James remembered belatedly, groaning inwardly at his own stupidity. "Where would the lad go? Come on, you're companions of his, are you not? Tell me where to find him!" he urged, eyeing them in turn.

The three exchanged unfathomable glances. "First," the old crone said, "ye must tell us what ye want with the lad. If ye were arter him for swiping yer fine cloak, we'll tell ye naught!"

James shook his head. "Nay, I was not. I was unaware of his identity 'til now. You see, his mother wrote to her sister, Mistress Nellie Flagg of New Orleans in the New World, saying that she was dying and begging her to return to London to fetch the boy. I am the captain of a merchant ship, and Mistress Flagg is an old and dear friend. She asked me to find the boy, to bring him to her to raise as her own. That is why I am here. The lad, young Chris, will have a fine life with her. His aunt is a wealthy woman, and a good and kind-hearted one, at that. He'll lack for nothing with her for a guardian, I promise you," he explained.

"Mmmm," the old crone pondered. "Well, the mistress o' this house do be long dead, nigh four years now. That letter must have taken its sweet time reachin' yer friend! We've been lookin' out fer young Chris these three years past. The—the lad were close t' death hisself when we found him, sick and all alone in this great old house. We've grown a mite fond o' the child, sir. We wouldn't be happy, no, not at all, if ye was t' treat him harshly!" she threatened, waving her pipe at him.

James was touched by the concern in their ugly faces. "On my word, I will not be harsh with the boy, though if I find him he will be disciplined when needs be. I am a fair man, I fancy, and you need have no fear that I will be cruel, however." He eyed them earnestly.

The old crone appeared convinced by his sincerity. "Then we must wait, sir! You'll not find him, not if ye was to search fer fifty years! The lad do be highly tempered, and he's run orf afore this. But he'll be back, never fear. He always comes home. Always," she vowed.

James nodded. "Very well. We'll wait, Mistress—?"

"Gran, love. Granny Rags, folks do call me, on account o' me fine clothes!" she cackled, primping her grizzled looks. "This one here do be named Lumpy Jack, on account o' his lumps"—her faded brown eyes twinkled— "and the other's named Coalie Joe, on account o' he used to work fer the coalyards. And yer name, lad, wot be it?" Granny Rags inquired, puffing on her clay pipe.

"James Mallory, Gran," James replied, inclining his head. "Captain of the *Fair Amanda*, and honored to make your acquaintance!" He grinned at the three of them, and the two men nodded eagerly.

"And us, yours, Cap'n," Coalie Joe wheezed, extending a grimy hand, which James clasped unhesitatingly. "Have yerself a seat and a warm at the fire while ye wait. If you do be lucky, young Chris will not be long."

The captain nodded and took the seat offered him on the sagging chaise. The fire was burning merrily, casting leaping giant shadows on the walls and warming the room as the blazing chair leg snapped and crackled, sending sparks flying up the chimney. Granny Rags set a black pot on a hook over the fire and cast pungent chunks of onions, turnips and leeks into its depths. In the half light, she looked, James thought, incredibly witch-like. She turned a toothless smile on him, and sat back on her haunches.

"There, my fine captain!" she pronounced, "Supper do be a-bubbling! 'Tis a right tasty brew of herbs and the like, wiv a wee bit o' mutton tossed inter the pot, for good measure. You'll honor us by sharing our supper?"

He gulped and nodded. "Aye, madam, with pleasure," he accepted gallantly, but with little enthusiasm. The stew smelled rich and savory, but he wished to God she had not said "brew" when referring to it! He stretched out his long legs to wait.

Three

James supped the mutton stew hungrily. Despite Granny Rags' eccentric appearance, he had to admit, albeit grudgingly, the old crone could cook!

He licked his lips and fingers appreciatively, there being no cloths on which to wipe them, and set his trencher down upon the floorboards. "My thanks, Granny," he pronounced, "it was a meal fit for King George himself!"

"Aye, lad," Granny Rags agreed, staring fixedly at him. " 'Twas the kind o' supper that put yer in mind of a good night's sleep, content and full-bellied, were it not." Her voice was low, soporific in tone. Her eyes held his like watery magnets.

James nodded, staring fixedly at her, aware now that a strange stupor was stealing over him. Even as he looked at the odd trio, their features blurred and grew indistinct. He tried to stand, but his legs would not hold him, and all of a sudden his arms felt weak and without strength. He flicked his head to clear it, to no avail. The trance-like state worsened. "Wh—what . . . about . . . Chris?" he mumbled thickly. "Je—Jenny Alex—ander, wha—what about—?" His head slumped forward on his chest and a loud snore buzzed from beneath his tricorn.

"He do be out!" Granny Rags chortled with satisfaction. "He'll not waken 'til the morrow, and by then, me lads, we'll be long gone!"

Coalie Joe nodded. "Aye, Gran. But why was it ye slipped the powder in his supper? Young Chris could have a fine life

28

in the New World, if what the cap'n says be true!"

"But it ain't, don't ye see, Coalie?" Granny hissed, puffing excitedly on her pipe, "for if it were, he would have *knowed*, don't ye see, about Chris! He would have knowed it all!"

"Ah!" Coalie grinned in understanding. "Ye are a right crafty old wench, Granny! I never thought o' that!"

"Aye!" Lumpy echoed, rubbing a hairy wart that sprouted alongside his nose. "The young cap'n were lyin, 'tis clear as day to me now!"

Granny flashed them a gummy grin. "Right! Now, let's get this here blanket out from under him, pack up our stuff and take t' the high road!"

Dawn was a great cat that slipped through the grimy windowpanes on cold, clammy paws. James shivered on the battered chaise. The demons were back in his skull once more, hammering on their anvils. A gnawing, dull ache clawed at his vitals. He groaned and sat up, rubbing the night's stubble on his jaw, and looked about him. The large, gloomy room was deserted. The hearth was empty, even the ashes gone! The scarred table was devoid of both tallow stub and wax puddle, the chinks in the windowpanes unstoppered of their rags. He frowned. Was it possible he had dreamed it all, conjured it in his mind? He stood and shuffled to the hearth. It was still warm to the touch yet. Nay, he had imagined nothing! What a fool the trio had played him for! "Never again," he vowed hotly, looking about him for his tricorn, but they had seen fit to divest him of it, along with his cloak. Thank God, they had at least left him his boots! Maybe they had proved too difficult to pull off, he thought with a grim, humorless smile.

He left the house without looking back, trudging through the crisp snow and cursing his stupidity as he went. The sun was up, a bleary, lemon-yellow haze behind a white sky that promised further snow. Servants were already about, shovelling the pathways clear or hurrying to the baker's for bread or buns with baskets over their arms, clogs clacking as they went. A sleigh, drawn by a sturdy dappled pony, swished past, bells jingling. The group of giggling young women inside it waved and called a friendly, "Merry Christmas!" as they passed, their smiles fading as the captain returned their greeting with a fierce, green-eyed scowl. Merry Christmas, indeed! he thought. What was merry about having to walk a good six miles across London with neither coat nor cloak, in weather cold enough to freeze your backside solid, he'd like to know? And all on account of that trio—nay, quartet, including that fiendish lad—of rogues! He'd been slipped a sleeping draft, he realized ruefully. His dark brown brows drew together in a frown. For some obscure reason, Granny Rags—if that was in truth the old witch's name—had seen fit to lace his portion of stew with a powder! His sea-green eyes narrowed. He'd find them, all of them, he vowed fervently. No one made a fool of James Mallory—and fool of him they had made, and royally!—without being called to account for it!

It was an hour's brisk walking before he saw the masts from the Pool above the rooftops and knew that he was nearing his destination. His pace quickened. Mister Wright, his first officer, was a good friend and a more than able officer, but somewhat of a worrywort. No doubt poor Ben would be sorely perturbed that his captain had failed to return to the *Fair Amanda* last night as promised, and was even now imagining him in the arms of some tavern wench, or hussy! *I wish that I had been*, James thought with a smile as he strode along. The smiled deepened. The dour Cornish officer considered no woman good enough for his captain, and more than likely never would.

He fought the hunger pangs in his growling belly as he passed the pie man on the street corner loudly ringing his handbell, crossed the cobbled street and started down

Harbor Lane. A beggar sidled up to him, a black patch covering one eye, one sleeve of his threadbare cloak hanging empty. "Alms fer the crippled, young sir?" he wheedled, a pitiful expression on his gaunt old face. James shook his head regretfully. "I've naught left in my pockets, old fellow," he apologized, hurrying on to the wharves.

Mister Wright, a stalwart, husky fellow with sandy hair and a worried expression on his homely face, hurried down the gangplank to meet the captain.

"Sir! I expected ye back long before this, sir! What happened? Where's the young Master Alexander?" He peered behind James.

James strode past him. " 'Tis a long story, Ben, and one best told over a tankard of ale and a trencher of hot victuals. First, fetch me another cloak, a hat, and a few guineas from the chest in my cabin."

Somewhat puzzled, Ben Wright nodded and did as ordered.

"Mullens!" James roared, pacing up and down the icy decks.

Silas Mullens, a small, wiry fellow and the bosun of the *Fair Amanda*, came at a run. "Aye, aye, sir!" he panted.

"Pipe the morning's watch abovedecks, Bosun," James ordered.

"Right you are, sir!" Mullens responded smartly.

The watch assembled before him, James took his place before them.

"I regret that there will be a delay in our putting back out to sea, men," he told them. "You are hereby given a few days more liberty. I have urgent business to attend to in the city, and will be gone for a few days." A cheer went up from some fellow, and James grinned. "In my absence," he continued, "I am entrusting the ship to Mister Wright, here. I want her provisioned and loaded, ready to sail by the morning tide of the twenty-sixth. For those of you that serve me well in my absence, I will effect a raise in rank and a week's extra pay at the end of our voyage. What say you?"

The men nodded and murmured their "ayes." They had been with Captain Mallory for nigh on two years and knew him to be an uncommonly fair man, a man of his word, and a worthy master of his vessel in all respects.

"What about them swabs what jumped ship, Cap'n?" asked Silas Mullens. "There'd be no crew for the sailing, if you were t' wait. There'll be plenty o' captains looking for men t' press into service if ye wait until after Yuletide t' find them!"

"Aye," James agreed thoughtfully. "Right you are, then, Mullens, go find replacements for us. Take Daniel Coombs with you, he's a good man, and mayhap Hardcastle, too. And Silas—I want volunteers, not pressed men, you understand?" he finished sternly.

Silas grinned. "Aye, aye, sir!"

After he had gone, Ben Wright hurried forward. "Here's your cloak, sir, and your hat. I—I took the liberty of fetching a coat, too, sir?" he asked with a worried frown. It was apparent, to the first officer's way of thinking, that his captain had been set upon and robbed, or more likely, fleeced by some pretty trollop while in his cups. He sighed heavily. It had happened before, in ports all over the world, and would no doubt happen again. In all respects, he admired his captain, save one: his frivolous attitude towards women! At times it seemed to Ben Wright that James was in love with the entire sex, bar none. And they, with very few exceptions on account of advanced age or addled wits, seemed to feel likewise about him. 'Twas a sad state of affairs, indeed it was, and he despaired of his handsome captain ever settling down with a good, honest woman of fine morals who was worthy of his otherwise admirable self.

"It was no lissome wench that robbed me," James said with a grim laugh, "but rather an old and conniving crow, so do not cast that gloomy look of disapproval on me, good friend! Aye, I can read your thoughts in your face, don't deny it!" he added, fastening the cloak's clasp. "Come, let's be on our way! There's a worthy inn not far from here, the Golden Goose, I believe it was called." He strode across the decks and back down the gangplank to the wharf with an eager stride.

Benjamin Wright smiled knowingly and followed suit. "I understand, sir," he murmured softly. "Is this one fair or raven-haired?"

"Neither, Ben, she's red-headed and a saucy, toothsome piece if ever I—!" James broke off, realizing he'd been duped into confessing his intent by the first officer. He grinned and slapped him heartily across the back. "You're a cunning fox, Ben Wright, but I confess, you know me well! Come, I will tell you what ills befell me since last I saw you, and mark you listen well, for the list is lengthy and plaguesome, to boot!"

James ran his hand across the generous globes of milk-white buttocks before him and grunted lusty approval. The wench rolled over and grinned up at him saucily.

"Ah, Lucy, my love!" he murmured, his green eyes roving the lush body beside him, "you are fashioned like a goddess!" He cupped a luscious, creamy breast in both large hands and flicked his tongue boldly over each swollen nipple.

"Goddess, now, is it?" Lucy giggled, stretching languourously to allow him easy access to her charms. Her hand ruffled the russet hair that curled crisply over his nape. "I never were called 'goddess' afore this, Jamie, love!" she purred, writhing on the rumpled pallet.

His hand trailed down to her waist, then across to stroke the silken plateau of her belly. "Aye," he murmured huskily, "the goddess of love!" His hands cupped the fiery red-gold bush at the junction of her strong white thighs, then were lost between them. His sea-green eyes were closed.

"Oh, sir!" Lucy gasped, wriggling in delight. "What a man you are! Oh! Oh!"

James laughed wickedly, burying his head between the valley of her ripe, full breasts. "And what a woman are you, Lucy!" he groaned, feeling desire rise up within him again like a swelling tide. Aye, the little wench *was* lovely, and fragrant as a field of newly-mown hay, with hair the color of autumn leaves, but a shade lighter than his own, and skin like clotted cream, tinted with roses. And, as he had said, she was fashioned like the goddess of love.

He lifted her onto him, pressing her down until he found himself buried fast within her strong, straight thighs. Her hair tumbled down in bouncing red-gold curls as she pleasured him, her full breasts jiggling madly, voluptuously, in a way that made him think of golden peaches on a wind-tossed tree. The lusty sight and scent of her, and the sound of her gasps and moans of pleasure sent heat coursing through him. He grasped her by the waist and arched powerfully upwards to meet her frenzied downwards thrusts, then gently rolled her beneath him and brought her to an explosive, shuddering release that turned the blue of her eyes to sapphire fire and her nails to talons and her moans to sated sighs. Yet still he was not done himself. Deeper he thrust, while her arms rose lazily to clasp about his neck and her strong legs locked about his lean, hard flanks to hold him fast. Her nails raked his broad back.

"Yes, oh, aye, yes, my lusty love!" Lucy whispered urgently. "Yes, my fine young captain!"

He ground himself one last time against her, shuddered and lay still after he had fallen to her side.

In the light of the flickering fire, there was a thin sheen of sweat dewing his forehead and upper lip, and his muscled, deeply-tanned shoulders gleamed damply in the light. Lucy leaned up on one elbow and brushed an unruly russet lock from his brow, running her finger along his high cheekbones and then down to trace the strong square set of his jaw. As her finger lightly brushed across his smiling lips, he growled and pretended to bite.

"Be still, mistress," he groaned, feigning exhaustion. "Was my loving not enough for you, you wanton vixen?"

"Ah, aye, sir, more than enough," Lucy murmured huskily, resting her head on his broad chest with its curling forest of red-gold. They had made love three times that night, and she had found more pleasure in the captain's arms than she had dreamed possible with any man, or at least, any of the many she had known date! All *they* had cared about was themselves, she thought, and never mind little Lucy! Jamie was different, aye, that he was! Why, in his arms, she'd *felt* like a blooming goddess of love, she had! She snuggled closer into the crook of his arm. "Will ye come again to see me?" she asked him hopefully.

"I might," he teased, looking across to the attic window. A bleary, pale blue sky filled the narrow panes. Another freezing day! He pulled the woollen blanket up over their heads, covering Lucy's thighs with his own leg slung carelessly across them. "And then again," he breathed in her ear, "I might never leave. We could hibernate up here like bears, and live on love until the first cuckoo sounds!" A soft giggle, followed minutes later by a warm, sleepy sigh, reached his ears.

He was almost asleep when a loud hammering pounded at the door. Lucy shrieked and leaped from the bed.

"Oh, Jamie, sir, 'tis my father, I know it!" she cried, casting about for her missing garments, tossed carelessly aside in the haste and heat of the night before.

James cursed and rolled from the bed, all but stepping into his breeches in the same move, and gathering up his own clothes with equal alacrity.

"Captain, sir!" bellowed a voice he knew well from

behind the door. More pounding. "Are ye in there, sir?"

James muttered an oath and flung open the door, buckling his broad belt as he went. "In God's name, man, of course I'm in here! What the devil is it?"

Wright's gray eyes flickered to Lucy, still only half-dressed and doubly charming in her wanton *déshabillé*. He coughed, reddened and looked smartly back to his captain. "Sir, ye asked me to waken ye at seven o' the clock, sir! The hanging is set for eight, and 'tis a fair ride from here to Tyburn flats."

James nodded, tucking in his full-sleeved white shirt. Last night, he had heard of the hanging to take place at Tyburn that morning. Though no ghoul, he had decided to attend. Executions attracted crowds, and crowds attracted cutpurses, pickpockets and trollops. If he were to find Granny Rags, Lumpy Jack and Coalie Joe—and thence Chris Alexander—in this rabbit-warren city, it was as good a starting point as any!

"Very well, Ben. Did you find me a horse?" he asked, pulling on his coat and then his cloak.

"Aye, Captain, and a worthy, spirited beast he is too, for a hired mount. He's saddled and ready for you, below in the stableyard."

"Right," James approved. "Give me but a minute more, and I'll meet you in the taproom."

Ben nodded and left. James strode across the room, lifted Lucy clear off the floor and kissed her soundly. "I must be off, sweet Lucy," he said regretfully, slipping a golden guinea down her bodice. "That is for you, my pretty, with my thanks for a night of sweet pleasures!" His eyes caressed her fondly.

Lucy smiled and shook her head, more than half in love with him already. "Nay, I don't want money, sir, not from you!" she whispered earnestly. "Will—will ye be back?"

He nodded. "Aye, sweeting, if I can. But take the coin, it would please me greatly. Purchase yourself a warm cloak against the chill—so I will not think of you shivering in this garret when I am far out at sea and unable to warm you." He smiled, and brushed the tip of her snub nose with his lips. "Until tonight, then, if I am able?"

She nodded and he left for the stableyard.

It was over three months since he had sat a horse, and the beast was spirited, as Ben had said. It circled nervously, snorting and stamping in the snow, until he was finally mounted.

He bade farewell to Ben, and turned the horse out into the cobbled streets.

Four

The snow lay gray and rutted on the cobbles and the crisp, cold air pained the lungs. The streets were busy and filled with the aroma of cooking as the people of London rose to break the night's fast. Ragged urchins shovelled the narrow pavements free of snow, and ladies in furred capes and muffs, their giant hoods pulled warmly over their bewigged heads, squealed in terror as two of the lads threw snowballs at the teetering, bell-shaped dames. The beggar was at his customary spot on the street corner, and James flipped him a threepenny piece, which he tested once in his broken teeth and slipped into a ragged pocket.

In one shop, James glimpsed a beefy butcher wringing the neck of a plump, white goose, and he realized with a start that there were only three days left to Christmas Eve!

His thoughts as he rode along turned to his family, as thoughts are wont to do at Yuletide. His father had passed away a little over three years ago, and only his mother and his sister, Caroline, younger than himself by almost seven years, lived at Havenoaks now. Havenoaks! James thought with a smile, a fine example of his father's dry humor. He had indeed found a haven there, from the English King George's wrath, and oaks aplenty, on the sprawling estates outside of Salem Town! Sadness gripped James momentarily as he rode on. He missed his father still, aye, they had been closer than men and their sons usually were. Richard Mallory had always been ready to listen, to give advice when asked and to stay silent when he was not. They had agreed on most things too, except on that one memorable occasion when James, a mere lad of sixteen, had calmly announced his decision to go to sea. James chuckled softly. The old man had nigh exploded! But after talking the matter through, he had realized that his son would not be persuaded from a seafaring life, and accordingly done his best to help him, even to the extent of having an old friend, Captain Lysle, take him on as cabin boy. And so it had begun, James thought, and he had never looked back, never regretted that decision to become a sailor, in all these years. Havenoaks and its wealth were now his inheritance, yet he was content to allow matters to continue as they had since his father's death, with the lawyers handling the estates and seeing that they were profitable and upkept as they had been during Richard Mallory's lifetime. His uncle, Lord Thomas Mallory, Father's older brother, deplored this state of affairs, but numerous letters had failed to bring his "wastrel nephew," as he had termed James, home from his beloved sea. Wastrel or nay, he had a tidy fortune amassed in letters of credit at his bank and a life he loved. He'd be a fool to want to change that!

He turned his thoughts now to the hanging. For two years, he had heard in the taproom last night, Michael Flynn, pirate and rogue, who it was rumored had gone by the name of "The Raven" while master of his ship, had languished in Newgate Gaol, awaiting trial. When it came, it had been speedy and his sentence without mercy. Captain Flynn had, during his infamous career of piracy in the Arabian Sea and along the West African coast, vowed many times that he was the bastard son of an equally infamous pirate executed some sixty years before, by the name of Capt. William Kidd. How this could be so, when Flynn was but a young fellow and Kidd had been in his dotage at the time of his death, James could not fathom. Yet the magistrate had obviously heard these same rumors and with merciless humor sentenced Flynn to the same death as Kidd: to be hung by the neck on the gallows 'til dead, his body to be exhibited in an iron cage until it had dried. After, his head was to be severed and impaled on a spike set by the Thames River, as a warning to all that piracy did not pay. James shuddered. He had had his share of run-ins with the dastardly pirates, as a merchant captain, and was a man of his time, used to a life filled with cruelties and hardships, yet no man deserved a death so utterly lacking in dignity.

He was nearing his destination now, for there were crowds all about, noisy and laughing. The atmosphere as he cantered across the Tyburn mudflats bore the tension and undercurrent of excitement he had learned long ago to expect at such gatherings.

Whole families had turned out, it appeared. There were mothers with squalling babes, bundled against the cold, and runny-nosed tots clinging to their skirts. Bewigged and powdered papas bore their young sons upon their shoulders, so that the lads might better view the gruesome spectacle. Street girls hawked piping hot pease-pudding, ladled up from kettles hung on yokes over their shoulders. The pie men in their white aprons and greasy jackets were there too, with their savory beefsteak pies dripping with gravy and wafting the odor of kidney everywhere in the damp, cold air. The muffin man was singing lustily in praise of his toasted and buttered fare. There were apprentices and shopgirls, greatcoats and capes hastily thrown over their aprons, and grand ladies who remained safely concealed in their elegant coaches as they awaited the exciting prospect of the hanging, and dallied with their lovers. It could have as easily been mistaken for a country fair on the common, James thought, as been recognized as a site where justice would supposedly soon be done! Tracts were being passed out, both religious and comical, some bearing bawdy verses in praise of Flynn's nefarious doings and sexual exploits, others condemning his soul to the flames of hell for his sinfulness. Peddlers sharpened knives and flaunted colorful ribands to the serving girls, or silken threads to their mistresses. A few dissolute young fops lolled, bored, against a pier, glimpses of elegant satin coats and breeches revealed beneath their cloaks as they pressed scented kerchiefs or pomanders to their noses, to keep out the stench of the rabble all about them like a sweating, unwashed sea. James' eyes scanned the crowd, but he could discern no sign of the trio that he sought, though there were many pickpockets and cutpurses in evidence, for barely a minute since his arrival had passed without a cry of, "Thief!" rising up from some unwitting spectator. The trollops were doing brisk trade too, for there was something about a hanging that excited lust in men and women alike. A celebration of life, James wondered, grinning? The tarts eyed James eagerly, their rouged and powdered faces, sporting velvet hearts and beauty spots, droll as mummers in the harsh light of day. He declined their services with a smile and thought with pleasure of Lucy. *There* was a wench who needed no paint or powder, who enjoyed a man between her sheets and never dreamed to pretend otherwise!

A great cry arose from the crowd as a colorful procession arrived and congregated about the wooden platform on which the ugly gallows stood, dark and ominous, before a wintry white sky. Michael Flynn, the condemned man, was on foot, surrounded by mounted guards, a priest, the hangman in his black hood and a drummer boy, having made the long trek from Newgate Gaol's foul confines, a lengthy march of some two hours. "The Raven" looked close to death already, his skin ashen with prison pallor, his shoulders shivering with an ague from the damp, vermin-ridden cell he had existed in these two years past. His hair, perhaps, had once been raven-black, but now was streaked with gray and white, which put James in mind of a badger. His nose was long and aquiline and gave an aristocratic cast

41

to his face, which was dominated by a pair of burning black eyes that looked out over the faces of the excited, noisome crowd with a mixture of despair and resignation.

Flynn approached his fate bravely; though shivering with sickness, he did not falter and took the thirteen steps up to the gallows without pause. The priest, robed in black, flapped up those steps behind him like a great, black crow, bending his beak eagerly over the manacled wretch to demand that he confess and make his peace before being dropped into eternity at the end of the rope.

The crowd roared madly with approval as Mick Flynn spat over the side of the gallows and refused, throwing their hats into the air along with the tracts to show their delight at his valor in the face of death. The drummer boy started his slow thrumming, while above his nervous beats the master-at-arms read aloud the crimes of which the prisoner stood accused and found guilty of, and for which he would soon die. The priest bent his ear once more to Flynn's mouth, hoping at the very last to extract his confession.

"Nay!" Michael Flynn roared, his voice surprisingly strong. "I am innocent! I asked no quarter of any man while I lived, and 'tis certain I am I will not ask it of God at my death. Let him be my final judge!"

The master-at-arms nodded to the black-hooded executioner, who lifted the noose over Flynn's head. An expectant hush fell over the crowd. All faces were upturned to the wooden gallows, their expressions eager, waiting. Children fidgeted nervously in the sudden silence. A babe wailed and was quickly hushed by its mother. Only the gulls' mournful mews broke the stillness.

The hangman kicked the ladder from beneath Flynn's feet. It fell to the mud with a hollow thud that was anticlimactic. A shrill, unearthly shriek rose from the condemned man as the rope tightened about his throat, but failed to break his neck. He dangled there, slowly strangling, arms and legs flailing grotesquely as he danced upon air like a ghastly marionette. A wet stain spread across his breeches' front, and the crowd hissed and booed their derision.

At a signal from the master-at-arms, the hangman stepped forwards once more. To James' horror, the ladder was propped beneath the frenzied pirate's feet once again, the faulty knot adjusted. For a second time, the crowd fell silent to a man, and all waited with bated breath. Again the ladder toppled but there was no inhuman scream this time. James looked back, disgust rising in his gorge, for Michael Flynn was quite dead now, his death mask frozen in the tortured grimace of his final agony. A sigh coursed through the crowd as the hangman cut down the dangling body, then several men-at-arms bundled it into a hideous iron cage. The cage was then suspended from the gallows. Gulls had already gathered on the masts and piers about the site, black eyes beady and gleaming in anticipation of the coming feast.

Sickened, James wheeled his horse away from the ghoulish scene. A few yards distant an ugly cur was advancing menacingly on a scruffy, long-haired little mongrel a quarter of its size, teeth bared in a snarl. The mongrel held its ground and yapped bravely at the much bigger dog. James made to ride past then reined in his horse. Was that the boy's hound? Aye, he was sure of it! It was the same mongrel he'd seen at the Alexander house on Darling Lane! He kneed the horse forwards at a mud-splattering canter across the flats, leaning low in the saddle and plucking the little beast into the air by the scruff of its scrawny neck. The animal rewarded his deliverer with a vicious nip on the hand.

"Ungrateful cur!" James cursed. " 'Twixt you and your master, naught but ills have befallen me." He cuffed the little animal, which stopped its wriggling and cocked its head on one side and eyed him curiously. Despite himself, James grinned. Though small, the dog was a game little fellow! He reached out to fondle its floppy ears but as he released the animal's scruff it sprang down from his saddle and scampered off into the crowd. Follow the dog and he'd find Chris Alexander, he was sure of it, he thought as he kneed his horse forward!

The pup led him on a merry chase far from Tyburn, tail held like the plume of an ostrich waved regally from side to side, small paws padding resolutely along the snowy cobbles, wet, black nose pressed diligently down to the scent. From time to time the dog would halt and look back in James' direction as if waiting for him to catch up.

The streets here were like an insoluble maze, twisting and turning in all directions between the mushrooming buildings. Refuse littered the open gutters and, despite the cold, slops of indescribably evil stench fouled the air; here, a dead cat, there a rat, stiff as a board with its feet straight up in the air. Further on he passed a pitiful, drunken old sot with a gin bottle pressed to her lips, and a pock-marked young bawd and a sailor coupling in a littered alley like animals in heat. Small children, blue with the cold and clothed in assorted rags, huddled together in a doorway for warmth. Their eyes held a deadness that all but froze James in his tracks. They had not even sufficient strength to hold out their stick-like arms to beg, he realized. He burrowed in his pockets and flung them all the coins he found there, not daring to halt for fear he'd lose track of the dog. When he looked back, the urchins were shuffling weakly to pick up the coins, but with such apathy he feared he had been too late with his charity.

The dog stopped finally at a narrow alleyway, and looked back expectantly. James swung down from the saddle and looked about him. The alley was far too narrow for a horse. He would have to proceed on foot from here, he determined ruefully. But what to do with the horse? The idea of leaving the beast in such an area unattended seemed foolhardy. When he returned he would as likely as not find it had been stolen. There was little option left open to him, however, for the dog was off and running once more! He looped his reins through a nearby bootscrape and sprinted down the alley after him.

At the back of the building, which appeared to be a warehouse, was a door. The dog scraped and whined at this door for several minutes, then yapped excitedly and waved his plume-like tail. James flattened himself against the wall. The door opened.

"Ah, 'tis you, Master Bones!" a young voice exclaimed. "You bad dog! Where have you left Granny? And where is Coalie, mmm?" The door closed.

James grinned. The hairy little beast had brought him straight to his master as he'd hoped, and apparently the lad was alone. It was now or never, he decided. He sidled up to the door, rapped sharply upon it and ducked back. After a few minutes he heard the scrape of the bolt being drawn again and the door opened.

"Gran? Lumpy Jack, is that you?" called the clear young voice again. Silence. The lad stepped through the doorway to see who had knocked.

In a flash James grabbed him under the ribs and flung him over his shoulder. He sprinted back down the alley the way he had come. The lad was overly light and his weight was negligible. He held the writhing, spitting lad while he freed his reins from the bootscrape, tossed the boy across the saddle and leaped astride behind him. Then he kicked the horse into a rapid trot and made off through the maze of backstreets. The little dog had followed his master out and raced after them, yapping furiously.

"Let me go!" the lad screeched, pummelling James' thighs and the unwitting horse's poor head and neck indiscriminately.

"Nay," James gritted through tightly clenched teeth, "and be still, else I'll box your blasted ears!" He pressed a heavy hand down between the lad's shoulder blades to hold him still, and forced a faster gait from the horse.

The boy bared his teeth, squirming his head in an effort to find some portion of the captain's anatomy on which to clench them. The direction of his intended attack appeared highly threatening, and not wishing to change his voice from baritone to falsetto, James made good his threat and cuffed the boy across the ear with a ringing slap.

"Be still, or there'll be more where that came from," he threatened harshly. "I've had naught but ill fortune since first our paths crossed, lad, and my temper is as thin ice—ready to crack!"

"Bastard! Kidnapper! Son of a French-pocked whore!" the boy cursed lustily, tears of rage spilling down his filthy cheeks.

James wrinkled his nose. The boy was not only unclean, he smelled. His mousy, straggly hair, he was willing to wager, had not seen soap or water in months, mayhap years, and was more likely than not the lodgings for more than one variety of lodgers. The rags upon his back were foul too, and horribly stained.

"You reek, boy," James growled, kneeing the horse which had slackened its pace. The boy ventured a retort, but beyond kindness, James shoved his head hard down against the horse's side, which effectively silenced him. James looked about him. The dome of St. Paul's Cathedral rose beyond the buildings. From there, he could find his way back to the wharves.

He turned the horse in that direction, coming out finally into a busy thoroughfare, where the beggars on the steps of the magnificent cathedral were as numerous as the snowy-winged pigeons fluttering and cooing in the frosty air. The little dog still scampered after them.

A beggar extended a tin cup to James for alms, but James growled a refusal without looking at him.

The boy's head jerked up. "Lumpy! 'Tis me, Chris!" squealed the lad suddenly. The man uttered an oath, flung his tin cup to the cobbles and lunged after the horse.

James looked hurriedly over his shoulder. Sure enough, Lumpy Jack was slouching after them, and hot on his heels came Granny Rags, her mobcap askew and her multi-colored skirts flying, and behind her, Coalie Joe was wheezing in pursuit. This was too much! James slashed the reins across the horse's rump and galloped off along the cobbled thoroughfare at dangerous speed, his cloak flying behind him. When at length he ventured a glance over his shoulder, they were gone!

Five

"Hold your tongue, lad, or I'll perforce tear it from your mouth!" James hissed under his breath as they clattered into the stableyard of the Golden Goose tavern.

An ostler hurried forward to take the horse, eyes askance at the tall captain's strange young companion slung across his saddle.

"A tragedy, is it not?" James murmured confidingly, handing the ostler his reins. "The young fellow is mad, a candidate for Bedlam Asylum, I fear. See how he glowers at me with murderous intent? Alas, what waste for madness to strike at the mind of one so young!"

"Indeed it is, sir," the ostler agreed fervently, edging away from the strange youth with frightened eyes.

"He has a fit on him now," James continued, fighting the desire to laugh, "and is of the notion I have abducted him. Strange fancies fill the poor lad's head, but they will diminish, God willing, think you not, if given time to do so?"

"Oh, aye, sir, I'm sure of it!" the ostler agreed hastily, appearing ready to bolt.

James lifted Chris Alexander, rigid with fury, from the horse. He winked at the man. "When he's taken this way, I play his game. Does it not look for all the world as if it were so, myself his captor and he the victim of some cruel plot? Aye, good fellow, I knew you would agree! Pray, hurry inside and tell your mistress the captain has returned. Bid her prepare my room, and quickly. Advise her of the lad's derangement and warn her that, come what may, if there be loud screams or the crashing about of furniture, or any such noise issuing forth from behind my door, she is on no account to force entry. Do you understand?" The ostler nodded, now utterly convinced the captain had a lunatic in tow. "Very well. When we are settled, I want a bathing tub brought to the room, hot kettles, cakes of soap, fresh linens and, if you can acquire them, clean clothes for the lad. And mind that I said *clean* ones. I want no stinking rags, of those he has plenty. Perhaps a stableboy's Sunday best? I'd be willing to pay him generously."

"I'll get right to it, good sir, and all as you requested!" Still boggle-eyed, the ostler beat a hasty retreat, tugging his forelock.

In minutes Mistress Annie Waller was leading the way up the gloomy flight of stairs, a stout candlestick held above her to light the way, although it was not yet dusk. She swung open a door at the end of the long passage and stood back to permit James to enter with his wriggling burden.

"There, sir," she said, brushing back a stray lock of dark hair from a pigeon-plump cheek, "I trust you'll find this to your liking. 'Tis bigger than the other room, and much more cozy, with the fire an' all."

"Yes, indeed," James declared, "Very comfortable. In one hour I should like a tray brought up with our suppers, if you please. Something hot and tasty and guaranteed to fill the belly. Instruct the serving girl to knock and leave the tray by the door, if you would. The ostler told you that the boy is not . . . well?"

"Indeed he did," Mistress Waller confirmed, "and 'tis no trouble, no trouble at all." She looked at the glowering youth hung over James' shoulder with kindly eyes. "Poor little lad!" she murmured sympathetically, "so young to be stricken! Your little brother, sir?"

"Nay, Mistress Waller," James said with feeling, "A nephew. Now, if you will excuse us? . . ." His arm and

49

shoulder had begun to ache and the garrulous woman had shown no haste to take her leave.

Mistress Waller sniffed her farewell and exited huffily. James dropped the boy unceremoniously—and none too gently—to the floorboards, strode across to the door and locked it. Then he went to the casement and peered out. It was a long drop to the street with no visible handholds to climb down, and nothing to break a fall. Perfect! He clipped the key onto the keyring at his belt and towered over the lad, his booted feet planted solidly apart.

"Get up," he ordered sternly, "I'll have none of your tantrums here, be damned if I will!" His sea-green eyes were stormy, like the greenish-gray swells he battled on the high seas. Yet the boy remained huddled on the boards, ignoring him. James bent down, meaning to drag him to his feet. As he did so, the boy jackknifed his leg and jabbed him hard in the groin.

An oath exploded from James as the pain shot in all directions through his middle, like red hot shot from a musket. "You black-hearted wretch!" he cursed, doubling over and sitting suddenly on the massive poster bed that dominated the room. "You have nigh ruined me!"

"Aye," the lad retorted, "indeed, I hope so!" He grinned fleetingly, scrambling to his feet, and eyed the livid captain with a crafty light in his dark blue eyes. "And 'tis no more than ye should expect . . . from a lunatic!"

Sparks blazed from James' eyes. Smoke all but poured from his nostrils. "I rue the day your aunt sent me to find you," he roared. "You are naught but a jackanapes and a mischief-maker, not to mention a cutpurse and thief. 'Tis my opinion the good Nellie would be better off without the likes of you."

"I never asked her to send for me," the lad answered hotly. "I've made my own way these four years past since my mother died. I've no need of your damned help, nor my aunt's—i' faith, I *have* no aunt!" He glared at James sulkily then crouched down in the corner, his head upon his knees and his arms hugging his legs, staring into the fire that spat and crackled merrily in the hearth and ignoring the captain utterly.

The silence hung heavily in the room, like a thick fog. James, too angered for speech, determined it was better to say nothing. He got to his feet, still wincing at his pained middle, and went to warm his coattails at the hearth.

Lord, he thought gloomily, what had he let himself be talked into? Yet he had given his word to Nell he would fetch the boy to her, and his honor would not permit him to renege. Indeed, he was 'twixt the devil and the deep blue sea — a devil that looked at him with twin storm clouds instead of eyes, dark and brooding. He raked a hand through his dishevelled russet hair. Where, in God's name, was the tub he'd ordered brought to the room?

As if in answer to his question there came a soft rap at the door. James unfastened the key from his belt and unlocked it. Lucy's father, a huge man with the burly build of a blacksmith, lumbered in with the brass-banded wooden tub upon his back, looking for all the world like an enormous turtle. Lucy tripped in after him, carrying two steaming kettles of hot water. She winked conspiratorially at James behind her father's back and blew him a kiss. James grinned and nodded faintly.

"Set the tub by the fire, Master Waller. Ah, Mistress Annie, let me take those heavy kettles from you!" James offered, crossing the room to help Lucy's mother.

"I'll be off to fetch the linens, Captain," Lucy said brightly, tossing her red curls.

"And me t' fetch a kettle or two more," Annie decided, bustling to the door. She caught James' long glance, both at the boy and then at the door and nodded in understanding before she went out, closing it loudly and pointedly behind her.

During all the comings and goings, the boy still huddled

in the corner.

At length all was ready: the water was steaming in the tub, the linens warming over a three-legged stool set by the hearth, their supper in covered trenchers giving off savory aroma on the table and two foaming tankards of ale next to it. They had even brought the clothes he requested for the lad, a rough, worn shirt and corduroy breeches, both old but clean and neatly darned. Mistress Waller bobbed a curtsy and left, and Tom Waller lumbered to the door and waited.

"There ye are, sir," Lucy smiled saucily," *everything* ye ordered sir!" Her blue eyes said that it was *not* everything, not quite!

"Indeed, Lucy, you and your good mother have done me proud," James said with a half bow. "My thanks to you bo—."

"Lucy!" bellowed the man by the door," get ye down t' the taproom, lass, and sharpish!"

"Aye, Pa, right away!" Lucy gasped. She scuttled from the room like a frightened rabbit without a backwards glance at James.

Thomas Waller glowered at the young captain. "I've seen how ye eye my daughter, sir, and I will warn ye now, sir, I'll not take kindly t' ye layin' a hand on the girl. Do I make myself clear, sir?" he asked nastily, balling his fists.

"Quite clear, Waller," James acknowledged.

"Right!" the man said sourly, and shut the door loudly as he left.

James relocked the door in his wake and sat himself down at the rough wooden table. "Come and sup, lad, 'tis good fare and will take the chill from your bones."

The boy eyed the food with longing yet he turned his head quickly away. "I'll eat none of it," he vowed, yet James thought he caught the glint of a tear in the corner of his eye, glistening in the light from the fire.

"As you wish," James said casually. He uncovered his own

trencher and bowl. Upon it lay three plump mutton chops, surrounded by lentils and onions and swimming in rich, savory gravy. A thick wedge of cheese and a crusty quarter-loaf, spread thick with honey and butter, accompanied it. From the bowl rose curls of steam and the aroma of a beef and barley broth. James attacked the repast with relish, with much exaggerated lip-smacking and groans of pure pleasure, for he was fully aware that the lad was eyeing him slyly when he thought him unaware of it.

James found himself appraising the lad, equally slyly. He appeared older, close up, than had been James' first impression, perhaps sixteen years, but short for a lad his age, and painfully thin. He wore a cap pulled down low over his filthy, matted hair, which was unevenly cut and hung about his shoulders in rat-like tails. There was a frailty about him that belied his wiry strength. His clothes consisted of a threadbare jacket, much patched and darned, and an equally worn pair of knee breeches. Beneath the jacket was a grimy, yellowed shirt, several sizes too large. The lad's feet and calves were bare and to James' mind, seemed sadly vulnerable. He remembered his own shivering after the lad had stolen his cloak. How much colder it must be without benefit of stockings and boots!

"On the morrow, lad, we'll see you properly outfitted. Shirts, coats, cloaks, everything you'll need. Your Aunt Nell sent a generous purse for your expenses. You need feel no gratitude to me, so rest easy on that account." He sucked on the mutton bone then licked his fingers noisily. "Come, Chris," he urged, "and sup. Never let pride stand in the way of a good meal—not when 'tis plain you are nigh starved. Only a dull-wit would refuse—and you strike me as a clever lad."

To his surprise, the lad got to his feet and came across to the table, dragging his feet in a great show of reluctance. He scraped back the chair and perched upon it, like a flighty bird ready to take wing. James hid a smile as the boy snatched up a mutton chop and tore into it with savage gusto. This was no time for lessons in manners—those could come later, when food was not a life and death matter for the youth. The boy's trencher was soon emptied, yet he scooped up the remaining crumbs of bread, wadded them into a tidy ball and sopped up every last vestige of gravy and mutton that clung to the trencher as if his life depended on it. He quaffed his tankard of ale with equal alacrity and slammed it down rudely on the table, as if daring James to comment on his lack of etiquette.

"Would you like more?" James asked kindly, "we can send to the kitchen for more victuals?"

The lad shook his head.

"Then," James said, standing, "we will see you bathed and to bed. The water should be cooler by—"

"No!" the boy hissed, jumping to his feet and knocking his trencher to the floor. "I'll not bathe, no!" He backed away like a cornered wild animal, eyes blazing.

James sighed and set his jaw firmly. "You will, Chris, if I'm forced to bathe you myself, you will bathe. You reek, lad, and I'll not take you to my ship in that condition, I swear it. Now, we've fought enough these past two days, what do you say? Give quarter, lad!"

The boy shook his head slowly from side to side. His arms snaked out and James ducked in the nick of time as the lighted candlestick—of heavy brass—hurtled over his head and crashed against the hearth, dislodging a shower of sparks to the floorboards. He ducked again as the trenchers, one after the other, followed the candlestick's flight. Before the boy could cast about for fresh ammunition, James leaped across the room, gripped him by the collar and breeches' belt, strode over to the tub and dumped him forcefully into it. The lad spluttered and coughed like a drowning cat as water slopped everywhere.

"Now," the captain roared, green eyes murderous, "scrub yourself, boy, else when I return I will thrash your scrawny buttocks until to sit will pain you sorely for a month! And then," he added, "I shall bathe you myself, and with the mood I have upon me now, I wager there will be little skin left on your bones. Take heed, lad, and do it. I shall be back shortly." He exited and locked the door securely and loudly in his wake. The little dog waited outside for his master, his head resting patiently on his paws.

Six

"Oh, Jamie, love, ye kept your promise!" Lucy breathed as he slipped into her attic room.

"Aye, my pretty bird," he answered softly, quickly crossing the room to her bed. He sat down and hurriedly hauled off his boots. "I cannot stay long. The lad—I dare not leave him alone, lest he escape." He briefly told Lucy of the mission Nellie Flagg had sent him on.

"Then the boy, he do be alright in the head, and not tetched as ye told me ma and pa?" Lucy giggled.

James grinned and nodded and slid into bed. Lucy's arms came up around his neck as he did so and pulled his head down to hers. He kissed her long and hard, his hands roving beneath her chemise and seeking out the soft, heavy weight of her full breasts. He fondled her gently, his lips still locked to hers, his tongue beginning a probing exploration of her mouth that was no less thorough than the voyage of discovery his hands were about. Lucy pulled him tighter against her, wriggling to feel her breasts rubbed against his hairy broad chest. He leaned back and unfastened the ties of her chemise, delighting in the sudden hot rush of desire that coursed through him as his hands touched her bared flesh. Lucy caressed his muscled arms, then his chest and finally rested on his taut flanks. She stroked him lazily, her laughter throaty, her eyes glittering sapphire pools in the meager light.

"Oh, James!" she sighed as his mouth fastened on a jutting, raspberry-textured nipple and tasted it greedily.

She pulled his hands down to her thighs, little moans breaking from her moistly-parted lips as he obligingly stroked the tender inner flesh of her thighs, first lightly, softly, then harder, all but kneading those lovely columns as he fought the fires of lust that raged within him. He plundered the secret portals of her womanhood with a gentle urgency that set her to writhing and bouncing on the pallet in eagerness for his taking of her.

"Now, James, my lusty love, now! Take me, sweet, oh, aye, aye!" she cried, tossing her head wildly from side to side in wanton abandon.

James took her with slow, lingering strokes, delaying his own throbbing release until Lucy reached hers with a loud, explosive cry that he feared would bring her burly father running. He dropped to her side and planted a hearty kiss upon her drooping eyelids, heavy with satiation.

"Noisy wench," he teased affectionately, drawing her to him, "your father bade me keep my paws off his darling daughter—and you all but called out the guard on us, sweet Lucy!"

"I do be right sorry, James, love, but I thought I were died and gorn to heaven, truly I did," she murmured contritely, snuggling against him.

"Now 'tis my turn to beg your pardon, sweet," James groaned, reluctantly turning away and fumbling in the dark for his breeches. "But the lad—I must go back to my own room."

Lucy pouted. "Not yet, Captain, sir!" she implored him. "Don't ye go yet!"

"But I must," James insisted, torn between duty and pleasure. He watched as Lucy scrambled from the rumpled bed and pulled a smock over her pretty nakedness.

"Get ye back t' bed, sir," she ordered cheekily," and give me the key. I'll be back in a shake of a lamb's tail, after I check on the lad for ye." She winked and grinned. "An' I do believe, sir that me appetite do be fast returnin'!"

James grinned too. "Hurry back then, you insatiable, lovely baggage!"

He waited in the darkened attic room, arms folded beneath his head, staring at the beamed ceiling. The sounds of merriment carried but faintly here, though he could make out the sawing of a fiddle and the wail of a concertina's rolling accompaniment to the jolly Yuletide carol quite clearly. He hummed to himself, the good humor he always experienced after a lusty bout of love-making coursing through him. Lucy was a rarity indeed. Though he knew very well that she had sold her favors on numerous occasions, she was unlike the other bawds he had met or bedded in that she enjoyed the act itself and never merely endured it for the coin as did many wenches of that ancient profession.

The door flew open suddenly, forcefully, and James sat up with a startled, "Whoa!" as it crashed back on its hinges.

Lucy hurtled across the room and rushed to stand before him like a bristling, red-haired terrier. She dealt him a stinging slap hard across the face.

"Get yourself out o' here, and sharpish!" she spat. "You lyin', scurvy rake! Be gone, else I'll call me pa, I will!"

"What is it, Lucy, sweet?" he asked, concern for her furrowing his brow. "Tell me what it is I've done to make you vexed!"

"Vexed! Pah! As if you didn't know!" she screamed, shoving him out of the door and hurling his clothes and boots into the landing after him, before slamming the door in his startled face.

Puzzled and shrugging, James hurriedly hauled on his breeches and boots and started back to his own room. He tugged on his shirt as he went. *Women!* he thought irritably. What temperamental creatures they all were! He thought back over the lusty interlude briefly, wondering if he had said something to cause Lucy's violent outpouring of displeasure, but could recall nothing. He stopped at his

58

door. The key was still in the lock! Had the lad taken flight? He flung open the door and strode swiftly inside, slamming and locking it hurriedly behind him in one savage motion.

His jaw dropped as he looked up. In the flickering firelight stood a young woman, her own expression equally astonished. Candlelight played on her moonlight-blond hair, touching the tumble of softly curling locks with warm light, and giving a golden sheen to the pale, almost pearly luster of her skin. She was slender as a willow, sylph-like in stature, and quite naked, her small but perfectly fashioned breasts set high above a dainty waist and almost boyish hips, which were crowned by a gleaming golden triangle of hair at the junction of her thighs.

"God's blood, woman, who are you?" James gasped finally, for once at a loss for further words.

A small, mysterious smile played about the young woman's lips, and she leaned down gracefully and retrieved her fallen towel, fastening it about her modestly.

"I?" she asked huskily, laughter dancing wickedly in her deep sea-blue eyes. "Why, Captain, don't you know me?" she inquired teasingly.

James shook his head. "No, my dear, I don't believe I have ever had the pleas—!" He stopped short, his own eyes narrowing as he fastened them on her dark blue eyes. Dark blue eyes, dark as twin storm clouds! "Strike me!" he breathed, "I don't believe it!"

The girl laughed. "Believe it or nay, Captain, 'tis true!" She curtsied mockingly. "Chris Alexander at your service, sir."

"But—but you're not a—a—!" James stammered.

"Boy?" she finished for him. "Nay, indeed I am not, in truth, though many times it was far safer to be a man than a wench!" She smiled. "I am in reality Chris*tianne* Alexander, your good friend Nellie's—nephew!" Her pretty lips twitched mischieveously.

"Holy Madonna!" James groaned. "Not again!"

Seven

"Again?" Christianne queried curiously. The captain appeared quite felled by his discovery, she thought! Indeed, the color had now fled the weatherbeaten tan of his face. Good for him, that bullying rogue! Despite her demeanor of compliance she had scores to settle with the good captain yet. Aye, indeed, she thought, remembering the stinging swats he had laid across her bottom as if she were a wayward child, she was not done with him yet.

"Your . . . surprise . . . put me in mind of something in the past, la—mistress," he amended hurriedly, his mind racing. "You need not concern yourself over it."

"I'm not concerned," the girl replied pertly, perching on the three-legged stool and holding out her hands, palms down, to warm them at the fire. She sighed dreamily. "This is the warmest and the fullest I have been since Mama passed on," she remarked wistfully to no one in particular.

"Mmm," James murmured absently, his own thoughts far from the girl. Instead his head was whirling with memories of another lass he had treated unfairly; another girl, this one with chestnut hair and eyes of darkest sable, who had stood with the lamplight burnishing her body and only a towel fastened about her, in the cabin of his first ship, the *Gypsy Princess*, and begged and implored him not to ravish her. Yet he, believing her a doxy procured for him by his men, had refused to listen to her protestations of innocence, and had taken her by force. Amanda! Pirates had overrun his vessel soon after, and he had thought the lovely Amanda killed when their ship, with he and Amanda and his men captive aboard her, had blown up. Yet the two of them had survived, neither knowing of the other's survival for many, many months. By the time he encountered Amanda again, she had lost her heart to her Miguel, Don Miguel de Villarin, borne him a son and was in terrible danger. Between them—Nellie Flagg, Amanda, Miguel and himself—things had ended happily. But there had been a brief time when he had wanted to marry Amanda and had even gone so far as to ask her to be his bride. She had gently refused, luckily for him, for belatedly he had realized he had no desire to settle down and restrict himself to one woman! Two years ago, that had been! It seemed a century ago and but a few days past at the same time.

"I said, Captain Mallory," Christianne repeated impatiently, "what garments should I don?"

James looked up, startled. "Garments? Ah, yes, your garments! Well—those on the bed, will they not fit?" he asked hopefully.

"No," she retorted. "I—I wore a binder to—to conceal my sex, and I have burned it along with my other rags upon the fire. These will not fit."

"I shall go directly in the morning to purchase you fresh garments for the voyage," he said distantly, his mind still whirling. "Go to sleep, meanwhile."

"I will not go with you on your ship," she declared, tossing her pale blond hair out of her eyes. But the captain was gazing moodily into the fire and seemed not to have heard her heated words, damn him!

She left the towel about her and crawled into bed, snuggling into the feathered pallet and goose down pillows and tucking the quilted counterpane and woollen blankets about her tightly. What luxury to be warm, she thought, stretching happily, and what luxury to be sleeping in a real bed! It had been—what? Aye, three years since she had slept anywhere but on piled rags of lice-infested blankets, too threadbare for warmth. After her mother's death, she had had nothing left but the furnishings and gradually not even those as she sold them, piece by piece, to purchase food and other necessities. Finally, with the coming of the bitterest winter she could recall in all her eighteen years, she had been forced to burn the remaining, mostly broken, pieces for fuel.

Life had been sweet and easy, she recalled, when she was a little girl. The man she had called Papa had come regularly and often to see her and her lovely mama, Jenny, at the house on Darling Lane. It was many years before she learned the truth; that her beloved parents had never been married, that her mother had, in fact, been Lord Christopher Alexander's mistress, and had merely adopted his last name for herself and her child. Oh, how it had hurt to learn she was Papa's bastard daughter! Nevertheless, he had loved both his daughter and his mistress dearly, and not a week passed that he did not come to see them. And then, his visits had stopped, suddenly and without warning. Weeks passed, and Papa came no more to the house, sent no word to reassure them that he loved them and to expect his continued support. At length, Jenny Alexander had bundled little Chris into a public coach and they had journeyed west across England, to Lord Alexander's country seat, Westlodge Manor in Somerset, to discover what had befallen him.

The answer had been painfully obvious. As they trudged the length of the elegant driveway, they saw that Westlodge had been draped in funeral crepe, even the windows shrouded in yards and yards of the mourning weeds. Her mother had dropped like a stone to her knees, sobbing out her grief, the little girl unable to console her. They had taken lodgings, the cheapest they could find, for that night, after stumbling from the imposing grounds of Westlodge. The next morning, Jenny had been pale but calm. Then, she recalled painfully, her cheeks flaming with shame at the memory, they had gone to the back door of the manor like tradesmen and begged the footman to ask Lord Alexander's widow if she would see them. She had condescended to do so. To Christianne's horror, her mother had flung herself at Louise Alexander's feet and begged the woman to see her way to grant them a meager allowance. How the woman had laughed! What awful, ugly names she had called her mother! Christianne had covered her ears and begged her to stop, to no avail. There would be no allowance for them. Lord Alexander's widow had instead cruelly suggested that perhaps they could both turn to the ancient trade at which Jenny had proved so adept in her younger days. Her mother had blanched but remained silent, and as little Chris had looked up into her mother's grief-stricken face, she had seen a hard, determined glint come into her pretty brown eyes. "What of the house on Darling Lane?" She had asked through tight lips. "Keep it!" Louise Alexander had hissed. "Keep that foul den where your bastard was conceived and your whoring with my husband took place." "Sign it over, then," her mother had insisted, and sign it over the woman had. They had left with the deeds to the house on Darling Lane in her mother's fist. "For you, my sweet Chris," her mother had whispered fiercely as they left, "for you, from your papa, who loved you dearly!" La! It seemed like only yesterday!

"What do I do with you?" the captain was saying, finally having emerged from his own reverie. "Mayhap we should hire you a companion or a maid of some sort?"

Lord, Christianne thought, covering her ears with the blanket, would he still not believe that she had no intention of coming with him to this New World? He was obviously a colonial himself, and she liked not his bold, brash manner, nor his easy ways, nor the slight peculiar drawl to his speech, any more than she had liked the cuffs and swats he'd dealt her, the brute! She did, however, like his warm bed and his good food, and for the night she was well content to stay where she was. Tomorrow she would let him know in no uncertain terms that she would take charity from no one. She might not have much left, but she still had her pride.

The wench had drifted off to sleep, James realized, going to stand over her. Small wonder Lucy had been outraged; seeing this pretty piece in his room, she no doubt thought his eagerness to return to his room had been on account of her. He frowned. That she was lovely was obvious to any who had eyes to see, yet what had she said? That it was "safer to be a man" than a wench, that was it. Was that why she had kept rags on her back and let her hair grow foul and filthy, for her protection? That same hair, which had been a drab and greasy mouse color when dirty, now fell in tousled, wispy curls about her delicately molded face, and was a silvery-blond hue, like moonbeams, he thought, a sudden flight of fancy taking him. A suspicion of a dimple lay in one cheek, rosy from the warmth of the feather bed and the firewarmed room, and her lashes were dark golden crescents against the almost translucent pallor of her skin. Her arms were slender—thin, in truth—and the hands that rested primly on top of the quilted coverlet were rough with calluses, which seemed incongruous on such a daintily-made young woman. Still, he mused, a few weeks at sea with regular victuals and few hardships, fresh air and relaxation would rid her of her pallor and put the roses back into her cheeks, and in time the calluses too, would disappear, and that wraith-like frame would fill out. He grinned to himself. What would Nell think of her "nephew," he wondered? He looked forward to seeing the look of shock on the madam's face and the first meeting 'twixt the two of them with wicked pleasure.

On the morrow he'd see Christianne properly outfitted and then comfortably ensconced in his cabin aboard the *Fair Amanda*. If Silas Mullens had hired the replacements for the few crew members who inevitably jumped ship at each port of any size they put into, he saw no reason why they might not get under sail forthwith. Aye, he had not delayed his departure by much. Christianne's recovery had been easy, thanks to the little dog. Belatedly remembering him, James crossed to the door and opened it. The mongrel looked up at him with mournful brown eyes and thumped his tail in greeting.

"Come on then, dog, she's in here!" he murmured.

Without need of a second invitation, the little animal scampered inside the room, padded across to the bed and jumped upon it. He circled once to get comfortable and then flopped down to sleep.

It was not until then that James realized; it was the floor or the straight-backed chair for his bed! Mistress Waller had presumed that they would share the bed, but now that was out of the question. He sighed, spread his cloak before the fire and rolled into it.

James awoke first the next morning. Christianne, he saw, was still asleep, her cheek cradled against her palm. In the gray light of dawn she was every bit as lovely as he had believed the previous night in the candle's flattering luminescence.

The first order of business was to obtain some suitable attire for her, and swiftly. He had no wish to have her awaken and flaunt her nudity as she had so brazenly the night before, knowing his own inability to resist a prettily turned ankle, or a rosy breast peeking o'er a bodice top! He hauled on his boots, stoked up the fire, then added a fresh log to it before he left, bound for a modiste's establishment he had noticed off Bond Street the day previous. No doubt he would have to gild the dressmaker's palms for getting her up at such an ungodly hour, but it would be worth it to get the wench outfitted speedily. He went with an eagerness that surprised himself, suddenly curious to see how Mistress

65

Alexander would look in feminine attire. He chuckled. She had certainly been most fetching without it.

Christianne stretched lazily and yawned. For several minutes she lay abed, letting foggy sleep thoughts disperse, before opening her eyes. At first she had to recall where she was. Memory flooded back quickly. The Golden Goose tavern. She grimaced. James Mallory. She groaned in disappointment. She had dreamed of her mother, dreamed of how it used to be when the house on Darling Lane had truly been a home, before Papa's death and before the long, lingering sickness had crept insidiously over her mother and cast its sickly pallor upon the bloom of Jenny Alexander's cheeks.

She had been a lovely woman, her mother, with auburn hair and green-flecked, hazel eyes. Her own silvery-blond coloring, her mother had said, had stemmed from her papa's side, from the Alexanders of Somerset.

Somerset, she thought, a happy smile curving her lips. Ah, how she loved that county with its apple orchards aflower with white blossoms, and filled with simple, friendly folk living simple, peaceful lives! Granny Rags had said that perhaps they might leave the house in Lumpy's care this summer and take to the roads. Most certainly they would visit that county if they did, and the county of Kent, with its funny little cone-roofed oast-houses where the hops were dried and made into ale. She frowned. It would be hard to leave London, though, with summer coming. She would miss the hustle and bustle of city life that she had always known: the colorful characters, the boatmen on the Thames poling their barges, the street-peddlers; the buildings that breathed with ancient life, the churches, colleges, shops; the pageantry of state occasions and magnificent processions. Leave England, the captain had suggested, blast him! Ha! It was *unthinkable* that she would leave her

66

beloved England for some outlandish spot that was in all probability savage and remote from any form of civilized life! And to do so to live off the uncertain charity of some unknown aunt, who was probably a spinsterish old dame in a lacy cap, and who had only sent for her out of a misguided sense of obligation—nay, never! She'd sooner die than accept charity from anyone.

She swung out of bed and went to peer out of the window. The mews below were deserted, save for a lone rider whose russet hair and tanned good looks she had come to recognize quite well. She watched his horse clatter out of the tavern yard down the street and out of sight before turning quickly to the fire. It was crackling merrily, eager flames devouring the fresh log the captain had fed it shortly before. Brr! she shivered. Away from the fire and the warmth of the bed, the room was decidedly chill, she realized, hugging herself about the arms. And she had no clothes. Dolt! Nitwit! Goose! she chided herself, regretting her hasty decision to burn the rags she had worn. Yet, rising from the tub, warm and sweet-smelling and clean, she had shuddered at the idea of donning them ever again. How long did she have before the captain returned, she wondered? An hour, two, mayhap? Whatever, there would be time enough to escape him!

Someone knocked at the door, a sharp, impatient rap, she thought.

"Come in!" she called hesitantly, dashing for the bed and scrambling beneath the counterpane.

The key scraped in the lock and the serving wench who had surprised her at her toilette the night before stalked in, a sulky pout on her fresh, pretty face this morning and her brows drawn together like storm clouds. Lucy, James had called her, Christianne remembered. The girl was carrying a tray of what smelled like porridge, well-sweetened with honey.

"The captain requested that ye be served the morning's

fare abed, mistress," she said sharply and with obvious disapproval, slamming the tray down upon the table with a loud clang. "And here it do be!" She bobbed a sketchy curtsy and made as if to leave.

"Wait!" Christianne cried after her. "Please, don't go!" she coaxed. "I—I need your help."

Lucy turned and sniffed disdainfully. "Help from the likes o' me?" she snapped. "You don't look like ye need no bloomin' help, ye don't!" Her eyes flickered jealously over the other girl's delicate beauty. She looked like a lady, she did. Her fair, fragile beauty made Lucy feel suddenly gawky and clumsy by comparison. Her own fresh, natural beauty must appear coarse when compared to the dainty loveliness of the young women in the bed. A sob caught in Lucy's throat. Little wonder Jamie had been so anxious to leave *her* bed, she thought angrily, hating him and loving him simultaneously.

Christianne read the expression on the girl's face easily. In the past, her ability to decipher expressions and the character they revealed had meant her livelihood, for when looking for an easy mark with a fat pocket to pick, it paid to choose one whose expression betrayed that he was lazily inclined and would quickly give up the fight. Accurately, she determined that Lucy had a fondness for the captain. She would have to play her cards carefully. A jealous woman was unpredictable, would be as easy to jump to the defense of her beloved as to condemn him, if not approached correctly.

"Oh, Lucy, I'm in terrible trouble!" she wailed, eyes downcast, lower lip quivering.

"Trouble?" Lucy queried, rising to the bait like a fine red salmon.

"Aye, indeed!" Christianne sighed heavily. "You see, my—my aunt in the New World has sent for me to come and live with her. The captain has been promised a fat purse to deliver me to her, and will stop at nothing to

68

obtain it. But you see, Lucy, dear, I cannot go with him, for if I do I must leave my one true love behind!" A lie served best when liberally laced with truth, she'd long ago discovered.

Lucy's anger melted fractionally. Christianne's words had, as the girl had cleverly calculated, advised Lucy that not only were her affections directed elsewhere, away from the captain, but also appealed to Lucy's desire to get even with him for his imagined slight by the harmless means of cheating him of the "purse" he sought. At the same time, Lucy could rationalize her desire to wound James by the worthy motive of helping a member of her own sex in trouble, and romantically believe she was assisting the course of true love at the same time!

" 'Tis a fair fix you do be in, indeed," Lucy agreed. But then her eyes narrowed suspiciously. "But then why were ye dressed like a lad?" she asked, hands on her hips.

Christianne played for time by dabbing at her dry eyes with the corner of the rough woollen blanket while her mind raced. "He stole my clothes!" she wailed piteously. "I had vowed to run away, to elope with my darling—er, Richard, you see. And James thought if he removed all my clothes, I would be unable to do so, an assumption in which he was quite correct, as you can see. La! What awful rags he procured in which to abduct me—did you not shudder at the sight of them? And then, to ensure no one would aid me when I cried for help, he told *everyone* that I was his nephew, and a lunatic to boot! I'faith, the man's a rogue!" She shook her head dolefully.

"Aye, he is that!" Lucy agreed happily, thinking entirely different thoughts. "But tell me, Mistress, what would ye have me do t' help ye?"

"Clothes, Lucy—obtain me some clothes," Christianne begged eagerly, "and I will vanish from this place as if I ne'er were here, and fly to the safe haven of my loving Richard's arms!" Poor Lucy, she thought, liking the serving girl and hating having to lie to her. But it was out of only the direst necessity that she did so.

Lucy pursed her lips thoughtfully, then grinned. "I'll do it!" she declared. "You're a fair bit smaller than what I am, but me clothes should fit if we fasten a belt about yer middle. Wait now, and I'll be back in a thrice."

Less than a half hour later, Christianne stood ready to go before Lucy's critical eyes. The little dog eyed the unfamiliar female garments curiously, ears cocked.

"Well, how do I look?" she asked, smiling and twirling about. She wore one of Lucy's mobcaps, an old skirt and blouse, a threadbare cloak of dark blue and much-darned woollen hose beneath wooden clogs.

" 'Tis a mite shabby, but 'twill serve." Lucy beamed.

"You have done me proud, Lucy!" Christianne exclaimed gratefully. "A thousand thanks! I shall return your clothes as soon as I am able. And, now, I must be off! Farewell!" she flung over her shoulder as she hurried to the door. Abruptly she halted. "Oh, if the captain questions you, tell him nothing, agreed?"

"Agreed," Lucy said, nodding. She'd tell that rascal nothing, all right! "Go on with yer, and Godspeed ye to yer Richard!"

"Richard? Ah, yes, my Richard," Christianne covered hurriedly. "Farewell! Come, Bones."

Despite the threadbare cloak, Christianne gasped at the cold air as she stepped out of the tavern onto the cobbles, slick with ice, Bones padding faithfully at her heels. The clogs hurt her feet, after so long without shoes, but she determined to battle it out and risk getting blisters. She cast about, looking for a likely coach or carriage passing by on which to commence her escape. There was one, and travelling rapidly in the right direction, to boot! She bunched up her skirts and clattered after it, Bones racing after her, leaped nimbly up behind and scrabbled for purchase, grimly clinging to its fancy gilded carvings for handholds. In no time at all, she thought happily, she would be back in Darling Lane! James Mallory would never believe her stupid enough to go back there, but Granny and Lumpy and Coalie knew her ways well, bless them, and would come there, looking for her.

"Perhaps the young lady would prefer dark colors, sir, if she is, as you said, very fair-complected? Darker hues would enhance the pallor of her skin, which is very much the fashion for the ladies now, sir?" the dressmaker suggested, stifling a yawn.

"No, no," James disagreed, frowning.

Several boxes of accessories lay scattered at his feet, feminine folderols he had no knowedge of and had allowed the dressmaker to select for him herself. But on the matter of gowns, he fancied he had an eye for color and would not allow the dressmaker to sway him. "Let me see that one, the red velvet in the corner."

"That? But, sir, it would need a great deal of alterations for a lady so slender! It was made for a much larger woman, you understand?"

"Nevertheless, I will see it," James insisted impatiently, drumming his fingers on the table. *Lord!* First he was a nursemaid, bathing babes and seeing to it that they were fed, and now, a lady's maid, be damned if he wasn't!

The dressmaker shrugged indifferently and spread the gown across the chaise of her salon. It was of deep scarlet velvet, the bodice cut severely with a high-buttoned neckline and long sleeves that were full at the upper arm and then tight-fitting from elbow to wrist. The waist was cut in a deep point over the stomach and the skirts fell in a simple, unadorned scarlet swathe to the floor that pleased him well. He nodded.

"I shall wait, Mistress Beckett, while you attend to the necessary alterations. It will suit admirably, I believe," he decided, congratulating himself. "Put it with the others."

"Very well, sir. There is a hooded cloak, sir, of matching velvet, that goes with the gown, if you would care to see it?" she added craftily.

A cloak, he'd forgotten the cloak! he nodded. "Very well."

The cloak was of the same flawless velvet but in a deeper shade of scarlet. The inside and the hood were lined with silvery fox fur. He ran his hands over the soft, luxurious lining, a sudden vision of that dainty elfin face and those flashing sapphire-dark eyes haloed by that silvery fur assailing him.

"I'll take them both," he pronounced firmly.

"As I thought, sir, a gentleman of impeccable taste, and a discerning eye for quality! If you would call back at twelve o' the clock, I will have them ready, sir," the dressmaker said, greedy eyes gleaming as he counted out many gold guineas into her palm.

"I said I would wait, madam, and I shall," James growled, "but for thirty minutes, no longer. And I give you fair warning, madam, that my impeccable taste is matched only by the foulness and brevity of my temper!" His green eyes brooked no refusal and the dressmaker gulped and fled to her sewing room, the gown spread across her arms.

When he emerged some twenty-nine minutes later, he carried with him only the boxes containing the scarlet gown and the cloak, shoes and certain frilly garments the dressmaker had deemed imperative for a young lady's underpinnings. The other boxes he had ordered delivered to the *Fair Amanda* immediately, by handcart.

Still, even with so few packages, riding proved difficult, and it was with relief he arrived back at the Golden Goose tavern and handed the horse to the ostler, who, remembering the captains suspicious arrival on the night previous, eyed him askance.

James took the stairs up to his chamber two at a time,

whistling merrily. He could scarcely wait to weigh anchor and put out to sea. All being well now, he could do so on the morning tide, he thought happily. He turned the key in the lock and stepped inside his room. A cursory glance told him everything. She had gone.

Eight

"I don't know where she be gone, James, and 'tis the truth, I swear it!" Lucy vowed, cursing the telltale color that seeped into her fresh cheeks and belied her words and her innocent expression.

"You are lying, Lucy," James said sternly. It was a statement rather than a question. He strode across the room and grasped her chin, turning her face.

Her eyes avoided his flashing green eyes and rolled about wildly in all directions in their sockets, looking anywhere but at him. "I do be telling the truth, sir, honest I am!" she sputtered breathlessly. "I done brought her victuals here this morning and she were gone, vanished off the face o' this earth!"

"Vanished, eh?" James murmured, brushing his lips over Lucy's. An instant response leaped through her, a response which he noted and pressed to his advantage.

His lips trailed sweet fire down the column of her throat, over the wildly throbbing surge of her pulse there. "When did she leave, eh, my Lucy?" he murmured, his lips still pressed against her skin.

Lucy arched her head back. "I—I don't know what you do be talking about, love!" she insisted, breathing heavily with rising passion.

"Mmm," James breathed, his hand sliding up the length of her body slowly, sensuously, to cup her full breast. His tongue traced the outline of her ear, his hot breath making gooseflesh rise all over her. She wriggled appreciatively.

"Oh, Jamie, you're a lad!" she sighed blissfully, tangling her fingers in his crisp, tousled locks.

"And you, my fine pigeon, are a toothsome treat fit for a lord!" he said huskily against her ear, reaching inside her bodice to entrap a swollen nipple in his fingers and tweak it gently. "And when did she leave?" he repeated smoothly, maintaining his handhold.

"Right—right after I brung the tray, Jamie. Oh, stop it, do, there's a good lad!" she squealed, but made no move to thrust his exploring hands away. Rather, she leaned forwards to offer him greater access to her now-unfastened bodice.

"I'll not stop, Lucy, love," he promised, laughter in his voice, "and nor do you wish me to, you minx! She left shortly after I, then?" he queried, more of himself than Lucy. "And how was she dressed?"

Lucy remained mute. He grinned and pulled down her bodice, fastened his mouth over a throbbing breast. His tongue teased the tingling peaks until Lucy writhed and all but lost her balance in her pleasure. "Oh! Oh, sir! How cruel to torture me so!" she cried. "She—she were dressed in a homespun skirt, sir, of brown, and me own old cloak, much worn-n-n!" The latter word came out as an anguished groan as Lucy felt herself lifted and borne to the bed in a pair of strong arms. "Oh, sir!" she cried expectantly, her blue eyes sparkling in anticipation of James' lustful assault on her person.

But to Lucy's dismay, James rolled her over onto her belly, flung up her skirts and thwacked her hard upon her plump buttocks in a manner that brought tears to her eyes.

"Bastard!" she shrieked indignantly, rubbing her posterior and glaring at him, red-faced, as he hurried to the door.

"Trollop!" he retorted fondly, blowing her a kiss and exiting swiftly. He was not a second too soon, for if he was not mistaken, a bowl of porridge crashed against the door in his wake.

Still chuckling, he leaned against the landing wall with his arms crossed over his chest and pondered what to do next. Of one thing he was certain: he was done chasing that slip of a girl hither and yon like a blasted will o' the wisp! He frowned. Wait! What was it Granny Rags had said so emphatically that night she had drugged him? He grinned. Yes, that was it, and he was willing to wager the old crone had not been lying about that. *He always comes home,* she had said, playing along with James' belief that Chris was a lad. *Always,* she had even added for emphasis. He descended the stairs two at a time, carrying the boxes, and raced from the tavern to the stables.

He had almost lost faith in his theory when he heard the rusty hinges on the garden gate creak mournfully, then the clatter of wooden clogs down the path. He stepped behind the door, listening intently as Christianne let herself into the house on Darling Lane.

Her footsteps clattered down the hallway, followed by the click of the little dog's paws on the scarred wood floor, then stopped outside the drawing room door. She turned the doorknob and stepped inside. In the same intant, James stepped forward and slammed it shut behind her and leaned upon it. Shock flitted across her face, quickly replaced by anger.

"You again?" she spat furiously, "are you dull-witted, Captain? Did I not tell you I would not come with you?"

"Indeed you did, Mistress Alexander. But you see, I made a grave error before. I implied that you had a choice of doing so or nay. This time, you have none. We are going to my ship and we will set sail forthwith."

"I shall not go with you!" she insisted, suddenly scared by the coldness of his tone. It was not a game anymore, she realized dully. He meant it, every word. That realization made her tremble.

"Madam, you will! he threatened softly. He crossed the room and picked up a box and held it out to her. "In here you will find suitable garments. I shall turn my back for the count of one hundred, no more. When I turn about, I expect to find you dressed and ready to leave. Do I make myself clear?" She glared at him defiantly and looked wildly about her. James hid a smile. "Looking for a weapon? You will find none! This house was thoroughly inspected by me prior to your arrival. There is nothing here that would serve your purpose, rest assured."

"What gives you the right to dictate to me?" she stormed. "Who are you to tell me where I may or may not go, and what I may or may not do?" She tossed her head angrily. "Damn your arrogance, sir!"

"I came here, Christianne," James said evenly, "at your aunt's bidding. Your mother's dying wish was that her sister should be your guardian. If I had found you well cared for, or married, or in otherwise good circumstances, it would be a different story. Then, the choice would be yours, to come with me or nay. But I find you neither well cared for, nor married, and certainly not in good circumstances, but with a company of thieves and cutpurses and with rags upon your back, half-starved. No, Christianne, I will not permit you to stay here! My *conscience*, if you prefer, will not permit it. Now, get dressed!" He turned his back, his booted feet planted aggressively apart.

Christianne opened the box with shaking hands. Tears sparkled in her eyes. She could see the wisdom in his reasoning, but knowing he was right did little for the sinking dread uncoiling inside her. She had not had much of a life lately, it was true—but it was all the life she knew, dear God!

The scarlet velvet was soft against her calloused hands. She drew the gown from the box and placed it carefully across the lid upon the floor. There was a cambric shift beneath it, soft silk hose of white, red-heeled slippers with pert red bows, and petticoats. In the other box was a cloak, the like of which she had never seen before, lined sumptuously with the silver fox fur. She stifled a gasp of delight. She was like a child before a peddler's box of fairings, i'faith she was! Her resolve had all but weakened by now, but suddenly surged through her hotly. She could have her pie, aye, and eat it too, she vowed! Yes, she'd don his fancy garb and still flee, the second, the very *second* his back was turned!

She glanced over her shoulder quickly to make sure he was not looking, then speedily undressed. She shivered in the chilly room until the shift and then the gown had been pulled on. She reached behind her, but could only fasten the bottom buttons. Damnation! she thought, biting her lip, she was forced to ask him to help her.

"Captain?" she asked self-consciously.

"Aye?" he said brusquely, without turning about.

"I—I am dressed, sir, but unable to fasten the buttons."

"Of course," James said gallantly. He turned to her. Her back was to him, a strangely vulnerable little back and a sweetly vulnerable exposed nape where she had lifted her hair so as not to let it get entangled in the buttons. He covered his wayward thoughts with a cough and hurriedly fastened each button. Then he lifted the heavy cloak from the box and draped it about her slim shoulders.

"There," he said uncomfortably.

"Thank you," Christianne murmured, fumbling with the clasp as she turned to face him.

The breath caught in his throat. The scarlet velvet glowed with the luster of priceless rubies and she, with the silver and golden loveliness of a Nordic princess! The rich, vibrant color gave warmth to her delicate coloring; the fur-lined hood haloed her dainty, oval face exactly as he had imagined it would. Lord, she was lovely!

"My lady?" he questioned, the formal address slipping off

his tongue unbidden.

"Captain?" she queried uncertainly.

Their gazes met and locked momentarily, both unable to look away. James came to his senses first. He smiled and offered her his arm.

"I asked if you were ready to depart, my lady?" he said softly, still under the magic of the spell that seemed suddenly, fleetingly, in the air between them.

She blinked and gave him a soft, bewitching smile, then inclined her head and murmured, "Yes."

Nine

The *Fair Amanda* gave every appearance of a vessel soon to set sail, if the number of sailors scurrying about their duties were anything to go by. The decks and the rigging fairly swarmed with men, and Christianne was momentarily overwhelmed by their numbers and the size of the trim, black-painted vessel and her immaculate appearance. A beautifully carved figurehead reared gracefully from her prow, a lovely woman with long, flowing hair painted a dark chestnut hue. The vessel's name was written in curlicued script across her bow. This Amanda for whom the ship had been named must have been someone very special to the captain. Was? Perhaps she is his wife, she thought suddenly, though he had not mentioned a spouse. No matter, she cared not a whit if Capt. James Mallory had as many wives as a sultan, nor if he kept them in a harem, to boot. She bit her lip anxiously. No chance to escape him had presented itself during the long ride to the wharves, for she had been seated before him on his horse, his arms about her waist and thence on the reins, making flight impossible. It appeared no more likely here, for a sailor of some authority was hurrying toward them down the gangplank.

"Here we are, Ben, at last," James declared, noting Ben's amazement with relish. "May I present Mistress Christianne Alexander."

"A pleasure, ma'am," Ben said graciously, doffing his tricorn. He turned to his captain, a question in his eyes.

"It appears Mistress Nellie and myself erred, Ben," James

explained, laughter in his voice. "We had expected a nephew, but we are delightfully surprised to find out that 'he' is in fact 'she'! Of course, Mistress Alexander will now be given my cabin for the duration of our voyage, and I shall be fortunate in sharing your own." He grinned.

"Very well, sir," Ben agreed dolefully. "Mullens has rounded up some new men, sir. Shall I have him assemble them on deck for your inspection?"

"Aye," James agreed, dismounting. "Have Mark take the horse back to the tavern, too, will you?" He lifted Christianne down to his side. He did not think she intended to flee, but he was taking no chances, not this time.

A feeling of panic swept over Christianne. Despite the cold, perspiration had beaded her brow and her palms were slippery. There was to be no escape, none whatsoever, she realized dully. She watched on disinterestedly while barrels of salt pork were rolled up the gangplank. How mournful, how bereft the gulls sounded as they wheeled about the masts! Their cries seemed to put into sound the anguish in her heart.

James' fingers still curled about her upper arm, their warm pressure light, a reminder more than anything that he was not going to trust her, not yet. Her heart thudded and skipped a beat. She had to try! She couldn't meekly walk up the plank onto this great ship like a lamb to the slaughter! She turned suddenly away, casting desperately about her for an escape route. Instantly those same fingers closed about her arms like a vise, cruel, powerful.

"Do not try it, lass," James warned hoarsely in her ear. He edged her forward up the gangplank.

Her feet felt leaden and unwilling to do her bidding. Tears lodged like a heavy stone in her breast. She stumbled as she walked up the gently swaying gangplank of the *Fair Amanda.*

At the rail she turned to look back. Low clouds that promised further snow hung brooding over the city of

London, over the steeples and towers of her churches and cathedrals, the rooftops of her taverns, her shops, her cobbled thoroughfares of bakers, haberdashers, goldsmiths and tailors. Farewell, England, she said silently, the tears in her breast dissolving suddenly and stinging her eyes. Farewell!

James was saying something. She looked up at him through a watery mist.

"Will you not take this little fellow with you?" he was asking.

She looked down. Master Bones wriggled wildly in his arms, his pink tongue joyously bathing the captain's face. She nodded and took the little dog from him, clasping him tightly to her breast and drawing comfort from his familiarity and warmth.

She followed James across the deck, dimly aware of the respect his men showed him, vaguely astonished by what seemed their genuine affection for their captain. He led her down a narrow gangway and stopped before a cabin door of oak. Ben Wright had followed them and now handed James a weighty key. Taking it from him, James unlocked and swung open the door.

The cabin within was very spacious but boasted only three pieces of furniture; a massive desk, a large four-poster bed, bolted to the deck and draped with brocade of deep blue and a matching coverlet, and an ornately carved chair. A window bellied outwards in one wall, framed by still more richly-carved wooden trims and paned with cloudy glass. An armoire and a cabinet had been built into the massive walls to accommodate the captain's clothing and personal items, and a huge sea chest sat squarely at the foot of the bed. It was bound with leather and studded with brass-headed nails. A fancy lantern hung above. There were numerous boxes and parcels on the boards, strewn haphazardly about.

"Here you will find your new wardrobe, Christianne,"

James said. "I trust my taste will be to your liking, but without your cooperation, I'm afraid I had no choice but to select for you." He smiled. "This cabin is to be yours for the duration of the voyage. It is my hope that you will be comfortable. Is there anything further you require?"

Christianne looked about her. "I see no bathing tub, sir," she said softly. "How am I to bathe?" The luxury of a bath was one she had all but forgotten the pleasures of until last night. If she was forced to endure this loathed voyage, it may as well be with every possible comfort at her disposal.

James frowned. "Of course. Mister Wright," he ordered, turning to Ben, "send someone ashore to find a tub for the young lady at once. Also linens, soap and an ewer and basin. On the double."

"Now where am I to find a bathtub?" Ben grumbled in his Cornish accent. His normally-kind gray eyes, eyes the color of the smoke from a wood fire, were angry.

"I have no idea!" James laughed. He turned to Christianne. "Make yourself comfortable, my dear. I must go aloft and see to my men and to getting us under sail. I will be back later to see how you are faring." He strode from the cabin. Ben Wright, still muttering under his breath, hurried after him and closed the door in his wake. It was not, as Christianne had feared, to be locked.

She set Master Bones down on the captain's fancy bed.

"Well, Bones," she sighed, "here we are!"

The dog thumped its tail in answer, tongue lolling.

She unfastened her cloak and lay it across the carved chair. Brushing a pale blond curl from her cheek, rosy with cold, she went to the piled array of boxes the young captain had termed her wardrobe and began unfastening the string about each one.

Such a quantity of garments she had never seen before! Delicate gossamer-thin shifts of fine lawn, warm but dainty chemises of lindsey-woolsey, quilted petticoats, silken hose in a rainbow of colors, two further pairs of shoes, a velvet drawstring purse, a portmanteau containing gloves, shawls, kerchiefs, garters and ribbons, and last but not least, the captain's choice of gowns. There was one of sky-blue satin with a low, square neck and pleated white lace sleeves, one a rich, mossy green, its skirts tucked up to reveal a rose-pink quilted petticoat beneath, another of prim dove-gray with a froth of white lace at the collar and cuffs. The last was her favorite, next to the scarlet velvet, of lavender, striped prettily with pink and silver bands, soft, muted shades that suggested delicate autumn sunsets or summer dawns.

She swung open the door of the armoire. The captain's clothes still hung there, cloaks, jerkins, shirts and breeches, along with several tricorn hats. After a brief moment's hesitation, she dragged them out and dumped them in an untidy pile upon the cabin floor, and set about installing her own new wardrobe in the armoire's interior. She admitted now that she had no choice but to go with James Mallory—but she would do so under protest.

James inspected his new crew members approvingly. Silas Mullens had done well, and he told him so. They all appeared to be strong and able men.

"Thank ye kindly, sir. And there is not a pressed man amongst 'em, sir, they do all be volunteers," Mullens added proudly, his weathered face crinkling in a grin.

James nodded his approval and stopped in front of one of the new crew members.

"Your name, man?"

"Jonathan Flint, sir!" the man sang out smartly. He was tall, rapier-lean, black-haired and wore a golden ring in one ear. His upper lip boasted a thin, wicked moustache. His eyes were as black as his wild, curling hair and very bold. They met James' scrutiny unwaveringly.

"You have sailed before?" James asked, though he

84

believed he knew what the man's answer would be.

"Aye, t' be sure, sir," Flint responded quickly. "I was first officer aboard the *Perdita* of the East India Company before."

"Under Captain Morrison?"

"Yes, sir."

"And why did you leave his crew?"

"On our last voyage, sir, the *Perdita* was overrun by buccaneers as we rounded the Cape. Captain Morrison and most of the crew were lost. Myself and a handful of others escaped and took to the longboats, scant seconds before they fired the ship. We worked our way back to England after many hard months, sir, and are now ready to go to sea again. 'Tis in the blood, I fear!" He grinned.

"I see." James nodded thoughtfully. "I have a first officer already, Flint, in Mister Wright here. Are you willing to serve me as one of the crew?"

"Indeed I am, sir! It is said in the taverns that you are a worthy captain, aye, and a fair one. I have no reservations. I'll serve you well, as will my companions here, Stephen Tancred and Pierre Le Chat. Tancred has some talents as a surgeon, sir, and Le Chat is the finest sailmaker that ever put needle to canvas, if I say so myself, sir. You won't regret taking us, Captain, I guarantee it."

"I am duly impressed, Flint, both by your companions and yourself," James said dryly. The man's loquaciousness was second only to the aura of self-confidence and cocky assurance he exuded! He stepped on.

"And who are you?" James asked, halting, forced to look upward by the massive height of the next man in line. If he were not mistaken, the fellow was close to seven feet in height and proportionately massive in breadth. Despite the bitter cold, he was clad only in breeches and a brown leather jerkin, and his bare arms were hugely muscled and almost as swarthy as a Spaniard's, forested with brown hair. He wore his hair long and straggly and had a rough, unkempt beard. His eyes were gray, a pale gray, and watched James sullenly from beneath a prominent forehead.

"I asked your name, man!" James barked, angered by the massive lout's silent insolence.

"Your pardon, sir, but the man is a mute. His tongue was cut out by the same scurvy pirates that overran the *Perdita*. We know him only by the name of Ox, sir, the name given him by the crew on account of his great size, sir," Jonathan Flint volunteered.

James nodded and curtly dismissed the men to their various duties.

"Well, sir, what do you think of them?" Ben Wright asked.

"Mullens appears to have done well," James said thoughtfully. "A sailmaker, a ship's surgeon to assist Matthew Locke should the need arise, and a powerful deckhand will doubtless serve us admirably."

"And Flint?" Ben asked shrewdly. "What think you of him?"

"To all intents, he is an able, intelligent man, but—!" He broke off, his green eyes narrowing as he frowned.

"But what, sir?" Ben pressed.

"But I do not like him," James continued, "nor do I trust him! Seafaring men, as you know, Ben, are a close-mouthed lot, for the greater part. Master Flint has a tongue as long as a carriage whip, and it will prove, mayhap, just as dangerous. Watch him, Ben, and tell Locke and Mullens to do the same!"

"Aye, aye, sir," Ben agreed. His own feelings regarding Flint were similar to his captain's. A chill slithered down his spine. A premonition? he wondered with true Cornish superstition. He shook his head and made for the gangway, unable to negate the feeling that someone had just walked over his grave.

* * *

James pondered his wisdom as to keeping Flint on as a member of the crew again that evening.

Twilight was deepening the misty amethyst of the sky to a deep, hard violet, in which the first evening star pierced through to twinkle frostily. The crew had gone ashore for a last drinking spree in the waterfront taverns, but Flint had declined to go with them.

"I beg your pardon, sir," he said in his soft, Irish brogue, "but I'm not much of a drinker, despite my origins in Ireland, sir. At the start of a voyage, at least, that is, sir!" His companions from the *Perdita*'s old crew had echoed his sentiments, though Ox seemed sullen at Flint's words.

James frowned, puffing on the pipe he often smoked aboard his vessel. Perhaps he should get rid of them and be done with it, and at least still the doubts he had. But good men were hard to find, and especially in the winter, most men preferring to find employment closer to a warm hearth than brave the high seas in wintry months. If he delayed their departure any longer, there was a good chance, too, that the Thames might freeze, as she did often in January, and then he would be forced to wait for a spring thaw in late April or May. The hell with it, he decided. He'd try them out, and if they proved unsatisfactory, off the ship they would go at the nearest port of call.

The voyage would be a circuitous one. The holds were as yet only half-filled with yardgoods from Lancashire, and lumber. In France he would take on brandy and laces; in Spain, finely crafted silverware and sherries by the bottle, barrels of almonds and exquisite leather goods and cigars. Then they would round the Cape of Good Hope and sail thence to the West Indies, he thought with a grin. Ah, the Caribees! Aye, warmer climes awaited them, islands of lush, emerald-green slopes and dazzling golden beaches, water of crystalline clarity and of such a brilliant azure hue that it pained the eyes with its vividness. And always, the odor of spices, rum and flowers that wafted to the ship, borne on balmy air, before ever the islands themselves were sighted! He'd had more than enough of an English winter, cold enough to freeze over the fires of Hades, by God!

He tamped out the bowl of his pipe over the rail and turned to go below. Ben had promised to have supper brought to his cabin—now Christianne's—so that he could sup with her. The little minx would be lonely, no doubt. He crossed the empty decks, lit only by the lanterns that hung from the yardarms. What manner of reception would he receive from her tonight, he wondered? He shook his head. No, he would not attempt to second-guess that silver-haired hellion's reactions! She was unpredictable, judging by the little he had learned of her to date!

He rapped upon his cabin door and a clear voice bade him enter.

"Good evening, Christianne," he began, his gaze falling on the pile of his belongings strewn haphazardly on the boards. His jaw tightened. "I see you have . . . availed yourself of my armoire?"

"Yes, indeed, Captain," she said sweetly. "I knew you would wish me to make myself comfortable in your absence, and I have most gratefully done so." Let him rant, and he would, after her carefully calculated little speech, appear not only cavalier but uncivil! She smiled innocently at him.

James bit back a scathing comment and instead strode across to the heavy oaken table. Platters had been set upon it holding a fine, roasted capon, a leg of mutton, a milky-white crumbling cheese and a full loaf of brown bread. A huge plum pudding, complete with holly-sprig, which despite its name held no plums but was instead studded with sultanas, currants and nutmeats, steamed on yet another platter. There was a golden-treacle tart, a game pie of some sort giving off a savory aroma, and several raspberry tartlets mounded on another trencher. James blinked. Such largesse, for just the two of them? Whatever had Ben and the cook been thinking of?

"I trust you will not object, Captain, but Ben—I mean, Master Wright—mentioned that most of the crew had gone ashore, and that those that remained would partake of some plain fare, poor lads. I requested that those few men might be permitted to join us here, at table, knowing you would not wish them to enjoy less than what their captain is about to enjoy. He has gone in search of a fine, fat goose to further enrich our Yuletide board." Under lowered lashes she awaited the captain's response, knowing full well she had sorely pushed his good humor to the limits by her actions and her words. She was not disappointed.

His green eyes flashed. A muscle twitched violently in his cheek. "Indeed, madam? You have not wasted much time in asserting your wishes on my crew, have you?"

"I have displeased you, Captain?" She frowned, pouting her rose-pink lips. "But in what way, pray tell?" Those same lips twitched, for James' knuckles were clenched white upon the chair back.

"Madam," he gritted, "I am the captain here! It is for me to decide who shall dine at my table, do you understand, not you!" He paced angrily, arms crossed on his chest, his handsome face set in a dark scowl. The leather of his boots and jerkin creaked loudly in the silence. He whirled on her. "I do believe you deliberately set out to anger me!" he accused, his green eyes stormy.

Christianne jumped to her feet. "I, Captain? And why should I desire that you be angry with me?" she demanded, tossing back her shoulder-length curls in challenging fashion.

"Resentment, you vixen! You resent my taking you to New Orleans against your wishes, and I have little doubt that you have determined, in your usual childish fashion, to prove difficult by way of retaliation!" He scowled, oblivious to the darkling look she flashed him. "Ah, you do not deny it!"

"Nay!" she retorted. "You will rue the day you entrapped

89

this *child*, James Mallory! You will rue it with every breath in your body, you scurvy whelp, you misbegotten, slimy—"

"Enough!" James growled, "Hold your tongue, madam, before I forget you *are* a woman," he said mockingly, "and thrash your buttocks like the child you behave like."

"My sex and my age need not concern you, sir," she spat, her navy-blue eyes flaring with dark fires. "I would hate you anyway, even if I were the lad you thought me at first. I give you fair warning: if you would deliver me to my aunt, you had best not turn your back, nor let slip your guard upon me, for I swear I will fly like a bird from a gilded cage if you but once slacken your surveillance. I swear it!" Her small breasts heaved with the ardor of her speech.

"Then it is still war, Christianne?" James said softly.

"It is!" she hissed, her eyes brilliant in the lantern's light.

The cabin door swung open. Ben Wright stood in the doorway, uncertainty in his expression. "I knocked, sir, but when no one bade me enter, I—"

"Yes, yes, Ben," James growled, "what is it?"

"The—the goose, sir," Ben stammered. "I was fortunate enough to find one at the tavern on Customs Street, ready-roasted and all, sir, as the young lady requested. 'Tis a fine bird, too. The men bade me give you their thanks in advance, Captain, for your generous gesture. They are looking forward to their Yuletide—" His voice trailed away as he spotted the expression of fury on James' face, and belatedly realized that the gathering had not been his captain's idea. He fidgeted uncomfortably, aware now, too, of the tension that fairly crackled in the cabin. His captain was livid, and so, it appeared, was the little wench. He sighed unhappily.

"I am overwhelmed that they appreciated the gesture," James snapped coldly. "Bid them enter for their repast. We must not keep our guests waiting, must we, madam?" he said mockingly.

"Indeed, no," she gritted. "Will you be joining us, sir?"

she asked, certain the captain would heatedly decline.

"But, of course!" James replied smoothly. "Since I am the host for our little gathering, I will of course be joining you." He made a half-bow that further mocked her, and leaned back with his arms crossed on his chest, a black scowl wreathing his handsome face.

Damnation, Christianne thought, muffling her displeasure as Ben ushered the crew members into the cabin, each bearing a chair, an empty trencher and a spoon. There were seven of them in all, with Ben, the captain and herself, and the cabin was crowded.

Jonathan Flint's eyes flickered over the young woman as he set his chair down. It was obvious from the gleam in their obsidian blackness that he liked what he saw.

The captain took his place at the head of the table and sat down, barely containing his temper and entirely forgetting his normally impeccable manners. The crew milled about the table, coughing nervously, still standing, as was Christianne.

Flint hurried to her side. "My lady?" he questioned, offering her his arm and withdrawing her chair.

She inclined her head graciously and allowed him to seat her.

"My thanks, sir," she murmured warmly, flashing him a bewitching, dimpled smile. "I had not expected one so gallant in such coarse surroundings as these."

Flint bowed over her slender hand and kissed it. "It is easy to be chivalrous, ma'am, when these coarse surroundings are graced by such loveliness as yours." He smiled, his dark eyes lingering on her lovely face. "Jonathan Flint is my name, ma'am, and I am your servant!"

"You are most kind, sir," Christianne said softly," please be seated, Master Flint." Her face was rosy from his compliment.

Inwardly, James seethed. He had not missed their exchanged glances, the warmth of hers. The little twit was seeking to make him jealous! He laughed inwardly. If she expected him to react to such simpering nonsense, she was in for a disappointment, he thought disgustedly.

"Flint, won't you take the chair on Mistress Alexander's left, since you have been introduced," he said easily, "and the rest of you, please, be seated."

There was much commotion as the party sat and the meal was begun. Despite himself, James glowered throughout it, while Christianne and Jonathan Flint conversed wittily and somewhat flirtatiously at the other end. James eyed his men moodily over the rim of his goblet. He could find no fault with Pierre Le Chat nor with the one called Stephen Tancred, although it was not for lack of trying, but the mute one, the one Flint had called Ox, was watching the girl as if mesmerized. His light gray, almost colorless, eyes followed her every move from within the shaggy forest of his hair and beard. The expression on his broad face was almost tender. A warning bell clamored in James' head. He'd have to keep a careful eye out for Christianne's safety, he thought.

Ben, on his left, noted the captain's narrowed gaze and coughed discreetly. "I don't believe ye need to worry, sir. This Ox seems much taken with the lass. I don't believe he'd harm her," he murmured in an aside.

"Aye, mayhap not," James agreed. "But should his adoration turn to lust, what then—?"

Ben nodded gloomy agreement.

Inwardly James cursed himself for his own misgivings. Damnation! He was like a spinsterish old dame who feared to find a man under her bed each time she peeked beneath it! He determined to relax and enjoy the remainder of the evening. After all, it was Christmas Eve!

"From where do you hail, Flint?" he asked casually, leaning back in his chair.

Flint, who had been recounting an anecdote to

Christianne—obviously an amusing one—looked up and smiled lazily. "From Ireland, sir," he supplied, "a wee village just a mile or two outside o' Dublin, t' be exact." He grinned beneath the thin, wicked dark curve of his black moustache. "And you, Captain, sir?"

"I am England-born, Flint, from the city of Portsmouth. But of late my family has settled in Salem."

"Ah," Flint said, nodding, "and why was it your family left fair England's shores, sir?"

"My father, Richard Mallory, was an honest man, and an outspoken one. When the colonies first began to mutter against taxation, he rashly—and publicly—sided with them, and incurred our late king's sore displeasure. Unfortunately, there were witnesses. Need I say more? He deemed it wiser to take his family to the New World before his sovereign's displeasure took some more positive turn," James recounted.

"A wise man!" Flint laughed, pouring himself another goblet of canary. "And you, Captain, where do your sympathies lie?"

James grinned, his expression deceptively open. "Why, Flint, my sympathies lie with those who have justice on their side, of course! And you?"

For a moment Flint's eyes seemed to burn with an ardent inner light that extinguished as swiftly as it had ignited. "I believe," he said mildly, as if his answer was of little import, "that my sympathies lie with the colonists, sir. I have little liking for the British. Your continued good health, Captain!" He raised his goblet and drained the contents in a single draft.

James raised his own. "And to yours, Flint. Merry Christmas, and a safe and prosperous voyage to all of us!"

Was he mistaken, he wondered afterwards, or had he really caught Flint and Tancred exchanging knowing, amused glances as the rest at the table raised their goblets in the toast?

Ten

A blustery, biting cold wind had buffeted the *Fair Amanda* on the first leg of her voyage, across the English Channel to the French port of Le Havre. Tears had stung Christianne's eyes, she recalled, as she stood on the cold, rain-swept decks and watched the white chalk cliffs of Dover receding into the fog. A lump had formed in her throat. To her surprise, James had come to stand at her side, and, sensing her misery, attempted to comfort her.

"Take heart, Mistress Alexander," he had said in a gruff but kind voice, "England has stood for centuries and will, no doubt, stand for many more. If at some later date you should still wish to return here, I am persuaded your aunt will not forbid you to do so. She is a kindhearted woman, Christianne, I promise you."

But her grief had been so great and her anger so new she could not find it in her heart to listen to the concern that underlined his words.

"You are persuaded, damn you! And what of me? What of my say in the course of my own life—that counts for naught?"

She had picked up her skirts and fled back to the cabin, unwilling to let him see the hot tears of defeat that spilled down her cheeks.

On nearing Le Havre, Captain Mallory had issued orders that she was not to be permitted to go ashore, no doubt fearing she would attempt to escape. And rightly so! she recalled with a wry smile, for she had been ready to fly at the first opportunity that presented itself, as she had vowed to the captain. Yet by the time the French coastline had appeared, escape had been the furthest thing from her mind!

She had been forced to take to her bed with a basin, and rid her belly of the captain's good victuals more times than she cared to number. How desperately she had wanted to stand once more on dry land, land that didn't roll and heave and lift and drop beneath your feet, or cause your belly to do likewise! James' refusal to let her go ashore became yet another grudge to be held against him, damn his soul, as if she needed more fuel for the fires of her hatred for him!

For four endless days she had suffered from the awful seasickness, until there was naught left in her belly to retch up. Limbs quivering, her head pounding, she had curled up in her bed, hugging her knees to her chest, and prayed for death to strike her quickly, suddenly, and thus put an end to her misery. On more than one such occasion, she had awoken from a fitful doze to find the captain at her bedside, a wet cloth in one hand and hot broth and sea-biscuits in the other. Patiently he had wiped her face clean and then sat and spooned the beef broth into her, insisting in no uncertain terms that she eat each and every morsel of the biscuit, too.

"You oaf!" she had screamed at him. "My wretched guts are rebelling at the mere odor of your swill, and will not permit it in my belly! Oh, ye gods and little fishes, take it away, please, I beg you!" she had moaned, pressing her hand over her mouth.

"Nay, Christie," James had insisted, "drink the broth and eat the biscuit. It is far worse to vomit on an empty stomach than a full one, trust me. This sickness will pass, and we'll make a good sailor of you yet, you'll see!"

Damn him, he had been correct on all counts! By the fifth day she had felt well enough to sleep the watch around. On the sixth she had been able to totter weakly from the bed and wash herself. On the seventh Jonathan Flint had come below and taken her up on deck to enjoy the fresh air, with his captain's permission. She had survived!

The weather was subtly warmer now that they were nearing Spain, she noticed. She began to hold out hope that, this time, James might permit her to go ashore when they docked at Barcelona. Spaniards! They were all sly, swarthy fellows, England's enemies more often than not, and therefore her enemies too, but still, she was curious to see their country. Her hopes had soared when James came to her cabin last night.

"On the morrow, Christianne, we reach Barcelona," he had begun. "I have old friends there I will be meeting with. It was my thought that perhaps you would enjoy coming ashore with me—or else you may stay here, under Master Wright's care, until I return. Would you care to come?"

Care to, you brainless dolt, she wanted to scream at him, of course I would *care* to! But she feared such a heated reply would anger him and cause him to withdraw his invitation, and so instead she only murmured that she would like very much to accompany him, and thanked him for the offer in quietly civil tones that appeared to give him considerable amusement, judging by the merry sparkle in his devil-green eyes!

"Ah, so you can behave like a lady when it suits your purpose!" he had exclaimed. "I had feared that only a foul-mouthed shrew lurked within that angelic exterior! Well, madam, we will go ashore together then. But first, I must have your sworn promise that you will not attempt to escape me. Swear it now, on your mother's grave."

Gritting her teeth fiercely, she had nodded. "I swear!" she vowed, almost choking on the words.

And so, she thought, here am I, and there is Barcelona!

She leaned over the rail and looked down. The ships were so clustered at dockside that James had been forced to drop anchor a half mile out. Longboats had been lowered to row the men to the wharf. The water was alive with small boats whose owners were doing brisk trade rowing impatient merchants ashore for a modest sum.

"Come, Christie, our longboat awaits," James said behind her.

She gasped in surprise as she turned to him. His curling russet hair was now neatly pulled back in a stylish queue, and a black tricorn braided with silver perched jauntily atop it. Over his full-sleeved shirt he had donned a dark blue coat and breeches of fine velvet, the breeches tucked into highly polished, black boots with silver buckles. A black cloak lined with sky blue silk draped from his broad shoulders, and beneath its folds she glimpsed a finely crafted sword and a matching dagger with a jewelled hilt, which her knowledgeable eyes instantly assessed at worth in excess of a hundred golden guineas! He looked very handsome, very dashing, and every inch a gentleman, she acknowledged with reluctance.

He grinned roguishly. "If I have passed muster, Milady Admiral, shall we go?" he asked her in a teasing tone as he offered her his arm. His eyes lit with approval as they noted she wore the sky blue gown with the ruffled lace sleeves beneath her scarlet cape.

Despite herself, she blushed under his intense green scrutiny. "Aye," she murmured, "I'm ready."

She negotiated the rope ladder down into the longboat with extreme difficulty, inwardly cursing her cumbersome female garb as she did so, for she was forced to accept James' offer of assistance. In minutes they were clambering up the stone steps of the wharf.

Christianne looked about her with avid curiosity. Young women with brilliantly-colored scarves tied over their heads and golden hoops swinging in their ears chattered volubly in rapid Spanish as they gutted the fish heaped in barrels before them. Their hands and their wickedly sharp knives flashed with amazing speed as they performed the messy task with the skill of years of experience. Swarthy dock laborers unloaded cargoes of fresh-hewn lumber, barrels of flour and kegs of salt from the ships at dockside onto waiting wagons, of which there were many. Merchants haggled with sea captains in various tongues over the purchase of their cargoes. Grubby urchins with enormous black eyes set in tiny, pinched brown faces, begged for pesos and eyed the fat merchants' purses with speculation! Christianne hid a knowing grin at the antics of the lads. There, but for the grace of God and my unknown Aunt Nellie, go I, she thought. Somehow, though, her supposed good fortune gave her little pleasure. The urchins, though obviously poor, ragged and in all probability but one step from starvation, were at least free. And freedom, she realized bitterly, was beyond price.

James strode eagerly across the wharf, weaving his way between the crowds trailing Christianne in his wake. He was headed, she saw, towards an elegant coach that bore an elaborate coat of arms emblazoned in gilt on its doors. She followed him at a slower gait.

The coach door flew open as James neared it and an exquisitely beautiful young woman leaned out. Her hair was the rich russet hue of chestnuts, yet her eyes were dark, with sweeping, seductive lashes.

"Dame Fortune be praised, he is here!" the young woman exclaimed delightedly. "Capt. James Mallory, in the flesh!"

Her accent was not Spanish but English, Christianne noted.

James all but ran to meet her, his handsome face alight with pleasure. "Indeed it is I, Amanda!" he declared, "and what a treat for a poor sea captain to feast my starved eyes upon your loveliness once more!"

Oh, ye gods, Christianne thought with a grimace.

James swung the young woman down into his arms.

"Aha!" proclaimed a deep, rich voice from within the

coach, "you are still a rogue, Mallory! See to it that it is only your eyes that rest overlong on my *pequeña* Amanda—and not your hands!"

Christianne could not stifle a gasp as the owner of that rich, Spanish-accented voice appeared in the doorway of the coach. The speaker was tall for a Spaniard with a lean, hard-muscled frame that was evident even beneath his rich garments. His fine head boasted blue-black, curling hair that fell crisply to his nape, and his face was the most darkly handsome she had ever seen, set with wicked, almost black, eyes.

James laughed, left the woman with one of his lingering smiles, and strode up to the man as he jumped to the cobbles from the coach. They clasped hands warmly.

"Don Miguel! By the saints, married life has done well by you, my friend!" he roared, clapping the Spaniard heartily across the back.

Don Miguel grinned. "And that of a bachelor by you, amigo, si? It is good to see you again! Tell me, how was your voyage?"

James snapped his fingers. "It was nothing," he declared. "I've seen millponds rougher than the ocean was this crossing."

Miguel nodded. His dark eyes glanced questioningly over James' shoulder to Christianne, who waited somewhat nervously behind him.

James caught his query and turned to her. "Forgive me, Christie," he apologized. "I am proud to introduce you to two very dear friends of mine. La Doña Amanda de Villarin, and Don Miguel de Villarin. Amanda, Miguel, may I present Mistress Christianne Alexander. Nellie's niece."

Amanda's lovely mouth dropped open. She hurried forward and clasped Christianne's cold hands in greeting. "Welcome to Spain, dear Christianne!" she said warmly. "Tell me, how is my darling Nellie? Lord, how I miss that red-haired—"

99

"Mistress Alexander has not yet had the pleasure of meeting her Aunt Nell, Amanda," James cut in quickly. "Nell is to be her guardian, since her mother, Nell's sister, Jenny, has sadly passed on. Nell entrusted me to fetch her while in London."

Amanda caught the warning in James' raised eyebrows and nodded. "Ah, I see." She smiled warmly at the girl. "Well, Christianne, you are indeed fortunate in having an aunt such as Nell. When I was in dire straits some years past, Nell was like a sister to me. You could not ask for a more loving, finer woman for your guardian."

Christianne grimaced. "Indeed, Doña Amanda," she said pointedly, "so I have been told by the good captain, on numerous occasions."

It was Miguel's turn to raise a dark eyebrow now. With the girl's words, it was as if a bolt of lightning had leaped between her and James, crackling the air with explosive tension. "Come," he invited hurriedly, "let's away to the inn. Amanda and I heard the *Fair Amanda* had been sighted and took the liberty of instructing Señor Cristobal, the innkeeper, to prepare a meal for us. You will join us, si?"

"Sil" James laughed. He offered Christianne his arm and handed her up into the coach with the de Villarins.

"Your letter reached us but two days ago, James," Amanda said as she spread her full skirts across the seat and settled herself in the luxurious, velvet-lined coach. "You said that you would be here at the end of January, and you are prompt almost to the day, for it is only the second of February."

James nodded. "Aye, it was a good crossing, and my business in London went well. If it were not for a little matter that caused me some concern while there, I would have been here even sooner." His eyes flickered to Christianne seated across from him. She glared stonily at him and haughtily looked away, and he hid a smile before continuing the conversation.

Christianne inwardly fumed. How dare he talk about her as if she were a child, as if she were not even there, that—that rat! She determined to ignore him and instead directed her attention out of the coach window while the trio exchanged pleasantries.

Barcelona was an old city like London, she saw, with narrow, winding streets above which the wrought-iron balconies that fronted the houses on either side almost met. It was far warmer than an English February was wont to be. The air smelled different, too, she noticed, inhaling, rich and spicy and filled with odors and aromas that even her astute nose could not identify. The pedestrians were dressed much like those in London, though for the most part they seemed to favor more somber colors and greater severity of styles. They were all dark-complected from the Mediterranean sunshine and had dark, flashing eyes. Donkeys were much in evidence, their panniers loaded down with pottery, fagots of wood or exotic, orange-colored round fruits that she had never seen before. She wanted to ask what they were called, but James was deep in conversation with the dark and handsome Spaniard and she was loath to show her ignorance before either of them. She stole a covert glance at the woman, Doña Amanda de Villarin. So, this must be the woman the captain had named his vessel for, she realized, and also the one he had mentioned that night at the Golden Goose tavern. He must have loved her, Christianne thought, yet if that were so, would he and the don be on such obviously amicable terms?

She shrugged irritably. What did she care who James had loved or had not loved! She wanted to be rid of him, that was all. Damn him for extracting her sworn promise not to escape him! Yet she had promised on her mother's grave, and she could not go back on her word. She bit her lip in concentration. Unless . . . Unless he were to do something so foul, so despicable, she could in all good conscience break it. Or unless he were *goaded* into doing so, she thought with an impish smile, remembering the lingering look he had given her that morning when first seeing her ready to go. Would it work? she wondered as an idea struck through the fog that had settled in her brain. I'faith, her wits were dulled by so much leisure time at sea, and her victuals being delivered up to her as easily as purses had been before! She needed a challenge such as this to sharpen them, she thought ruefully. She was becoming as slothful as a slug with this life of ease! Aye, her idea was worth considering.

The coach halted in the stable yard of an inn and the ostler came out to take the matched pair of black horses. The de Villarins and James climbed down, and then James reached inside to lift her down after him. She shot him a grateful smile as he did so, which he returned with a bemused inclining of his head.

By God, James thought, leading Christianne into the gloomy taproom, the wench could bewitch a man with those small, mysterious smiles of hers when she wanted, and cause him to forget that she was ever a shrew!

Señor Cristobal, a barrel-bellied, balding Spaniard, came bustling forward to greet them and ushered them to his finest table. He snapped his fingers and sent his many daughters, all buxom, sloe-eyed Catalonian wenches, flying for his wealthy guests' meal. Since it was Friday, and the de Villarins were, of course, of the Catholic faith, meat was naturally not included in the fare. Instead great platters of fish, simmered with onions and tomatoes, spices, wine and olive oil, were set before them. Loaves of golden-brown bread, still warm and crusty from the oven, pats of butter and flagons of red wine accompanied the meal, which, Christianne soon discovered, was delicious and quite unlike anything she had ever tasted before. Saffron-colored rice, tossed with shrimp and red and green morsels of peppers, followed. Christianne ate heartily, oblivious of the kind but amused glances exchanged by her hosts and the captain. At length she pushed back her platter and sighed with satisfaction.

" 'Twas the finest victuals I ever did taste!" she declared, reverting to her urchin's phrasing in her relaxed state.

Amanda smiled. "Indeed, it is very good," she agreed. She looked up as a plump Spanish matron entered the taproom, trailed by two small children, laughing and chattering in a mixture of Spanish and English. "James," Amanda said as the trio reached their table, "I would like you to meet Señora Bonita Viernes. And this young man I believe you already know, though he has grown just a little since last you saw him!" She laughed.

James gaped at the little lad before him. The boy returned his stare boldly from bright, black eyes. His hair was an unruly mop of blue-black curls, his chin as square and stubborn as the don's.

"Michael?" James picked the lad up and tossed him into the air, eliciting a delighted peal of laughter from him. "Why, lad, you are your father's son!" he declared as he set the boy down. "He's a fine little fellow, Miguel," he said warmly. He crouched down and peered around Bonita's skirts. "And who might you be, my poppet?"

The little girl surveyed him solemnly from the safety of her nurse's skirts. At length she extracted a chubby thumb from her mouth and smiled shyly. "My name is Marianna," she said, "and I'm two." She tossed her auburn curls proudly and held up two fingers as proof of her words.

"Indeed," James said gravely, "I can see that you are, and a very pretty little señorita you are, too, like your mama." He burrowed in his pockets and withdrew two silver sixpences. "For sweetmeats, children, from your Uncle James!" he declared, handing them over.

"Tío James?" Amanda laughed. "You do not look like anyone's uncle, James Mallory!" she declared, "though mayhap you might pass for a roguish, black sheep brother

103

of some noble family!"

"And you, my dear Amanda," he rejoined, "do not look like the mother of these two. You have changed not a whit these few years past!" He ignored Miguel's and Christianne's scowls and kissed her hand fondly.

Miguel coughed. "Enough, Mallory," he said with mock severity, "or I shall be forced to call you to account! Tell me, can you return with us to Villa Hermosa for a few days before you continue your voyage? My brother, Fernando and his wife, Miranda, are most anxious to meet you. They would have travelled to Barcelona with us, but my sister-in-law has just been delivered of her third child, a fine girl, this time, and was unable to travel."

James shook his head regretfully. "No, I'm afraid not. I have cargoes to deliver and take on in the Caribees, and time is of the essence these days. It is the fleetest vessels that carry the richest cargoes—and the richest captains, eh, Miguel? And besides, I am sure our Nell is most anxious to meet her lovely niece." He grinned. "Almost as anxious as Christianne is to meet her!" Christianne's expression shot daggers at him, which he studiously ignored. "However, I believe we may spend an enjoyable day together, recounting old times. I have a trustworthy first officer who will see to the loading of your almonds and oranges and sherry, never fear."

Miguel nodded. *"Muy bien, amigo,"* he said approvingly. "Today we in *España* celebrate the feast of Candlemas. There will be dancing in the plaza, and many entertainments, too. I am sure our ladies would enjoy it, especially little *señorita* Christianne, here." He smiled at her, and she blushed under his dark gaze.

James nodded. "I am sure she would. Christianne?"

Christianne nodded mutely, feeling decidedly strange. She looked, James thought suddenly, a little green about the gills. Amanda appeared to have noticed it, too, for she stood up and took Christianne gently by the elbow.

"Come, we will go upstairs to my chamber to freshen ourselves for this afternoon, while the gentlemen enjoy their brandy." The men rose and bowed as the ladies withdrew.

Christianne tottered up the stairs, grateful for the doña's gentle support as she went. Once inside the chamber, Amanda sat the girl down on the bed and hurried to dip a cloth in water.

"I'faith, I ate too much!" Christianne groaned, sinking gratefully into the feather bed while Amanda patted her face with the damp cloth.

"I'faith, Christianne, I wager you did!" she teased. "Lie down for a few moments and it will pass. The rich, Spanish fare lies very heavily on the English belly, I have found!"

Christianne smiled wanly. "Aye, it does indeed," she agreed. A dark scowl crossed her elfin face. "No doubt Captain Mallory will think me a glutton and a babe," she said woefully.

Amanda smiled. "And do you care what the captain thinks?" she asked lightly, perching on the bed at Christianne's side.

"Nay!" the girl retorted vehemently.

Amanda's amused smile deepened. "Then who cares! Let him think! James Mallory was ever a teasing rogue. If you ignore his taunts, they will cease."

Christianne sat up. "You know him very well," she observed, overwhelmed with curiosity.

"Yes, I do, very well," Amanda said with a smile. "He asked me to marry him once. I refused, for I had already lost my heart to Miguel. If not, I fancy I might have accepted. James is a fine man, though a devil for the ladies! You see, to the captain, women are a separate species of rare, exotic creatures. And he loves the *entire* species!" She sighed. "I despair of him ever settling down."

Christianne, remembering Lucy Waller at the Golden Goose tavern, nodded vigorous agreement with her first words. The doña was right. James Mallory was a rake, that's what he was!

Amanda stood up. "Well, if you are feeling a little better I will leave you to take a nap, what we call a siesta. Here in *España* it is the custom, you see, to rest during the hottest part of the day. When you awaken, we will go to the fiesta, as Miguel suggested. I will send Bonita, the children's nurse, to help you dress," she offered kindly.

Christianne smiled. She liked the doña enormously. "Yes, thank you, Doña Amanda."

"Call me Amanda," Amanda insisted. "The other is much too formal, and you will find when you come to know me better that I loathe formality!"

"Thank you, Amanda," Christianne amended.

"*De nada*, Christianne," the young woman said as she left the room. The girl's eyelids were already drooping.

But despite what the lovely Doña Amanda thought, Christianne was, in truth, far from sleepy. Now that her nausea had passed, her mind raced with the idea she had half formed en route to the inn, and which her conversation with Amanda had made seem even more feasible than she had at first thought: how to goad James Mallory into doing something, *anything* that was a serious breach of honor, so that she, with a clear conscience, could break her vow to him not to attempt an escape. And that something was now so obvious, she could not believe she hadn't thought of it earlier! All she had to do was to entice James into attempting to seduce her! Then, pretending great outrage and upset on her part, he would beat a hasty exit, probably stammering and asking her forgiveness on bended knees. Then, the very second he left her alone, she would run away from him and from Spain, back to England! It would be simple, as the best plans always were, and knowing what she did of his character and what Amanda had unwittingly added to reinforce her already low opinions of the captain's morals, it would not take much to inspire a rake such as he to attempt to press his attentions on her! Now, all that remained was to concoct a means to bring him here, to this chamber, alone. She pondered this knotty problem for but a few seconds before an impish grin lit her face. Of course! He already believed her ill. All she had to do was to feign further illness, great pain and distress, and he would come running. It was perfect!

She lay back on the bed, still smiling. But then the smile faded, to be replaced by a worried frown that creased her dark gold eyebrows in concern and wrinkled her pert little nose. What if James failed to find her desirable? What if he proved immune to her honeyed smiles and seductive glances and merely summoned a physician to attend her "illness." La! That would never do! She lay down and critically ran her hands down the length of her body, trying to feel it as if she were James the Lecher, instead of Christianne the Temptress.

Since she had shed her boy's clothing in London and grudgingly donned female attire, her figure had seemed as if it, too, was trying to shed its boyishness and become less angular, more rounded and feminine. She cupped her breasts and pressed them upwards until they almost spilled from her bodice. She was not nearly so well-endowed by nature as that Lucy at the tavern in London had been, and James had seemed mightily taken with *her* charms. Oh, if only she weren't so boyishly flat, she thought wistfully! Still, there was nothing she could do about that. She must either discard her plan or carry through with it as best she could and hope that James had at least noticed she was a woman and that he did not just consider her his good friend Nellie's plaguesome niece. After all, she did not intend that he should *really* ravish her, only that with her help, he should attempt to! She didn't care if he really found her desirable or not.

Liar, Christianne, she snorted, disgusted with herself, your pride would be sorely pricked if he scoffed or scorned you. You wonder what it would be like to see his devil-green eyes ablaze with passion for you, to know how his strong, tanned hands would feel upon your body! Though she was quite alone in the room, she blushed. Aye, she did wonder, just a little, and James was the first young, attractive man she had ever met to fasten her fantasies upon, for fantasies was all these wild imaginings were, she told herself seriously. She muttered a curse and swung off the bed, purposely rumpling her hair into what she hoped was wanton disarray, then practicing a woebegone, stricken expression and another of sultry passion before the mirror as she passed it. Now would be the perfect—perhaps the only—time to set her little plan in motion. She would wait just a few minutes longer to guarantee James was taking his—what had Amanda called it?—his siesta, and then give it a try. After all, what had she to lose by trying?

Impatiently, she paced the chamber, which was spartanly furnished in dark, heavily-carved furniture. A crucifix gleamed dully in one corner; a statue of the Blessed Virgin, a rosary and a Bible stood upon the dresser. She gulped. La! Could she attempt such wickedness with the Virgin smiling so serenely at her? She guiltily turned the statue to face the wall, then stepped out into the hallway.

One of Señor Cristobal's plump daughters was carrying a brimming chamberpot carefully along the landing, no doubt on her way to empty it.

"Please, could you help me?" she cried after her, grimacing furiously.

The girl turned, grinned in a friendly fashion showing small, white teeth, and shrugged. "*No hablo ingles, senorita*," she apologized.

Drat and damnation! She had forgotten that, Christianne realized belatedly. She'd have to mime her wants. She did so, waving her arms about and holding her belly while expressions of torment screwed up her lovely face. It seemed an eternity before the chambermaid nodded in understanding.

She grinned broadly and rolled her eyes. "Ah, si, *el capitán ingles!* Aiee, *qué hombre! Un momentito, por favor."*

Christianne nodded and pointed to her room before the girl scuttled off. Then she hurriedly sped back inside her chamber and shut the door without sliding the bolt. Once inside, she quickly unfastened her sky-blue gown and, having partially done so, squirmed out of it and flung it aside. Then she unfastened the strings that laced her bodice over her bosom halfway down, so that the tops of her breasts swelled provocatively through the gap. Breathing heavily with her haste, she pinched her cheeks to make them rosy and hopped into bed.

It seemed forever that she lay there, her hair sprayed fan-like across the pillow, her arms outspread upon the coverlet in a pose of wanton abandon, before she heard the heavy tread of booted feet on the landing outside her room. A heavy fist beat upon the boor.

"Who is it?" she cried wanly.

"Captain Mallory. You sent for me?"

"Yes, indeed. Please, come in, Captain," she murmured just loud enough for him to hear.

He strode inside the room, stopped short in his tracks by the sight of the lovely Christianne sprawled seductively across the bed. He and Miguel had consumed a brace of brandies before retiring to their respective chambers for this damnably strange custom that the don had called siesta, and the sight of her lying there, her breasts half-spilling from the unlaced bodice of her embroidered lawn shift, quickened his pulse and thickened his breathing.

"The chambermaid told me that you were ill, Christianne?" he asked in a level voice, trying to control his wandering eyes. Had the wench taken leave of her senses, he wondered? What mischief was she about now?

"Aye, indeed! My belly—it plagues me cruelly, sir!" she cried, wailing piteously and screwing up her lovely face, while at the same time trying hard not to laugh.

But to her dismay, it was James who laughed last.

He snorted and grinned. "So, that's your game, is it?" He laughed, his fists on his hips, his green eyes merry.

"Game?" she echoed weakly, her heart suddenly racing.

"Aye, game," James repeated, striding across the chamber and looking down at her from what seemed like a towering height. He sat upon the bed at her side. "What was to have been your next move?" He frowned thoughtfully. "Would you perhaps have asked me to place my hand here, like so," he pondered aloud, laying his rough, warm palm flat on her belly, "to gauge the exact spot where this plaguesome ache was? Or would you, mayhap, instead have pressed my hand to your heaving bosom, so that I could feel for myself the racing gallop of your heart?"

She thrust his hand away. Color flamed in her cheeks. "I intended nothing of the sort!" she lied. "Why would I do anything so, so foolish?"

James shrugged. "It was my fancy that maybe you intended to seduce me, madam, or rather, that I should attempt to seduce *you!*" He laughed softly. "Either one would be a very tantalizing prospect."

"Either one would make me ill, Captain!" she retorted hotly, turning redder still with guilt.

"Liar!" he accused. "If it served you, you would try anything, my little vixen! I have no illusions as to your character. I would wager a hundred crowns that you intended that I should attempt to ravish you, so that you—with a clear conscience—could break your sworn promise to me not to escape." Her mouth dropped open. He tweaked her rosy cheek. "Ah, yes, I see that I was right!"

He was a devil, in truth, Christianne thought, numb with disbelief. He had plucked her very thoughts from her mind! Would he now order her returned to the ship posthaste? She tried to read his expression, but found that in the handsome captain's case, she could not. His green eyes revealed nothing but his amusement at her.

"I hate you," she said clearly, and meant it to the very core of her being.

"That is your prerogative, madam," James replied evenly. "However, let me give you a little advice, for it appears that your years spent masquerading as a lad have left you sadly ignorant of the wiles of your sex. Firstly, a man likes to be the hunter, wench, he enjoys the thrill of the chase! Spreading yourself upon the bed like a sacrificial lamb upon some pagan altar is no challenge, lass, to the hunter in every man. Now, sit you up," he urged, raising her to sitting. "Better, much better. Now, your bodice. 'Tis far too low, you see, my pigeon, and leaves no mystery to be explored. Raise it just a mite, like so," he advised wickedly, doing so for her. His fingertips grazed her bare shoulder as he did so, and he flinched at the inviting warmth and softness he felt beneath them, and at the leaping response that surged throughout him. Mild astonishment flitted across his rugged face. Had he been so long at sea that this pretty child-woman could so arouse him? He shook his head very slightly and hid a grin. If such was the case, Yolanda, the innkeeper's youngest daughter, had seemed—he chuckled—interested. Mayhap he should seek her out?

Christianne, meanwhile, perched upon the bed beside him with a crestfallen expression on her elfin face.

"It appears I have gone about this badly," she said bitterly, the timbre of her voice husky with unshed tears. She felt wounded to the quick by his mocking lessons on the art of being a woman, and small with shame that he had seen through her scheme so easily. "I should have known better," she murmured to herself, "aye, indeed I should! I am no sheltered, innocent chit!"

James noticed her deflated expression and the unshed tears that swam in her long-lashed, deep blue eyes and felt a stirring of pity for the little wench. She appeared so fragile, so forlorn sitting there with her slim hands clasped protectively in front of her, her unusual ash blond tresses falling untidily about her lovely face. He had wounded that fierce pride he so admired with his thoughtless teasing, he realized belatedly.

"Nay, not so badly," he murmured consolingly, wanting to take the sting out of his "lessons" in the art of seduction. "This wanton tumble of silvery tresses—'tis perfect! It invites a man to fondle it, tousle it, to lose his fingers in its softness." So saying, he ran his hand lightly across her shoulder and did so, burrowing beneath her curls to idly stroke the nape of her neck. "And your lips, they are perfection, too, rosy red and ripe for kisses! A man would be a fool not to want to press his own lips upon them." With a smile, he leaned over and pressed his lips over hers, intending but a brief, teasing kiss to restore her pride. If it angered her, so much the better, he thought, for he much preferred her a tempestuous hellion than this teary-eyed milquetoast miss!

But her response took him completely by surprise, for as he pressed his lips to hers, her slender arms instinctively rose to clasp about his neck. One hand rose still higher and ruffled his hair. The light pressure of his lips was returned by equal pressure—and more— from hers!

If her reaction had surprised the captain, it astounded Christianne! James' lips tasted warm and sweet as brandy, aye, his kiss was very pleasurable indeed, and not at all the distasteful, even *loathsome,* experience she had expected when he had leaned over and she had guessed his intent. Delighted by her delicious discovery, she quite forgot that it was the hated captain whose kisses she was returning so eagerly, and completely in innocence of the devastating effect her ardent response was having on him, she closed her tawny-lashed eyes and kissed him with even greater fervor.

She was quickly made aware that a kiss was not, as she had always thought, a thing of the lips alone. Nay! It did strange things to the breathing, made her blood course through her veins like a racing river of fire, made her breasts tingle and tauten in some magical way she did not understand, and spread a tide of such warmth through her belly and loins that she blushed hotly to feel it! In truth, she felt more than a little giddy—like when one staggered from the swingboats at a country fair. It was as she imagined being drunk must feel, though she had never been drunk in her life until now, drunk on the sparkling wine of his kisses!

James' thoughts whirled in delighted chaos. Where was the icy, hostile Christianne now, the Nordic princess of silver and white with glaciers in her veins and blue ice chips for eyes, and words that could cut and pierce like frozen splinters wrested from an iceberg? The girl-woman in his arms was all that was warmth and fire, glowed like a flame of incandescent brightness, clung to his lips with her own burning lips and sighed her pleasure with every honey-sweet kiss in a way more provocative than any woman he had ever known—and he had known many! She had said that she was no innocent maid, and her actions assuredly echoed her impassioned avowal. It seemed probable that he could spend a hot, lazy afternoon in some pleasurable dalliance with the little spitfire. But no sooner had the thought entered his head than he severely quelled it. Lecher! he upbraided himself sternly, the girl was Nellie's niece, not a tavern slattern or a lusty bawd, for all that she was no virgin maid. Aye, in truth, how could the poor, orphaned lass have guarded her maidenhead when she had lived alone, uncared for and unprotected, but inches from the gutter—and gutters that teemed with lecherous, two-legged vermin only too willing to relieve her of the burden of her virginity! He gently disentangled himself of her arms, unwilling to take advantage of her as had they. Yet as he pulled away, she strained forward and followed him, her lips still fastened to his, her small breasts provocatively crushed against his chest in a way that was highly unsettling

113

and inordinately pleasurable. Even through the cloth of his shirt and the gossamer thinness of her shift, the heat of her lissome body was fiery. His manhood surged and answered its burning plea, overwhelming his scruples with the urgency of that answer.

With a low growl, he parted her lips with the tip of his tongue and gently explored the secret recesses of her velvet mouth. His hands laced in her wispy mane and arched her head back beneath his conquering mouth. He drank at the fountain of her lips like a parched man at an oasis, and still found himself thirsting for more. He covered a soft breast with his hand and felt it stir like a trembling dove in the cup of his palm. As his thumb traced circles on the satiny crest, it rose and pressed firmly into his touch against the fine lawn of her shift. Desire raged through him. He wanted to feel that sweet flesh bare against his flesh, he thought, his breathing unsteady and husky, without these hampering garments between them!

He bore her down to the bed beneath his broad chest and divested her of that gossamer shift without taking his lips from hers for so much as a second. Hungrily, his hands enfolded her perfect breasts, breasts like rosy pillows of the finest silk from the Orient. With reluctance, he broke the kiss and trailed his lips down to the treasures in his hands, pausing to nuzzle the little hollow of her throat where her pulse throbbed erratically and the smooth, satiny curves of her shoulders, before parting his ardent mouth over them and tasting their sweetness like wild honey on his tongue.

Christianne, for her part, seemed taken by a fit of madness, for what else could explain the dizzying maelstrom of wondrous sensations assailing her? His caresses sapped her strength and made her limbs heavy and languorous, while at the same time her body sang and vibrated like the plucked strings of a mandolin! She wanted . . . oh, Lord, she wanted! But what it was that she wanted so desperately she could not name, knew no word to describe that hunger of the body, that bittersweet aching of desire.

He parted her thighs with tender hands and learned the secrets of her woman's body with his touch as surely as his lips had learned the secrets of her mouth. She gasped and laced her fingers in his tousled, russet hair, arching upwards as his delicate, stroking caresses drove her to a fever pitch of yearning.

"I want . . . I want! . . ." she gasped aloud, tossing her head from side to side, unable to voice what it was she so ardently wanted, for in truth, she did not know herself.

"Aye, my sweeting, I know," James murmured huskily against her fragrant hair, "and you shall have, never fear." He slid atop her, summoning every means at his command to temper the burgeoning pressure of his desire for her with tenderness, though his body clamored for a speedy release from its sweet torment. Aye, he wanted to be tender to the little scrap of loveliness beneath him, to show her the ecstasy of her woman's part in making love. God knows, her other swains had like as not been tender as rutting stags! He kissed her breasts, her throat, her eyelids and finally her lips as her mouth parted under his once more. As it did so, he thrust between her thighs. Sweat stood out on his forehead, more beaded his upper lip, as he found his entry barred. Time seemed suspended in that second or two while he hesitated. His desire for her was ungovernable—like a river swollen with the spring thaw that gains in volume and threatens to overflow its banks. Like a river of crimson, molten magma that must seek release from the fierce pressure of the volcano's core, so was his passion for Christianne! He could not bring himself to draw back—nor did he want to, in his heart of hearts. A groan of anguish tore from his lips as he felt her stiffen beneath him at the same time as he thrust forward. He heard her cry out with an instant's pain, and then her small fists were pummelling furiously at his chest in a display of resistance that had

115

come too late.

The sudden sharp pain as James entered her had brought her back to reality more forcefully than a bucket of icy water thrown in her face. What had she done? What had she permitted him to do? What madness, what *madness* had possessed her?

"No!" she cried raggedly. "No, please, I beg you, stop!" Tears spilled down her cheeks.

James gathered her up into his arms as he continued to love her, kissing her tear-streaked face. " 'Tis too late to stop, my sweet," he murmured gently, his tone filled with remorse. "Fate has decreed that you be mine for this moment in time, and I will teach you the delights of love that can be ours. There will be no more pain, I promise you."

Despite his reassurances, she clawed at his muscled back, raking his flesh with her nails, her ferocity like that of a mountain leopard cornered in a cave. But it was to no avail. As he had said, it was too late to undo what had been done. A second's mindless pleasure, and she would pay for it with a lifetime of regret! She had dared to play with fire, and she had been royally burned. She should have known that the lusty captain, with all his experience in such things, far outmatched her in her innocence. He had not hesitated to take advantage of that innocence! Women were all alike to him: ripe plums to be plucked at random from the tree—and never mind whose orchard, she thought bitterly.

In the afternoon sunlight that slanted through the narrow casements over the red-tiled rooftops of Barcelona, James' hair gleamed like a fiery helmet. His eyes were a glittering green with desire, a striking, unforgettable green against the weather-beaten tan of his ruggedly handsome face. Aye, he was a handsome scoundrel, for all that she hated him, she acknowledged reluctantly. The first stirrings of pleasure trickled through her as he continued to move rhythmically, powerfully within her. Her blue eyes darkened with confusion and desire. The warm languor that had begun with his first caresses returned and eroded her resistance as surely as a sea erodes a mighty cliff. Her pleasure spread to every corner of her being! Damn his soul! This was the final humiliation; to find herself yielding, nay, worse, *loving* the ravishment of the man she hated, she thought miserably.

James interspersed each powerful thrust with lingering kisses and soft caresses, murmuring love words in her ears. Gradually he felt the tension ebbing in her trembling frame beneath him, felt a surging response within her body to his own that was like a leaping pillar of fire.

"Hellion!" he murmured. "Sweet, wild hellion, love me!"

The husky command sent racing shivers of excitement dancing up and down her spine. He leaned up and smiled down at her, his broad shoulders blocking out the light, his pleasant, masculine scent filling her nostrils, his body possessing hers 'til he filled her world, 'til it began and ended with his sight, his touch, his scent, his taste! He was tanned a deep bronze from his rugged seafaring life, and those powerful shoulders that filled her vision tapered to a hard, flat belly, lightly forested with curling red-gold hair. His flanks were lean and well-muscled, flexing powerfully as he drove deeply inside her, and elicited gasps of delight despite herself. The bittersweet aching, the wanting, built again. She was poised, quivering, on the brink of something wonderful, she sensed — some mystery that he had promised to reveal, something that would ease the knot of tension that lay coiled in her belly like a whip. She moaned as her passion soared, her legs enfolding his hips to keep him fast within her. Arching upwards, she hesitantly matched her rhythm to his.

With a low laugh of pleasure and triumph, James kissed her deeply as waves of throbbing pleasure engulfed her, her cries of ecstasy staunched by his lips.

"Damn you! Damn you!" she gasped when he rolled to her side, himself utterly sated.

He laughed again. "Damned am I?" he growled in mock displeasure, his eyes roving her creamy flesh, now tinged with the faintest blush of rosy color. With her hair spilled wantonly about her face, and her eyes wide and dilated blue pools, and her lips a deep, moist coral from his kisses, she was breathtakingly lovely—the epitome of every woman he had ever wanted! And she little more than an innocent maid, for all that she was eighteen. "Damned, eh?" he repeated. " 'Tis a strange endearment from the captain's . . . mistress." He smiled and casually lifted her hand and kissed the palm.

Somehow, his affectionate kiss had a possessively intimate quality, as if having once taken her he could touch or kiss or caress her at will. She drew her hand away as if scalded, rolled onto her side and offered him her rigid back, thoroughly riled. "I am *not* your mistress, despite what has happened!" she stormed, her voice muffled against the bolster. "Nor will I ever be!"

"No?" James queried mildly, tracing his index finger down the narrow ridges of her spine and causing goose-bumps to rise all over her creamy flesh. "We shall see!" he taunted. "A lengthy sea voyage lies ahead of us, my snow fox, and the nights are long and lonely to the Caribbees. I fear a hot blood runs swift beneath that frosty countenance and manner you present to the world. And passion is like the forbidden fruit—once tasted, the appetite is never quenched!"

He swung his legs over the massive bed and reached for his breeches. Guilt pricked him fleetingly as he flung aside the sheet and saw proof of her virginity there like an accusing crimson finger pointed straight at him. He dressed quickly while Christianne lay on her side, silently seething, no doubt, he thought ruefully. He would have liked to offer her some comfort, some reassurance that her world had not

118

ended with the loss of her maidenhead, but he sensed that any such overture would be fiercely rebuffed at this time. She needed time for reflection, to lick her wounds in private. He bent and kissed her bared shoulder.

"There's water in the ewer, my sweet, for you to bathe yourself. I will return shortly to escort you to the fiesta. Sleep for a little while." She would not answer him, nor did she even acknowledge his words. "Christianne?" he asked, lightly touching her arm.

She turned on him, eyes aglitter with unshed tears. "Don't touch me!" she cried, gritting her teeth. "I vow that you will never have me again, Captain! Turn your back on me, and I will kill you, I swear it!"

James buckled on his sword and dagger. He gave her a long, unfathomable green-eyed stare, deliberately turned his back on her and left the room.

When he had gone, Christianne sank back down to the bed, staring blindly at the closed door for many long moments. She shook her head slowly from side to side. It hadn't happened . . . no, no she had just imagined it all . . . all of it! she denied numbly. Then she covered her face with her hands and wept, wept as if the end of the world were nigh, for she knew that she lied to herself. She wept for her lost virginity, irrevocably, irretrievably lost; for her pride, momentarily displaced; and she wept in shame and bitter disappointment at the betrayal of her own, treacherous body. Sobs racked her slender shoulders, tears splashed like falling rain down her cheeks, ravaging her pale face and dampening her pale hair. Her heart felt like a leaden weight in her breast—i'faith, heavier!

Limbs still quivering, she stumbled to the washstand and unwound the sheet she had tucked about her. She washed herself vigorously, trying desperately to remove all traces, visible and invisible, of James' ravishment from her body. Yes, it *had* been ravishment, she told herself time and time again, even though she had thrust herself into his arms, dazzled by the sweetness of his kisses. He had used his lips like a silken scarf to keep her silent, caresses instead of blows to subdue her, and his arms had been bonds that held her fast, but nevertheless, it had been ravishment! He had used her very innocence against her, that heartless rogue, and she, like a fool, had thought to use him! How could she have ever believed her silly scheme would work? For all his honor, the captain was still only a man. But she had counted on his honor as being stronger than his lust, or his friendship to her aunt as being more valuable to him than a few moments of pleasure! Men! They were all animals, rutting animals, she thought bitterly, wiping her tears away with the corner of the sheet. At least, she realized, she now had her wish; she could flee James without the least bit of a guilty conscience! Small consolation, indeed, but it would be better to cut her losses and run at the first opportunity that presented itself.

"Christianne! Christianne!"

There was someone knocking at the door, she realized.

"Yes? Who is it?"

"Amanda de Villarin. Would you like me to send Bonita to you now to help you dress?"

Christianne looked wildly about her. The bedchamber was strewn with her clothes and the tangled bedcovers.

"Thank you, but I believe I can manage," she called quickly.

"Very well! We will attend you below. Don't be long—we don't want to miss anything!" Amanda called with a merry laugh.

"I will be but a minute, I promise," Christianne answered.

The fiesta—she'd forgotten that! Her jaw came up resolutely as her misplaced pride was suddenly recovered. Aye, she'd go to this fiesta, and she'd turn that damned captain's triumph into a defeat that would be as bitter as gall. By midnight, she vowed hotly, she would be rid of him— forever!

Eleven

The Plaza del Rey was already thronged with people by the time the de Villarins, James and a still-seething Christianne reached it.

A troupe of gaudily-costumed mummers were performing a masque on one side, and their ribald antics had attracted a goodly crowd of jostling onlookers. Still more people had gathered to watch as a mangy bear with a grizzled snout pranced about to the merry jig his master was sawing on an old fiddle. The air was filled with savory and sweet aromas: marchpane and gingerbread, mulled ale, steamed shellfish and the like. The merrymakers licked sticky, greasy fingers as they wandered from stall to stall. There were jugglers, tumblers, and conjurers from Arabia, tinkers and dancers and wrestlers, all clad in colorful garb. The little pavilions and booths that had been erected for the fair made still more splashes of silken color against the somber cobbles and galleried houses of Barcelona.

Candelmas! The celebration brought back happy memories to Christianne and dispelled a little of the doom and gloom she had fallen prey to. She trailed after the rest of her party, looking avidly about her. Candlemas was the feast day in celebration of the purification of the blessed Virgin after the birth of the Christ Child. There had been processions as part of the celebrations in London, she recalled, the worshippers each bearing a lighted candle to place at the Madonna's feet. The sight of those solemn faces, lit by the wavering light of the myriad candles, had filled her with wonder and awe. Would they do likewise in this barbaric country, she wondered? A small smile curved her lips. The feast and the resulting fairs that always attended such religious festivals had also offered enormous opportunities and pickings for cutpurses and pickpockets. She and Granny Rags, Lumpy Jack and Coalie Joe had done brisk trade, spending their ill-gotten gains on fairings and sweetmeats the very second they left their victims' pockets for their own!

She paused at one stall, a pavilion of billowing dark blue silk shot with threads of silver and gold and embroidered with the moon and stars and other mystical signs. An old gypsy woman lifted aside the curtain that was the entrance and beckoned to her with a claw-like finger.

"Would ye learn your destiny, my pretty?" she wheedled, her black eyes gleaming like jet. "Would ye learn what the fates and life have in store for ye?"

Christianne smiled and shook her head. "I regret not, old woman. I have no silver with which to cross your palm."

"Here," said a deep voice behind her, "I have silver aplenty. Tell the little lady's future, and mark you tell it well, señora."

Christianne looked up into James' teasing face. He had, she realized belatedly, been keeping a watchful eye on her, despite appearances to the contrary.

"Go on," he urged, "discover what fate has in store for you." He grinned. "Mayhap the old crone will forecast a speedy parting 'twixt you and I, and give you cause for hope!"

Christianne scowled. "Nay, 'tis foolishness. I believe not in such things."

Amanda, who had retraced her footsteps to their sides, nudged her. "Oh, do go on!" she urged, "listen and remember all she tells you, and then after, I will take my turn. We will have great sport recounting all *la gitana* tells us! 'Tis all in jest, so what harm can it do? Go on,

Christianne!" Her sable-dark eyes danced merrily.

James flipped a coin to the old woman who caught it deftly and tested its silver with yellowed teeth before slipping it down her bodice.

"Come, little mistress," she said, and beckoned again.

Christianne reluctantly followed her, ducking her head under the low-hung curtain.

Inside, the pavilion was gloomy. The old woman gestured her to be seated on a pile of worn Persian rugs that were strewn on the cobbles. She squatted cross-legged upon them herself next to the girl, and took her slim, pale hand in her own dark, gnarled one, peering intently at the palm.

Christianne waited impatiently, wondering why she had allowed James and Amanda to persuade her to take part in this foolishness. While she waited, she curiously inspected the old gypsy woman—*la gitana*, Amanda had called her.

The fortune teller appeared very ancient, for her skin was crisscrossed with countless lines, etched deeply like the seams in a well-worn piece of leather. Her complexion was nut-brown and weathered. Heavy gold hoops swung from her ears, and curiously-wrought gold bangles adorned her scrawny wrists and ankles. About her wrinkled neck draped several strands of cornelian beads, red as blood. Her hair was a yellowed white, held back in a vivid kerchief of crimson and yellow, the same brilliant colors that embroidered the hem of her full black skirts and the fringes of her black lace shawl.

At length the crone lifted her eyes to Christianne's, sloe-black, bright with cunning and intelligence, undimmed by her advanced age.

"I see a life of happiness ahead for you," she cackled with a toothy smile, as if she had said those same trite words to countless other gullible, superstitious young women. "I see a wealthy husband here, and a babe or two, and a life of luxury and love. The man that you marry will be kind and good to you, señorita, if you will but give him the chance.

123

But he is not, I regret to say," she murmured with an apologetic smile, "that handsome, green-eyed *gorgio* you are with today. That one, he will bring you only heartache, yes?"

How apt, Christianne thought with a wry smile. Mayhap the old crone knew of what she talked, and was not a charlatan! She made to withdraw her hand and leave.

"Not yet, *pequeña*, not yet!" the old crone said, refusing to relinquish her hand. She peered once more at Christianne's palm, and when she looked up again after several long minutes, she was no longer smiling. "You have many miles yet to travel and much time will pass before this happiness I have promised you will come to be, little one. There is grave danger in your path, countless obstacles you must overcome to attain your prize of happiness. You must have great courage, for the carrion bird of death will sit on your shoulder every step of the way!" She closed her eyes and rocked gently back and forth, muttering all the while under her breath in a strange tongue that Christianne assumed to be the gypsies' own peculiar Romany language. "Beware the dark one and the sign of Scorpio! Beware the mystery within a mystery—for if not, it will prove your undoing. Trust not the flatterer's smile, for it hides the grin of the tiger. Though in the guise of an enemy, great Taurus will prove a friend. By the words he does not speak shall ye know him." Her grip tightened about Christianne's wrist until her bony fingers were like talons in her tender flesh.

"Look beneath, child, look beneath! Trust nothing and noone to be as they appear, for in your life up will be down, and down up. Good will hide evil and evil will conceal that which is good. Learn to strip away that which is not so, to find the hidden truths within. Do not let false pride stand in your way, or you will postpone the fulfillment of your destiny." She suddenly thrust Christianne's hand away. "I see no more," she said abruptly, "but what I have told you will suffice, if you mark well my words."

She lifted a strand of the blood-red cornelian beads from her neck and placed them gravely about Christianne's own. "Take this necklace, child," she urged, "for it will protect you against harm. Let these beads be your talisman against adversity, an amulet against the evil that will threaten you, for it is said:

> 'Cornelian is a talisman
> It brings good luck to child and man.
> It drives away all evil things;
> To thee and thine protection brings.
> From such a gem a woman gains
> Sweet hope and comfort in her pain.'

"Take it, child, take it and go!" the old crone whispered fiercely. "I am done for this day." Her glance dismissed Christianne.

Somewhat mystified, Christianne scrambled to her feet and exited the pavilion.

James and Amanda and Don Miguel were waiting for her. They gathered around her, smiling expectantly.

"Well?" Amanda asked eagerly. "Did she promise you great riches and an indulgent and loving husband?"

Christianne smiled. "Aye, indeed she did! But not until after I have endured great dangers and adversity to win him, of course!" She fingered the string of cornelian beads about her neck. "She gave me these, as a talisman against those evils she prophesied," she finished, her expression pensive.

Amanda inspected the necklace carefully. "Why, it is quite pretty! Do you suppose she will give me one, too, if my future threatens to be sufficiently hazardous?" She smiled as she turned back to the pavilion. "Señora! Señora!" she

N.B. Poem taken from a collection of poems by Johann Wolfgang von Goethe, entitled *Westösterlicher Divan I*. No permission required.

called, but there was no answer. When she lifted the curtain aside, they saw the tent was now empty. "Oh, well, I shall never know now! Come on, all of you. Bonita promised to meet us at the swingboats with the children, and there are fire-eaters and sword-swallowers from Arabia that I am just dying to see!" She slipped her arm through her husband's and they set off ahead of Christianne and James.

James smiled down at her. "There, my sweet," he said teasingly, gesturing at the necklace about her slim throat, "today has not been completely without its rewards, has it?" He lifted her hand to his lips and kissed it. His green eyes caressed her upturned face with tenderness.

She jerked away. "I would call this necklace of beads a miserable recompense for what you stole from me this day, sir!" she flared, tossing her blond mane like a high-spirited filly.

James frowned. "You mistake me, sweet. I meant to imply no such thing. If I had but known beforehand—"

"—If you had known beforehand that I was yet a maid, it would not have happened? Do not play me for a fool, Captain! The choice was yours. As I recall, you left *me* none! You are a lecher, a heartless rake who will take any woman he chooses, with neither thought nor care for the consequences, as casually as you don your tricorn or fasten your stock." Her angry face was flushed scarlet.

He scowled at her, his guilt pricked by her words. "If I recall correctly, you did not seem unwilling until our sport was well begun, madam," he pointed out cruelly. Her belligerent hands-on-hips stance had brought more than one curious stare from the crowds milling about them, he observed.

Suddenly she dashed her hand across his face with a ringing slap that rocked his head back. "There!" she cried. "Take that, you scurvy rat! There was but one thing the gypsy told me that pleased me mightily—and that was that

126

I would never marry you!"

She kicked up her heels and fled, clutching up her skirts, weaving in and out of the fair-goers and knocking a basket from the arms of one stout matron in black as she went.

James roared at her to halt, then careened after her, his booted feet pounding against the cobbles.

Christianne hopped nimbly between the stalls, ignoring the angry outcry raised by the stall holders. She was determined to escape the sea captain! She sped along the rabbit-warren streets that twisted and turned, the buildings on either side almost forming a tunnel above her. She flew like the wind past wine sellers and water carriers, sausage vendors and flower girls until she was well away from the Plaza del Rey and in the quiet backstreets of Barcelona that dozed sleepily in the afternoon sunlight. Still, James' dogged footsteps hounded her path!

It was late afternoon and the brilliant blue of the morning sky was fading and taking on the amethyst and lavender hues of evening. Nightfall was imminent. If she could but evade him until it grew dark, he would never find her in these maze-like streets! But, damnably, those heavy footsteps still pounded the cobbles in her wake.

Her breathing was ragged as she rounded yet another corner and pulled up short. An ornate black wrought-iron gateway blocked her escape, reaching across the street. Beyond it she glimpsed elegant gardens and courtyards. There were no alleys running off this thoroughfare, nor opened doorways or arches in which to conceal herself. Unless the gateway proved unlocked, she was trapped, and right well, she realized, sprinting towards it. She grasped the elegantly twisted bars in her fists and shook them soundly. The metal clanged and reverberated but the gate remained securely closed. Christianne whirled about, her back pressed up against the gate. No! James had turned the corner and was racing towards her at considerable speed.

She turned back to the massive, tall gate and reached up,

getting her grip, then started climbing up with all the speed she could muster. Damn her petticoats and skirts! she cursed with gritted teeth, they made an easy climb a perilous undertaking. At last she reached the top and gleefully swung her leg over the row of tall spikes that topped the gate. Now she had only to let go and spring lightly to the grass beyond to make good her escape! This climb would have gained her considerable lead over that damned James! Confidently, she let go and jumped. But a sharp jerk beneath her armpits and a loud ripping sound resulted, and she found herself hanging in midair, dangling from the spikes by her skirts like a fairground marionette! She flailed her arms and legs, wriggling desperately to free herself, but all her efforts were useless. Trapped!

James threw back his head and roared with laughter as he looked up into her furious face and saw her ungainly position. "Good afternoon, milady," he mocked, doffing his tricorn and sweeping her an elegant bow. "I had hoped you might wait for me, so that we might continue this 'stroll' together, and I see you have indeed waited—and in considerable style!" His slanted green eyes twinkled merrily.

Seething, Christianne said nothing in reply to his taunts. Instead she wriggled and squirmed, still vainly trying to gain a hand or a foothold that she might free herself.

James lounged against the wall that housed the gate, his arms crossed on his chest, watching her frantic antics with great—and undisguised—amusement. After a lengthy period, he strode across to the gate. "Do you, mayhap, wish some assistance, my sweet?" he asked with feigned chivalry.

"Why, no, sir!" Christianne ground out sarcastically through clenched teeth. "It has often been my habit to pass my afternoons hanging from gateways by my skirts!"

James smiled doubtfully. "I had not noticed! Then, I shall be off back to the plaza, and the sweetmeats and the fairings, and leave you to enjoy your peculiar pastimes." He turned to go.

"Wait!" Christianne wailed. "You can't leave me here, dangling like a spider in a web! Where is your honor now, Captain, your compassion, your chivalry?"

One eyebrow rose inquiringly. "You ask my compassion, madam? You, who, not many minutes ago slapped my face and called me a scurvy rat? You, who, knowing full well what you were about, enticed me to your room so that you could attempt to persuade me to seduce you, so that you could go back on your sworn promise? Well, my lovely, you got far more than you bargained for, did you not? And I am tired of forever chasing after you, wench!" He patted her dangling ankles. "At least now, I know where you are!"

She lashed out to kick him in the face, but the kick missed.

"You have angered me now, wench!" he growled. "It would take a far gentler tongue than yours to persuade me to free your trapped skirts!"

Christianne seethed. She'd cut out his heart and roast it on a spit once she got down, she vowed hotly; she'd tear out his tongue and use it for a penwipe, she'd—

"Well, then, my little spitfire, will you ask me to assist you in a civil fashion, or . . . shall I leave?"

"Leave then, damn you!" she screeched. "I'll give no quarter to the likes o' you, you scurvy bilge rat, nor beg you to free me with pretty words!"

"As you wish!" James blew her a kiss and turned smartly on his heels, headed for a nearby tavern. In his opinion, Mistress Alexander had been sadly spoiled by her doting mother and her overindulgent father prior to becoming an orphan. She was, in essence, a tempestuous brat, even if a very lovely one! Her upbringing had been heavy on pride and short on discipline. She would come around and learn that he was not a man to put up with her tantrums, given a little time, he decided. A grin creased his handsome face. After all, she could go nowhere! A few minutes could well do wonders for her temper and give her pause to reconsider running from him again.

Christianne craned her neck to watch him. He had meant it, the brute—he was striding off down the street and leaving her like this! She struggled anew, breathing heavily, squirming and worming from side to side until her armpits ached where her skirts dug into them from her weight. She was exhausted! There was nothing to do now but wait and hope, hope that either someone else would come to her aid or that James would relent and return, she realized, the tastse of her defeat bitter on her tongue. Please God, let it not be that damned captain who next came down this street, but someone, *anyone* else! she prayed fervently.

But no one did.

James returned at length, two leisurely, foaming tankards of ale beneath his belt from the tavern the next street down. Feet braced apart, his fists on his hips, he looked up at her. "Well?" he asked with a wicked grin.

"I—I should like to get down," Christianne spat through clenched teeth, averting eyes that were blazing with fury.

"Indeed? Well, you can ask me more civilly than that! Do I hear a 'please' mayhap?"

"I should like to get down, *please!*" Christianne sputtered, murdering him inch by inch with her eyes in a thousand glorious, exquisitely agonizing ways.

"Better, much better! So, you wish to get down from there, do you? And who is it you wish to assist you?" James asked innocently. Lord, she looked fit to be tied!

"You, you great oaf! Help me down, *please?*"

James shook his head.

"Please, *James,* will you help me down from this damnable gate?" she said slowly and distinctly, almost choking on the words.

He grinned in triumph and nodded. "Without delay, madam!"

He climbed agilely up the gate and swung over it, drew his sword and cut her skirts free in a single slash.

She dropped suddenly like a stone to the grass on the opposite side of the gate, the breath knocked from her. James sprang down to her side, gripping her firmly by the wrist before she could recover her breath and wits and take to her heels once more.

"Now," he said sternly, "we shall climb back over into the street again together. After you, my sweet—and hurry. The de Villarins will be wondering what has become of us."

Muttering curses that cast severe doubts as to the legitimacy of James' parentage, the profession of his mother and his dam's forebears, she did as he ordered.

They neared the plaza as night fell at last in sudden purple splendor. The sky was a velvety black studded with myriad stars like diamonds that twinkled fiercely in its folds. The pungent scent of gardenias, laden with night dew, and the heady sweet perfume of carnations wafted on the sultry night breeze from a hidden courtyard nearby. The rich, throbbing chords of a guitar and the furious clacking of many pairs of castanets and as many wildly stamping heels on the flagstones changed James' easy stride to a swifter gait. He had heard much of the fiery flamenco dancers of Spain and intended to see them tonight, whether Christianne were willing or nay. He all but hauled her after him.

"Slow your pace, damn you," she panted, trying to wrest her wrist from his grip. Her wispy locks now tumbled all about her face in disarray, adding to the elfin quality of her beauty. James halted in his tracks so violently that Christianne, held securely in his grip, was jerked into his arms. For a fleeting second, she looked up into his eyes, and saw a kindling there as she was pressed firmly against him. She colored, feeling heat rush to her face, for a sweet warmth had encompassed her too, feeling her bosom crushed momentarily against his broad chest and recalling a time not too long past when they had been lovers! Her heart began to race, but to her relief the bright flame that had leaped into his eyes extinguished as suddenly as it had flared.

"If you cannot keep up, I must carry you," he said firmly, and swept her into his arms despite her protests.

By the time they reached the plaza proper, he had almost decided to forego the dancing completely. The feel of her soft, rounded form nestled against his chest had stirred him more than he cared to admit. A sudden urge to repeat the delights of the afternoon asserted itself strongly.

"Let us retire to your room," he whispered huskily against her hair, "I still have much yet to teach you of the arts of love."

"Let us not, you rogue!" she retorted in fierce whisper. "I would rather remain unversed in such arts!"

Amanda and Miguel were coming towards them, James noticed. Though they were old friends and he had not seen them in over two years, he cursed their bad timing — bad for him, that was, but very fortunate for Christianne, who smiled with relief. He let her slide from his arms to standing, only belatedly realizing how delightfully dishevelled she appeared with her hair tumbled every which way and her skirts torn. He wrapped his arm firmly about her waist and pulled her against him to conceal the rip as the de Villarins approached.

"There you are! We've been looking for you everywhere!" Amanda exclaimed. "These crowds — I've never seen the plaza so filled with people!" She eyed the pair with a suspicious gleam in her dark eyes. James looked decidedly guilty and little Christianne seemed somewhat *rumpled*, to her eyes. She and Miguel exchanged knowing glances. "The flamenco has already begun, as you can see, and after there is to be a procession to the cathedral, with everyone bearing a lighted candle to put at the Blessed Virgin's feet. Miguel and I had thought perhaps we could all join them. Christianne will be as entranced by it as I was the first time I saw it, I am sure!"

Miguel de Villarin frowned. "Hush, *querida mía*, I only said that we should ask Christianne and James. Perhaps our *capitán* has made other plans for this evening? We must not presume too much, since he has but the one night in our city. And besides, *mi estrellita*, it has been a long day, and I am tired. Shall we instead retire to the inn?" He yawned, a studied, transparently false yawn. His expression, as it rested on the lovely face of his wife, left some doubt as to the truth of his plea of fatigue, for his dark eyes were blatantly sensual. Amanda's cheeks crimsoned with color.

"Well," Christianne exclaimed brightly, "I am not a whit tired! I'faith, I believe I could dance the night away!" Aye, and she would, so long as that hungry gleam remained in James' eyes! She shivered. He'd not take her again. She turned on James with a pleading expression. "May we please watch the dancing, sir?" she implored him softly, "we have but this one night in Spain, and I shall never have the chance to see such dancing again. Please?"

Amanda almost laughed aloud at the matching scowls the two men turned on Christianne. James' was, if anything, the fiercer of the two, even darker and fiercer than her own lusty Miguelito's. So, that was the way of it! she thought. You are burning for her, James, and your little Christianne will have none of it! Her smile deepened. Unrequited passion burned ever fiercer when it remained unrequited, as well she knew.

"Of course we will not allow you to miss such a colorful tradition of our country, Christianne," Amanda declared. "And I am certain that neither James nor Miguel would want you to miss it. Would you, Miguelito, *querido mío?*" She fluttered her sable-dark lashes, raised her eyebrows almost imperceptibly to the other couple and offered her husband her arm. With an equally faint nod of understanding, he grinned and led her gallantly away towards the crowds gathered about the troupe of dancers performing in the plaza.

Triumphant, Christianne likewise offered James her arm and he grudgingly led her after them.

The music was loud and exciting, the crowd noisy and wildly enthusiastic, roaring, "Ole!" for every well-executed step. James murmured something, but in the hubbub she failed to catch his words. She reached up on tiptoe to listen as he repeated himself, shouting this time.

"I said, Christie, that you have outfoxed me this time, but that tomorrow we return to my ship. There'll be no Amanda there to intercede for you, nor any place to run to, minx! After a week of lusty nights, you will plead with me to take you again and again!"

It wasn't until he had finished shouting his wicked and amorous threat that he noticed the music had stopped and the crowd had fallen silent. He had shouted his intent for all to hear!

They were several days out to sea before he realized that his chagrin had been unnecessary, for the crowd—with the exception of Amanda and Miguel—could probably not have understood him!

As Christianne lay sleepless in her spartan chamber at the inn that night, James' lusty threat repeated over and over in her mind, and it seemed that each repetition mocked her further. "Nay, sir," she whispered fiercely into the gloom, "nay, I will *never* beg you to take me! I'faith, I would die before I asked anything of you, least of all that you should bed me!"

She heard the uneasy cooing of the pretty gray doves that roosted in the rain gutters, disturbed by the thud and scrape of the crippled night watchman's uneven tread as he shuffled along in the alley below.

" 'Tis twelve o' the clock, and all's we—ell!" *el sereno* cried in nasal, drawn-out Spanish.

It must be midnight, Christianne realized, though she

did not understand him. She slipped from her bed and went to the casement, catching a glimpse of the old man's crooked silhouette as he continued on his rounds down the Calle de los Pobres, before he was swallowed up by the shadows as if he had never been.

Midnight! she thought again, sighing heavily as she turned from the casement and back to the bed again. She had vowed that by midnight she would be far, far away from this inn and from James. Ha, she thought bitterly, there was little hope of escaping him now, for he prowled the landing outside her chamber door like a red wolfhound to ensure she would not do so, a flagon of wine in one fist, his other clamped securely over the ring of keys at his belt. Nor was it any more likely that she would have opportunity to run away tomorrow, for he had warned her that at first light they would be returning to the *Fair Amanda* and would put out to sea immediately, wind permitting. She might as well accept it; he had won, for now at least. She shivered and hugged herself, though the chamber was warm yet from the day's stored heat. Was she just imagining it, or had that shiver of dread that trickled down her spine been accompanied by the faintest twinge of anticipation?

Silvery moonlight lit the pearl-and-ruby-encrusted handle of James' dagger where it lay upon the dresser. She lay there, looking at it, until she drifted into sleep.

Twelve

Despite Christianne's fierce determination to resist James' love-making and to make a mockery of the lusty threat he'd made in the Plaza del Rey, she realized to her chagrin in the weeks since they had left Spain that he *had* made good that threat in all but one facet: that she would beg him to take her. Nay, she had never begged him, or at least, not in words, she thought uncomfortably—but her resistance had grown steadily less with every passing night of delight spent in his arms in the bed of the great cabin, until, like the very stars themselves, her protests had paled into insignificant murmurs which he had quelled soundly with his ardent lips. Her feelings for the wicked, amorous captain vacillated from intense dislike, fury that he could so easily cajole her treacherous body into willing surrender, to other, warmer feelings of affection for her handsome, russet-haired lover that to her way of thinking were far more dangerous emotions on account of their tender nature.

With increasing frequency, she was annoyed to find her eyes drawn to watch James at the enormous ship's wheel while she strolled the decks to take the air in the mornings with Jonathan Flint as her escort. She ruefully found she enjoyed her covert inspections of the handsome captain, realized, to her dismay, that she found him very attractive indeed with his unruly hair tousled by a freshening breeze, loved his sea-green eyes, now fastened gravely upon his vessel's course, even envied the wind that flapped his white silk shirt about him and pressed against his well-muscled chest and powerfully-corded arms. Aye, he was every inch a man, from the jaunty silver braid of his tricorn to the toes of his black boots, and all that lay betwixt them! Hot on the heels of such favorable appraisals came recollections of a highly inflammatory nature: of how pleasantly crisp but silky his wavy hair felt between her fingers, and how exciting it was to see the sea-green of his eyes darken and become dreamy and heavy-lidded with desire for her; of how safe and protected she felt with his arms about her; and of how sweet and potent his kisses were upon her lips. She would find her heart thudding crazily after such reflections and her face flushed.

Angered at herself for being so fascinated with a rake such as she knew James to be, she would turn to Jonathan, her most bewitching smile curving her mouth, and bring all her newly-found talents at flirtation into play in an attempt to convince herself that she found the black-haired, dashing Irishman equally fascinating, and that therefore her feelings for James were nothing more than a passing physical attraction, and consequently of little import.

In truth, Jonathan Flint was a most handsome man in his own right, with his wild, curling blue-black hair and his dark, almost black eyes. His moustache and single golden earring added to the wicked, buccaneering look of him, she thought, looking up into his face with a smile.

Inwardly, Jonathan was delighted by the attention she paid him. Each day he drew her a little closer to his side as he escorted her about the decks to take the air. By St. Patrick, he thought, the little colleen was as fragile and as dainty as a faerie, aye, and as lovely as an angel with her creamy hair and her deep blue eyes, eyes as clear as the lakes of his native Ireland on a hot midsummer's day! She bristled like a wee terrier every time that damned Mallory came near to her, she did, he thought with a grin. Aye, the captain wanted her, 'twas clear, but she'd have nothing to do with him! His smile faded as he glimpsed that silent, lumbering oaf, Ox, hovering close by. Although the shaggy-haired giant held a pot of varnish in one hand and a brush in the other, Jonathan was not fooled. The sailor had a soft spot for the girl, he was sure of it, for he constantly appeared whenever he escorted Christianne of a morning, like a blasted mother hen anxious for her chick, he thought angrily. Sometimes he wondered if he could trust the shaggy brute, if he was for him, or against him.

Ben Wright, for his part, was even dourer during this leg of the journey than he was wont to be.

Raised in Penzance, Cornwall, by a true Cornish-bred mother, he had been suckled on her country superstitions and beliefs in fairies and hobgoblins along with her mother's milk. These beliefs were now as much a part of him as were his sandy hair, his young-old, kindly face, and his large, square hands.

Since his presentiment the night before they had left London that someone had "walked over his grave," no one thing he could put his finger on had given him cause to expect misfortune to come his way, yet he could still not negate the strong feeling that there was an ill wind blowing, one that boded trouble for himself and all aboard the *Fair Amanda*. Nor could he completely rid himself of the notion that this something would be connected with the Irishman, Flint, even now walking little Christie Alexander about the decks. He frowned. Aye, he'd observed soon after Flint came aboard that the man was left-handed, and everyone knew that the left hand was the one preferred by the pawns of the devil himself!

A series of mishaps, minor in themselves, had deepened his feelings of uneasiness. A small mirror he had used when scraping his beard of a morning had slipped from his hand

and shattered. He had spilled salt in the mess countless times, and of late it seemed that the ship's cat called, appropriately enough, Beelzebub, who was a black, scrawny beast with amber eyes, seemed constantly to cross his path. As if that was not enough, he had accidentally walked under a ladder while seeing to the loading of the de Villarins' cargoes in Spain, and broken the trinity it formed with the wall! The only superstition he refused to subscribe to was a sailor's one: that a woman on ship was a sure guarantee of bad luck for all aboard her. His smoke-gray eyes lightened when he thought of Christianne. Noting her loneliness, he had gone out of his way to offer the poor little wench his companionship when able, in the form of conversation or in playing at cards. She had returned his kindness with gentle smiles and shy words, and he thought her sweeter and more thoughtful than any other young woman he had ever known. He recalled his captain's professed dislike of her and shook his head. Could James not see further than the end of his nose? Could he not put himself in the girl's place and try to understand her, see that her fierce pride and her hostility were just defenses thrown up about herself as barriers against hurt? He smiled. Her confidence was growing daily and she had already thrown off her urchin's way of talking. Given time, he was persuaded she would soften further and reveal the underlying compassionate and loyal nature that was now hidden, become, in fact, the woman he had come to know in their private moments, one worthy of his captain in all respects! They had already discovered a mutual attraction in other ways, he knew well. Aye, he was as sure as he was that the sun rose and set every day that the lass aboard ship could cause misfortune to no one.

As for the captain of the *Fair Amanda*, James had grown more short-tempered every day. His men endeavored to steer clear of him when they could. Those that knew him well, as did his officers, Mullens, Locke and Ben Wright, recognized the signs and would look from the girl and back to their captain with knowing expressions on their weather-beaten faces. The lass had more than just taken his fancy, they'd wager; he was in love with her, perhaps really in love for the first time. It was his frustration that she seemed unimpressed by him that caused his ill humor, for in the past, women had tumbled eagerly to his bed.

James would have been the first to angrily deny these conjectures. True, he felt an unbridled desire each time he saw Christianne, but nothing more. He eyed her now, strutting the decks on the arm of that damned sailor, Flint, with a jaundiced eye. Flint had humbly asked his captain's permission to escort Christianne on her airings each day. Not wishing to appear jealous or overly possessive of her in any way, like a fool James had agreed! What pretty compliment had Flint paid her that had brought that rosy blush to her cheeks, that lively sparkle to her eyes? He scowled and forced his eyes away from the pair, determined to give the handling of the massive ship's wheel his undivided attention from here on. He would, however, have much preferred for his fingers to be knotted about the cocksure Irishman's throat than upon the wheel's wooden spokes.

Yet even with his eyes steadfastly on the glittering crystal-blue of the ocean this morning, a vision of Christianne floated up before his gaze, her dimpling elfin face bewitching him with its fragile loveliness of eye and nose and sweetly pink lips, framed by a wanton tumble of pale blond, curling tresses falling in silky wisps to her shoulders. He cursed angrily beneath his breath. He *wanted* her! Had she in truth ensorcelled him, that lovely, tempting witch? No matter how he tried, there was no escaping the reality of his hunger for her, no denying it when his body's lustful, urgent assertions were all to the contrary. Even on the rare nights they now slept apart, she tormented him in his dreams, causing him to rise from his bunk in the first officer's cabin and go abovedeck to relieve Ben hours ahead of his time. And, he recalled grimly, even there she followed him! He saw her hair in the phosphorescence of the moon-frosted sea, her eyes in the deep, dark sapphire of the ocean, the creamy luster of her skin in the curling sea foam, and the rosy pink of her lips in the clouds at dawn—and still he hungered for her! Did she part those rosy lips for Flint's stolen kisses in the shadows of the gangways, he wondered jealously? Did *he* stroke the sea-foam pallor of her silken skin and lose himself on the turbulent sea of her eyes, while her shimmering mane cascaded like surf all about them?

His fists tightened on the wheel until the knuckles were bleached white. His jaw hardened. If he learned Flint had so much as laid a hand upon her, he would kill him, he vowed silently! The white-hot anger evaporated as suddenly as it had surged through him. What right did he have to dictate on whom she should shower her favors? She still put up a token protest each time *he* began to make love to her. He sighed heavily. He had never had to force any woman to his bed before this, and though he knew he had used his skills as a lover rather than his strength to have her, the knowledge that she was still unwilling rankled, for the former lovelies he had been fortunate in bedding had tumbled into his bed with quite alarming eagerness. Nay, he had not intended, despite his lustful threat, to take Christie by force of any kind, but his desire for her had proved ungovernable. It had kindled and burned ever fiercer with his successive beddings of her and still showed no sign of becoming extinguished or of burning itself out, as he had hoped! Damn, he would rather she had come to him willing or not at all than this way, if he could have helped himself. He scowled darkly. He fancied it would have been not at all.

His green eyes narrowed as he glanced back towards the pair on the upper deck. Was it just jealousy rearing its ugly head, or was Flint indeed holding Christianne far closer than was necessary to steady her walk across the rolling decks? Aye, he thought so!

"Mister Mullens, the wheel, if you please!" he barked.

Silas Mullens jumped smartly to the duty, offering his stern-faced captain a questioning look which James studiously ignored. He strode down the stairs to the lower deck, towards Christianne and that silver-tongued Flint. Expressions of displeasure at his intrusion were written clearly on both her pouting face and on Flint's. The latter quickly covered his with a smile.

"Top o' the morning to ye, Captain!" Flint sang out, doffing his tricorn. " 'Tis a fair day and a fine breeze, is it not?" He grinned. Despite the removal of his hat, there was none of the usual deference shown a captain in his manner, but rather a cockiness that fueled James' ire still further.

"A fine day indeed, Flint," he agreed curtly. "You may return to your duties now. I shall escort Mistress Alexander forthwith."

"But, sir, I was but—!"

"That is all, Flint," James dismissed him softly.

Flint shot an apologetic look at Christianne, who smiled one of her rare, bewitching smiles at him in return. He glowered fleetingly at his captain before leaving as ordered, but with obvious reluctance.

Christianne scowled fiercely up at James. "There was no need for that, Captain," she flared. "Jonathan was doing nothing wrong! He was but regaling me with tales of his native Ireland. He has been a most entertaining escort." Unlike some, she added silently.

James snorted. "Madam, this is a merchant vessel, not some townhouse withdrawing room where anecdotes may be exchanged over dainty cups of tea. Your Master Flint is not a fop in silks and satins, but a sailor, with other duties to attend to."

Christianne's tawny eyebrows rose. "And you have none, sir?"

"I," he said deliberately, "am captain of this vessel."

"Ah, now I see!" Christianne said crossly, brushing an errant curl of fair hair from her stormy, deep blue eyes, "Your men may not dally with female passengers, but for the captain it is permissible!" She pouted sulkily.

James glowered. "Flint is a member of my crew, madam—not your damned lap dog! Does that little beast not serve you well in that role?" He cast a jaundiced eye on poor Bones seated at her feet, tongue lolling and panting with the heat.

Christianne shrugged and tossed her hair over her shoulder in an angry gesture. Her slim hands, now free of calluses, gripped the varnished taffrail before her. She fastened her gaze upon the rolling blue swells rather than upon the captain.

"Bones is of great comfort to me," she said stiffly, "but he cannot provide me with sufficient companionship to break the unending monotony of this voyage, nor can he help the endless, boring hours to fly by. Now that you have forbidden me Jonathan's company, the days will seem even longer, I fear."

"Perhaps it is a more intimate companionship you seek from Flint?" James suggested jealously. "I see no lack of companionship for you otherwise! Ben Wright passes his free time playing cards with you; between the two of them, your every whim is attended to. Nay, I would not have thought you lacking, madam!"

Her face flamed scarlet. His tone was insulting. " 'Intimate companionship,' indeed!" she stormed. "Why, I do believe you are jealous, sir! Could it be that it is your intimate companionship you wish me to accept?" she asked, smiling sweetly. "For if it is"—her smile changed to a scowl—"you may go to Hades, my lord captain, aye, and your lecherous companionship with you! I vowed I would never willingly become your mistress, and I meant it!"

"You also vowed you would never leave England," James pointed out, chuckling softly now at her furious expression.

The look she shot him was withering and gave him peculiar pleasure. He leaned over the railing beside her, brushing her arm with his own as he did so.

She moved a few inches away, both to underline that she had no liking for him, or his nearness, and to attempt to still the erratic fluttering of her heart. When their arms had touched, gooseflesh had risen all along the length of hers, despite her irritation at him, and an image of his sea-green eyes afire with desire for her had flashed through her mind in a most unsettling fashion. It was not the first time her treacherous body had reacted so violently to his nearness, she recalled furiously, trying to force her wayward thoughts back to the wide expanse of blue before her over the rail, and failing miserably. Every time he looked upon her, she felt naked in the emerald blaze of his eyes, as if yet again he was threatening to make love to her, with or without her permission.

They sailed with the African coast not two miles off their bows, and the hot, sultry breeze carried the scent of spices and steaming vegetation to their ship. They'd passed more than one vessel in the past few days, but James had hailed none of them, nor returned their captains' hailings. Instead he had kept his eyes stonily on their course, or on the churning white trough in the wake of the *Amanda*'s stern. She determined to ask him why this was so, to steer her thoughts elsewhere than on the unsettling fact of his nearness.

"Because," he said in answer to her question, "those vessels that we passed are blackbirders, slavers trafficking in human flesh and misery. I will acknowledge no man who calls himself master of such a vessel! The coast that you see beyond is known as the Slave Coast. There it is that the unwitting Africans are abducted from their villages or sold by their own treacherous chiefs to the slave traders and herded into pens like cattle. There they await the black-birder, into the hold of which they will be loaded like bales of fustian crammed tight. Less than half of them will survive that hellish voyage to see their destination! And their misery does not end with their arrival," he finished darkly, "but rather it has just begun."

Christianne nodded. Though slaves were not as common-place in London as they appeared to be in the New World, she had seen black men, dressed in gaudy, lavish livery and paraded about by their mistresses like some freakish attraction at a country fair.

"It is obvious the subject of slaving upsets you, Captain," she observed. "You like not this traffic where human beings are denied their freedom, do you?" He shook his head, and she smiled in triumph. "Then why is it, sir, that you so heatedly deny me my own?"

He spun to face her, gripping her arm so roughly she yelped in startled pain. "You compare my guardianship of you with those poor devils' lot? What an innocent little fool you are!" he said scathingly, and she flinched. "At least, my poor, *enslaved* Christianne," he mocked, "your imprison-ment has a foreseeable end in New Orleans, while theirs," he paused, a bitter glint in his green eyes, "can end only in death, and if the fates are merciful, swiftly!"

Christianne had the grace to look somewhat ashamed of herself. What he had said was right, she knew, and she shuddered though it was a warm breeze that bellied the *Fair Amanda*'s sails. She could imagine the stifling black-birder's hold, crammed with bodies: the wails and moans of the sick and the dying, the despair and the misery that permeated the hold. I'faith, she had truly but spoken in anger and without thought, and she wanted desperately for him to understand her feelings. "I—I'm sorry," she stammered, "I spoke without thinking." She wetted her lips. "But whether it angers you or nay to hear me say it, I *feel* like a prisoner, Sir Captain! Mine has always been a restless nataure, as is yours, I fancy. But whereas you have your ship and your crew to run, I have nothing to do but twiddle my thumbs day in and day out. Is it not said that the devil finds work for idle hands to do? So will it be with me, I fear!" She rested her fingertips against his arm in supplication. "I beg you, James, set me some task to perform! Any task will serve to make the tarrying hours pass more swiftly and restore some small measure of content-ment to me. Anything!"

James anger melted and he chuckled. "Are you certain you will not reconsider the post that I have already offered you—as my mistress?" he offered teasingly. "I would guarantee you many far-from-boring hours in that particular duty!"

"You tease me again, sir," she cried, her face flaming, "as you are ever wont to do when I am serious!" Her face flamed. "If you can think of nothing more important for me to do than to become your—your *bedwarmer,* I suppose I will have to content myself with doing nothing at all!" She would have flounced angrily away, but James stayed her.

"Wait, do not be hasty," he reproved. " 'Tis no easy task to find some labor suitable for a wench in a man's dominion such as this vessel. And one in which you will come to no harm, to boot." He leaned down and ruffled Bones' silky ears. "What say you to a fetching new apprentice at your rat-catching, eh, dog?" The little dog whined and thumped its feathery tail on the deck. James laughed, then noticed Christianne's furious expression and attempted to maintain a more sober expression. "All right, all right, you vixen, I

146

am done with my teasing!" he promised hastily. "I will think on it and do my best to find something for you to do."

"My thanks, James," she said, favoring him with one of her rare smiles.

He nodded. "My pleasure, Christianne, to be of service to you." His green eyes caressed her. "It suits me well that we have at last agreed upon some common end, however small, for since we met, we have done little else but fight"—he winked—"for the greater part. If you would but give me the chance, you would find I am not the merciless brute you believe me to be," he finished in a gentle tone.

"No?" she murmured, her tawny brows raising in inquiry. "Then what manner of man are you, Captain?" she asked candidly.

Her frankness took him aback. He threw back his russet head, hooked his thumbs in his belt and laughed. "What manner of man am I? Why, lass, I'll be damned if I know, having never given the matter thought 'til now! I consider myself a fair man, I suppose. A man who is inordinately fond of the fair sex," he added with a grin. "A man who sees much of life as it is these days as being far too grim a matter to take seriously all the time. An ability to see the amusing side of things is a sanity-preserver, I believe. Humor is the leavening in the hard bread of life. Without it, we would all break our teeth on its crusts!" He stepped closer to her. His warm breath stirred the tendrils of fair hair about her ears. "You have such a bewitching smile, my sweet, such a lovely, silvery laugh!" He rested his palm lightly on her hip. "It would please me to see that smile and hear that laughter more often."

He intended to kiss her, she sensed, and broke nervously from him like a startled gazelle. In her demure gray gown with its froth of white lace at the collar and cuffs, and with her wild, creamy mane neatly fastened in a narrow black ribbon, she looked for all the world like a prim Quaker

147

miss. Ah, how deceptive appearances could be, James thought. He knew well what a passionate and tempestuous nature lay beneath that cool facade. The memory of her scent, her taste, flooded through him hotly.

"If you sincerely wish that we be friends, sir," she said huskily, noting the ardor in his eyes, "you would not make so bold with your hands! I am not chattel, to be handled at will by you or any other man!"

"Indeed?" James asked, his good humor dwindling. "Not even by your Jonathan Flint? If my eyes were not deceiving me a while ago, he deemed it necessary to hold you overly close as you promenaded, and yet I heard no outraged protest from you then?"

She reddened guiltily but chose to ignore his implication.

"Will you not tell me all that you know of my aunt, sir?" she asked, changing the subject. "It has occurred to me of late that I know little of her. If I am to live with her, the more I know the better, think you not?"

James nodded, taken aback by her question. Should he, *could* he tell her that her Aunt Nell was the richest madam in all of New Orleans? That Nell Flagg's "girls" had the reputation of being the most beautiful and highly-accomplished in their ancient profession in the entire town — a town that prided itself on the sinfulness of its reputation to boot? Nay! If he did, she would curse him as a hypocrite for his numerous affirmations that her new life with her aunt would lift her far from the gutter life of London she had known! Having never met Nell, having never witnessed the true beauty of the indefatigable, feisty, generous little woman's character, she would not see that the manner in which Nell chose to make her living counted for naught. That, in the fashion in which Nell ran her bordello, there was an innate honesty and justice that gave a measure of decency to this oldest of the world's professions. Nell's girls were free to come or go as they wished — in fact, many had left the Royal Street house to become respectable wives to the settlers that poured daily into New Orleans. While they were with her, Nell saw that they were paid fairly, fed regularly and well, and received a physician's care when necessary. As a result, many formerly destitute or orphaned young women now called Nell's house their home, and meant it in the fullest sense of the word, for like a mother she shared their joys, wept with them in their sorrows and gave timely advice and scoldings when needed. But how could he impart all that in a few words, however carefully chosen or honestly felt? No, it would be wiser to wait until they reached New Orleans, James decided, and then the revelation would swiftly be followed by meeting her aunt in the flesh, and she could learn for herself the fine caliber of Nell Flagg, madam *extraordinaire*.

"Your aunt, I am honored to say, is one of my dearest friends, and has been so these past two years," he said carefully, his eyes fixed resolutely on a colorful shoal of *pintados* a few yards over their side. "She has a merry wit that I believe you will enjoy, and a strength of character that all who come to know her admire. She is of a generous nature, and if she decides that you are indeed a friend, you could trust her with your life."

Christianne smiled politely. It would not have surprised her if he had added that this paragon of virtue had sprouted wings and a halo! "And she is wealthy, it appears, to have put up such a generous purse for my wardrobe?"

"Indeed, yes," James admitted uncomfortably, "a very wealthy woman. But," he added pointedly, "one not easily gulled."

La! Christianne thought indignantly, did he expect her to murder the old battleaxe in her bed and rob her of her gold? The nerve of him to even think such a thing! Nevertheless, her curiosity outweighed her irritation, and she

149

made no angry retort.

"Is she not married?"

James sucked in a deep breath. Christianne's questions were becoming a little too specific for his liking. "No, no she is not."

"Then how is it she has made her fortune? My grandparents were hard-working folk, but poorer than church mice!"

James frowned. "Well, she, er, she is the proprietor of a large—a large house," he hedged, "that caters to a wealthy clientele. Through hard work and shrewd investments, she has, er, accrued considerable fortune." There, he thought, let her make of those ambiguous statements what she would!

"Ah, I see," Christianne said, nodding in understanding, "so, my aunt runs a hotel. Would you not consider her a spinsterish old dame then?"

James choked, covering his laughter by coughing. "Nay, indeed I would not!" He grinned. "There is nothing of the 'spinsterish dame' about your aunt! She is a comely woman, aye, and a lively one! Now, do not concern yourself overmuch in regards to Nell Flagg. You will meet her soon enough and be able to judge for yourself."

"Yes," she agreed with little enthusiasm, "I suppose that I will." She turned from the rail. "Lord, 'tis so hot! I believe I should like to go back to my cabin now."

"As you wish," James agreed, relieved that the sticky subject of Nell's profession had been smoothly covered.

"You will not forget what I asked you—about finding me some task with which to fill my hours?" she reminded him.

"I will not," James promised solemnly, offering her his arm.

A day later, hands blistered, Christianne was sorely

regretting her rash promise to do "anything" the captain cared to set her.

In her sore fingers she held a sailmaker's needle of sharpened whale bone, and about her on the deck spread seeming acres of billowing, bleached-white canvas, the huge rents in which she was supposed to repair! She wiped her brow with an already sodden scrap of a kerchief and kneaded her aching back. Her feet had long since gone numb in her cross-legged posture and her eyes ached from the unaccustomed sewing and the brilliant light.

The crew of the *Fair Amanda* seemed to find her labors highly amusing, and made no effort to hide their grins as they passed, damn their souls! She viciously jabbed her needle into the heavy, unwieldy canvas, and began repairing yet another tear. "Mend them well, lass," Silas Mullens had cautioned, with a wink of his one eye, "for the storms we do be expecting come we reach the Caribee Sea will tear these beauties hither and yon like the hounds o' hell rent them in their jaws!"

She had nodded in understanding. After many of her and James' passionate interludes, he had talked at length and with greath enthusiasm of the Caribees. He had described them as a string of isles set like dazzling gems in the azure sea. He'd talked of white sand beaches and verdant greenery, of the smoking volcano, Pelee, fertile sugar and tobacco plantations and exotic plants and flowers so vividly she could see them in her mind's eye. He'd also described in terrifying detail the hurricanes that could flatten an entire island in mere hours, wrest palm trees from the ground like a gardener removes weeds, whirl houses into the air with less effort than a roué flips his cards onto the gaming table. He had also mentioned a plantation that had caught his fancy, *La Reine du Ciel,* the Queen of the Sky, in glowing terms, adding that if it had not already been purchased, he intended to bid on it when they arrived in Martinique. It was, he'd said, the one place where he felt he might be happy when his seafaring days were done. The plantation house was set on a steep rise overlooking the ocean, and commanded an unobstructed view of half the island from its widow's walk. The two-storied house boasted a spacious white-railed veranda to its upper story and a fine, colonnaded lower floor with steps leading up to the main doors. The gardens, he'd said, were filled with butterfly-bright blossoms, purple and magenta bougain-villaea, yellow hibiscus and plumeria, *roses d'Inde* of vivid scarlet and luminous white moonflowers, as well as curly ferns and plantains and cacao trees. She sighed. It all sounded like an enchanting fairy-tale palace and part of her envied the woman who would share this tropical para-dise with James—though not her Prince Charming, nay, never!

She sucked her finger, which had begun to bleed, and looked up as a low whine drew her attention. Bones padded to her side, wagging his feathery tail. His chocolate-brown eyes were mournful as they peered out from under the pepper-and-salt curtain of hair that almost covered his wet nose.

"What is it, Bones?" she asked, petting him fondly. The dog whined and lay down, his muzzle resting on his paws, looking up at her soulfully. It was then she spied a drying spot of blood on his nose. "Oh, poor Bones! We are both wounded from our labors, are we not? What was it, old fellow, a plaguesome rat? Did you catch him, mmm?" The dog thumped his tail and yawned hugely. Christianne laughed. "I think not, else you would not appear so dejected! Now, go back to your rat-catching, and leave me to my work!" After a few moments, Bones grew bored with his mistress' industrious mood and padded off across the deck. Christianne smiled as she watched him go. Faithless hound! she thought with a rueful smile. When she had returned to the ship from Barcelona, it had been debatable whether that hairy little beast had been more overjoyed to see her or James, for he had greeted them both with equal amounts of excited barking, tail wagging and vigorous swipes with his pink tongue!

She was just about to go forward to the scuttlebutt for a well-deserved ladle of water when she heard voices rising up through the grilled hatch-cover of the fo'c's'le hold where the crew had their quarters. Grinning, she silently sank back down, for the snatches of conversation she had just caught had been too scandalously juicy to miss! She muffled her groans as blood rushed back to her numbed feet and cocked her head on one side, the better to eavesdrop.

"Aye, ain't it true though!" she heard one gruff voice exclaim. "Our cap'n do be a lucky rogue t' have the like o' Mistress Christianne to warm his bunk and feast his eyes upon! Pretty as a bloomin' angel, she is, an' all, with her silver hair. Jack, I tell yer, just t' look at her makes me come over all queer, it do!"

Ribald laughter followed this, and Christianne smiled impishly.

"Take a hold o' yer tongue, Todd, lad, and mark ye don't let our Irish 'lord' hear ye talkin' that way about the cap'n's lady! To hear Flint sing her praises, she's the Holy Madonna and good, virgin Queen Bess combined!" said a second man. "Come we reach the Caribbees, there'll be wimmin aplenty, all willin' t' share a pallet with a handsome tar like yourself—if ye have the coin to go with yer good looks!" More raucous laughter. "For meself, I've a mind t' wait until we reach New Orleans. There's a little gal in a Royal Street house what took a fancy ter me last time we put inter port, make no mistake. Her hair were the color o' yeller gold, and her teats were right big!" Hoots and more laughter. "I do declare, she were that amply endowed, I wished I had two pair o' hands, I did!"

Someone snorted. "Well, I'll tell yer wot! Next time I'll go with yer ter see yer yeller-haired gal—and ve'll have that second pair o' hands ye wished fer!" He roared with laughter.

"Get along with you, Todd Hawkins! This gal's a fancy piece—she won't look at the likes o' you, and that's a fact!"

"Fancy piece, my arse!" Todd, apparently, responded scornfully. "She be one o' Ma Whitehouse's doxies down by the levee, more likely than not, I'll wager, else she wouldn't have been so taken with the likes o' you! Her poxy bawds would tumble a bloomin' monkey, if he had coin t' pay!" Todd sniggered.

"Poxy bawds be damned!" Jack retorted indignantly. "My li'l Mary ain't one o' Ma Whitehouse's tarts, I'll have ye know. She do be at Nell Flagg's place, on Royal Street—the fanciest bleedin' bawdyhouse in all o' New Orleans! None o' them farthing tarts in a cot on River Street fer me, no sir! Nell's house do boast of its clean wimmin, fresh linens every week and . . ."

Christianne never heard the rest. The blood drained from her face until it was chalky white. Her fingers froze in midair about the needle. *"Nell Flagg's place on Royal Street—the fanciest bleedin' bawdyhouse in all o' New Orleans!"* The words echoed over and over in her mind. No, it couldn't be! she told herself. She must have heard wrongly. There *must* be another Nell Flagg, she rationalized, desperately hoping against hope that somehow her suspicions were wrong. Why, just yesterday, James had as good as said her aunt kept a hotel . . . though come to think of it, he had never actually said so in words, but she had assumed—! A hotel? Nay, a *whorehouse,* she realized! That lying rogue! That—that hypocrite! That devil-whelped sea serpent! she screamed inside her head, wishing he were there, right that very second, so that she could carve his face to shreds with her talons, pluck out his eyes

154

with her fingers and hurl them to the gulls, wrest his traitor's heart from his breast and feed it to the sharks! She flung the canvas and needle aside and marched furiously across the decks to the wheel.

"Your captain, Master Mullens," she demanded, tapping her toe impatiently, "where might I find him?"

Mullens shoved back his tricorn, scratched his head and grinned. The little miss were right riled up about summat, an' no mistake! He didn't envy James' lot when she found him. Her eyes were aglitter like sapphires and there was a fearsome high color to her cheeks and a grim set to her jaw that promised a right good—.

"If you please, Master Mullens," she snapped through gritted teeth, "I would know where he is *today*, not tomorrow night!" She glowered at the bosun fiercely, and the feisty Mullens reddened like a callow boy.

"He do be below, Mistress Alexander, ma'am," he stammered, "in Ben Wright's cabin. His were the grave watch last night, yer see, and he were just finishin' up when ye came abovedecks this mornin' and—"

"My thanks!" she spat at him and stormed back down the stairway, skirts twitching.

"By St. George!" Mullens muttered under his breath, "you'd best look out, James, lad! It seems we do be in fer our first squall this voyage—aye, an' a regular tempest it do promise to be!" He shook his head gloomily.

Christianne's fury was not one whit abated by the time she reached Ben Wright's cabin. Rather, it had increased in volume, and her expression was murderous. She wasted no time on such niceties as knocking, but simply hurled open the door so that it flew back against the cabin wall with a reverberating crash.

James slept on in his bunk, not so much as flinching at the sound. He had rolled himself into a woollen blanket and only his face showed above it, a face that was the very picture of male innocence as he slept, she saw, livid now. She clamped her fingers over the edge of the blanket and tore it from the captain.

"Wake up, you lying, two-faced, lily-livered rogue!" she screamed, scant inches from his ear. "Wake up, else I will brain you!"

James' eyes flickered open, still a little glazed with sleep. He grinned lazily. "Christianne, my sweeting," he exclaimed warmly, "what brings you down here?" He patted the rough wooden bunk beside him and smothered a yawn. "Come, there is room enough here for two," he promised, a sensual expression on his sleepy face that she now knew well.

"Aye, damn you, James Mallory, I'll warrant there's *room*—room enough to teach me all the tricks I'll be needing in New Orleans, no doubt!" she railed, her fury uncontrollable. She whirled about, grabbed up his sea boots and hurled them at him full force, her aim wickedly accurate.

James yelped and sat up, fully awake now. "By all that's holy, woman, what's wrong?" he sputtered, dodging missiles as they rained across the cabin at him. "Have you taken leave of your senses?"

"Nay, I've not!" she snorted, flinging her creamy hair out of her blazing blue eyes as she snatched up a weighty candlestick, "I have found them, rather!" The candlestick arced through the air with a brassy flash.

Hurriedly, James threw up a hand and deflected its deadly weight in the nick of time. The candlestick thudded to the boards. "Enough!" he roared. "Blast you, vixen, cease this nonsense and tell me what has angered you!"

She cast about her for another weapon, but the small cabin's meager supply of missiles had already been depleted. Breathing heavily, hands on her hips, her small breasts heaving, she advanced on him like one of the Furies.

156

"I'll tell you what's wrong," she spat. "I've learned the truth, that's what's wrong! What was it you promised me, my fine *honorable* captain—a better life with my aunt, was it not? My Aunt Nell Flagg who owns a hotel, I believe you led me to understand it? Well, mayhap you should have said whorehouse, should you not? And all the love-making and flowery phrases you plied me with in your cabin—what were they? My preparation for my new life as a doxy in New Orleans? Part of my education in how to please my aunt's 'wealthy clientele'? Aye, you played your part well, you—you—*whoremaster*—and I, like a silly twit, an innocent chit, had begun to enjoy your attentions! I had begun to believe that you were in truth fond of me! What a fool you must have thought me! How you must have laughed at my sighs and my kisses! Damn you!" Her fists came up from her hips to rain blows on his head with such unexpected speed he was totally unprepared for them, or their ferocity.

"Damn you!" she panted again. "Damn your lying soul!" Her small fists flailed at him. Her anger gave her added strength and each blow told. "I'll play the whore for no man, sir, no man, I tell you!"

Ducking, James stood and tried to grasp her wrists, but it was much like trying to grapple a cornered wildcat, writhing, spitting curses, clawing for his face and yelling lustily as hot floods of tears spilled down her crimson cheeks. When at last he had trapped both hands and wrestled them down to her sides, she brought up her knee and jabbed him wickedly in the groin.

"God's Blood, vixen!" he groaned, "careful lest you unman me!"

"I can think of nothing I should like better!" she hissed through gritted teeth. "Count yourself lucky you awoke when you did, or I would have taken a knife and made your present condition permanent!" There was enormous relish in her tone.

Despite his pain, James grinned lopsidedly. By the gods, she was a hot-tempered little hoyden, if ever he'd seen one, and, he realized guiltily, quite righteously furious! He enveloped her in a bear hug and pushed her backwards down onto the bunk. Her knees gave way against the wooden edge of it and she sprawled beneath him, howling with fury.

"Now," he panted, still atop her as the only means to keep her still, "listen to me and listen well, for I will say it but once, and no more! How you came by your information, I know nor care not, but it is—"

"Aye, deny it, damn you!" Christianne cut him off, glaring into his hated face just inches from hers.

"—But it is true," James continued calmly. "Your Aunt Nell is indeed the madam of a sporting house in New Orleans, aye, and a very successful one it is, too. But you, my dove, were never destined to serve its patrons, my word on it."

"Your word? You ask me to take *your* word? Pah! Your word is as good as a—a snake's, with its forked tongue, you serpent!" she retorted, wriggling and squirming to rid herself of his heavy weight.

James pressed still harder down on her, for once impervious to the pleasant proximity of her body. "Your aunt and I believed you to be a lad, Christianne, as well you know. The reason I let you believe your aunt owned a hotel was because I feared just such an outburst as this from you if I told you the truth—aye, and rightly so!" he added with feeling. "I didn't wish to prejudice your opinion of your aunt before you met her by telling you of her house and her position as its madam, for Nell is a fine woman, a decent, loving woman, whatever her profession. You will find naught but kindness in her care, even if she does keep a bordello."

"No doubt you speak from experience, sir," Christianne said acidly, still endeavoring to writhe free of him. "I see it all now—your frequent singing of my aunt's praises, your numerous comments that she is kind and loving! No doubt you have taken her to bed more times than I have fingers and toes to count! But your fancy pleas sway me not a whit. I still consider you a liar, Captain, a liar and a scoundrel without a morsel of decency in you! If you were as honorable as you profess to be, you would have told me all and let me, *me* be the judge of whether I sailed with you or nay!"

James shook his head. "Nay, not so. You are young in years, my sweet, and life has dealt harshly with you. You would have determined to stay in London with your motley band in Darling Lane, living from the gutters, for however hard a life it was, it was safe in its familiarity. Sooner or later you would have been caught at your cutpursing and had your pretty neck stretched on the gibbet at Tyburn, or perhaps worse, been consigned to a living hell in the hulks while you awaited deportation to Australia's penal colonies, falling prey to filth and disease and rape and all the other miseries of those poor devils' lot. Nay," he said fervently, caressing her lovely, angry face, "I could not leave you to come to such a pass!" She jerked her head away from his hand. "Hate me if you will, but your only hope for a better life lies with your aunt, madam or nay."

A sob lodged in Christianne's throat. "You gave me no choice," she whispered fiercely, "none! And you lied to me! I'll never forgive you, never. I'll hate you forever, for as long as I draw breath, I'll hate you. Hate you! Jonathan Flint is ten times the man you are!"

James' handsome face hardened. He swung himself off her, stood up and looked down at her small, dishevelled figure with its tumbled mane of silvery hair with something like pain in his eyes.

"As you wish," he said flatly. "I have said my piece; I can do no more. I had thought you were at last a woman grown, Christie, but I see now that I was wrong. You are still but a child, after all." He bent down and retrieved his tricorn from the jumble of items strewn on the floor. "See that you return everything here to its proper place before you return to the great-cabin." Without further words, he left.

Christianne felt peculiarly deflated after he had gone. She scrambled off the bunk and surveyed the cabin's ruin without remorse, before picking her way delicately through the clutter to the door. Once there, she smoothed her ravaged hair, wiped her tear-streaked face on the back of her hand and straightened her skirts before slipping out into the passageway. If James wanted this cabin set to rights he could do it himself, she vowed, a flash of her former defiance returning.

She stalked quickly down the passageway to the foot of the stairs and brought up short. James was there, tall and stern, his arms crossed over his chest and his feet planted aggressively apart. His expression was dark and scowling.

"Not so fast," he growled as she tried to thrust past him, "you have work yet to do. You will go back and restore that cabin to its original state as I ordered." He blocked her path.

"And if I will not?" she flared, her deep blue eyes flashing sparks at him.

"But you will," James said firmly, "sooner or later! If you will not do it now, you will remain there until you do so. I will place a guard on the door and not a trencher of food will you have until it is done." He smiled, but she did not care for the quality of it. "Now, be a good little wench and repair the results of your . . . tantrum."

"You will not treat me like a child!" she vowed. "I'll die before I touch one item in that cabin," she swore recklessly, but with enormous pride.

"So be it," James acknowledged, not a trace of mercy in his tone. "Luke!" he roared, then turned back to Christianne. "Your guard will be here shortly," he said with a grin, "now, back to Ben's cabin, if you please, infant."

With murder in her heart, Christianne turned and walked back down the passageway.

Three days passed. Three days in which neither James nor Christianne showed any indication of giving quarter to the other in their war of wills. As James had vowed, not a trencher of food had been delivered to the first officer's cabin, though water had been. An attempt by kindly Ben Wright to smuggle a ration of salt pork and sea biscuits in to the girl had been severely punished on its discovery, and the shamefaced Cornishman, caught red-handed by his captain, had himself retired to a hammock in the men's quarters without victuals that night.

As Christianne had vowed, she had not set the cabin to rights, and her missiles—oddments of clothing, seafaring journals, a chamber pot and the candlestick—still lay where they had landed three days before.

"Ah, 'tis foolishness," Silas Mullens remarked dourly, late into the evening of the third day. "I know the cap'n well. He's a kind lad at heart, but he won't be giving in to a chit of a girl! She'd best do as bidden, an' there's an end to the matter."

"She'll not," Luke Hardcastle, on guard yet again outside the cabin door, said with conviction. "She mutters and curses him from dawn t' dusk without no sign o' letting up. I wager Cap'n Mallory has been bested by the wench."

"And would ye care to back your wager, son?" Mullens asked shrewdly. "I've a hogshead of arrack in my gear, what I got when we provisioned in Morocco. My hogshead says the lass will relent afore eventide tomorrow," he challenged.

"And I've a pouch of 'baccy and a pair o' good worsted stockings to match your wager, that says she won't!" Luke matched him with a grin.

"Done!" said Mullens firmly, a smug smile wreathing his weathered, gnome-like face. He could almost taste that 'baccy now, smell the fragrant smoke of it spiralling up from his pipe. And the stockings would be right welcome next time they had cold weather. He grinned. They were both as good as his already!

If anything, the wager she had heard while her ear was pressed to the cabin door only served to reinforce Christianne's determination not to give in. She had fought down first the flutters, then the growls, then the gnawings of her hungry belly, and whenever exhaustion and her pangs permitted, she slept. But by the afternoon of the fourth day she was light-headed and feeble-limbed and felt more than a passing weakness. She kept to her bunk and lay there listlessly, half tempted to try at chewing on the corner of the woollen blanket to stave off her hunger. Damn James! she thought, tears filling her eyes, she couldn't give in, couldn't let him win! However, even she admitted to herself that she felt this with far less conviction than she had felt before!

Meanwhile, James, a trencher in one hand and a spoon in the other, paused in his eating and set the food aside. He scowled at it, pushed back his chair and paced across the great-cabin, his again now by default.

"Is it not to your liking, Jim?" Ben asked with a knowing grin. He had, piece by piece, extracted all the details of the present state of siege between the pair both from James and from Christianne, through whispered, tearful exchanges through the locked cabin door. Privately, he sided with the little lass. James had not been straight with her, not by a

162

long chalk.

"It is to my liking," James snapped curtly. "I find I have little appetite, that's all."

"Ah," Ben nodded, "I understand. It makes you guilty to fill your belly when the poor little lass is nigh dead from starvation, does it not?" He stood and began stacking the wooden trenchers to take back to the galley.

"It does nothing of the sort!" his captain growled, his green eyes glittering angrily. "And as for the 'poor little lass,' as you and Mullens persist in calling her, I would not waste your pity on her, or you'll regret it, mark my words! She would deliver the pair of us up into the devil's hands to further her own ends—aye, Ben," James insisted as he caught the Cornish man's expression of disbelief, "Even you, who have shown her only kindness, without second thought!"

Ben clicked his teeth reprovingly. "Now, sir, don't harden your heart against the wench. You've taken your pleasures in many a port, aye, and with many wenches, but this one calls for different handling, sir, don't ye see? For all that she's brave and fierce on the outside, inside I do believe she is—"

"—As hard and unbending as leather pickled in brine and baked in the desert sun!" James supplied hotly.

"Nay, sir," Ben continued, unruffled and shaking his sandy head, "just a frightened slip of a girl t' whom life is yet a stranger and terrifying to boot, on account of its strangeness. We've spent some time in these past few weeks conversing and playing cards, as you know, sir, and she has told me much of her former life and the woes that befell her. 'Tis a story that would tear your heart to hear, sir!" James grunted in disbelief. "For all the girl's brave masquerade as a lad, and her rascally friends, 'tis a sheltered life she has led, in many respects. Such as knowing what transpires 'twixt a man and a woman in love. She knows

163

only what she has witnessed of men in the backstreets, sees them all as lecherous animals—and you, sir, if I may make so bold, have done little to change her impressions with your actions of late!"

James blinked. It was probably the longest speech he had ever heard from the taciturn Cornish Ben, and by far and away the most heated! It was a mark of his security in his friendship with his captain that he dared to take him to task so boldly, for despite their friendship, James was still the captain, his word aboard ship, law unto all. That Ben should champion the girl infuriated him!

"She told you?" he roared, incredulous. "She told you that she did not come willingly to my bed?"

"Aye," Ben confessed calmly. "Who else had she to confide in—she has no mother, no sister, no friend here. With all due respect, sir, 'tis my opinion you've treated her badly."

"Respect be damned!" James exploded, slamming his fists down on the table. "Does it show respect for a first officer to take his captain to task for a personal matter? That vixen! She has turned her talents to coming betwixt you and I, now, my friend! Well, she has made her bed, and now she must lie in it. She acted like a naughty child not long out of swaddling and I treated her accordingly. If she would be treated like a grown woman, she must act like one. Nay, Ben, she will not best me in this!" he said grimly.

"I expect you're right, sir," Ben said smoothly, heading for the door. "Right is on your side, as captain, I realize. But the way I heard it told, she had grounds to be angry, did she not, sir?"

"Ben—!" James growled in warning. "Do not press me!"

"I wouldn't dream of it, Captain," Ben denied with a guileless smile as he opened the door. "And by the way, sir, there's another matter I think should be brought to your notice, a matter of missing stores, sir."

James frowned, still angry at Ben. "Missing stores?" he echoed. "What of them? Explain yourself!"

"Cook says supplies are vanishing. I wanted to ask what you would have me do about it?"

"Do you think someone is stealing food for the girl?"

Ben shook his head. "No, sir. According to cook, this has been going on for a while, now. He wanted to be sure before he told me, so he set some pork and biscuits out. Sure enough, they disappeared the next day!"

"Mmmm," James murmured thoughtfully. "Well, I would suggest a guard be placed on the stores until we catch whoever it is. What say you?"

"I say 'aye,' sir. Good evening to ye."

"And to you, Ben," James agreed as the first officer left him.

He lit his pipe and paced up and down the cabin. The first officer's accusations had bothered him more than he cared to admit. He sighed heavily. Christianne's fragrance lingered yet in the air, the fragrance of roses from the soaps he had bade Ben fetch in London along with her bathing tub. Even now, he recalled how sweet she smelled, the roses mingled with her own subtle, intoxicating scent, and how she felt under his hands, soft and warm and infinitely arousing. Devil take the fair sex, he thought. Who needed them anyway, the devious emotional creatures? You tried to protect them from danger and from themselves, cherished them, loved them, and in what coin did they repay you—with curses and hurled candlesticks and insults, that's what! He sat down and angrily poured himself another goblet of wine, then a second, hot on the heels of the first. As he looked irritably about him, his glance fell on a hefty wedge of cheese, bread, and a juicy leg of capon still on a trencher on the desk. Ben must have missed it, or else left it in case his captain's appetite returned, James surmised. Or had he, that sly rogue? Well, no matter what Ben's intent had been, James thought with a grin, the trencher of food had given him an idea of how to bring that vixen Christianne to her knees!

He gathered up the trencher and yet another goblet of wine and strode with them belowdecks to Ben Wright's cabin, giving Luke on guard there permission to take an airing and stretch his legs.

"She'll not eat it, Cap'n," Luke said with a jerk of his head at the food.

"Indeed she will not, Hardcastle," James agreed, smiling broadly. "This platter is for me, not her."

" 'Tis a sly one you are, sir," Luke said sourly, the hogshead of arrack he had expected to win on the morrow seemingly gliding out of his reach. He stomped off down the passageway, bent on persuading Mullens to forget their wager.

James grinned wickedly, then set his features in a serious expression and let himself in the cabin.

His single-minded desire to win the war of wills between himself and Christianne for winning's sake alone evaporated when he saw her. She was now as slender as a wraith, and as pale: pale hair, pale flesh. Her eyes, dark and shadowed with violet, were the only color in her face. He muffled an oath on his own rigidity, and instead nodded cordially.

"Good evening, Christianne," he murmured, setting the trencher on the rough-hewn table. "I have brought your supper myself. Please, eat it."

Christianne eyes him sullenly. What trick was he up to now? The floor was still strewn with clutter. She had done nothing to earn this "reward" of food! Did he mean to torture her by offering it and then snatching it away and eating it himself while she looked on? Her eyes narrowed. Lord, it smelled so good—better than any food she had ever smelled before, she was certain! Her stomach muscles squeezed agonizingly. The temptation to spring across the cabin, snatch up the victuals and cram them into her ravenous mouth like a wild animal was all but overwhelming! She clenched her fists and fought the urge, turning to face the bulkhead so she would not have to look at the capon, gleaming with its own tasty sauce and drippings, or the cheese, sweating a little in the heat, nor the crusty loaf.

James scowled. The wench was as stubborn as a long-eared ass, he thought, irritated that his gesture had been rebuffed. What did she expect—that he go down on his knees before her and plead with her to eat? Damn her, no, she'd not make a mouse of this man, as she had Ben, Mullens, Flint and even that mute lout, Ox. They had all proved so much clay in her hands! Nay, one last chance and he was done, he decided firmly. Let her stay here, sulky and starving, 'til she died, if that was what she wanted.

"Christie, enough of this foolishness," he began, obviously uncomfortable in his role of olive branch extender. "You have won, as you intended you would, I admit freely. Eat the victuals I have brought."

" 'Tis a trick!" she retorted, still not looking at him.

"Nay," he replied wearily, " 'tis no trick." He straddled the cabin's only chair backwards. "I confess, when first I came in here, I intended to tempt you by eating the victuals myself but—"

"I knew it!" Christianne crowed triumphantly.

"—but now, no," he finished.

She scrabbled to sitting and regarded him warily, her brows wrinkled in concentration, arms wrapped about her bent knees and her chin resting upon them. "And why not now?" she pressed. "What has made you so willing to accept defeat? You do not strike me as a man accustomed to losing in any facet of life," she observed suspiciously.

"Ordinarily, no," the captain conceded. "But there are times when a judicious surrender is preferable to a victory.

My first obligation is to ensure the safety of my crew and my vessel. The second, to your aunt, and hence also to you. I promised her that I would see you safely to New Orleans and I will do so. She would not take it kindly if you were to arrive there looking like a skeleton with female attire!" he said with a grin. "And Nell Flagg is not a woman I would care to cross. A family trait, mayhap, this shrewish tongue and virago-like temper when angered?" His eyebrows rose in inquiry.

She shrugged. "Your crew have wagers on who betwixt us will win this war of wills, you know. You will lose their respect if they learn you have —" she smiled fleetingly — "surrendered to a mere wench!"

"They may think what they will," James answered. "But since I am captain of this ship, they will obey me whatever their feelings on this matter, or suffer the consequences! The wiser amongst them will realize that if to continue a battle will cost the life of one more man needlessly, it is preferable to accept an honorable defeat and surrender. At times, a leader shows his integrity more by the battles he does not fight than those that he does." He stood, a smile on his lips and sparkling in his green eyes. "And I, Madame Victor, will now beat a very judicious and timely retreat! You are free now to return to my—your cabin, when you are ready to do so. Goodnight, Christie. I hope that you enjoy your supper."

He left and Christianne waited expectantly for the heady rush of triumph that should have followed his exit. There was none. Her victory was hollow, somehow. By winning, she had, in some peculiar fashion, lost miserably. She walked to the table and sat down to eat, but the food had none of the ambrosial qualities on her palate with which she had endowed it in her imagination. After a few bites only, she shoved the trencher aside and pensively sipped the wine.

A soft scratching and whining at the cabin door brought her thoughts back to the present. She rose and let Mister Bones into the cabin. He barked joyously and bounded up against her, tail waving furiously, pink tongue ecstatically lapping her face. She crouched down and flung her arms about his shaggy neck, a dam of tears released as she buried her face in his silky, gray hair and hugged him close.

"In truth, Bones, you are my only friend," she sniffed woefully, "my only friend in this whole, wide world!"

She stood, feeling more than a litle sorry for herself, intending to set the cabin to rights. A gentle hand on her arm sent her whirling about.

Jonathan stood there in the doorway, an adoring smile on his handsome face. "Nay, mavourneen," he said tenderly, pulling her into his arms, "that hound is not your only friend. You have me, me darlin'! You have me." He lowered his head to kiss her.

From his hiding place beneath the table, Bones growled deep in his throat.

Thirteen

James tossed aside the charts strewn all across the desk and reached for his quill. "Pass me the log, Ben, there's a good fellow."

"Aye, aye, sir," Ben said with a grin, handing him the ship's log, a heavy book bound in scarred leather. Their easy friendship of before had gradually been reinstated over the past three weeks and it was as if he and the young captain had never exchanged heated words. "There you are, Captain."

James grinned. Ben seemed as determined to forget their altercation as was he. Aye, he was well content to let sleeping dogs lie, as the saying went! The only one who was not, it appeared, was Christianne. Though she was polite and answered when spoken to, the exchange was so stilted and formal that soon James gave up all overtures towards friendship and restricted the occasions when he spoke to her to the absolute minimum. Needless to say, he had not made love to her either in those three weeks, a condition which, though sorely regretted and sadly missed, he had no recourse but to accept. He had determined, after leaving the first officer's cabin and Christianne in judicious retreat that night, never to bed her again unless she implied that she was willing. Perhaps when Hades iced over? he wondered with a wry smile, scratching the date in the left-hand column of the log. Ben leaned over his shoulder and read the entry he had made.

"Friday the thirteenth!" the first officer gasped. His ruddy face paled. "Holy Madonna!"

James shook his head and grinned. "Come now, Ben!" he reasoned, "superstitions are for old dames with naught better to worry about! The thirteenth is but a date, and Friday a day like any other. Put this nonsense from you, friend! What say you to calling this day the twelfth yet again? Aye, the twelfth of May will fall twice this year!" He grinned again but Ben did not return his smile.

The first officer shuddered. When he had read the date in the log, the hackles on the back of his neck had risen and an icy slither of fear had slipped down his spine.

"Nay, sir!" he whispered hoarsely, " 'tis Friday the thirteenth, and you and I cannot change that! Bad fortune will strike, you mark my words!"

Jonathan Flint laughed inwardly as he looked about the circle of men gathered around him. It was just like before, aboard the *Perdita,* yes, to be sure it was! For all that the men pretended loyalty to their damned Captain Mallory, the seeds of mutiny had been sown amongst them, he could tell by their expressions.

"Come, lads, think of it! 'Tis not you poor devils who will profit from this voyage, but the captain. 'Tis not he who will work his fingers to the bare bones, not he who will toil in this stinking heat 'till his muscles scream with the pain of it—but yourselves! Follow me, and there will be riches beyond your wildest imaginings, sufficient for each and every one of you to live out your lives in leisure and luxury. Think on it, me boyos, think on it! Never having to take an order again, t' be your own master!"

A murmur ran around the handful of crew members gathered about Flint in the hold.

"Nay, Flint," Hardcastle argued. "Cap'n Mallory has always been straight and fair with us. I, for one, will stand by him. The devil take you and your promises of riches!" Luke elbowed his way out of the gloomy fo'c's'le hold and several followed him. Those that remained shifted uncomfortably under Flint's penetrating black eyes.

"So," he said softly, "you've all signed over your manhood along with your 'X' in the captain's log, have ye? So be it, then, lads! The *Fair Amanda* will have a new name and a new master 'ere long, mark my words—and 'tis a long memory I have. The next time I 'ask' you to join me, you will. Right, Tancred, right, Le Chat?"

"Right!" his two cronies agreed with sly smiles, and the half dozen men remaining exchanged nervous glances and wetted their lips.

"Well, well, what have we here?" Silas Mullens asked, shinning agilely down the rope ladder into the crew's quarters. It took a few seconds for his one eye to adjust to the gloom after the glare abovedecks. "Ah, Master Flint is it? And what is it you're havin' here, Flint? A choir practice? Seems ter me 'tis your watch, is it not? Get moving, lad, and look sharp as ye go!" The little bosun had caught the latter part of Flint's little speech prior to climbing down into the hold, and had liked the sound of it not at all.

Jonathan Flint favored Mullens with a cocksure smirk. "In my own good time, Bosun," he said casually, and the other men gasped at his insolence. Flint hooked his thumbs in his belt and lounged against a timber. "I know when my watch is well enough, I'm no fool. I have no need of a one-eyed monkey t' tell me what to do, nor when to do it, and that's a fact."

The "one-eyed monkey's" fist came out of nowhere and drove like a pile driver into Flint's nose with a loud crunch. The men groaned in unison. Blood streamed in twin torrents from Flint's nostrils, running down into his moustache and dripping off his chin. He lunged at the little bosun and gripped him by the cloth of his striped jersey, slamming him up against the bulkhead. He doubled Mullens over with a barrage of vicious punches to the belly, following with a hefty upper-cut to his jaw which snapped his head back and cracked it into the timber behind him. Mullens spiraled to the deck. Flint leaped after him and would have beaten him to a pulp if Ben Wright's shout had not stayed him.

"Enough, Flint!" Ben roared, "Break it up, I say, you scurvy swabs!" He hauled Flint, who was breathing heavily, off the prone man. After a few moments, Mullens staggered dazedly to his feet, wincing and hugging his bruised belly.

"All right, you lot, who started it?" Ben demanded, his angry gray eyes travelling around the circle of men. "Speak up, damn your souls, or it's the brig and crusts and water for the lot of you!"

They shifted uncomfortably, but no man would point an accusing finger at Flint.

"Mullens?" Ben demanded.

"He refused an order, sir," Mullens volunteered reluctantly, "but I struck the first blow."

"You, Walters, summon the captain t' the foredeck," Ben snapped. " 'Tis for him to deal with this pair."

"Aye, aye, Mister Wright, sir," Walters agreed, hurrying to do the first officer's bidding.

"Flint, Mullens, you follow me. The rest of you, back to your hammocks. Any more trouble and we'll see if a few days' extra duty will take the vinegar out of you!" Ben growled, clambering up the rope ladder.

The captain was pacing the foredeck when Wright and the two men reached it. Christianne, who had been enjoying the air, hovered by the rail. The tension in the air was palpable and communicated itself to her. She saw

173

Flint, blood still streaming from his nose, and hurried forward to help him.

James' arm was suddenly there, blocking her path to him.

"Stay out of this, madam, it does not concern you," he said sharply. "Go back to your cabin and wait there."

Christianne backed away but remained on deck, defiance in her eyes. James nodded to Ox nearby, and the huge, shaggy-haired man obediently took her elbow and led her away.

"Trouble, it appears, Mister Wright?" James inquired.

"Aye, Captain. The pair of them were fighting in the quarters," Ben supplied grimly.

"I see," James said with a curt nod. Hands clasped behind his back, he strode to stand before Silas Mullens, who still appeared somewhat green about the gills. "Well, Bosun, let's hear what you have to say about this!"

Mullens muttered something under his breath, refusing to meet his captain's eyes.

"Louder, man!" James barked, those green eyes flashing angrily.

"I said it weren't nothing, sir. A bit o' tomfoolery is all. I took exception t' something Flint said, an' I took a swing at him. I'm sorry, sir."

James nodded. He didn't believe for one minute what Mullens had said. The little bosun was a good man, a fine sailor, and not one inclined to tomfoolery. If he had swung at the Irishman first, it was not without good cause, he'd wager. "And your side, Flint?" he asked, turning to Flint.

"It was all as Mister Mullens said, sir," he said in his silky brogue. "A bit o' tomfoolery between us lads that got a wee bit out o' hand, 'tis all. It won't happen again, sir."

"Captain, if I might have a word?" Ben murmured, frowning.

Flint's eyes narrowed as James nodded and bent his ear to his first officer. That damned Wright! he cursed silently, always poking his blasted nose in where it wasn't wanted.

James listened as Ben described the scene he had come upon and repeated Mullens' comment that the man had refused an order and been insolent. James noticed Flint's cocky smile had wavered a fraction as Ben spoke up. At length he turned to the men once more.

"Refusing an order is a serious offense, Flint," James said sternly.

" 'Tis a lie, sir!" Flint insisted.

"Careful, Flint," his captain cautioned. "If you would call Mister Wright a liar, you had best have witnesses who will come forward to support you."

"Aye, sir, I have," Flint insisted. "I have all the witnesses I need in Bosun Mullens here. He told you we were just larking about. There was nothing about refusing an order, sir!"

Mullens' head jerked up at this, but he said nothing. Inwardly, Jonathan laughed. The bosun was afraid of him, as he'd thought.

Silas Mullens blinked his one eye furiously. Keeping his silence was one thing, but what Flint expected of him was an outright lie, and he had little liking for the Irishman!

"Now look ye here, Flint," he began, "I will not—" He stopped himself.

"Go on, Mullens," James pressed.

"Nothing, sir," Mullens mumbled.

"Then you are saying that Mister Flint is telling the truth? That you gave no order to Flint and that he could not have refused an order because none was given? You agree with Flint that Mister Wright is a liar?"

Mullens looked at the first officer uncertainly. Ben, who was a friend, met his eyes unwaveringly. The captain sounded more riled than he'd ever heard him before, the bosun thought miserably, and there was a chance he might vent his spleen on the first officer if he supported Flint's lies.

And after all, who was Flint, anyway? He owed him no debt of silence!

"I'm waiting, Mullens," James threatened softly.

"You did *what?*" Christianne whispered incredulously an hour later in the great-cabin.

James stepped past her to the carved cabinet and poured himself a stiff measure of rum. He downed it in a single quaff before turning back toward her to answer her question.

"I said that Flint has been given five lashes," he repeated levelly. The flogging, only his second in all his years as a sea captain, had disturbed him. Although necessary in this case, he had not ordered it carried out with any relish, despite his dislike of Flint.

"But—but why?" she demanded, stepping to stand in front of the captain.

"For refusing an order, and on suspicion of attempting to incite a mutiny amongst the crew." That had come out when he had pressed Mullens further for the truth of the incident.

Christianne laughed harshly. "Suspicion?" she echoed. "You ordered a man whipped because you *suspected* him guilty of something? I cannot believe that even you could be so cruel! Where is he now? I must go to him and see to his wounds," she cried, attempting to brush past him. James' fingers closed about her wrist.

"You'll do nothing of the sort," he barked. "We have a ship's surgeon to see to his stripes. And as for my 'cruelty'—"

"Aye, cruelty!" she repeated hotly, her deep blue eyes stormy.

"—It was necessary. He refused an order. He insulted one of my officers, as well as making certain statements that smacked of mutiny, as I told you. I have in excess of a hundred men aboard! To have let Flint off with only a tongue-lashing would have been taken as a sign of my weakness as a captain, and I have no intention of ever letting that happen." His jaw hardened. "I did what had to be done, and that's an end to it. I don't expect a woman to understand my reasons, being of a softer nature, so do not argue the point with me, Christianne."

Christianne shook her head. "You are right, sir, I do not understand it, but that is not an end of it! I will go to Jonathan whether you gainsay me or nay. Let me pass!" She sprang for the door.

James gripped her again by the wrist. This time he pulled her back inside so forcefully she lost her balance and sprawled to the boards.

"How dare you!" she stormed, picking herself up. "What gives you the right to—!"

"My captaincy of this vessel gives me every right, vixen, to do anything I wish with you or any other person aboard her. If you cannot accept my discipline, then you will suffer the consequences," he said coldly.

"I will not!" she fumed. "Your men may be bound to answer to you, but I am not!"

"Oh, but you are, my dear!" he gritted. His eyes were glittering green slits, his mouth but a thin, lipless line with his anger. Fists on hips, he towered over her.

"You cannot make me, sir," she challenged him recklessly. She tossed streamers of creamy hair over her shoulders and glowered at him, her small bosom heaving against the green silk of her gown in her fury.

James laughed. "Indeed I could, madam, was I of the mind to bring you to heel! You overestimate your strength against a man." Aye, he thought, he could break her, could break that indomitable pride and fiery spirit of hers and bring her to her knees, but he was loath to do so, for these were qualities he admired in a woman but rarely found. However, she must learn to accept his discipline, bow to his authority for the duration of the voyage. The situation was delicate now, for he had no way of knowing just how far Flint's talk of mutiny had been spread. If his men saw Christianne, whom they considered their captain's lady, ministering to Flint, it might convince them that Flint was a worthy leader.

She noticed his hesitation and mistook it for a sign that her words had struck home. He could not force her to obey him, and he knew it! "How?" she taunted, throwing caution and discretion to the wind, "How could you bring me to heel? Would you flog my back bloody, too? Pray, do not let my sex deter you, Captain, I am a match for any man! Aye, tie me helpless to the mast and flay me as you did poor Jonathan!"

Anger roiled through him. She was pressing him to the limit, by God, she was! "Continue this tantrum and I may yet do so," he warned. "Your 'poor Jonathan' is a dangerous man who stirs up trouble wherever he goes, sowing the seeds of dissension then standing back to watch them flourish like tares. Without discipline, this vessel and all upon her are destined for disaster! Flint had to be made an example of. That is an end to the matter."

"Perhaps for you, Captain, but not for me," Christianne cried. "You are beneath my contempt! You call yourself an honorable man? Ha!" she mocked. "Where is your honor now, Capt. James Mallory, seducer of virgins! Where was your honor when you ordered another human being, another man, flogged at your whim? You speak so loftily against slaving, but you are little better than the masters of the blackbirders you so deplore!"

The blood drained about James' mouth. A muscle twitched in his cheek. He had never struck any woman, but by all that was holy, he wanted to now! "When you play

178

with fire, vixen, do not be surprised when you are burned," he said softly, mastering his temper only by supreme self-control. "When you spread yourself across a bed and entice a man to your chamber, it should not come as any great surprise when he avails himself of what you so brazenly offered him."

Angry tears sparkled in her eyes. "Aye," she said heavily, "you are right about that first time. I was a fool! But what about the second, and the third, and those that came after? I made you no such offer then, sir! You took what you desired without thought for my wishes to the contrary. Do you recall what I said that time in Barcelona? I vowed that I would kill you before you had me again!"

He nodded warily.

"Well, Captain," she said deliberately, "I fell for your kisses and your endearments, until I learned that you had lied to me about my aunt. The oath I swore still stands! 'Tis time now for you to settle your debts!" Something flashed in her fist and he saw it was a dagger, *his* dagger, the hilt afire with rubies and pearls in the meager light that slanted through the cabin windows. He had missed it when they returned to the ship after going ashore in Spain.

"So, you had it. I should have known," he said quietly.

"Aye," she agreed. "You should have! I slipped it from your belt as we watched the dancing in the plaza at Barcelona. You never even noticed!" She stepped closer to him and slapped the wickedly sharp blade across her palm. "Now, sir, do you still have a mind to bed this wench? For if you do, I guarantee you'll never bed another!" She smiled sweetly, but dark fires glittered in her eyes.

James frowned as if seriously impressed by her brave threat.

"Put down the knife, Christie," he said very softly. "It is a

179

pretty toy, but such toys can be dangerous in the hands of a child."

Pretty toy, indeed! she thought indignantly. He would see! Her smile widened, deepening the dimple in her cheek, and for a split-second her concentration wavered. In that second James dived at her. Her fist came up; the dagger flashed downward in a silvery arc, then clattered to the boards as his fingers clamped about her wrist in a steel-like grip that threatened to snap the delicate bone.

She yelped in pain. His face, she saw, fear sweeping through her, was dark, dark with fury, his eyes a fierce, glittering emerald-green. The impetus of his attack bore her backwards across the bed, he falling heavily atop her. She clawed and writhed at him, but he held her wrists easily in one fist above her head. His lips parted over hers, lips that were hard, almost bruising with the pent-up ardor of his desire for her. He broke the kiss briefly, breathing heavily, and reached over the edge of the bed and retrieved the dagger, his body's weight holding her immobile. He hooked the dagger's tip in the neck of her gown and slit the cloth from its lacy fichu to the waist. Her shift followed the gown. Desire—or was it but lust?—surged ever fiercer through him as she lay bared beneath him, her pale flesh pearly in the gloom.

"Now you will see," he threatened huskily, "that it does not pay to draw a dagger on me, wench. You will learn anew who is master of this vessel, and all upon her—be they man or maid!" He knew he used his anger, in part, to rationalize his taking of her by force when he had sworn never to do so again, but knowing that did not deter him. His craving for her was ungovernable, fiercer than any desire he had felt for any woman before her, even Amanda, whom he had thought he loved. Damn her soul! Was she Circe, that she could so bewitch him? Delilah, that her loveliness could shear him of reason and caution as surely as

Samson was shorn of his locks? He laughed thickly and pressed his lips to her throat. Aye, she was both of those wicked temptresses—and more, far, far more!

Her hands fluttered to shield her nudity from his eyes, eyes that burned with a fiery green, like the fires of St. Elmo that flickered about the masts and spars in a storm. That red-haired Lucifer, she thought furiously, he would not take her now! She struck him across the face as his large hand slid possessively down the length of her body, following its curves with searing warmth. He grinned as she struck him, as if the blow had been a caress. Her legs, clad now in only her white silk hose and fastened with frothy white lace garters, flailed furiously at his middle. She scratched and squirmed and arched from side to side in a vain effort to escape his weight and his vice-like grip. Her eyes, he saw, were murderous, killing him inch by inch in a thousand torturous ways. Her nails were talons that scored his cheeks and drew blood. He brushed aside the remnants of her gossamer-thin lawn shift as if it were but a cobweb and turned her effortlessly onto her belly.

She roared with rage against the feather bolster, pummelling her fists into the goose down pallet with impotent fury as she felt his weight bear her full force face-down into its softness. God in heaven, what was he about? What cruelty, what perversity did he intend to inflict on her now? She tried one last time to dislodge him as he unbuckled his belt, but it was useless.

He lay upon her and parted her trembling thighs with his powerful knees, entering her in almost the same fluid movement. She gasped at the unexpected direction of his entry, then again as she felt the warmth of his lips against the back of her neck as he rained kisses on the sensitive nape and across her creamy shoulders. His fingertips traced the delicate knobs of her spine. Her frightened gasps changed to desperate moans as he began to move, filling the heated sheath of her womanhood with his hardness. Her flailings gradually ebbed to convulsive clutchings at the coverlet beneath her. He reached beneath her and cupped her breasts in his large hands, teasing the aching crests while he nuzzled her ears and kissed her burning cheeks and whispered endearments.

She tried without success to quench the insidious flaming tongues of desire that ignited and spread like wildfire out of control through her veins. The fire blazed through her, fanned, in some peculiar way, by the anger of scant minutes before. Her surrender was unconditional and complete — she knew it, and so did he, that rogue!

But then suddenly he fell back to her side, grinning at the blatant expression of disappointment and unrequited passion she flashed up at him. Her rosy lips were pouting, her flushed cheeks darkening with outrage, her deep blue eyes as stormy as a wind-whipped ocean as she rolled onto her back and glowered up at him. Still without speaking, he lifted her astride him, murmuring heated endearments as he arched upwards to possess her anew.

The sun streaming through the cabin windows bathed her uplifted face with golden light as she closed her tawny-lashed eyes and leaned back, glorying in this new pleasure. James' breath caught involuntarily in his throat at her loveliness, at the sleek line of proudly-tumescent breasts, taut abdomen, and flat velvety belly before him. In the lovely, fluid curve of her throat was revealed the wild, erratic throbbing of her pulse. Her hair tumbled down her back in a profusion of spun-sugar curls. Her lips were slightly parted and moist, little cries breaking between them as her passion soared. All this he saw with the heightened sensitivity of passion, as he arched to possess her, conquer her, know her — love her.

"You are beautiful!" he cried. "Do not fight me, Christie, love me, love me!"

When ecstasy came, it was a shower of rainbow-colored stars that filled her vision and dazzled her. It seemed, for those few, wondrous seconds, that she could soar like a bird to the azure heavens. She felt lighter than air as the throbbing pleasure engulfed her. Yes, surely she could fly, she mused dreamily as she fell exhausted across his chest.

James smiled as he rolled her beneath him. Her expression as he attained his own sweet release was heavy lipped and heavy eyed, the face of a woman who has soared to the heights on the wings of desire and found what she quested for.

Sunlight winked off the cabin's brass trims and glistened on their bodies. James looked down at Christianne, nestled in the crook of his arm. *Will you ever come to me willingly,* he asked her silently, brushing his lips against her brow, *or must I always find excuses to make you mine?* An aching clutched at his heart, and he realized that despite all he had ever said against her, his feelings for the little scrap of womanhood beside him far surpassed anything he had ever felt before for any woman. Maddening she might be, and a hoyden to boot, but the thought of their parting wounded him to the quick. She had burst into his life like a Roman candle erupting, disrupting his senses, exploding his orderly routine and fragmenting every facet of his life, yet the thought of returning to that orderliness, that routine, in which she would not be a part, did not bear thinking about. Why, he wondered, why her? Why not one of the many lovely, willing women he had encountered before? Why not a woman who returned his feelings, who was mature and worldly-wise, instead of this child-woman who hated him? He sighed heavily. If he knew that, he thought with a wry smile, he could revolutionize the world!

A soft rapping came at the cabin door. Cursing softly he swung out of bed and pulled on his breeches and boots. It was Mark, the cabin boy, with an urgent request that he meet with Mister Wright below in the ship's stores. Grunting agreement, he turned back inside the cabin and quickly dressed.

He found Ben crouched down between barrels and kegs and crates ranged tidily along the walls. James strode to his side and looked down. A woman sprawled face down on the deck, quite motionless. Her hair was matted and dirty, her clothes stained and wrinkled horribly.

"I found her like this, Captain, a while ago. It's her what's been after our rations!" Ben said indignantly.

James nodded. "Aye, I should have guessed we had a stowaway, but the trouble with Flint put this little matter clean out of my head." He crouched down, turning the woman gently onto her back. Surprise, then concern flitted across his features in rapid succession. "By the gods!" he exclaimed, " 'tis little Lucy!"

"Lucy, sir?" Ben queried.

"Aye, Lucy Waller from the Golden Goose tavern in London. Lord, the wench is weak, Ben! Stand back while I lift her."

He scooped Lucy into his arms and carried her down the passageway. Ben hurried after him, his face furious. The lass had been so thin, so dirty, he had not even recognized her.

They made her comfortable in Ben's own bunk. The first officer surveyed her dolefully. "Poor little wench!" he said, clicking his teeth, "what a time of it she must have had. She was a comely lass before, but to look at her now, no one would believe it."

James nodded. He carefully pulled up Lucy's upper lip and inspected her gums. If they were angry and swollen, it was a sure sign that the first stages of scurvy—the scourge of a seafaring life—had set in. Next the gums would turn black with rot and rank with a foul pus, and the unfortunate victim be doomed to a slow and agonizing death.

There was no sign of any swelling in Lucy's mouth, thank God!

"Have someone fetch up some oranges from the hold," James suggested to Ben. "I believe we have found her in the nick of time, but if not, they'll help her. I believe she suffers only from her deprivation as a stowaway. Plentiful victuals, water and a place to sleep should bring her around in no time. Have Matthew Locke examine her, just to be sure." James grinned. "He's had little enough to occupy his time this voyage, save for doubling as our sailmaker. This should serve to sharpen his skills as our ship's surgeon! Ah, and Ben, good fellow," he paused, "see that the lass is bathed, too, will you? I swear I itch all over just to look at her in such a state."

"Bathed? By who, sir?" Ben caught the devilish glint in James' green eyes and shook his head. "Oh, no, sir, not me! I'll not bathe a lass, be blowed if I will, sir!" He appeared ready to bolt.

James frowned. "But who else is there to do it? I'd trust no one save you with the lass, Ben, with your fatherly ways. Mayhap you can pretend sweet Lucy is your own dear daughter?"

"Nay!" Ben retorted with a shudder. "Why not you, sir, seeing as how you're accustomed to—to young ladies, sir, and I am not?" He reddened furiously.

"That is precisely why I cannot do it," James argued. "You know full well, Ben, my weakness when it comes to the fair sex!" He shook his head gravely. "Nay, I cannot trust myself with the lass—and it would not endear me to Christie any further if she learned I had bathed Lucy here, and Lord knows, she is little enough fond of me now! I'll see if she has a spare chemise for the girl. Go to it, Ben, lad, on the double!" He winked roguishly and hurriedly exited the cabin before Ben, still sputtering, could think of words to stay him.

The first officer stepped reluctantly over to his bunk, angrily resigned to his fate. He looked down at the sorry creature lying so still on his pallet for some time, before reaching out to the laces of her bodice with shaking fingers. It seemed indecent, it did, he thought, his face red with embarrassment.

"Oh, sir!" Lucy mumbled weakly, her blue eyes fluttering open. "Whatever are you about?"

Ben dropped the bodice strings as if they were red hot and jumped back guiltily.

"I—I was about to fetch the ship's surgeon to ye, Mistress Lucy," he stammered. "I'll be back shortly," he muttered as he fled to the door.

"Oh, no! Wait up, kind sir!" Lucy cried after him, weakly raising herself onto her elbows. "Don't ye go! I got t' talk t' Jamie. It's ever so important, it is, an' I'll only tell it ter him, got it?" she cautioned.

Ben nodded and sent Mark, the cabin boy, running for the captain. James came immediately.

"Well, Lucy, my pigeon," he said fondly, towering over her, "how are you faring?"

"Pay no mind t' me health, love," Lucy admonished, "there's more serious stuff afoot than the state o' me bloomin' health!"

"And what could be more important than that?" he asked, grinning.

"Mutiny!" Lucy said darkly, her normally merry face very grave.

James and Ben exchanged glances. "Explain yourself," the captain pressed.

"Aye, I will!" Lucy said. "I know who, and I know when. I heard it all down below, I did!"

Later James and Ben stepped from the cabin into the gloomy passageway.

"Well, sir, 'tis no longer but a suspicion," Ben said

186

heavily. "You have a witness now who will speak up against Flint."

James nodded grimly. "Aye, I do indeed."

"Shall I have him thrown in the brig?" the first officer asked.

"He's in no condition to try anything at the moment, Ben," James said thoughtfully. "First thing in the morning will be soon enough."

He strode off to the stairs and left Ben alone, little knowing that his decision to wait until the morning to have Flint thrown in the brig had already set in motion a chain of events that would prove disastrous to more than one man aboard.

Ben shook his head as he watched him go and crossed himself. "Friday the thirteenth!" he muttered worriedly. "I knew no good would come of this day, I knew it!"

Fourteen

Christianne awoke on the morning of May fourteenth with a headache that would have done credit to a giant. Her limbs felt stiff and achy and her throat was sore, as if she were coming down with a bout of the ague or a grippe of some sort.

She lay there in the enormous bed, the coverlet pulled up about her, eyes closed against the morning sunlight that streamed through the great-cabin windows, reluctant to get up. And why should she, she thought crossly? What was there to get up for? James had forbidden Jonathan to escort her for her airings about the deck, and was hardly likely to change his mind after the events of the previous afternoon, so there was little to look forward to but yet another monotonous day. Poor Jonathan! How was he? she wondered. Did it take long for such wounds to heal? James Mallory must be mad—or insanely jealous—to take such harsh action against a man of Jonathan Flint's character! The Irishman had always been charming, gentle and considerate to her. She smiled as she remembered how he had kissed her in Ben Wright's cabin after she had woefully declared she had no friends in the world save Master Bones. How wrong she had been! A warm glow infused her. Jonathan was indeed her friend, and try as he might, that damned James could not alter that! She had never considered herself a vindictive person, i'faith, to date she had always thought herself of too soft-hearted a nature for her own good, but since James' cold-hearted seduction of her in Barcelona, learning that he had lied to her in regards to her aunt, and his continued assaults—aye, assaults, she thought firmly—on her person, she had learned what it was to want to hurt, to wound. Her new-found femininity had given her a powerful weapon to wield to that end that she had never before considered, and wield it she would against that lying, hypocritical captain, she decided.

Did she love Jonathan, she mused? That he was fond, inordinately fond, of her was obvious to any who had eyes to see. But did she love him? She pursed her lips and wrinkled her pert nose in concentration. No, she thought not, she decided at length, but she did like him very much. She liked his compliments, and, she thought, blushing despite being quite alone in the cabin, she liked the way he looked at her, a mixture of masculine desire and adoration in his black eyes that was almost as blatant as those of that one the crew called Ox. Before Barcelona, she had not realized what that burning, hungry look in men's eyes when they looked at a woman meant. Now she knew only too well! It was not love, as she had naively imagined, but lust! Love? Ha! She had no wish to be in love, nor to be loved, by any man.

Last spring, a troupe of mummers had come to the common by St. Martin's Field and performed a masque, followed by one of Master Will Shakespeare's plays, *A Midsummer Night's Dream*. In it the doltish lovers had seemed taken by a sort of madness. She scowled, her normally deep blue eyes turning even darker. She had no wish to become mad, nor to behave as foolishly as they, she decided with distaste, whatever the cause of that "madness." Besides, she had witnessed the slow decline of her mother and, finally, her death as a result of losing her beloved Christopher. If that was what love did to one, she had no desire for it, none at all. There was no room in her plans for such frivolous, painful pleasures. Quick wits, light fingers and swiftness of foot were what one needed to survive in this hard world. Not love!

She had not merely been shouting into the wind when she had sworn she would escape James yet. Indeed not. She would bide her time until they put in to some port or other and try again when he least expected it. If he thought his lustful love-making, however pleasant, had changed anything, he would be sadly mistaken! She'd been able to escape him in London. She could do so again! Men! she thought wryly. They fancied themselves the stronger, more intelligent of the sexes, but they were foolish, easily gulled creatures, even the best of them. All, that was, save her papa. There had been no man, to date, who could compare with Lord Christopher in her eyes, aye, and likely never would be!

He had died leaving no issue save herself, his bastard daughter, and upon his wife's—the proud and cold-hearted Louise Alexander—death, the estates and Westlodge Manor itself would pass on to distant relatives in Norfolk. Christianne had determined, on that one unforgettable visit she and her mother had made to beg charity from Papa's widow, that *she* would one day be mistress of Westlodge, as was her due. After all, was she not Papa's only issue, albeit born on the wrong side of the blanket and not rightfully bearing his name? *Why, oh, why, did you not acknowledge me as your child, your own flesh and blood, Papa?* she wondered for the thousandth time. Her mother had had an answer to that question, she recalled.

"Your papa was a fine man, my dear Chris," she had said, "and he loved you dearly, loved us both, in fact, as much and as fully as he loved life itself. His marriage, you see, was one of convenience, with no love on either side, as is common among the nobility. Your grandfather, Lord Charles, sought to extend the family estates to the west, so the marriage between his son, Christopher, and his neighbor's daughter, Lady Louise, was an expedient and sensible means to do so. So it was that your father married a woman he did not love, and that is why he sought love elsewhere.

"My own father was a cobbler, until his eyes grew dim and he was unable to sew his fine leather shoes and pattens. He took to the alehouses and drank himself into ruin before he died, bitter and defeated by life. My mother was yet a young woman, but worn down and old before her time from the bearing and the burying of the sickly babes she bore. There were eight children born to her, but only two of that eight survived their second year, your Aunt Nell and myself. My mother became a washerwoman to support us, but, when I was younger than your four-and-ten years, she, too, died and I determined that I would not follow in her stead and find an early grave. I vowed I would use whatever means I had at my disposal to better my station in life. I was young then, and men—men thought me comely. I entered a sporting house, little Chris, where wealthy men such as your papa go, in search of . . . love. It was there that I met him. He adored me! He bought me this fine house to live in and tutored me himself so that I would have all the accomplishments he sought in a companion. I learned quickly: how to speak well and to assemble my thoughts with intelligence and wit; how to dance and sing and play the harpsichord and flute; and how to walk, talk and dress in the manner befitting a lady. In return for his support, I gave him solace in his times of sorrow, amusement when he wanted to laugh, and most importantly, my heart! In time, his infatuation with me turned to true love, a love as deep as mine was for him.

"But your father had one fault, my dear. He believed himself immortal; he was certain that, in the vigorous prime of his life, he had many years left to him in which to acknowledge you as his daughter. He was wrong! He died without doing so, my poor child."

Christianne sighed. Mama had never really recovered from Papa's death. The sparkle had fled her pretty eyes like a doused candle, and never been rekindled. With each passing month, she had grown more sickly. The physicians had called it a consuming fever of the lungs, but Christianne fancied that Jenny Alexander had died of a broken heart. With no funds to run the large house, and with no means available to them to work in her sickness, Jennifer had, piece by piece, sold the jewels, the gowns, the very silverware that Lord Christopher had lavished upon her during their long affair of the heart, to support herself and her daughter. And then, one foggy, dismal morning, Mama had gone to a pauper's grave in a potter's field, she recalled bitterly. *Thank God for Granny Rags!* She had found Christianne huddled in a ditch by the roadside exactly one year from her mother's funeral.

She had gone to put flowers on her mother's grave. It had been a dreary, wet November day and she faced a long, long walk. Against her better judgment, she had accepted the offer of a ride to her home from a smooth-talking young toff in a very fancy black carriage boasting a matched pair of grays. He had seemed so genuinely concerned for her welfare that she had gladly clambered up into the coach. Too late, she realized her folly! Before long, the red-headed rogue had attempted to force himself on her, a mere child of fourteen years, in no uncertain manner. She had leaped from the vehicle, preferring the risk of injury to rape, and found herself miles from the house on Darling Lane. All that night she had wandered in the fog, unable to find her way, until shortly before dawn, she had huddled in a ditch, too exhausted and now too ill, to carry on. Gran had found her there and seen her safely back to her home, had stayed and tended her through the ague that had been a consequence of her night's exposure. Christianne had been grateful, and asked the old dame to stay with her, and so their friendship began. Granny Rags had taught her the hard lesson that to survive meant being craftier than the next fellow, swifter of foot and sleighter of hand, and Christianne had proved an adept pupil in the arts of cutpursing and pickpocketing and, in times of direst necessity, the dubious skill of picking a lock. She had joined the little band of thieves as an alternative to starvation, the workhouse, or—her last recourse—the selling of her body for a farthing or two countless times a night to the filthy rabble of London Town. Without second thought, she had opted for the life of a thief! Her experience with the young, sly gentleman in the coach had taught her that she would not care for the doxy's lot. She had seen enough of whores and trollops, with their haggard, poxed faces and disease-riddled bodies, to know she wanted none of that life. I'faith, she would sooner die first! If James harbored any faint hope that he could force her to work in her aunt's bawdy house, he would be sorely mistaken.

She scrambled off the bed and threw a wrapper over her nakedness, aware that there was a loud knocking at the great-cabin door. She pressed her ear to it. "Yes?"

"Open the door, Christie, me darlin'! 'Tis I, Jonathan! Quickly, now!"

Christianne hurriedly flung open the door. She smiled eagerly up into Jonathan Flint's face, her eager expression swiftly changing to one of consternation for he looked scarce able to contain his anger.

"What is it? What's wrong?" she cried, her deep blue eyes wide, anxious pools. She stepped out into the gangway beside him. Angry shouts and bellows carried from abovedecks. Whatever was going on, she wondered?

"That bastard captain, damn his soul! He has accused me of plotting mutiny against him!"

"What!" she gasped. To suspect a man of mutiny was one thing, but to accuse him of it was far graver, for it was punishable by death or marooning, she knew well!

"Aye, 'tis true!" Jonathan confirmed. "In the captain's twisted mind, I am an agitator, my love. Even now he and his crew are searching this vessel for me. They mean to throw me into the brig!"

Christianne wrinkled her brow. "Nay, it cannot be! James is a fair man, I fancy, for all that I have no liking for him. He would not do such a thing—unless he has some proof?" she insisted, regarding him doubtfully.

"Did he need proof to have me flogged?" Jonathan hissed fiercely. "Aye, you know he did not! His jealousy over you and I has twisted his reason, my love. He means to maroon me on some godforsaken island, or have me hung from the yardarms, I know it! You must help me, mavourneen! I have friends out there—" he jerked his head towards the ocean—"friends with a fine, fleet vessel who will see us safely away from here, if you'll but help me, me darlin' girl!"

His urgently whispered words rang false to her ears. "What friends?" she queried. "And where?"

"My name is not Flint, lass, but Flynn. My brother was hung at Tyburn Flats shortly before we sailed."

"Michael Flynn!" she gasped incredulously. "But he was a pirate, was he not?"

"Nay," Jonathan denied heatedly, "he was not! No finer, more decent man ever sailed the seas than he! He was wrongfully imprisoned by the British. For two long years he rotted in Newgate 'til we heard he'd been sentenced to death. Three of my men and myself went to London, in the hopes that we could free him. We bribed the executioner with a hefty purse o' gold to feign his hanging. The lily-livered scum reneged! Now he feeds the fish at the bottom of the Thames, and my brother, the worms in some unhallowed grave!" He noticed that she shuddered. "It was planned that the four of us would sign on some ship plying these waters on leaving London, and would rendezvous with my own ship off the cape in the month of May. She is out there, somewhere, just waiting for my signal. Come with me to a new life, me darlin'! If you would be a captain's lady, be mine! Capt. Jonathan Flynn of the *Red Scorpion* offers you his heart and his hand!"

Stunned, she gaped at him. Of a sudden, her chance to flee James and this damnable ship was here! Yet, for some obscure reason, she was suddenly loath to take it. She shook her head. "No. No, I can't go with you."

Anger contorted Flynn's face. His arm snaked out. His fingers fastened about her throat. Her hands fluttered to break his grip, but could not. Darkness hovered on the edges of consciousness, threatening to close in.

"You'll help me, colleen," he hissed in her ear. "For if not, every man and jack-tar aboard this fine vessel will die—including its fancy captain!" He chuckled softly. "Aye, me darlin' girl, I've seen the way he looks at you! 'Twould give me great pleasure to slit his damned throat! If you would save this miserable crew, you will come with me, do all that I ask of you—or watch while I kill them one by one before your pretty eyes!" He released her abruptly.

Dizziness washed over her as the blood surged back into her brain. Despair flooded her. What option did she have?

"If I help you, you'll leave this ship and all aboard unharmed?" she asked weakly. Her eyes were dark pools of shock and disillusionment as she rubbed her bruised throat. "There must be no bloodshed—promise me, Jonathan?"

He nodded. "I swear it!" he said in a gentler tone.

She heaved a shuddering sigh. "Very well, then. Tell me what I must do." Despite the African heat that enveloped the ship, her hands and feet were suddenly icy.

"Tonight, when it is dark, take the lantern up on deck

and swing it over the bows three times to left and right. 'Tis the signal, and my ship will come for us. Meanwhile, my lads will free me from the brig. We'll take a longboat and flee to the *Scorpion!* I'm sorry I scared you, lass, but I couldn't bear t' think of leaving without ye," he purred silkily.

"I—I'll do it, never fear," she stammered.

He nodded and lifted her hand and kissed it. "Until tonight, mavourneen!" he whispered. "I must be gone now, before they find me here and suspect!"

She nodded numbly as Jonathan Flint—no, Flynn, sped swiftly away. She heard a shout above, then the sounds of a fierce scuffle and much cursing. They'd caught him, she realized dully. She shivered and leaned up against the wall of the gangway, fingering the painful bruises on her throat. How was she to do Flynn's bidding? There was no way she could simply take a lantern and give the signal, not without being stopped and questioned. But if she didn't—! An image filled her mind: of James, his laughing, devil-green eyes dimmed in death, his handsome face frozen in its death mask. Of Ben Wright, gentle Ben, with his throat cut . . . she *must* do it, she had to! What was her life worth, when weighed against the lives of so many? Men who had been friends, in their clumsy fashion. Tears filled her eyes. Aye, they had all tried to be her friends, she realized too late. And James—! Why did her heart ache so at the thought of never seeing him again? He would think she had betrayed them all when he learned she had gone with Flynn. A sudden thought struck her. His was the evening watch! It was he who would be up on deck when she went to give the signal! He would never let them flee without putting up a fight, and Flynn had no liking for the captain. Her mind raced, desperately seeking a plan of some kind. A sleeping draught! Aye, that was it! She would plead a head-ache and beg a powder from Matthew Locke, the ship's

196

surgeon. Somehow—and she believed it would take little persuasion—she would persuade James to come to her cabin that night and drug his wine, then she could slip away to do her Judas' work.

"Mistress Christie? Are you ailing?"

She opened her eyes to see Ben Wright standing there.

His gray eyes noted her ashen pallor and ragged breathing with concern. They had caught Flint abovedecks, very close to the stairs that led up from the great-cabin. His eyes narrowed. Had he bothered the little lass in some way? But Christianne was smiling now.

"I am quite well," she lied. "For a moment the heat overwhelmed me, and I believe I have a plaguesome headache starting. Would you ask Master Locke for a powder for me? I think I will lie down and rest for a while more."

He nodded, his fears partially abated. "Aye, lass, 'twould be best," he agreed. "Rest ye for a while. I'll see t' the powder."

She smiled warmly. "Thank you, dear Ben," she murmured tremulously, "I am grateful for your concern and your friendship."

She turned and slipped inside the cabin, but not before he had glimpsed the tears that had shimmered in her eyes. He pursed his lips. It probably meant nothing, nothing at all. Girls were ever wont to be teary-eyed for little reason, as well he knew, having four sisters. But just in case, he determined to tell James of her upset.

Fifteen

"Good day, Christianne," James said almost curtly as he strode to where she stood, leaning against the rail. "I regret I bring news that you will certainly deem unpleasant, yet I would ask your understanding of my predicament." His tone and his manner were clipped.

"But of course, Captain. What is it that you have to tell me?" she asked, intentionally not permitting her tone to be too compliant. He knew full well that she was still furious at him for taking her the previous afternoon, and would become suspicious if she made a sudden about-face.

"Your friend, Master Flint, has been confined to the brig. I have a witness that will testify to hearing him conspire to mutiny with several of my men." He carefully watched her face. "It seems my suspicions were well-founded after all."

Christianne feigned shock. "What! But he seemed so charming, and so loyal to you, Captain! Jonathan—a mutineer!" She shuddered delicately, her wispy, pale blond tresses stirring about her face. She clasped her hands demurely in front of her. "But of course, if you have a witness, I suppose it must be so."

His eyebrows rose. "You do not protest his innocence? Pray, to what good fortune do I owe this happy state of agreement?" The wench, to date, had missed no opportunity to cross him, irk him, or otherwise anger him. This was a turnabout!

Christianne muffled a curse. She had overplayed her hand somewhat, she realized. She must tread very, very carefully, for James was nobody's fool. She smiled wryly. "A restless, long and very thoughtful night, Captain," she said in answer to his question, "spent in weighing all that has happened to me since I left London. I realize now, to my regret, that I have wrongfully blamed you for everything, for taking me away from my beloved England, in particular, when you are but trying to do as my mother wished, upon her deathbed, that I should do. I—I have decided that I, too, must honor her last wishes, sir. I would like to suggest a truce between us for the duration of our voyage, a voyage that will be long and arduous enough without adding our mutual animosity to those hardships. If we cannot be friends, can we not at least be *cordial* enemies?" There was a heavy lacing of sarcasm to her words, as she had intended, and James seemed more convinced of her sincerity because of it.

"Indeed we may!" he said with apparent enthusiasm. "And may I say, Christianne, that I could not ask for a fairer . . . enemy?"

She laughed, a merry, silvery laugh, though inside she felt like crying. "Now, now, Captain, I said friends, not lovers! But thank you for the compliment anyway, sir!" she said, a becoming blush staining her cheeks. "Well, now that that little matter is settled, I will keep you from the running of your ship no longer. My . . . thanks for breaking the news about Jonathan to me in person, sir."

A faint smile caught the corners of James' mouth. How dainty and fragile she appeared, with her hair like a spun-sugar cloud about her face and shoulders, and her lips, naturally a deep rose hue, set in a serious but provocatively pensive bow. She was the kind of woman who put a man in mind of woodland dells and moonbeams shivering through the trees, while Pan-pipes played seductive, silvery notes and she flitted amongst the woods clad only in a diaphanous wisp of silk, like a wood nymph. If, that was, a man knew her no better than to accept what appearances suggested. His smile deepened.

"You are more than welcome, sweet," he murmured. "I only wish my news could be of a more pleasant nature."

After a few moments more of semi-flirtatious conversation, she left to go belowdecks. Ben Wright joined his captain on the upper deck.

"Well, sir?" the first officer asked.

James grinned. "I told her our Master Flint was in the brig, and she not so much as batted her lovely eyes!" His smile seemed one of satisfaction.

"Ah, 'tis well, then, Cap'n," Ben said, his relief obvious. "Your suspicions that the little miss and Flint had conspired were unfounded! Ah, did I not tell you they would be!"

"Nay, Ben, they were not unfounded," James disagreed. "Our Mistress Alexander is a vixen, indeed, the perfect mate for our foxy Flint. She is a part of this somehow, or I am not captain of the *Fair Amanda!*"

Ben's expression showed utter confusion. "But if that's so, sir, why is it ye see fit to find such merriment in it?"

James smiled grimly. "I laugh because for all her fragile air, I admire the icy courage that flows in her veins, the steel in her nerves! She played me well, Ben, and if I had not known her vixenish ways, would have taken her bait and swallowed it whole. Ben, lad, what a performance she gave! I would have paid gold to see it! 'Tis my belief the minx intends to try to free Flint from the brig."

Ben paled. "No, sir, I will not believe it of her!"

James grinned, but there was a cruel glint in his eyes that

200

Ben had never seen before, and hoped never to see again.

"We shall see, Ben," he said softly. "I shall give the lady the benefit of the doubt. We have a rendezvous tonight, in my cabin. Take my watch, will you, friend? I do not intend to miss it!"

Christianne gnawed her lower lip nervously as she awaited James that evening in the great-cabin. Everything had proceeded without incident, almost too smoothly to be true. She had, with a feigned, wistful air, remarked casually on the loneliness of her condition now that Jonathan was not able to escort her for her airings, and since Ben Wright seemed too busy to play cards with her of late. She had bravely expressed the hope that Lucy Waller would prove a companion and friend when recovered suffi- ciently from her exhaustion, but said that meanwhile she would make do with what little companionship Bones could offer her. As she had anticipated, James had taken the bait and quickly suggested that they sup together that night and exchange "conversation and companionship," as part of the new conditions of their truce. Ha! She had little doubt as to what form he would expect that companionship to take, but she had determined to go ahead, despite it. What, she thought bitterly, could he possibly do to her that he had not done already, or take that he had not taken already? She could withstand his lustful love-making if it meant that by doing so, Jonathan would be able to quit the ship without incident or bloodshed and without harm coming to any man aboard.

She concealed the vellum envelope containing the sleeping draught in the dark recesses of the carved cabinet where James kept his wine. From there it could be removed and stealthily slipped into his cup. All that remained now was to prepare herself.

She bathed, then dressed with extra care in the ruby-red velvet gown that she knew the captain favored above all others, for the admiration in his devil-green eyes each time she had worn it had been obvious. So had the blatant admiration in the sailor Ox's eyes when he had carried out the bathtub earlier, she recalled. If only she had a larger mirror in which to review the results of her toilette! she thought as she lifted the necklace of cornelian beads that the gypsy had given her in Spain over her head. She sighed. The silver-handled looking glass James had purchased with the rest of her wardrobe in London would have to suffice.

She brushed her freshly-washed hair vigorously until it shone with shimmering gold and silver highlights in the amber lanternlight that winked off the brass trims and fittings of the cabin. The wispy mane surrounded her delicately boned face like a gleaming halo, shot with filigrée threads of precious metals. Spitting in the soot from the chimney of the lantern, she dabbed her grimy fingers against her tawny lashes to darken them. Nibbling at her lips in her nervousness had already caused them to take on a pretty, deep coral hue. She need only pinch her cheeks to impart the seductive rosiness of vibrant good health to them, and she would be ready!

She finished not a second too soon, for a hearty hammering on the cabin door signalled the captain's arrival. Taking a deep breath, she counted to ten and walked slowly across to it.

"Why, Captain!" she exclaimed in mock surprise, "I had not expected you so soon."

James grinned charmingly, slipped inside and closed the door behind him. He was dashing and very handsome in a white silk shirt with full, lace-trimmed sleeves, a leaf-colored vest of satin and breeches to match, with golden

202

buckles on the cuffs of his boots. Because of the heat, he wore neither coat nor hat.

"You may interpret my earliness as a compliment, Christianne," he said, his eyes roving over her in obvious pleasure at what they saw, "for I was most eager to sup with you tonight, and impatient for the afternoon to end." He picked up her hand and kissed it gallantly.

Christianne smiled. He was as easy to gull as a simpleton! "As was I, Sir Captain!" she confessed huskily, permitting him to retain his hold on her hand. Their glances met. Christianne was hard put not to burst into merry peals of laughter at the besotted expression on James' face as she gazed steadfastly into it.

They both looked up, startled as a second knock sounded on the cabin door.

"Ah, our supper," James declared, throwing the door open.

Mark Duggan, the cabin boy, entered, bearing a tin tray on which platters and a heavy candlestick were set. He quickly arranged them atop James' desk and exited as speedily as he had entered.

"There," James said with a smile, seating Christianne, "a finer meal could not be ours, I'd warrant, if we supped in London Town."

"Indeed not, Captain," she agreed sincerely, eying the succulent leg o' lamb, stuffed capon overflowing with grapes and sauce, and the fresh-baked bread. "But pray, what is this?" she queried, holding up a round, brightly colored fruit and inhaling its warm, tangy fragrance.

"That is called an orange, my dove, a rarity in England unless one is affluent enough to pay a sixpenny piece for it. Don Miguel de Villarin has orchards of this fruit, as well as vineyards and almond groves." He withdrew the jewelled dagger from his belt and sliced the orange into segments, handing them to Christianne "Here, try it," he urged. "When I found that Lucy Waller had stowed away aboard *Amanda*, I had a barrel of these oranges brought up from the hold for her. For some reason, these fruits and others like them seem most beneficial to the sick. I hoped that you might enjoy them too. Their flavor is very pleasing and refreshing."

He grinned as Christianne's eyes rolled heavenward in pleasure at her first taste of the luscious, tangy fruit. Her lovely, pink mouth devoured it greedily, and he found her very blatant enjoyment strangely arousing. He coughed and forced himself to look away, damning the heat that coursed through his veins.

"Here," he said gravely, handing the jewelled dagger to her by the blade, "since we have determined to fight no more, I am giving this to you, for your protection, you understand. With this business with Flint as yet unresolved and without knowing just how widespread his mutinous mutterings have been seeded amongst my crew, I would rest easier knowing you had a means to defend yourself, should the need arise. That is," he amended, grinning, "if you are sure you no longer harbor any murderous intent in your heart for me?"

"None whatsoever, Captain," she lied with a disclaiming little laugh. "Now, shall we sup?" She set the dagger down on the table with a great show of indifference, and James smiled as he averted his face. How far would she go, the minx, he wondered?

"We will indeed. But first, some wine to sharpen the palate." He went to the carved cabinet and poured them both a measure of porter in silver goblets. Christianne's heart was in her mouth momentarily, for she feared he would discover the vellum envelope, but he turned to her with a smile, bearing the goblets.

As they dined, James watched Christianne over the rim of his goblet. She seemed perfectly at ease, doing justice to her appetite or alternately conversing with light, flirtatious repartee and what appeared to be genuine enjoyment of his company.

He pushed back his chair and came to stand behind her own. His large hands molded her slimly-rounded shoulders above the smooth velvet of her gown.

"Never have you appeared more lovely than you do in the lanternlight, my sweet," he murmured, leaning down and losing his lips against her hair.

Christianne stiffened, then forced herself to relax.

"My thanks, James," she responded in a husky voice, "I have greatly enjoyed both our supper and your companionship." She turned her head and looked up at him seductively from beneath her darkened lashes. "Perhaps," she ventured, "perhaps we might make this the first of many such pleasant evenings, think you not?"

"Without reservation, my sweet," James replied easily, raising her to standing. He cupped her face in his hands and covered her mouth with his own. Her lips parted in sweet surrender beneath his and he explored the silken recesses of her mouth with a gentle ardor that stunned her. His hands caressed the soft mass of her hair, burrowing beneath the silky tresses to stroke the vulnerable nape of her neck. A delicious tingle spread throughout her as he did so. Involuntarily, a small satisfied murmur broke from her lips as he ended the kiss, a murmur that was like the sleepy purr of a kitten. He kissed her again, this time drawing her firmly against the lean, hard length of his body in the circle of his arms. His lips drifted languorously down her throat to cover the throbbing pulse in the sensitive hollow there. Of their own accord, it seemed, her arms reached up to clasp him about the neck, then roved upwards, her fingers tousling his reddish-brown hair. It felt crisp and vibrant to her touch, she observed dreamily, as vital and alive as the rest of his muscled body hard against her. He nuzzled at her ears, his breath creating racing shivers that eddied up and down the length of her spine. The unsettling but highly pleasurable sensation darted through her, ending, in some mysterious fashion, as a warm glow in the very pit of her belly.

He reached behind her and deftly unfastened her gown, his eyes a sensual, murky green as they held hers willing captives. The ruby-red velvet slipped to her ankles. As if in a trance, she stepped from its folds and stood there mutely in her shift. Only the rapid rise and fall of her bosom betrayed the extent of her passion for him. The lantern glow cast a golden sheen on her bared arms and shoulders, her lips were now a deep, provocative red from his ardent kisses, her hair a shimmering tousled mane from his caresses. She eyed him doubtfully, as if astonished at the sudden, bittersweet rush of desire that quickened her pulse and made her step silently toward him. He finished his undressing of her with the same unhurried gentleness, interspersing each action with still more kisses and inflaming caresses until she stood unclad before him. The necklace of crimson cornelian beads glowed against her creamy flesh like droplets of blood strung together on a chain.

James stepped towards her, inwardly marvelling at her petite loveliness, at the perfection of her milk-white breasts, rose tipped, and her slender waist, the dimpled perfection of her buttocks. He lifted her and carried her to the massive bed.

As he lay beside her, his hand slid caressingly up the length of her body to capture a soft breast and a low growl escaped him as the petal-soft tip swelled and tautened beneath his impassioned caress. He tasted her lips again,

206

lips that were as heady as the wine they had shared and doubly potent. He swept aside the last vestiges of her resistance with the probing urgency of his mouth. Her passion soared as his lips moved downwards to tantalize her breasts, first softly and persuasively, then hungrily, then softly again. The delicious torture continued as he traversed the flat plane of her belly and grazed across the mound of her womanhood. Another moan broke unbidden from her parted lips as he kissed the satiny inner columns of her thighs, then finally pressed his lips against the very fount of her womanhood. She gasped and knotted her fingers in his hair, tossing her head from side to side as he brought her ever closer to the brink of release. When it seemed she could stand no more of his maddening caresses, would go mad with delight if he did not take her, he suddenly loomed above her and slipped between her trembling thighs. He moved deeply within her, his mouth buried in the angle of her neck and shoulders. She arched upwards convulsively, crying his name again and again. He plundered her lips with his own and showed her the full measure of his desire as he possessed her fiercely, fully, totally the master of her body. She sobbed with release as waves of ecstasy lifted and carried her over the crest, bore her exultantly from the bittersweet aching of desire to the drowsy realms of utter satiation. Moments later, James found his own release and she gloried in the final, surging thrust of his body against her before he fell exhausted to her side.

She stayed immobile, a weakness in her limbs, the racing beat of her heart ebbing to a steady, even rhythm as her composure returned. She glanced across at James. He lay on his back beside her, staring up at the cabin beams above them, his handsome face serious. He turned to smile at her, feeling her eyes upon him, and reached out to draw her against his chest. She lay there, his heartbeat steady and even beneath her ear, his hands toying lazily with her tousled hair. She felt suddenly overwhelmed by guilt at these signs of his affection. Could she do Jonathan's bidding now, she wondered doubtfully, after that intimate exchange of pleasure they had shared? She felt somewhat akin to Judas Iscariot, her freedom the thirty pieces of silver she would receive for his betrayal. A deep sigh followed her thought.

"Did I pleasure you, my sweet?" James asked teasingly, peering down at where she nestled against his chest like a sleepy kitten.

"Aye, Captain," she confirmed, still perplexed. "You pleasured me beyond my wildest imaginings!"

The sea captain grinned and struggled to remove his arm from beneath the drowsy weight of her body. "Then wake up, my sleepy-headed minx," he urged, "for the night is yet young and ours to share. A goblet more of wine will revive you, I wager." He swung out of bed and crossed the cabin, as at home without his clothes as with.

He was beautiful, she thought reluctantly as she watched him, if a man could be considered beautiful. Every inch of his frame was well-muscled and lean, and all of him golden-tanned in the lantern's light. He moved with the lithe, virile grace of a Greek athlete, whose pictures she had seen in her schoolroom textbooks long ago when her papa had yet been living and tutors came daily to the house on Darling Lane.

James returned to the bed and held a goblet out to her. He raised his own. "To us, and our continued delight!" he proposed roguishly, quaffing a generous mouthful.

"Aye, aye, sir!" she murmured cheekily, raising her goblet in response with an impish grin curving her lips.

He sprawled on the bed beside her, leaning on one elbow with his goblet held lazily in his other hand. He kissed her shoulder lightly.

Christianne steadfastly sipped her wine, refusing to look at him, afraid if he saw her eyes he would be able to read her thoughts. What should she do, she wondered in confusion? If she intended to do as Jonathan had instructed, she must act quickly, and soon. But James' tender love-making had shown him in a different light to her, not as a rutting young rake in pursuit only of his own pleasures at her expense, but as an ardent and considerate lover who had gone to great lengths to ensure that she experienced the delights of passion too.

"A farthing for your thoughts, my lady?" he teased, kissing her again lightly on the arm.

She shook her head. "No, Captain, you first. A half-penny for your thoughts—I raise your bid!"

He grinned. "I am not sure you will want to hear them, or think your coin well spent."

Christianne feigned a pouting expression. "In faith, sir, I won the bidding. A man of honor as you profess to be would pay the price without delay," she bantered.

"The halfpenny first then, Mistress Alexander," James insisted.

"Nay, I have none!" Christianne confessed ruefully. "Will you accept a single kiss in payment for your thoughts?"

James rolled over, a laughing glint in his green eyes. "Indeed I will—and shall consider it a bargain well struck on my part!" He lay on his back, his arms crossed under his head. "Pay me, wench, or suffer the consequences of your failure to honor your debts!"

With a throaty laugh, she leaned over him. Her hair brushed in light, tickling strands against his hairy chest as she slowly lowered her rosy lips over his firmly chiselled mouth and kissed him. To her surprise, she found she enjoyed the sweet sensation, her new role as the initiator of their love-making. When at length she broke away she was breathless and James' expression registered delighted astonishment. She pulled the sheet primly back up to cover her and rocked back on her heels self-consciously.

"Now," she demanded, her head cocked on one side like an inquisitive child, "I have paid, and well. Tell me your thoughts!"

James shrugged and drained his goblet. "I was merely thinking, Christianne, that of all the women that I have bedded, you fascinate and pleasure me the most. You excite me, my lovely Christianne, with your silvery tresses and your mysterious dark blue eyes and your rosy lips. A pristine beauty that hides a passionate tigress! To your beauty and to a long and pleasure-filled voyage, for the two of us!" He raised his goblet, realizing only belatedly that it was empty. He made to get from the bed, but Christianne hurriedly stayed him.

"No, my lord captain, I will fill it for you," she offered lightly, holding out her hand for the goblet.

A frown creased his forehead momentarily, followed closely by a grin and a nod of assent.

She took both goblets to the carved cabinet and set them down while she unstoppered the crystal decanter. Her hands shook with rage as she poured the blood-red wine. Damn his soul, she thought furiously as she did so, she was but another conquest to him, despite his flowery compliments and his gentle caresses. Just another woman who had warmed his bed and whiled away the boring hours, to be bragged about in the next port o' call, no doubt. Her mind was made up! With shaking hands she palmed the vellum envelope she had hidden earlier in the cabinet, then deftly emptied the gritty powder into James' goblet and stirred the contents hurriedly with her finger. She sensed a movement behind her and whirled about, the scrap of vellum spiralling to the deck as she did so. She held her breath, her heart hammering.

James, who had come up as silently as a cat behind her on his bare feet, noted the paper's fluttering descent but said nothing. He smiled. "The bed was lonely without you beside me," he said caressingly.

She laughed, the sound brittle with her nervousness. It sounded forced even to her own ears. "Well, sir, I am done. Here is your wine. Shall we return to our bed and sip it together?"

James nodded, a deceptively lazy, hooded look to his eyes, a look she presumed to be the same one she had come to know well. "I can think of nothing I would like better," he said softly.

They lay side by side in silence, James sipping his wine with a stern, brooding expression, seeming unaware of Christianne's furtive side-glances in his direction. His eyelids wavered, closed, then flitted open. "Lord," he said drowsily, "I . . . I can scarce stay awake!"

"Sleep, then, my captain," she murmured soothingly, running her hand lightly across his brow. "There will be other nights, as you said, will there not?"

James nodded, his head barely moving, his eyes closed. His arm slid off the bed, his grip slackening. The remains of the drink splashed to the boards, then the silver goblet clattered after them. Seconds later, a loud snore buzzed from the apparently-sleeping captain.

Christianne waited several minutes to be sure that he was truly asleep. Satisfied he was, she sprang from the bed and hurried to the sea chest at the foot of it. She flung up the lid and hastily withdrew the first garments she found inside, a man's shirt and knee breeches and one of James' light capes, more suited to the hot climate than her own fur-lined one. Breathing raggedly with fear, she hurriedly

211

donned them, slipping the dagger James had given her into her waistband. She touched the cornelian beads about her throat for good fortune, cast a last sweeping glance about the cabin, then slipped through the door. Master Bones thumped his tail and yawned sleepily.

"Stay!" she ordered, a lump in her throat, stepped over where he lay across the threshold and quietly closed the cabin door behind her.

James watched her go through slitted eyes.

Sixteen

Christianne crept stealthily along the gangway to where a lantern hung on a hook to light the pitch-black passage. Its glow concealed by the flowing cape, she hurried up the stairs to the upper decks.

The decks were shadowed and silent save for the slapping of the waves against the bows. She glanced furtively up into the rigging. The watch's profile was a blurry silhouette against the indigo night sky. She breathed a sigh of relief. The moon, supposed to be full this night, was wreathed in streamers of cloud, her light hidden. If she were swift, she could pass silently beneath the watch without being seen.

Like a shadow, she wove in and out of the masts and coiled lines, headed for the bows as Flynn had instructed. Once there, she looked about her. There was no vessel out there that she could see, nothing but inky blackness all about the *Fair Amanda* like a great confining wall. She dropped the cape and held the lantern aloft. With trembling hands she swung it left, then right, then left again. She waited several seconds, then repeated the signal. There! Far to the east an answering light flashed, repeating the signal she had made. She almost laughed aloud. She'd done it! Jonathan truly had friends out there in the silent darkness. But where was he? She crouched down on the damp decks to wait, concealed by the heavy shadow of the gunwales.

James waited until Christianne had left the cabin before donning his breeches and slipping out after her. He had surmised her intention was to free Flint and it seemed he had been right. That Jezebel! She had lain in his arms, sated by his loving, and all the while she had plotted to betray him to that silver-tongued rogue, he thought as he strode up the stairs, across the deck and down into the fore-and-aft gangway toward the brig. There was neither sight nor sound of Christianne. Apprehension clawed at his gut as he leaped down the last stair. The lantern that usually illuminated the gloomy gangway was unlit, though its brass fittings felt hot still to the touch. He strode on, his bare foot coming up against something heavy and soft in the gloom, and he knew without doubt that it was a man's body, sprawled there. The barred door to the brig hung open. Flint had gone! James tore down the gangway and leaped up the stairs, cursing his lack of a sword as he went.

"Rouse the crew, damn you, Andrew!" he roared to the watch in the rigging above. "To arms, all hands!"

The watchman's whistle sounded shrilly. James whirled about, plumbing the darkness for Christianne with eyes that glittered with fury.

In seconds, the *Amanda*'s crew came pouring up from the fo'c's'le, bleary-eyed with sleep but bearing swords or pistols or daggers.

"Flint and his cronies are about a mutiny this night," he barked, "and I want them found! Jump to it, lads!"

Men dived left and right to do his bidding. Ben Wright sped to his captain's side. "What's happening, sir?" he gasped.

"Flint's escaped the brig," James said harshly, "and I want him found, and now! Get a lantern, Ben, and go down to the brig. There's a body there. Find out whose it is. I'll warrant it's Hardcastle's, and not our Irish friend's! There are ten golden guineas," he bellowed loudly, "for the man who brings me the woman, Christianne—and mayhap," he added in a lower voice, "he may have her, too, when I am done with her."

Despite its lowness, his voice was chilling, Ben Wright noted. He hurried off in the opposite direction to the brig.

Christianne trembled as the men's coarse voices, raised in excitement, grew steadily nearer. Dear God in heaven, where was Jonathan? Her palms were slippery on the lantern's handle, her heart thudding so violently it seemed ready to leap from her chest. She stood up hesitantly, her back pressed hard against the rail for support. Despite her former bravado, she had never been so frightened in all her eighteen years.

Suddenly Jonathan appeared out of nowhere at her elbow. She almost cried out in relief to see him there.

"Take off the cloak, lass," he ordered harshly. "We must swim for it! Ox and the others have lowered a longboat. They will pick us up. Come on."

Christianne shook her head and nervously licked her lips. "No! I cannot! I cannot swim!"

"You don't have to. We'll jump together. Quickly, up onto the rail with you, they're coming for us!"

Trembling all over, she nodded and unbuckled the clasp of her cape and let it fall to the decks. Jonathan's eyes fastened on the dagger stuffed carelessly into her belt. He hauled off his sea boots. "Give me your knife, me darlin', and climb on up," he urged.

"My knife? But—why? You promised me there would be no bloodshed!" she gasped, clambering up onto the rail and

215

steadying herself by hanging on to a ratline that hung within reach.

"Just give it here, woman," Jonathan growled. "These waters are thick with shark. We might need it. Give it here!"

Understanding now, Christianne tossed the dagger to him. He caught it easily and thrust it into his own belt before climbing beside her on the rail.

"Flint, no!" cried Ben Wright, sprinting across the deck towards them. "Go if ye must, but leave the lass, I beg ye!"

"Nay, Wright, she goes with me!" Jonathan crowed, laughing at the first officer's concerned expression.

Ben shook his head. "I can't let ye take her, Flint, and ye know it!" He lunged towards them.

Jonathan reached for the dagger. It sang through the air and Christianne screamed as Ben dropped like lead to the deck, a scarlet spider spreading from where the dagger lay buried deep in his belly.

"You promised me, damn you!" Christianne cursed. Her small fist hooked up to strike Flynn. "Liar!" she shrieked.

Jonathan spat, shoved her over the rail with a foul curse and dived after her.

She hit the water with a mighty slap and sank like a stone beneath the surface. Terror panicked her and she screamed into the black void, filling her lungs with salt water. Her arms flailed uselessly. The darkness closed in.

Drowning . . . she was drowning . . . a watery grave had claimed her! Oh, please, God, no, not like this! Not like—

She gulped air as her head broke the surface. In that moment a shaggy head, streaming water, appeared not inches from her own. 'Tis the devil, she thought hysterically, Lucifer himself or one of his demons, come to carry me off to purgatory for my wicked ways! The demon made strange, garbled noises that sounded unlike any earthly tongue she had ever heard. She thrashed desperately, trying to get away, far away, from that horrible apparition, water spewing from her mouth and mingling with her sobs. A sharp blow thudded across the back of her neck and everything went black.

When she came to, she lay huddled in a longboat, a greasy leather jerkin covering her. Beside her, she recognized the sailor, Ox, by his massive bulk. His arm was stretched protectively across her, heavy as an oaken timber. She could barely discern Jonathan's profile in front of her. The two men that bent to haul on the oars must be the one they called Tancred and the other, Le Chat. Loud, angry shouts carried from the darkness behind them. Twin explosions boomed, then a third and a fourth. Spray burst all about the boat as the musket balls fell scant inches short of their mark. Jonathan threw back his head and laughed triumphantly.

"Row, my bullies, row!" The *Scorpion* awaits!" he roared.

Christianne struggled to sit up, coughing and spluttering. Ox peered into her face anxiously. It was he, she realized belatedly, who had pulled her out and whom she had mistaken for the devil himself. "My thanks, Ox," she whispered, shivering with cold. "My thanks for saving me."

Ox grunted and nodded. He was bare-chested and his hair and beard as streaming wet as she, but he shook his head vigorously when she held out the jerkin to him and pushed it back toward her.

"Ah, Christianne, you're awake," Jonathan exclaimed. He scrabbled across to her side. " 'Twas a grand escape, was it not? And Mallory left like the fool he is!" He picked up her icy little hand and would have kissed it if she had not wrenched it away.

"Satan's spawn!" she spat, anger broiling through her. "You vowed there would be no bloodshed, you *promised* me

217

there would be none, you lying, two-faced whoreson!"

Jonathan shrugged carelessly. "He came at me and I killed him. Say no more! It was him or us, and I chose you and I, me darlin'." He chucked her beneath the chin.

Christianne jerked her head violently away. "Nay, Flynn, lay not a hand on me! I'll not be touched by a coward. Ben Wright was unarmed—you killed an unarmed man! James was right. You are a silver-tongued rogue, and you have a winning way, and I, like a babe, fell for both, you lily-livered scum!"

The two men rowing laughed at her vehemence. Jonathan silenced them with an oath.

"By the gods, woman, you have a shrewish tongue, and no one, be he man or wench, calls Jonathan Flynn a coward. Another of your "compliments" and lovely or nay, 'tis over the side you go!" he threatened, turning from her. "Row, you swabs, row!"

The longboat swiftly glided through the water, toward a lantern that seemed suspended in a void. Yet as they neared it, Christianne could discern the massive bows and the tall masts of a mighty vessel against the night and the ocean. The moon came out from behind the clouds, casting silvery light on the dark swells. She looked back over her shoulder. It was as if the *Fair Amanda* had never been. A heavy, shuddering sigh coursed through her and she determinedly turned to face ahead. "Look to the future, not the past," her mother had always said. The future, she thought uneasily. What would it bring?

The creaks and groans of the *Scorpion*'s hull seemed alarmingly loud in the silence. Pale moons of faces appeared over the rail and a booming, gutturally-accented voice hailed them. Jonathan shouted back, then seconds later a rope ladder was tossed over the rail.

"Ox, take the wench," Jonathan ordered, starting up the

ladder first.

When he had climbed over the rail, Ox picked her up with surprising gentleness and slung her over his shoulder. Despite his girth, he managed the swinging ladder with little difficulty, and in no more than a minute or so, Christianne was standing on deck.

Whoops and whistles of coarse appreciation greeted her appearance. The air was filled with the sickly-sweet odor of grog. She looked about her. The crew of the *Scorpion* were a rag-tag bunch, ranged in a wide circle about their captain, Jonathan Flynn. Some were as swarthy as Spaniards, others blond and stocky like the Dutch were wont to be, but the majority appeared to be English. Her eyes flickered from one to another. The look in every pair of eyes was the same, and that look boded ill for her. Instinctively she edged toward Jonathan, feeling the devil she knew was preferable to these devils she didn't.

He noted the move and clapped his arm about her possessively.

"Your captain has returned, my bullies!" he cried. "Another keg, for the captain and his lady love! We'll celebrate our safe return. Mendoza—a tune, man, strike it up, and lively now!"

Obediently, a short, swarthy man stepped forward with a concertina and began playing. Several of the men stamped their feet and clapped their hands in time to the lively sea chanty. A belligerent-faced man thrust his way through the circle and faced Flynn with a querulous expression. The music wheezed to a halt.

"A celebration, is it, *Captain* Flynn?" he jeered. "And what's there to celebrate—your new doxy? Where's the ship you promised me and the booty to be had from her holds—that's what I would like to know, *ja?*"

Many of the crew echoed his sentiments, muttering,

219

"Aye!"

Jonathan grinned. He clasped the man's shoulder.

"And you shall have them, booty and vessel both," he vowed. "You see, my friend, Captain Mallory of the *Fair Amanda* that we just quit is that rarity among seafaring men—an honorable fellow!" The men laughed. "It will go against his noble grain that we have jumped ship, killing two of his men in the process, and that I have the woman here that he wanted for his own, to boot. He will thirst for revenge as a leech thirsts for blood! Let him pursue us if he will, to the Red Island, friend Wilhelm. There we will relieve him of his ship and her cargo both, with ease," he paused, "Or will you risk the promise of a worthy new vessel on a skirmish on the high seas, my friend, and continue to sail your worm-riddled hulk?"

The man scowled. His blunt-featured face set deep in thought. At length he smiled. "*Ja*, Flynn, we will wait. Good ships, they are hard to come by in these waters, *nein?*" He clapped Jonathan across the back.

Christianne thought she saw relief flicker briefly in Jonathan's sloe-black eyes.

"Aye," he agreed. "Mendoza, play on!" he ordered. "Ox—take the wench below, to my cabin." His dark eyes raked Christianne's body in its plastered-down boy's garb. "I will join you shortly, me darlin' Chris," he murmured, "and this promise I shall keep!"

She shot him a withering look and followed Ox across the decks. The fiercely defiant expression faded as she left the captain's line of vision. "*Beware of the sign of Scorpio!*" the old gypsy crone had warned her in Barcelona. Was it possible her gift of prophecy had been genuine—that she had confused the zodiac sign for the name of this pirate vessel, the *Red Scorpion?* And if that were so, could the rest of her warnings also be believed?

Seventeen

James paced restlessly in his cabin while Matthew Locke, sailmaker and ship's surgeon, tended to Ben Wright. The shirt they had cut from him lay upon the boards, soaked with blood.

Matthew stood up, stretching his aching back.

"How is he?" James asked grimly.

Locke shrugged. " 'Tis hard to say, sir. If the blade missed his vitals and there's no poisoning, he'll live, Captain," he said quietly. "If not—?" He sighed heavily. There was no need to finish the sentence. A fleeting grin crossed Locke's face. "I sewed him up finer than any canvas I ever put needle to, sir, and Ben here is hardier than most. God willing, he'll survive."

"I pray you're right, Matt," James said. "And the girl, Lucy, what of her?"

"Weak as a suckling babe, sir, but mending right fast. The oranges were what did it, sir, I'd wager my eyes on it."

James nodded absently. He'd seen too many men die needlessly from scurvy for want of citrus such as limes or oranges not to have realized what the girl had lacked in her two months as a stowaway. Although the benefits of such fruits in the rations had yet to be proved, there were several shrewd captains like himself who swore by it to prevent the killer, scurvy, on lengthy sea voyages. They had found Lucy in the nick of time, before her gums had started to swell and blacken, fortunately for her, he thought, his mind still on Flint's escape. And Christianne. His face set sternly and Matthew was glad the captain's ire was not directed at him.

"My thanks, Matt," James told the man. "Have Mullens come down here, will you? I'll sit with Ben meanwhile."

Matthew Locke nodded, gathered up the sailmaker's needle and twine he had used to sew up the first officer, and left.

James sat at Ben's side. "You damned fool!" he said gruffly to the pale, still man. "Did I not warn you she'd not let your kindness turn aside her ambitions, my kind-hearted Ben? Ah, but you would not listen, and she repaid your friendship with a dagger in your breast." He shook his head, disgust curling his lips. He had not believed himself she could have harmed Ben, until he had seen the dagger protruding from his belly and realized the depths of her black-heartedness. His eyes burned with green fires. "I vow, Ben, that she will pay for her treachery," he murmured, his fists clenched. "There will be no sea, no ocean, no continent large enough to hide her from me, for I will chase her to the ends of the Earth and beyond if I have to, to call her to account and bring her low. Would she were a man, that I could slit her murderer's throat!"

He stalked across the cabin to the desk, unrolled a chart and spread it across its surface, scanning it thoughtfully while he rubbed his stubbled chin. A knock sounded at the door. He bade Mullens enter and poured them both a measure of rum.

"Sit down, man," he ordered, seating himself. "I called you here because I have need of your help. You've sailed these waters before, have you not?"

"Aye, sir, more times than I care t' count." Silas Mullens

grinned. "I were with the East India Company afore I signed on with yourself these two years past, under Cap'n Fitzpatrick. Our ship was the *Helen* and our route, India, sir. I could sail these waters with a patch on both me eyes, sir, that I could, instead of just the one." The short, stocky man winked that one eye roguishly.

James grinned. "That was my hope, exactly. Now, take a look at this chart. Flint must have hoped to make a landfall or else planned to rendezvous with a vessel of some kind. What say you?"

Mullens pursed his lips thoughtfully and took a swig of his rum. He smacked his lips and wiped them on the back of his hand. "A ship, I'd wager, Cap'n. Talk belowdecks is that the rogue had it all planned—even hinted, like, that the *Amanda*'d have a new master right soon! You cut his dealings short, sir, by throwing him in the brig, yes, sir—and it were right fortunate for us you did!" Mullens traced his stubby, calloused finger across the parchment. "There's few vessels these days what sail these waters. Them what do be blackbirders or merchants or privateers. Now, sir, I don't reckon our friend Flint for a merchant, and he talked a mite too loftily of freedom for a slaver, which leaves us, by my reckoning, Cap'n, with but one choice."

"A pirate ship?"

"Aye, sir, pirate, privateer, whatever you care to call them sea wolves—don't seem to make much difference if they be licensed to raid or not, that I can see. Now, sir, if he do be a pirate, we'll likely as not find him holed up . . . here." He jabbed his stubby finger at a large island on the chart, an island off the west coast of Africa that angled toward the east. "Madagascar, sir, or the Great Red Island, as some do call it. 'Tis been a favorite lair of the sea wolves for many a year," he chuckled, "believe me, sir, I know!"

James cocked an inquiring eyebrow at Mullens. Mullens

took another swig from his tankard before continuing.

"Well, sir, like I said, I sailed with the *Helen* under Fitzpatrick. On one voyage a storm hit and we were run aground on the reef, right here, sir, or near as I recall. Of the six of us that the captain sent ashore for provisions, the natives killed two straight off with their spears. The rest of us hot-footed it as best we could, but it were no use, us not knowing the country an' all. We were taken, sir, and it were a year before we escaped and made our way on a missionary ship to rejoin the *Helen.*"

James nodded. "And what of that year spent on the island?"

Mullens grinned again. With his leathery skin, he looked like a wizened little monkey of a man. "At first, the Malagasy, as the natives is called, made slaves o' the four of us. Then we lost two men to the flux, which left only John Fox and meself. But"— he tapped his head—"we was determined not to follow arter the other poor lads. We ate what they ate, them natives, and we did what was asked of us and"—he paused and eyed James craftily—"we took uselves a couple o' them dark, little gals as wives, pretty little woolly-haired pieces they were an' all. And, when their relatives got careless o' guarding us, seeing as how we were respectable married men an' all, we scarpered! Reckon there's a coffee-colored, blue-eyed Mullens bastard left there an' all, along o' John Fox's little 'un." He winked. "I do hope that me missus in Richmond don't never find out!"

His captain laughed. "Then, Mullens, you know this island well?" he asked eagerly.

"Aye, sir, better'n most, anyways. But it ain't no piddlin' little island, sir, 'tis three times the size o' England! If they've gone ashore an' holed up there, 'twill be the very devil to find them!"

"We'll worry about that when we get there," James said,

casting a concerned look at his first officer in the bed who had still not moved or made a sound. "First, we must go after them!"

Mullens grunted agreement.

James continued: "I would like you to take Ben's place as first officer, for the time being. I want the *Amanda* rigged with all the sail she can handle. We will press the men to the limit. No man rests more than a half hour in ten until we sight Flint and his ship. Any of the crew tells you nay, Master Mullens, he'll feel the lash on his bared back, be damned if he won't," James vowed grimly.

"Aye, aye, sir," Mullens agreed solemnly. He had never seen his captain so stern-faced before, or threaten such harsh measures. "You have my loyalty, sir, and 'tis my belief the rest of the men will stand behind you. Those," he added slyly, "what might be after refusing, can be persuaded, like!" His grin stretched evilly from ear to ear, and with the black patch covering his right eye, James thought that Mullens could easily pass for a pirate himself.

"Good man!" James grinned. "We'll sail east with the dawn and pray for a fair wind."

Christianne awoke from one of many fitful dozes she had fallen into during the remainder of that night since her flight from the *Fair Amanda*. Escape, she thought wryly? Ha! She had not so much escaped as leaped from the hot kettle into the fire! She shook her head in disgust. Little Chris, street urchin and cutpurse without equal in the back streets of London Town, whose talent for picking a safe mark by the lines in his face had meant her life, had allowed her assessment of Flynn's character to be gravely inaccurate: had been tricked by his handsome looks and his pretty speech and gentlemanly ways into believing he was a man of honor and truth. James Mallory, for all his arrogant, domineering ways and his lustful appetites, had never reneged on his word, or pretended to be anything other than what he was, she realized with reluctance.

Thankfully, the sounds of carousing and drunken laughter had lasted until the pearly shades of dawn had pinked the eastern sky. Jonathan—probably as deep into his cups as his crew—had either forgotten her or fallen asleep dead drunk. She looked about her, suddenly aware of her surroundings, for last night it had been too dark to take note of much, and Ox had left her neither lantern nor candle.

A broad bunk of rough-hewn timber flanked one wall. A thin pallet stuffed with stale straw and a rough woollen blanket were its sole coverings. Into that bunk it was that she had tumbled last night, half numb with shock and fear and shivering still from her soaking in the Atlantic Ocean.

The little panes of cloudy glass in the cabin's solitary window were murky and let in little light. A rickety chair, riddled with woodworm holes and a battered captain's table in like condition, a sea chest bound with brass straps and a ship's log set upon it were all that furnished the cabin. The air had a fusty odor as if it had remained unstirred for many weeks, perhaps months, and millions of dust motes eddied and swirled in the fragile bars of sunlight that filtered through the murky window. Christianne wrinkled her nose in distaste as she stiffly swung her feet out of the bunk and stood up. Her shirt and breeches were stiff with salt, as was her hair. Her clothes were still damp in places. She raked her fingers through her matted tresses, ruefully aware of how quickly she had accustomed herself to her brushes and her combs and her baths. I'faith, she had become softer than the dainty dames who teetered to the wig shops on Bond Street of a morning in their petticoated gowns and high-heeled slippers of fine kid leather, and who swooned if they misplaced a button or a bow, or spied a mouse!

She slipped across to the cabin door and lifted the latch. The door groaned as it swung inwards on rusted hinges. Across the threshold, like a shaggy, faithful hound, sprawled Ox, snores reverberating through his beard. Gratitude swept over Christianne, an emotion she had rarely experienced before and found herself ill-equipped to deal with. Childish, foolish tears stung her eyes. That this great bear of a man had passed the night thus to protect her, she had no doubt. Any vestiges of fear she might have had of him after his diabolical appearance in the water last night vanished like smoke. She crouched down.

"Ox! Ox, wake up! Do you hear me?" She wondered fleetingly if the man were deaf as well as mute, for the two afflictions oft went hand in hand, she knew. She shook him by the shoulder. He rolled heavily over, blinked in puzzlement, grinned and lumbered to his feet. He nodded and touched his forelock to her in the manner of a servant to a lady.

"No, Ox, no, there's no need for that," Christianne said self-consciously, embarrassed by his gesture. "I am no fine lady, I promise you!" She smiled, gamin-faced.

Surprisingly, Ox shook his head and made a deep half-bow to her, followed by another silly grin. Christianne sighed. "Very well, if you must," she said resignedly. This was no time for disagreements, especially one conducted in mime. "Tell me, where is Captain Flynn?"

Alarm lit Ox's pale gray eyes. He shook his head and motioned Christianne back inside the cabin. There he raised his hand repeatedly to his mouth as if lifting a tankard to it, then jiggled his head about drunkenly in a way that needed no words for explanation. So, she had been right, she thought. Jonathan Flynn had passed the night away carousing with his men. What would be his mood this morning, she wondered, after such a lengthy bout?

Ox broke into her musings, making signs that he would go to the galley to find some victuals for her. After he had left, Christianne was of a mind to lock the door in his wake—not for protection against the gentle giant but against Flynn. She bit her lower lip worriedly, refusing to acknowledge the fluttery tremors of fear in the pit of her belly, yet her deep blue eyes reflected the growing panic inside her like fathomless dark pools. She paced back and forth, furious at the trembling of her knees, hugging herself about the arms as if it was a chilly English autumn morn rather than a fiercely hot day off the coast of Africa. Dolt! Ninny! Lily-livered goose! she upbraided herself mercilessly. Yet it was hard to be brave or defiant when she felt so terribly alone and in unfamiliar circumstances. She felt more alone than she had before Granny Rags and Lumpy Jack and Coalie Joe had come to live in the house on Darling Lane after her mother died. At least then her surroundings had been familiar and safe, after a fashion.

The door groaned again as it swung inwards, and she whirled about, the smile freezing on her lips as she saw it was not Ox, as she had expected, but Jonathan Flynn standing there. He smiled his charming smile, but this morning its charm was wasted on Christianne, for she knew it to be the smile of the tiger in the second before it pounces on its prey.

"Here I am at last, me darlin' girl," he declared, lounging against the door jamb. "Is there t' be no loving welcome for your captain?"

His speech, she noted, was faintly slurred, and his breath reeked of rum even from across the cabin. She turned her

228

back to him, her mind racing for words, wishes, thought, *anything* she could say to keep him talking and away from her.

"A good morning to you, Jonathan," she said lightly, stepping over to the cloudy window, " 'tis a fine day, is it not? I declare, the fair weather gives me an appetite. Might I trouble you for a bite of something to break the night's fast?" She knew she was babbling on, but the sick, queasy feeling in her vitals refused to be quelled.

"Later," he said softly. He reeled away from the door and lurched towards her.

He was, Christianne realized, much drunker than she had thought at first.

"The captain and his lady must become much better acquaint—acquainted," he said with a lazy smile. "With an edge to our appetite, the victuals will ha-have the taste of ambrosia about them!" He reached out suddenly and caught her about the waist, pulling her against him with such slamming force the breath was almost knocked from her. He gripped her chin in his hand and arched her head back before his mouth fastened hotly over hers.

His drunken kisses repulsed her. She raked her nails down his cheeks, pushed against his face in a frantic effort to force his lips from her own. She kicked and writhed, but despite Flynn's whip-lean build, he had a wiry strength that seemed invincible. Her kicks pained her bare feet far more than they appeared to deter him! He released her at length and stood there, breathing heavily. His black eyes were glazed with a mixture of lust and rum, and the scratches that scored his handsome face were livid against his tanned complexion.

Christianne backed away, realizing suddenly that even should she succeed in fending him off, there was nowhere to run to, unless it was abovedecks, to the *Scorpion*'s woman-

229

hungry crew! Her legs felt rubbery, ready to buckle, damn them. In God's name, what was it that ailed her? Was fear the sole cause of this kittenish weakness that churned her belly like butter and dewed her face with sweat?

Jonathan peeled off his shirt and tossed it carelessly across the cabin. He swayed a little as he advanced on her, his black eyes glittering. "So," he purred, "you swore you would not suffer the touch of a coward, did you, my dainty Chris?" he crowed, stalking her deliberately and relishing the chalky pallor of her face and the fear in the dark pools of her eyes. By St. Patrick and the Snakes, she was a queenly piece with her web of silvery hair and the soft thrust of her regal breasts outlined by her man's shirt! He chuckled softly. How Mallory must have burned to possess such virgin beauty as he was about to possess! He would writhe on a spike of jealous rage when he learned that the girl had given her chastity to he, Jonathan Flynn, instead of himself. Just like Michael, he was, that damned Mallory, always wanting the best for himself, to be first in all things, even with their lying harlot of a mother. But in this, he would be first! He licked his lips. Aye, Michael had always been their mother's favorite—but Michael, dear Michael, was no more.

He dived at her suddenly, the suddenness of his move startling her, making her shriek in fear. Christianne cast about her desperately for a weapon. The pursuit seemed to heat his blood still more, for his breathing was thick and heavy now.

"There's nowhere to run to, me darlin' girl, nowhere at all," he taunted. "Come here, t' Jonathan."

"No!" she defied him, shaking her head. "I—I am not well! In truth, a dizziness overwhelms me, and—and my limbs, they are shaking! Do not force me, I beg you! I will be your woman, I swear it," she lied, "but not this night.

230

Give me more time, I beg you!"

Stubbornly Jonathan shook his head, grinning wider. "Nay, my lovely queen, I will have you now. For two long months I have hungered for you, imagined the feel of that creamy flesh under my hands. I lay in my hammock at night, half afraid to sleep, certain Captain Mallory would make you his woman before I ever had a chance to make you mine," he said heatedly. "I offer you more than my bed, Christianne, more than myself—a kingdom of your own! Your chastity will be your dowry. My wedding gift to you will be my island, Paradise, your place at my side as her queen, and the heart of her king, Jonathan Flynn!"

Christianne frowned in puzzlement. The grog caused him to talk in riddles, yet the way he raked her body with his shining black eyes needed no deciphering. Did he not know that James had taken her to bed? A faint hope stirred in her breast. He seemed to prize her nonexistent chastity greatly. If she confessed that she were no longer a maid, mayhap he would leave her alone!

"No, Flynn, don't you see? I have no 'dowry' such as you speak of left to give you. I was the captain's woman, Jonathan—how else had you imagined I could have opportunity to drug his wine? Now, please, leave me be! Let me go back to England!" Perspiration ran in rivulets down the valley between her breasts; more broke out on her brow and her upper lip. She shivered violently and all but crumpled to her knees with weakness.

The blood seemed to drain from Jonathan's lips and about his mouth as the import of her words registered through the drunken fog that clouded his brain. A cold, cruel fury glittered and danced in his eyes. He lunged at her with a snarl like a rabid dog.

"You were that damned Englishman's woman? Then by God, you will also be mine!" he spat.

Instead of backing away from him, Christianne stood her ground and slammed hard at his chest as he leaped at her. The impetus of his own assault rocked her violently back on her heels and snapped her jaws together, yet the unexpected forward thrust served to hurl Jonathan off balance. He keeled over, lost his footing and fell, cracking his head against the sea chest. He groaned and lay quite still. The sudden weighty silence was deafening.

At first Christianne stood there numbly. It had all happened so fast! One minute he had come at her like a madman, and in the next he lay at her feet like a broken mannequin. She covered her gaping mouth with her hands, horror flooding through her. *She'd killed him!* The blood roared in her ears like a raging sea. Dear God, she'd killed him, killed a man! What would happen now—what would the *Red Scorpion*'s crew do to the woman who had murdered their captain? She swayed dizzily, dread uncoiling in her gut like a sinister, hooded cobra rearing its ugly head. She knew full well what they would do! She'd welcome death long before it came, of that she had little doubt.

The door swung inwards. Christianne looked up numbly as Ox lumbered in with a wooden tray. His pale eyes flickered from her own ashen face to the crumpled figure on the boards. His bushy eyebrows rose in inquiry.

"He—he's d-dead," she whispered, her hands fluttering aimlessly like giant, pale moths. "I on-only meant t-to s-stop him, but he . . . he tried . . . and I—!" She couldn't go on. "He—he's dead! Dear Go-God, what can I d-do?" she sobbed.

Ox set the tray aside and knelt at Flynn's side. He rolled the man over and leaned down, putting his cheek close to the captain's mouth. He looked up at Christianne, and nodded his head and pointed to the captain's heart.

She gasped. "He's still alive?" Ox grinned and nodde again. Despite her horror at what she thought she ha done, it was with mixed emotions that she absorbed th realization that Flynn was but unconscious. When he cam around, he would kill her, she knew!

Ox lifted Jonathan as easily as if he were a child an carried him to the bunk. He motioned for Christianne t tear the captain's discarded shirt into strips for a bandage She quickly did so. Ox wound it about his captain's head neatly binding the bloody gash just above the temple. H turned to the trembling girl and held her face securely i his large palms until she had calmed. Then he released he: and began making clear, easily understood motions to her

Her chest pained her and that awful weakness stil fuddled her head and made her feel rubbery about the joints, but at length she grasped his meaning.

"Stay at his side, nurse him, you say?" she frowned. "But why? I have no liking for the man!"

Ox gesticulated again.

It transpired that Ox was convinced the Irishman would recall nothing of the incident when he awoke. He urged her to pretend great concern for the man, to minister to him as if he were her sun and moon and stars! The captain would have only gratitude for her when he awoke, and would not harm her.

"Very well," she agreed doubtfully, "if you think it will work, I shall try it. Yet I fear he will be none too forgiving if he recalls what I confessed—and that it was me who caused him to fall!"

And what, she wondered, would she do then?

Eighteen

Three weeks passed since the morning Jonathan had collapsed at her feet. In that time, thanks to Ox's sound advice and a miserable bout of the ague that had laid her low, Flynn had been unable to make good his threats to ravish her.

When he had come around from the combined effects of the blow to his head and his drunkenness, he had found a sweetly smiling Christianne perched at his side, soothing his aching head with a dampened cloth. As Ox had so craftily mimed, he recalled nothing of the incident that had caused his fall, and was embarrassingly grateful for her ministerings. In his eyes, she had acquired a status bordering on sainthood! The next night Christianne had herself taken to the bunk, hot and cold sweats and a hoarse, hacking cough racking her body. She blamed her falling asleep in her cold, wet clothes the night of their flight from James' ship as the cause of the ague, and the reason for her weakness and trembling when Jonathan had lunged at her. But it was not Jonathan who had reciprocated and tended her in her sickness. Nay! The captain seemed mortally afraid of catching it from her, and had ordered poor Ox to see to her, an order the shaggy-haired giant seemed only too pleased to comply with.

In his fondness for Christianne, Ox had nursed her like her own mother. Having, it seemed, few medicinal supplies aboard the *Scorpion,* he had dosed her with toddies of hot rum, well-laced with the juice of a tart yellow fruit that caused her mouth to pucker with its sourness, with hot beef broth and with gruel. Now she felt well enough to stand and although weak, her mind was clear again and free of the hallucinations the fever had caused her. She shuddered. What awful visions they had been! She had imagined herself a little girl again in the house on Darling Lane, having her dancing lesson. Her instructor, strangely, had not been M'sieu Balmain, but Ben Wright, first officer of the *Fair Amanda.* He had taken her hand and led her through the stately steps of the minuet. Then a gong had sounded and her papa had appeared, his back turned to her across the room. Happily she had run to him, begging to be carried on his shoulder. But when he turned around, she saw her dear papa wore James' face, and that his eyes had seemed on fire. She had flung about, horrified, to find Ben Wright there, asking her to dance, a gentle smile curling his lips and a dagger with a hilt of rubies and pearls jutting obscenely from his belly. His shirt had been a river of blood.

The music of an unseen harpsichord, flute and violin had soared and swelled to fill the room, and awful Ben and her papa with James' face had made her dance and dance and dance. The room and the music and their faces had run together in a spinning, dizzying whirl of horrible sensation until at length she had been flung headlong to the floor, their mocking laughter ringing in her ears. She had awakened in Jonathan's bunk, her shirt soaked with perspiration, her parched lips cracked and painful, to Ox's gentle nursing.

And now, she thought with mixed feelings, it appeared

they were about to go ashore. Since dawn she had sensed an undercurrent of excitement in the coarse voices that carried to the cabin from abovedecks. Even Ox had seemed jumpy and had gestured that soon they would be taking to the longboats. He had pressed a wooden comb into her hands, crudely carved, she was sure, by himself, and a battered rectangle of shiny tin for a mirror. Her toilette had taken but minutes and though she longed for fresh clothing and a proper bath, she had done her best with only a bucket of water and a cloth. All that remained now was the waiting, she thought with a grimace.

Her wait ended sooner than she had anticipated. Not an hour later, a sailor came to summon her abovedecks, where Jonathan awaited her with an eager smile on his handsome face. He took her hand and kissed it. Christianne was acutely aware as he did so of how his men ogled her in her revealing boy's garments. She was comforted to note that Ox hovered nearby, pretending to be busy coiling some lines. The bond of friendship they had wrought during her illness was a strong one, and she knew that he would do all in his power to protect her, should the need arise, just as she would endeavor to help him in any way she could.

"We are home, me darlin'," Jonathan declared, using the almost reverent tones he had adopted to address her. "My island within an island will be our paradise in fact as well as in name, and you shall be her queen!" He swept her an elegant bow and caressed her cheek fondly. "Come, Queen Christianne, survey your kingdom!"

Over the bows some fifty yards off where the vessel had dropped anchor lay a small island. Beyond it loomed a larger land mass, its outline a hazy rust in the brilliant sunshine: Madagascar, known as the Great Red Island to sailors from the West, as the Island of the Moon to the Arabs who came to her shores in search of slaves to fill their slaveships.

Discovered by Portuguese captain and navigator, Diégo Diaz, when his caravel rounded the Cape of Good Hope in the year 1500, the large island had alternately been claimed by the Portuguese and the French over the 260 years since. Several attempts at colonizing the island had met with little success by either country, for one reason or another. Hostile Malagasy natives and a steaming climate that proved inhospitable to the Europeans, the bloody flux, other diseases and numerous typhoons had defeated even the hardiest colonist. Many had simply given up and sought passage on the swiftest vessel homeward bound, thankful they had escaped alive. Now Madagascar had little more to offer than a few trading posts, run by men of dubious character and uncertain origins, where passing vessels en route to India might put in to trade for provisions.

Ile Ste. Marie, the tiny island that lay across a narrow channel off the northeast coast of Madagascar, had also formerly been an offshore trading post, manned by the French, who claimed sovereignty over her. Unfortunately, no one had informed the Malagasy Merina tribe that they were now citizens of *la belle France!* They rose up and massacred the French settlers to a man. Now the island had reverted back to the natives, in effect if not in fact, and the ravaging wolves of the sea, the pirates, who made the isle their lair.

"Ile Ste. Marie," Jonathan gestured, inhaling the silky tradewinds that wafted across the *Scorpion*'s bow, "St. Mary's Island, my love. A veritable heaven on Earth! Fish and turtles, bananas and coconuts, honey and beef and chicken will all grace our board here. We shall live like Solomon and Bathsheba, little Chris, and never want for aught." He put his arm about her shoulders and drew her to him.

Grudgingly, she saw that Flynn's description of the island was not exaggerated. It was enriched by the glittering sapphire-blue of the Indian Ocean that lapped lazily at shores of dazzling white sand. Groves of verdant palms with feathery fronds scraping the cobalt-blue sky fronted a lush, jungle-like wall of vegetation. It seemed a fairy tale isle, she fancied with a sudden rush of pleasure and anticipation, though she would reserve her judgment until she had seen Jonathan's land of milk and honey first-hand. She forced her attention back to him. He was still talking on and on with a look of boyish excitement on his face, and she thought with a little shiver that he bore little resemblance to the ruthless murderer who had hurled a dagger into an unarmed man's chest with less compunction than squashing a beetle.

"—All that we lack can be traded for from the natives, you see, me darlin'—or stolen from passing ships!" He grinned evilly. "We are in constant need of powder and shot and liquor for the men. Your Captain Mallory's fine cargo will replenish our stores admirably."

"The *Fair Amanda?* But how?" she queried, her brows drawn together in a frown. "Did we not leave her behind nigh a month ago?"

Jonathan chuckled nastily. He turned from her, leaning against the ship's rail His obsidian-black eyes danced with wicked anticipation. "Aye, t' be sure we did. But I am certain, knowing much of the noble Captain Mallory's character, that he will even now be pursuing us here—both to avenge the death of his two men, and the stealing of the woman that he lusted for! And the *Scorpion*'s crew will be ready for him, aye, and with a sting in its tail!"

Christianne said nothing, uncertain of what, exactly, she felt about this new revelation. She had as much desire to set eyes on an undoubtedly livid James again as she did to stay here, with the murdering Flynn and his crew!

"I see," she murmured, deciding the safest course was for her to steer their conversation in a safer direction, "and that land beyond St. Mary's—what is that?"

"Madagascar," Jonathan supplied readily. "An island of great beauty and plenty, and of stark wastes and towering escarpments combined, whose natives are of murderous inclinations. The brown-skinned Merina men and women of my island have more temperate dispositions." He turned from her. "Lower the boats! Lower away, lads! Your women are waiting, and I'll warrant their blood runs hot!"

Hoots and whistles from the *Scorpion*'s crew echoed his wager.

Jonathan turned back to Christianne. "Their women are dark-skinned harlots, every one of them," he sneered. "They will envy me my lovely, virtuous Chris! Come on!"

Not long after, they were standing on the shore with the powdery white sand hot beneath her feet. The crew of the *Scorpion* were bringing ashore their belongings in the longboats, and the beach was a hive of activity.

Black-skinned men wearing only loincloths, their women bare-breasted save for colorful silk shawls and sarongs knotted about their hips, crowded forward to inspect the newcomer, to greet the returning crew and to help with the unloading.

Christianne, despite her trepidation, gazed upon everything with avid interest. Truly, Jonathan had not lied nor exaggerated when he had described his island as beautiful! If anything, his glowing descriptions had fallen short of the breathtaking loveliness all about her. City-born and London-bred, the lush foliage and brilliant colors of the scenery were dazzling to eyes used to the pastel prettiness of the English countryside and the drab hues of London. Here it was as if an artist had determined to paint a landscape using only the raw primary colors: red, yellow, blue. Even the shadows were sharply cast by the blazing sun, the fronded coconut palms forming an inky fretwork on the pale, powdery sand, like the carved fretwork of an eastern temple. Gaudy butterflies flitted aimlessly about in the balmy air, airborne exotic blossoms. Hermit crabs scuttled fearlessly over her feet.

In back of the thick grove of curved-trunked palms lay a heavy wall of foliage, a jungle of great, fan-shaped palms, liana vines and tamarind trees. It was toward the jungle that Jonathan headed, motioning two men to follow him. They were Pierre Le Chat and Stephen Tancred, who had also been aboard the *Fair Amanda*. Christianne had no liking for either of them. Though Stephen was an attractive enough young fellow, there was something in his eyes that sent a shiver of distaste down her spine. Le Chat was a sly piece of work who moved as light-footedly as any feline she had ever chanced to meet, whose habit it was to come up upon one soundlessly and smile when you jumped in surprise. Aye, Flynn and his cohorts were as well-matched as triplets. All men carried muskets slung over their shoulders.

They moved in single file along a narrow path cut through the vegetation, weaving in and out, twisting back and forth in a fashion that was bewildering. Ox led the way, then Tancred, Jonathan, and herself with Le Chat bringing up the rear. Christianne, still weakened by her illness, soon found herself exhausted and longed to rest. The steaming heat of the jungle was draining. Just when it seemed she would drop with weariness, they came out into a clearing. A wide, blue lagoon gleamed in the brilliant sunshine. Rectangular huts of a native appearance were dotted beneath the trees and several coffee-colored half-caste children stood wide-eyed and grubby there and watched the little party approach.

Christianne shaded her eyes and looked across the lagoon. Another small islet lay in its center like the pearl within an oyster, completely encircled by water. The white walls of what appeared to be a small fortress rose above the treetops.

"There!" Jonathan pronounced proudly. "Did I not tell you that my island within an island was a paradise? My men, for the most part, live here about the lagoon with their native women. But you, my queen, shall have your own kingdom, your castle and your king." He smiled. "There was a man named Misson, it is said, whose dream it was to found a new republic at the Bay of Diégo Suarez on the island of Madagascar. His ideal was that there all men might be free and equal and live in democratic peace. He called it Libertalia. But the natives did not share his doctrines and attacked the colonists. His Libertalia failed—but mine shall not," he vowed hotly. "My brother Michael and myself spent many months laying the foundation of our republic. Now he is gone, killed by the British, but I shall carry on alone." He paused, smiling. His words had a lofty, noble ring that pleased him. He could almost see himself as that founder, puffed up with noble visions!

Christianne mistook the wicked gleam in his eyes to be one of a fanatic. "And you will found your new . . . Libertalia on the spoils of bloodshed and piracy?" she asked mockingly. "Nay, Captain Flynn, there is no true liberty when it is founded on such an economy as yours." Her vehement tone surprised even herself, but appeared to faze Jonathan not a whit.

"When men are denied the right to earn an honest wage by honest means, they still must live, my soft-hearted girl," he said blithely, leading the way to a ramshackle landing where a raft of lashed poles was moored.

Christianne said nothing, for what he had said, in essence, was true. Had she not been forced to live outside the law herself in order to survive?

Ox poled the five of them across the lagoon, where several gray-green, lichened logs lay half-submerged. Yet as Christianne idly watched those logs, one of them opened a cavernous mouth and threshed a mighty tail, whipping the still water to white foam. She shrieked and stepped quickly backward, rocking the raft dangerously.

Jonathan smiled at her fear. "Careful, my lady," he rebuked mildly. "I have no wish to feed the crocodiles— have you?"

She shook her head, all blood drained from her face. What other manner of dangers might lurk in this savage place?

As they neared the tiny islet, Christianne saw that the fortress was little more than a ruin in places but that for the most part it appeared undamaged. The raft secured to yet another wooden jetty, the party started up the sloping, sandy banks that gave way to hardy grass underfoot as they neared the fortress. Chickens fluttered and clucked and flapped frantically back under the archway of smooth blocks of bleached stone to sanctuary. The five followed beneath the arch in their wake.

Christianne's mouth dropped open in astonishment. The pirates' lair she had expected had been a foul rats' nest, devoid of all comforts and offering only the barest necessities for survival. Believing none of Flynn's boasts, she had steeled herself to endure the privations she had known before James' entrance into her life. Yet it appeared not only likely but highly probable she would be in quite comfortable surroundings as he had promised.

A square, stone-flagged courtyard opened up around them. A cookhouse of adobe was tucked in one corner of it.

Several arched doorways led off a covered walkway. Stone stairs reached to the upper story where again many doorways led off a long balcony that encircled the second floor and was bordered with ornate wrought-iron work. More stone steps led from this floor to ramparts that were level with the red-tiled rooves. There the fact that this was a fortress and no stately villa was forcefully brought home, for several fat-bellied cannons poked their squat, black snouts out through apertures in the white stone walls.

She sucked in a breath. If James did indeed come after them, as Jonathan anticipated, he would find this little island virtually impregnable. Surrounded by the lagoon, defended by cannon, then shielded all about by the jungle of St. Mary's proper, and then the Indian Ocean about that—it would withstand all onslaughts, save a lengthy siege. An "island within an island" indeed, as Jonathan had said.

He swaggered up to the heavy, oaken main door that stood open. He raised his hand with a proud flourish, his black eyes shining. "Queen Christianne, your castle!" he declared loudly, making a sweeping gesture at the fortress. "Is it not magnificent? I call it Paradise. It is the corner-stone of a new way of life, for all of us here on Ile Ste. Marie. It is the heart of our republic, a republic that will know no class, no nationality, no religion. Where all will live as one!"

"Then how may you set yourself up as king, Captain Flynn?" Christianne asked pointedly.

His broad smile changed to a scowl. "Until my new way of life is established, the people will need a leader. As I captain the *Scorpion* so shall I rule here, with you at my side. Our children will be born here, in freedom. Come!"

It was her turn to scowl now, but she made no comment. She followed Jonathan as he swaggered beneath the imposing arched entrance into an equally impressive hallway tiled with squares of black and white marble. Wrought-iron sconces hung on the walls. Jonathan beckoned to her to follow him. The other three men he waved away, ordering them to find someone called Isabella and see about a meal for himself and Christianne.

"I will show you your chamber shortly, me darlin'," he promised, "but first I have a little surprise for you." He withdrew an iron ring from his belt, from which suspended several large keys. Selecting one, he fitted it into the lock of a low door at the farthest end of the entrance hall. Taking her hand, he drew her after him down a short flight of spiral steps cut from stone. The air was much cooler as they went down beneath the fortress and smelled of damp. A weighty door lay opposite the foot of the stairs. He opened this, too, and stood aside to allow her to enter before him.

Christianne gasped, bedazzled as she stepped inside the small chamber. She had wondered if sly Jonathan had intended to imprison her here in the bowels of his fortress, but though the narrow, heavily-barred window confirmed that the room had, at some point, served as a cell, it now appeared to be a treasure trove!

Chests and caskets ranged against the walls, their lids open. Gold and silver coins, candlesticks, goblets, bowls and crucifixes spilled from their depths. Necklaces and bracelets were strewn on the cold stone floor, aglitter with the fire of priceless rubies, emeralds, diamonds and sapphires, and the creamy luster of pearls. Exquisite bolts of shimmering satins and silks, lengths of velvet and lace, jewelled swords and silver-stamped Arabian saddles were heaped carelessly in the corners. The array was dazzling and left her speechless and open-mouthed! It was a thieves' dream come true, she thought dazedly. But how many men had paid with their lives to fill the pirates' coffers? A great many, judging by the enormous size of the booty. In all her years of cutpursing no man or woman had ever died because of her thievery. It seemed suddenly as if she could smell the copper stink of blood on these riches, the stink of death.

She shivered. She felt no avarice in this room, no urge to fill her pockets or toss handfuls of coins over her head like so many autumn leaves. How strange it was to find oneself suddenly confronted by the stuff of dreams and to learn you had no desire for any of it. She was changed, she realized, from the girl who had blithely stolen James' cloak that wintry morn. That Christianne would have loaded herself to the gills with these baubles.

Jonathan noted her silence with a sly smile, mistaking her lack of comment for delight and disbelief.

"A king's ransom and more!" he crowed softly, his eyes, black as obsidian, flickering fondly over his treasures. He strode across to one of the caskets and withdrew a necklace of priceless sapphires, set in filigree gold like teardrops of deep blue on a dainty golden chain.

"For you, me darlin' girl," he breathed, holding them out to her. When she made no motion to accept them from him, he came to stand behind her and lifted the necklace over her head, fumbling with the clasp.

Christianne shook her head. Her hands went to her throat and grasped the necklace, intending to tear it from her neck. "No," she insisted, "I want no part of your riches. They are stained with blood."

She could not have chosen her words more foolishly, for his face contorted with anger. He knotted the necklace in his fists and pulled it tight about the slim column of her throat like a garrote.

"You *want*," he hissed. "If *I* say that you want, you *will* take it."

Her hands fluttered up to her throat. Tears of pain swam in her lovely eyes. "Yes, yes," she gasped, fighting for her breath, "it's . . . it's lovely, Jonathan. Th-thank you."

Abruptly, he released her and pressed his lips against her hair. "Aye, my lass," he murmured, "it is lovely, but not as lovely as you. I shall shower you with these jewels, clothe you in silks and satins befitting an empress." He pulled her into his arms and kissed her brow, then softly, full upon the lips. Her flesh crawled, but she forced herself to remain still until he had finished. He gazed adoringly into her face, toying with the wispy, spun silk of her hair, feasting his eyes on her delicately molded features. "My ice maiden Christianne, so slender, so very fair, I adore you!" he vowed. "We must be wed, and soon, else the desire to have you will overwhelm me. Aye, I do not trust myself with you. the sooner 'tis done, the better." He fingered the sapphires about her throat. "If you can be patient but a day or so, I will send some men to the Red Island, to Madagascar, and the trading post at Fénérive. There is a missionary priest there. I will have him brought here to perform our nuptials, then truly you will be my bride. Come, I will show you to your chamber and we shall find other clothing for you. These rags are not fitting for the queen of Paradise."

He strode from the room and Christianne followed, her thoughts in turmoil. As he locked the door behind them her fingers strayed to her throat, bruised from when he had pulled the necklace tight against it. She had not fought him, deeming it wiser to pretend compliance for the time being. Yet she had no desire to be his queen, especially the queen of his garden of Eden, in which he seemed more the serpent than Adam. She followed him up the spiral stairs.

The bedchamber that he led her into was sumptuously appointed. A massive poster bed, hung with crimson brocade embroidered in gold, dominated it. The floor was of cool, pink-veined marble, strewn with Persian rugs in vivid blues and reds, beiges and violets. The casements, which stretched from the high-beamed ceiling to the floor, opened out like doors onto a balcony of wrought iron after the Spanish design she remembered from Barcelona, and were hung with dark blue tasselled draperies. Beside one was a silk-covered divan, upon which were numerous fringed satin pillows. A sea chest with gilded designs of Neptune and mermaids, whales and sailing ships, and bound with fancy brass straps and brass studding, stood at the foot of the bed.

"This will be your chamber, until after we are wed," Jonathan declared. "The chest contains many gowns, from which you may choose whatsoever you desire. I shall send Isabella to assist you." He smirked and drew his finger along the line of his moustache. "Do not be alarmed if she should seem less than—how shall I put it?—amicable, towards you. It was her hope, you see, me darlin', to become my wife. That foolish trollop!" he laughed derisively, "whoever heard of a harlot for a queen?" He blew her a tender kiss and closed the door softly behind him, leaving Christianne alone.

Nineteen

James lifted the spyglass to his eyes and scanned the glittering Indian Ocean. A fresh breeze ruffled his reddish hair and flapped the full sleeves of his white silk shirt. When he lowered the glass, his green eyes were lit with excitement. The lust for revenge sent his blood racing, by God!

"Sail ho!" he roared. "Mullens!"

The new first officer raced across the decks. "A sail, Cap'n? Where away, sir?" he cried.

"Here, see for yourself," James offered, handing him the glass.

The man lifted it to his single remaining eye. "Aye, sir, 'tis canvas indeed," he agreed. "Due north and shifting her bows right smartly, by the looks of it. She's headed for the island, sir, I'd wager, not Madagascar but St. Mary's, the little 'un."

"St. Mary's—you know it?" James asked eagerly, grasping the varnished taffrail.

"Nay, sir, only of it. I ain't never bin there."

"A pity," James murmured with a frown. "We'll need provisions before long. Which would be the closest of the trading posts you mentioned on Madagascar?"

"I reckon Fénérive, sir. Seems I recollect there was a

trading post or two right across the channel from St. Mary's, an' a mission an' all, but 'tis all very primitive, sir."

"Then Fénérive it is. Open a cask and give each man a double measure of rum. They've earned it these past three weeks, by God! There were times, Mister Mullens, when I feared we were chasing a mirage!" The captain grinned. "We'll maintain our present distance from them. I don't plan to come any closer to them than we are right now. We'll hang back just long enough to be certain of their destination, then head for this trading post you spoke of for provisions, before going after her."

"Aye, sir," Mullens nodded, winking his single eye merrily over James' shoulder. "Good day, Mistress Lucy."

"Morning, Mister Mullens, sir," Lucy sang out, giving Mullens a cheeky smile, which he returned.

James grinned and lifted Lucy's hand and kissed it.

In the past three weeks, Lucy Waller had recovered her blooming health and vitality and seemed harmed not a whit by her several weeks of deprivation as a stowaway, other than having lost several pounds off her once delightfully voluptuous figure. With her tenacious spirit and her merry, oft bawdy wit, she put him in mind of Nell Flagg, be damned if she didn't!

Lucy, on feeling stronger, had explained tearfully to James how she had decided she loved him and determined to follow him to the ends of the Earth, if needs be, hence her decision to stowaway. But by the time they had rounded the cape, hunger had reared its ravenous head, and Mistress Lucy had decided that no man, not even her handsome Captain Jamie, was worth the misery she was enduring. Accordingly she had opted to throw herself on James' mercy.

"But then, Jamie, love," she had said, her saucy blue eyes unusually solemn, "I heard a bunch o' the sailors awhisperin' in secret, like. I was afrightened they'd find little Lucy, and so I snucked back to the bulkhead an' waited." She paused dramatically.

"And what was it you heard?" James asked curiously.

Lucy Waller had pushed herself up into her elbows. "I heard," she said darkly, "them sailors plannin' for to take this ship, and one o' them — Flynn, they called him — were all set to be her master in your stead, Jamie love. 'Mutiny!' says I. ' 'Tis mutiny they do be after plannin'!' But then me head started in ter spinnin', and me knees they were wobbling like calve's-foot jelly, and then ev'rything started spinnin' like a bloomin' whippin' top. The next thing I knowed, I was here in Mister Wright's bunk, and there was Mister Wright himself, ministering ter me like me own bloomin' guardian angel, he was, bless his heart."

James had nodded. Flynn. Had she meant Flint? For some reason, the name Flynn struck a bell in his memory, but he was damned if he could recall where he had heard it before.

"And how is Ben this morning?" James asked, coming back to the present. Concern was written on his face.

"He seems ter be mending, Jamie, but slower than what I'd like. The fever ain't abated none, neither. Hotter than Hades, he is, mumblin' and talking on something terrible."

James nodded grimly, and Lucy thought she caught the glint of a tear in his eye, though true men didn't shed tears, as well she knew, so of course it could not be, since Jamie was all man.

"He'll weather it out, Cap'n," Mullens said gruffly, clapping his hand over his captain's shoulder. "You'll see, our Ben'll pull through. These Cornish lads are a hardy breed an' it'll take more than the likes of a blade to send him to Davy Jones' locker, I'd wager me liberty pay on it!" He grinned. "And what man 'ud do something as daft as dying with a lovely lass like Mistress Lucy here t' tend him? A veritable sister o' mercy she is, and as pretty a one as I ever did see!"

Lucy blushed. "Get on with ye, Mister Mullens! Your flattery is making me all flummoxed, it is." She sniffed primly. "Besides, caring for Mister Wright is the least I could do, seeing as how he cared for me in my sickness, or so Jamie said."

"Indeed he did, Lucy," James confirmed solemnly. "He tended you with the devotion of a father."

"Ha! I reckon it were more than that!" Lucy said with a toss of her fiery locks. "Me own pa would have turned me out at first sign o' sickness, if'n it were bad enough that I weren't able to work no more." She scowled. "Proper hard, he was, and no mistake!"

Mullens tutted. "Now what father would treat his lovely daughter like that? Shame on ye, Mistress Lucy, for saying such a thing. 'Turn ye out,' indeed!"

Lucy sniffed again. "Nevertheless, that's how he were, when he weren't after trying t' tumble me. Not me natural pa, he weren't, see. Nor was me mother, neither, though she were a good and loving soul, unlike Tom Waller. Nay, I were a foundling babe, left on the steps o' the tavern some eighteen years ago. The Wallers took me in an' fer that I'm grateful, seeing as how there's many what wouldn't have taken ter having an extra mouth t' feed."

James and Mullens nodded sagely and Mullens patted Lucy's shoulder in a fatherly fashion. "Well, now, 'tis a new life you'll be after having in New Orleans, lass, so put the past where it belongs, behind ye, an' look to the future. I'll be seeing to the grog for the men, sir," he finished, turning to James. The captain nodded and he left.

"Well," Lucy said brightly, "I've had my breath o' fresh air, and now I'll be off t' tend Master Wright. Good

251

mornin', Jamie, love."

"Good morning, Lucy. And my thanks to you. I don't know what we would have done without you." He smiled at her affectionately.

She nudged the captain with her elbow and grinned.

"Think nothing of it, ducks. I'm just awful pleased ye didn't toss me overboard when ye found me!" With a merry laugh she strolled jauntily away from him.

They dropped anchor off Fénérive late that afternoon. As Mullens had thought, the other vessel they had sighted had headed for Ile Ste. Marie, St. Mary's Island, as straight as an arrow. It was decided by James to attempt provisioning the ship first at the trading post, and then to go after Flint or Flynn or whatever his name might be.

Longboats were lowered, James and Mullens in one and a few trusted crew members in the other. The remaining space was crammed with goods to barter for provisions.

Lucy had not argued when James had told her she must stay aboard the *Fair Amanda,* both to care for Ben and for her own safety, in the event the Malagasy natives should prove hostile, as they had many times in the past according to Mullens' story.

They beached the boats and started up the sloping beaches in the direction of several log-hewn cabins, enclosed by a wooden stockade, beneath the trees. All ten men kept their hands lightly on either their muskets or pistols, or on the hilt of a dagger or cutlass, for it was possible their reception at the trading village might be less than friendly.

A bearded giant of a man came out to welcome them, flanked by several dark-skinned natives with woolly black hair, worn full like a bush about their heads. They were clad only in *salakas,* loincloths, and each carried a wicked-looking spear in his hand. Beads of a blood-red color decorated their oiled black chests.

"Greetings, friend," James said, extending his hand to the bearded man. "We've come ashore to purchase provisions, if you have them. I'm Capt. James Mallory of the *Fair Amanda* you see anchored beyond the reef, out of New Orleans by way of London Town."

The man pumped his hand vigorously and grinned.

"Greetings to you, Captain Mallory. You've come to the right place, sir. This strip of land 'twixt here and the Bay of Antongil is the richest there is for trading and the like — the envy of our less fortunate neighbors, we are. And Fénérive is the most affluent of all the coastal villages. New Orleans, you said? Ah, lad, you've come a fair few miles of ocean, Captain! Where are you bound?"

"Home, sir, by way of the Caribbees, after I conclude a certain matter in these parts to my satisfaction. And your name, sir?"

"Your pardon, sir," the man apologized. "Nicholas Drew's my name, I run the trading post here. Bety, take the captain's coat! You, Rahena, see to the captain's officers. Ah, 'tis a climate that saps one's strength, is it not, Captain?" He murmured some strange words in the native tongue and gestured to the longboats drawn up on the beach. "The Malagasy lads will bring up your goods and we'll discuss your provisions. But first, you'll refresh yourself, I trust? We have food aplenty in Fénérive." He laughed. "Though there's times I'd give it all and my soul with it for a pipe o' 'baccy."

James grinned as Drew rolled his eyes woefully. "Consider it given, then, Master Drew!" He withdrew a pouch of tobacco from his shirt and his own pipe. "We'll smoke a pipe together first and discuss our trade later."

Drew fairly beamed. He clapped James across the back in a comradely fashion. "I like the cut of your jib, Jim, lad, indeed sir!"

Some two hours later, James leaned back and surveyed the trader thoughtfully. " 'Twas a fine meal, Nick," he declared. "My thanks, both for myself and my men."

Drew nodded and sucked on his pipe. "And thank you, Jim. 'Tis the finest 'baccy I ever drew breath on. From Virginia, you say?"

"Aye," James nodded. He looked across the crackling fire at the circle of his men gathered about it, seated on mats strewn on the bare earth. They appeared relaxed, but none had imbibed too freely of the trader's liquor, as he had instructed prior to leaving the *Amanda*. There was not a man among them drunk. He grunted with satisfaction.

Mullens had warned him the night previous that the majority of traders in these parts were but a shade more honest than the pirates, and that some were in fact pirates as well. It would be best, he'd advised, to take a cautious stand if they intended to leave with both their lives and their provisions—and without being pressed themselves into the pirates' ranks, as pirates were wont to press innocent seamen. At the first sign of trouble, James had instructed Matthew Locke, into whose hands he had given the command of the *Amanda* in his absence, they would fire three shots in rapid succession. On hearing this signal Matthew was not to attempt to rescue the landing party but to set sail and proceed on to the Caribbees without a backward glance. Matthew Locke had solemnly promised to do so.

Nicholas Drew had done them proud for victuals. Fresh sides of beef, succulently roasted on wooden spits, yams, chicken, rice and coconuts had all been set before them by Bety and Rahena, Drew's women, who had been named after Malagasy princesses, he had said with a grin. Both women were beautiful, an exotic combination of the Asian and the Moor in their broad features, with liquid dark eyes and full, sensual lips. James had politely refused one of the dusky, bare-breasted beauties to share his sleeping mat that night, pleading fatigue and a slow recovery from a bout with the flux as his reasons for refusing, both of which were, of course, lies. Nay, he would not carouse and wench this night. He intended to keep a surreptitious watch on both his men and their trading goods: six head of fine, healthy cattle; several wicker coops each of twenty chickens; ten sacks of rice; ten baskets of coconuts; barrels of palm oil and salt. In return he had given Drew a barrel of cannon powder, precious ship's stores such as flour, lanterns, buckets, breeches and shirts and a few carpenter's tools, five barrels of rum, two quarter-casks of fine Madeira and a chamber pot. All in all, not a poor trade, James thought with satisfaction as he tapped out the bole of his pipe against the hard-packed red earth.

The coastal village consisted of a wooden fort and several artisans' buildings scattered about it where Drew kept his trader's goods and where his men lived and worked. There was also a rough, wooden mission run by a Father Luis Quintana and his assistant, Father Pedro Cardenas, both Portuguese. These two pious souls came at length to the gathering to pay their respects to the newcomers, or so it appeared at first.

"Good evening, my sons," Father Luis said in nasal, heavily-accented Portuguese-English. He benevolently motioned his index finger over the seated gathering in the sign of the cross. The men all muttered and fidgeted uncomfortably after the priest's blessing, which effectively dampened their festive spirits.

Drew greeted them blithely. "Good evening to you, too, Father Luis, Father Pedro. Will you sup with us, or share a mug of the Madeira that the good captain has brought to our heathen land?" He grinned at James and winked slyly.

Father Luis shuddered delicately. "As you are well aware, Master Drew, we will not imbibe your devil's brew. We came but to seek your assistance. It appears we must travel to St. Mary's, for Capt. Jonathan Flynn of the *Red Scorpion* has happily decided to take a wife. We are to perform the holy service of matrimony, that he and his bride may be joined according to God's law."

James all but choked on his Madeira.

"Indeed, Father? And how might I be of service?" Nicholas Drew asked congenially.

"Provisions for the journey will be needed, of course, and native porters to carry them," Father Luis said.

Drew nodded. "I'll see to it, Father, never fear. When do you leave for the island?"

"On the morrow, at dawn. The good captain has sent two of his crew to escort us."

"And where are these men of his?" Drew asked innocently. "Bid them join us and sup."

Father Luis scowled and slipped his hands into the sleeves of his dark, cowled priests' robes. "They have each taken a native woman into the jungle, Drew, as well you know, to indulge in fornication and strong liquor this night." With pious disapproval his dark, beady eyes swept over the gathering. "Evils that I trust you will not permit our guests to fall prey to, Master Drew?"

"Indeed not, Father!" Drew grinned and slipped an arm around Bety and Rahena's shoulders, blatantly fondling their dark-nippled breasts. "As you know, I myself would never indulge in such depraved and lecherous doings!"

The crew of the *Amanda* laughed bawdily.

Father Luis snorted his disdain and cast a frosty eye on Drew. "I shall expect the provisions and porters outside the stockade at first light, Master Drew," he said coldly, and started off toward the mission with Father Pedro faithfully dogging his footsteps.

"Aye, aye, Father!" Drew called after him. "Have a lustful night with little Marta meanwhile!" He quaffed his Madeira, wiping his beard on his sleeve. "Hypocritical, pious old bastard!" he snorted. "He preaches chastity and continence to myself and my men, but I wager he has tumbled more native wenches than I've had mugs o' ale in my life. This Marta is a Malagasy wench, barely twelve summers old, whom he professes to give 'religious instruction' of an even'." He nudged James and winked lecherously. "But I wager 'tis something firmer than a Bible tract he is after slipping her—especially since her belly's swelled up like a pig's bladder!" He roared with laughter and gave Rahena and Bety a bear hug and a smacking kiss.

James laughed too. "No doubt you're right, Nick," he agreed. "But this—what was his name—Jonathan Flynn, who is he?" he asked innocently.

Rubbing his beard, Drew laughed. "He is captain of the *Red Scorpion* and as two-faced as Janus. He and his men fancy they'll build a new republic on the island, where all will live in harmony and justice, or some such rot. He calls his islet in the lagoon Paradise, and has set himself up in an abandoned fortress there." He frowned. "This news of his wedding is fresh to my ears, though. He's lived with a comely Spanish wench by the name of Isabella for months. The tale has it that he raided the colonist ship she were on and carried her off for his own. He said he'd make her the queen of his paradise," Drew snorted, "but when he found she had already lost her maidenhead, he made her his *puta*. When he tired of her he handed her over to his men. A strange fellow, is Captain Flynn. Had a brother, he did, name of Michael. Seems he disappeared one night and ain't been seen since."

James grunted noncommittally, well aware of Mullens' excitement at his side as he hid his own. He had a plan to regain the treacherous Christianne, and to settle the score of his dead crew member and ailing Ben Wright simultaneously. Was it she, he wondered, whom Flynn planned to make his bride? He smiled grimly. In the leaping flames of the fire his green eyes glittered. She'd be a widow before she was ever his wife, damn her soul, he vowed!

Twenty

Christianne paced restlessly back and forth across the pink-veined marble floor of her opulent prison, twisting the necklaces of cornelian beads and the one of sapphires about her fingers in her distraction.

I'faith, this was a fine mess she was in! And how to get out of it? She cursed under her breath, picked up a silken pillow from the divan and hurled it across the chamber. She had as much desire to marry Flynn as she did to dangle from the hangman's noose at Tyburn flats!

She paused by the floor-to-ceiling casements, lifted the latch and stepped out onto the little balcony. If she tried to escape that way, there was nothing to break her fall, and nothing to climb down but solid stone, she realized with a heavy sigh. She turned back inside the room, her eyes widening as she saw a young woman standing there in the now-opened doorway, her hands on her hips and hatred flashing in her dark eyes.

The young woman wore her blue-black glossy hair parted in the center and falling over one shoulder in a heavy swath. Her peasant blouse was of a rough woven cloth in its natural hue and exposed her tanned shoulders above several rows of colorful embroidery. Her skirts were full and of swirling colors and reached to her bare feet, where silver anklets clinked as she advanced on Christianne, hips swaying insolently.

"So!" she spat. "You are the English *puta* Jonathan has chosen for his new bride!" She laughed throatily.

The sound put Christianne in mind of the low snarl of a cat about to spring. She put her own hands on her hips, angry color staining the pale gold of her cheeks. The Spanish insult needed no translation. Its meaning was obvious.

"And who the devil might you be?" she demanded, her stance as aggressive as the other woman's. She tossed back her pale mane and glared at her fiercely.

The girl swept her a deep, mocking curtsy, spreading her colorful skirts and inclining her head. "I am Isabella — first queen of *Capitán* Flynn's Paradise," she hissed. "Look upon me senorita, and see yourself when he has finished with you — if you last that long, with your puny little body!"

She came across the chamber and stopped directly in front of her.

"I have no wish to replace you, Isabella," Christianne said quietly.

"Liar!" Isabella spat. Her hand snaked out and knotted in Christianne's hair. The second followed. She fiercely tried to grapple the smaller woman to the floor by her hair.

Christianne, with years of a street urchin's wiles and dubious skills at her disposal, instantly retaliated. She stomped down hard on the arches of the girl's feet, following it with a sharp crack across the shins.

Isabella hurriedly released her hair, tears of pain springing into her dark eyes. *"Puta!"* she shrieked.

"Slut!" Christianne countered. She sprang back as the girl reached to her waist and withdrew a wicked-looking dagger.

Isabella brandished it in one hand, the other outstretched for balance. She smiled in triumph as she sidled towards Christianne. "It is good that you are afraid, *chica,*" she purred, "for I shall kill you, I swear it! Jonathan will have no woman but me, Isabella!" She lunged suddenly and the knife flashed in the air.

Christianne ducked and twisted sideways. Both women were panting heavily when they faced each other again. When Isabella again advanced, she retreated, casting about her for a weapon or defense of some kind. She wetted her lips. The divan was at her back now. A smile flitted across her face.

She beckoned. "Come on then, Isabella, come on!" she taunted. "If you mean to kill me, come on!"

The girl did not move, yet her eyes still glittered with hatred. Her hair had come free of its ribbon and jet-black streamers tumbled all about her shoulders. Her breasts heaved with pent-up fury.

"Spanish *puta!*" Christianne goaded. "Little wonder Jonathan cast you aside—you are as ugly as a witch, a black-haired hag!"

With a shriek of fury, Isabella leaped at her. She stepped nimbly aside and the girl toppled forwards across the divan. Christianne dived on her, one knee in her back, the other on the wrist that held the dagger, plunged into one of the silken pillows. She wrested it from Isabella's grip. Feathers flew everywhere from the rent in the pillow.

Isabella writhed and squirmed but could not unseat the English girl. Christianne hurled the dagger safely away across the room, forcing Isabella's face down into the silken divan. "Now, listen, you scurvy she-cat," she panted hoarsely, "I've no liking for your damned Jonathan, nor for being his queen, do you hear me?"

Isabella howled with frustrated rage, the sound muffled in the silken coverlet of the divan. Her legs thrashed wildly.

Christianne muttered an oath. She knotted Isabella's black mane in her small fist and ground the girl's face into the divan once more. "I said, do ye hear me?"

"Let me up!" the Spanish girl hissed when Christianne gave her breathing space at length.

"Nay!" she retorted hotly, grinding her knee into the young woman's back. "Not 'til you ask for quarter I'll not let you up!"

"I'll ask no mercy of you, *inglesa*," Isabella swore, still wriggling.

"Then you'll stay where you are," Christianne said firmly, "and listen! The ship that I was on sailed out of London Town. Her captain—*lie still!*—her captain was my . . . my guardian, of sorts. He was to take me to the New World to live with my aunt. I hated him, and I did not want to go with him, and so when Jonathan told me his plans to jump ship, and threatened that if I did not come with him he would kill her crew, I felt I had little to lose by joining him. I thought I could somehow get back to England, you see, but it appears Flynn had other ideas. He says he will make me his bride, that our sons will be born here, on Paradise. If you would prevent that, we must be allies, not enemies, don't you see? Perhaps, señorita, if we combine forces, we can do something. I swear by all that is holy, and on the grave of my mother, that I want no part of Flynn's plans—nor of him! Isabella?"

The Spanish girl lay very still. Christianne wondered fleetingly if she had rendered her senseless, but quickly dismissed the notion. Isabella was either catching her wind, she decided, or feigning unconsciousness—and she could wait just as long as Isabella could. Several tense minutes passed. Finally Isabella craned her head to one side.

"You do not lie, *inglesa?*" she gritted through clenched teeth.

"Nay, I do not," Christianne confirmed.

"And you do not love Jonathan?"

Christianne snorted. "No, I do not!" she cried. "You may have him, Isabella, aye, and gladly!"

Several more minutes passed. Her back was beginning to ache from her uncomfortable position when Isabella sighed heavily.

"Very well. Let me up," she said in a calmer voice. "We will talk, yes?"

"No tricks?"

"No, no tricks. I, too, give my word."

Christianne nodded and stood up. She did so warily, unconvinced as yet that the girl's word was good.

Isabella sat up, rubbing her bruised wrist and her aching back and casting a reproachful eye on Christianne.

"You fight well, *inglesa*," she said with grudging admiration.

"In the past I've had to, many times," Christianne confessed ruefully.

Isabella nodded, her lips still set in a sulky pout. She tossed her dark hair over her shoulder with a defiant flick of her head. "So, what now, eh? You have said you will not become Flynn's wife, but he is determined you shall. He has even sent two of his men to Fénérive, to bring the priest here to perform the ceremony. They left immediately."

"Mmm." Christianne scowled. "Is there no way off this damnable island without the captain's say-so—no regular packet ship I might beg passage on that puts in here?"

"None. If there were, I would have done so many months ago." She sighed. "But now I must stay here, come what may, because of the little one."

"Little one?"

"Si. I am with child. Jonathan's child, though he will not acknowledge the child as his own flesh and blood," Isabella explained bitterly. "You see, there were six of us girls, all orphans, sent here from Madrid a year ago, to marry the men of a new Spanish colony on the big island of Madagascar that you see from your window. The *Red Scorpion* and Captain Wilhelm's ship, the *Voyager*, attacked our poor vessel and overran it. What they did to my five companions is beyond description, senorita, though I am sure you can imagine. But I, Isabella, felt myself luckier than the rest, for *el Capitán* Flynn seemed very taken with me. He—he said he thought me beautiful and vowed he would marry me when he carried me to his bunk aboard his ship. There he—he quickly learned that I did not come to him chaste. He took me many times that night, called me his queen and promised me this island as my kingdom. Yet when he tired of me after a few months, it was a different story. I could never be his bride, he told me cruelly, for I was nothing but a *puta* who had sold herself to many men before him. It was a lie! He refused to listen to my pleas, and gave me to his men. By then, I knew I carried his child. So you see, he must marry *me*, to give the child his rightful name. I will never leave here until he acknowledges that the child I carry is his!" She sighed. "He was kind, at first, as he is to you. When he held me in his arms then, he could convince me that I was his sun, his moon and his stars combined!"

Christianne said nothing. She could well imagine Jonathan plying the girl with his pretty compliments and softly-murmured endearments, both of which she had been gullible enough to fall prey to on the *Fair Amanda*, the silver-tongued wretch!

"When do you expect his men to return with the priest?" she asked.

"In four, mayhap five, days, at the most."

"Then we have that much time to come up with a means

of escape," Christianne said thoughtfully. "Until then, we must appear to go along with his plans and his grand notions, think you not?"

"Si. But in that case, you must get dressed! He sent me to help you, *inglesa*, and to bring you down to sup with him. Come, we must hurry! I will fetch you water to bathe, and then we must choose you a gown. Get out of your dirty clothes, quickly!" Isabella darted out of the chamber, her silver ankle bracelets tinkling as she went. She returned minutes later with a pitcher and basin of warm water.

Christianne peeled off her stained rags, and quickly made her toilette. Afterward, Isabella led her to the sea chest at the foot of the poster bed and flung up the lid. Christianne crouched at her side. Vivid silks and satins, brocades and velvets gleamed within it, all women's garments and all of varying styles and sizes. Pirate booty, she realized, like the treasure.

The Spanish girl rummaged among them, finally pulling out a gown of shimmering sky-blue satin with billowing skirts and a low, lace-trimmed neckline. The sleeves ended in deep, pleated flounces just below the elbows.

"Here, put it on," Isabella urged. "I know it will fit, for once I wore all of these, and this was a little too tight for me." She smiled impishly, and Christianne realized for the first time that the girl was very pretty indeed, without hostility souring her features.

She slipped the gown over her head. The cool satin felt like the brush of a hand down her body as its folds billowed about her, and for a fleeting second she was sharply reminded of James. The cloth had felt as sensual as his caress upon her bared flesh. She smoothed down the skirts with an angry gesture. La! What was this madness she was thinking? She turned and waited while Isabella fastened the numerous hooks at the back of the gown.

"Well, how do I look?" she asked nervously, turning to face the Spanish girl.

Isabella scrutinized her up and down and turned her this way and that. "If I did not trust you," she said at length, "I would tear out your eyes, you are so beautiful!" She pouted.

"Just remember, I am doing this for both of us, and for your child. I have no wish to please Jonathan, believe me, however it may appear, only to lull him into trusting me," Christianne reminded her.

"I do believe you," Isabella said. "Hurry now, follow me."

She followed the Spanish girl down the stairs and through the large entrance hall she had seen before. They traversed a long corridor running off it with several closed doors on either side. Isabella stopped before polished double doors and rapped softly upon them.

"Enter," Jonathan commanded grandly from within.

Isabella squeezed Christianne's hand to reassure her. "Go on," she whispered conspiratorially, "I must see to the food. Go on—and *buen suerte,* good luck!"

Christianne nodded. She took a deep breath to calm herself and swept through the doors with a haughty carriage befitting the queen Jonathan wished her to be. She paused halfway across the room, partly for dramatics' sake and partly to assess her surroundings. The dining room was high-ceilinged, as the bedchamber had been, and also marble-floored. Twin crystal chandeliers hung from that ceiling. A long and highly-polished oak table dominated the room, set with silver candleabras and silver platters and goblets for two. The casements looked out onto a small courtyard and beyond was the wall that surrounded the fortress, a vine with pungent, white blooms trailing down it.

Jonathan rose gracefully to meet her and she muffled her surprise at the handsome figure he cut. In the past she had only seen him in the nondescript sailor's breeches and jersey, but today he wore a tail coat of black velvet and breeches to match. A vest of gray satin worked in elegant silver and black embroidery, and a white silk shirt that was heavily ruffled with lace at the collar and cuffs set off his lean body and sleek, dark good looks perfectly. But the effect was wasted on Christianne, who could cheerfully have torn his heart out. Each time she had looked at him since leaving the *Fair Amanda* she recalled the look of disbelief and horror on Ben Wright's face when the dagger had plunged into his belly, and her gorge rose up in her throat. She hid her disgust from him with a forced smile and languorously extended her hand to the pirate captain.

Jonathan kissed her hand dutifully. The admiration he held her in was evident in his shining black eyes.

"You are a vision, me darlin'," he purred silkily over her hand, "even more beautiful than you were before, aboard the *Amanda*. Come, let me pour us some wine and I will drink a toast to your beauty and to our future." He led her across to the long table and seated her before pouring two goblets of ruby-red claret from a heavy crystal decanter. She took the goblet from him with a murmur of thanks. He raised his own.

"To my lovely bride, and to our Paradise," he said huskily, and tossed off his wine in a single quaff.

Christianne mutely raised her own goblet but only pretended to sip. She'd not toast their marriage, nay, never, she vowed. " 'Tis a fine claret, Jonathan," she observed in an attempt to draw his conversation away from the favorite topic of their wedding.

"Indeed, yes," he agreed, lounging comfortably in his carved chair. "It was destined for the wine cellars of an Eastern mogul, a gift from the governor of Madrid. I saw fit to 'relieve' the governor's vessel of such worthless cargo." He chuckled and winked.

She forced a smile. "You have excellent taste," she remarked.

"Aye, lass," he nodded, "and expensive ones. It took several years and two score of treasure ships for Michael and I to fill that storeroom below to satisfy those expensive tastes. If I never raided another vessel I could still live out my days in luxury and ease, and still satisfy each and everyone of your heart's desires." A gloating expression wreathed his face momentarily, followed by a frown of irritation. "There are but a few things we cannot acquire by purchase here."

"And what are they?" Christianne asked curiously, fingering the jewels encrusted into the stem of her goblet while she awaited his answer.

"Ships, my lass, seaworthy vessels to replace our own. And arms and powder."

"But can your men not rebuild or repair your vessels?"

Jonathan shook his head. "Not so fast as the Toredo worms can bore their timbers and the tropic storms can wreak their damage. Perforce we must take what ships we can to replace them! Captain Wilhelm's *Voyager* was badly damaged these two months past by a cyclone while she lay at anchor and is now but a patched and leaking hulk. The *Fair Amanda* will provide admirable replacement for her"—he scowled—"and serve to keep friend Wilhelm off my back."

"I see," Christianne nodded. "But what will happen to the *Amanda's* crew?" She forced her voice to sound light and unconcerned.

"The crew? Why, they will be given a choice, me darlin'! Of joining our happy republic of free spirits, or—!"

He smiled, yet she noticed the cruel smile never reached his dark eyes and she did not need to hear more to know what other "option" would be theirs. A heavy silence lay between them and it was with relief that she heard a light tapping at the door.

Isabella entered, bearing a heavy tray. Ox followed, carrying a silver soup tureen. Both kept their eyes lowered as they set the dishes on the table, not so much as glancing at either Jonathan Flynn or Christianne. Isabella's expression, however, she observed, was one of fiercely-controlled anger. The pair exited as silently as they had entered, closing the door in their wake.

"Spanish witch!" Jonathan spat after Isabella's exit. "I am of a mind to rid myself of her and her unborn bastard whelp. There are Arab slavers aplenty that come here in search of slaves who would take her off my hands. She is as sullen and as poisonous as a viper!" He poured himself a second measure of wine and drained his goblet angrily, wiping his mouth on his sleeve.

"No, please don't," Christianne said a mite too quickly. "I . . . I shall need a . . . a lady's maid, shall I not, Jonathan, as queen of Paradise? I believe Isabella would do nicely," she covered.

Jonathan leaned back in his chair and pressed his fingertips together to form an arch. A slow, unpleasant but very satisfied grin creased his face. "Ah, yes, I like that! I like it very much! It will teach the Spanish bitch her proper place."

Christianne leaned forward and ladled the steaming soup into their bowls, busying herself to hide her anger. *Swine! Scum!* she thought, averting her face so that he would not read her expression.

The soup, of some sort of shellfish, spices, rice and slivers of vegetables, proved delicious.

"Tell me," Jonathan asked as they dined, "what of your family, little Chris?"

"My mother and father are both gone," Christianne said levelly, chasing a morsel of rice with her spoon. "James Mallory was to escort me to my Aunt Nell in New Orleans. She was to have been my guardian."

He nodded. "Your beauty and your bearing bespeak a noble birth," he said confidently, the idea of her being well born obviously appealing to him.

"Aye, indeed," Christianne lied. "My father was Lord Christopher Alexander, and his country seat was Westlodge Manor, in Somerset." It was not so much a lie as a half truth! She had no need to add that her parents had not been wed!

Triumphantly, Jonathan nodded. "I knew, lass. 'There,' said I, the first I set eyes on you, 'is a fine lady of quality, to be sure!' "

Christianne almost choked on her soup. She covered well and murmured, "My thanks for your compliment, sir."

She took a meaty drumstick from the silver platter and nibbled at it delicately. In truth, she had little appetite. This risky game of verbal cat-and-mouse was draining. She feared that at any second a slip of her tongue or a careless remark would give away her true feelings for him, or her relationship to James!

Jonathan helped himself to his own drumstick, tearing into it with gusto. "I am of a mind," he said between mouthfuls, "to also give you Ox for a bodyguard. The oaf seems taken with you and as you are the loveliest colleen on this isle, you must have protection from my rutting crew. What say you?"

Inwardly delighted, Christianne forced herself to shrug nonchalantly. "If you consider it necessary, of course, Jonathan. But are you not afraid that Ox himself will harm me?"

Jonathan laughed complacently. "Nay, me darlin', you'll

have nothing to fear from him! You see, that wretch can never be a man in aught but name, for he can never bed a wench! When he was but a stripling lad on his first sea voyage as cabin boy, our Ox was taken captive in the Arabian Sea by one of the slavers I spoke of earlier, or at least that is what I believe from what little I have been able to learn from him. His captain and his crew were butchered before his eyes, but because of his tender years, his life was spared. He was taken prisoner to become one of the guardians of a sultan's harem. And all such guards are eunuchs, lass." Jonathan chuckled.

"Eunuchs?" Christianne echoed, frowning in puzzlement.

"Aye—gelded like stallions! His tongue was cut out, too, so that he could never tell of the beauty of the sultan's ladies. And nor will he speak of my lady's charms."

Color suffused Christianne's cheeks. "I see," she whispered, afraid she would gag at the horrors that had been inflicted on poor Ox, before he had ever grown to manhood. "Thank you for telling me, Jonathan, I see I shall be quite safe with Ox to attend me. Am I permitted to roam freely about the island, or must I consider my chamber a lovely prison?" she asked, giving him a dazzling, bewitching smile that belied her anxiety over his answer. The possibility of her escape rested solely on what he said next. If she were confined to the chamber upstairs, there would be little opportunity to flee.

Jonathan reached out and rubbed one of her silver, fair curls between his fingertips, captivated by her loveliness and the brilliance of that smile. That she adored him was obvious to any who had eyes to see. "But of course you may go wherever you wish on our little island—with Ox to attend you, of course. 'Tis your home now, after all. I ask only that you do not cross the lagoon to St. Mary's proper, for the time being. The men of the *Red Scorpion* and the

Voyager have been too long without bedding a white wench, you see, and I would not wish any harm to befall you, my lovely."

Christianne deliberately lowered her lashes seductively and gave him a sidelong glance. "And when will our wedding day be, my dear? she queried breathlessly, hoping he mistook her nervous breathlessness for impatient longing for that day.

He pushed back his chair and came to stand behind her. "Soon, very soon! I expect my men to return here with the priest from Fénérive across the channel in four days." He lowered his lips to her bared shoulders and kissed her above the neckline of the sky-blue satin gown.

Her flesh crawled as his lips travelled upwards along the line of her throat and finally crushed her mouth beneath them. She cried out and broke away, fighting the urge to vigorously rub her lips clean of his kisses with her knuckles. "Nay, Jonathan, you must be patient!" she cried. "Four days, my love, and we will be man and wife. Then I shall be yours and yours alone! It will be torture for both of us, I know, but we must wait for the priest."

He nodded, lifted her hand and kissed it. "You are right. By the gods, how lucky I am to have found you, my angel! I had thought all women were but faithless harlots, as Isabella proved and my mother before her long ago, that adulterous slut. Ah, there was a harlot, Christianne, if ever there was one! I vowed that the woman I made my wife would be pure of heart and body—and at last I have found that woman in you, me darlin', my chaste and lovely Christianne!"

Christianne gulped nervously, a sudden image of James, striding across his cabin towards her, his well-muscled naked body burnished and so very male in the lanternlight, filling her mind. Dear God, if Jonathan but knew, if he so much as *suspected* she had been James' woman, she was doomed!

"Aye, Jonathan," she murmured, "as chaste and pure as the driven snow!"

And just as cold where you are concerned, Captain Flynn, she added silently.

Jonathan returned to his seat. He swirled the wine in his goblet and leaned back in the carved chair, his legs propped up on the table. Christianne noticed that his expression had a faraway, dream-like quality, as if he saw something in the candle flame's steady luminescence but with the mind's eye rather than his own brooding black ones. That expression, she recalled, had come over him since the mention of his mother earlier. Still seeming remote, he began to talk in a low, almost monotonous voice.

"Did I tell you about my mother, Christianne?" he asked without turning his head to see if she said yes or not. "Ah, she was a comely woman, that one, with hair so glossy and black it reminded me of the blackbird's ebony plumage in the sunlight, when he sat and warbled in the hawthorne tree. Her eyes—her eyes were bluer than a lake and sparkled with life, with laughter. Aye, she laughed a lot, and men were drawn to her as the moths to the flame before you. She was as beautiful as the Blessed Virgin herself, she was, yet her beauty only served to cover the evilness of her harlot's heart." His grip tightened on the goblet in his fist, and a muscle or a nerve twitched violently in his cheek. "There were three of us before. My brother, Michael, that I've told you of—he was the eldest, then myself, and little Timothy, the baby of our family." A smile flitted across his face. "Little Tim," he repeated, "who followed me everywhere. I cared for him, ye know, Christie, cared for him like the father he never had, and I was only a lad o' nine years myself."

"He must have loved you dearly," Christianne observed, sipping her wine and watching his face.

He smiled. "Yes. As I loved him."

"Your father—he had passed away?"

"Father? Ha! Nay, Christianne, we had no father, or at least none that was married to our mother, the lovely Maureen. If she was t' be believed, we all had different fathers—we were all bastards!

"Most nights she'd leave us at dusk and go down to the village tavern. She'd not come back 'till dawn and often as not, not even then. The three of us would wait for her, too afraid of the dark to sleep, our little bellies growling with hunger and with cold. Little Tim suffered the most, for he had been sickly from birth, and though I tried my best to care for him, he was always ailing. Well, one night Ma left us just after dusk and we huddled by the fire, frightened of the wind howling outside. Michael teased little Tim that it was a banshee, trying to find a way into the cottage, and the little lad was frightened, too frightened to sleep. He had been even more sickly than usual, and so I sat up with him until he nodded off. I'd stayed up with him the night before, too, and was tired. Try as I might, I could not stay awake!" A tear glistened in his eye. "I awoke from a heavy sleep to hear Timothy's screams. The poor, wee lad had risen from his pallet and in his sickness tumbled into the peat fire! I pulled him out and Michael and I did what we could, but Tim was dead. I ran through the dark and the wind t' the tavern, t' find my darlin' mother. I found her sure enough—in the bed of a damned British soldier, selling her favors. I begged her to come home! I screamed at her that Tim was dead, but it was no good. She was too fuddled with British gin t' mark my words. She came back at dawn with taties and a wee bit o' mutton she'd saved for

274

her favorite son, her darlin' Michael. I watched her as she looked at Timmy, all burned and stiff, where I'd laid him on his bed. I tell ye, Christianne, there was not a tear in that woman's eyes, not one! She seemed almost relieved he had gone! ' 'Tis for the best,' she said, 'for he was ever a sickly lad.' " He tossed off the remainder of the wine and glowered at the candle flame. "She was a harlot, my mother, a harlot through and through!"

Christianne said nothing, though a thousand questions clamored in her head. His story had explained much of his character, but not all. She watched as he rose to refill his goblet. His expression was still cold, angry, with a brooding malevolence she had never noticed in him before.

"After Timmy's passing, she favored Michael all the more. 'Twas him that always got her quick pats and her kisses, the treats she'd begged or stolen from her men. I might not have existed, for all that strumpet cared! She and Michael began whispering together, and I knew they were up to something, and that I was not to be a part of whatever it was. But I found out their little secret!" He grinned wolfishly. "I learned they planned for Michael t' travel to England, and there to take on with the crew of a vessel bound for the colonies. Once settled there, they planned he'd send for our mother and the pair o' them would start a new and better life there—without me. I decided I'd go with him, whether he wanted me to or nay, yet I had no coin for the passage to England. I went to the squire of our village, an English lord by the name o' Philip Rawley, and begged him t' see his way t' lending me the passage fare on my bended knees. I thought he'd not refuse me, since he'd had a glad eye for me mother for many a month."

"And did he give you it?" Christianne asked.

Jonathan shook his head. "Nay, he laughed in my face!

He said he'd lend no money to the son of a two-farthing whore who'd not even lift her skirts for an English gentleman. And so I had no choice."

Christianne cocked her head on one side. "No choice but to what?"

"To kill him, and t' take what I needed." He spoke in such a level tone she thought at first she had misunderstood him.

"You murdered him?" she whispered incredulously, paling in the candlelight.

His eyes narrowed. He bristled. "Murder? Nay, not murder, Christianne! You cannot call what I did murder, for Rawley had long deserved to die." He scowled. "But let me continue. I followed brother Michael to England and told him I meant to come with him t' the New World. He argued but I kept to his coattail like a cocklebur to a hound's pelt! We were taken on as crew aboard the *Perdita*. The voyage was a troubled one from the first, and the men had little respect for their captain," he continued, and Christianne could have wagered he lied by the shifting of his eyes, "and plotted mutiny against him. I saw little option but to join them, and was duly chosen as the new captain, after the old one was set adrift in a longboat by the other members of his crew." He glanced sideways at her craftily. "I knew we were all destined for the gallows by the *Perdita*'s crew's foolishness, and that we now had no choice but to become . . . privateers. I demanded of the crew if they would follow me or nay. They pledged to do so to the last man. And so we sailed on, finally coming to this lovely isle and making the pearl at its center our paradise on Earth. We renamed our ship the *Red Scorpion*." He sipped his wine, a smug expression on his darkly handsome face.

She regarded him doubtfully across the table. Privateers? Pirates, more likely! She sensed that much of his tale was

276

true, but that he had gilded and altered much of his part in it to show himself in a more favorable light to her.

"But—what of your brother?" she asked hesitantly. "Did not Michael resent his younger brother being captain over him?"

"Indeed he did!" Jonathan chuckled wolfishly. He scraped back his chair and paced. "It bothered him cruelly that I now ruled the roost, when he had always been the favorite of the family. And so he plotted with my men, Christianne, *my men*, to oust me from my captaincy and from my leadership here on St. Mary's."

"But I thought that you were close," Christianne exclaimed. "What of that treasure you amassed together, the risk you ran in voyaging to England to attempt to save your brother from the gallows?" The pieces didn't fit, nay, not at all!

He smiled, cat-like. "You're as shrewd as ye are lovely, me darlin'," he murmured and laughed softly. "I let him believe we were equals here, right up to the end! A British frigate put in to St. Mary's for provisions and to ride out a storm. Her captain was a pious soul, one of our good king's little covey of captains sent in search of freebooters and unlicensed privateers to bring them to justice for their crimes." He paused and regarded her expectantly. "Now, my clever colleen, can ye not guess how I revenged myself on dear brother Michael?" His smile was chilling.

"You betrayed him!" she gasped. "You gave him over into this captain's hands—your own brother!"

"Aye, my own brother!" he sneered, and smiled broader still. "And my voyage to London was to ascertain that his damned neck was well stretched, not to save him!"

She was stunned into silence. Jonathan had now revealed himself in all the foulness of his colors. How could she have ever trusted him, felt any fondness for this, this *abomination* of a man! Her desire to escape him strengthened in direct proportion to her disgust, a disgust she dared not let him so much as suspect she harbored for him!

"Ah, now I see," she said after a lengthy silence. He seemed to expect some comment on his cleverness, but she was at a loss for further words.

"I knew that you would," Jonathan approved warmly. "From the minute you agreed to jump ship with me, I knew we'd make a worthy pair."

Christianne clenched her fists until her nails had gouged her palms and drawn blood. A worthy pair! Did he forget so soon his threats to kill the *Amanda's* crew—or did he prefer to believe she had come with him willingly? She averted her eyes to conceal the tears of rage sparkling in them, rage at her own gullibility as much as at him. St. Patrick, she thought grimly, had rid Ireland of all serpents save one: Jonathan Flynn!

"Another wee draft of wine for you, me darlin'?" he asked.

She nodded. It would take many such drafts to bring her to the oblivion she sought this night, she thought miserably.

The wine glistened red as he tipped the flagon. Try as she might, she could not negate the awful fancy that it was blood he spilled into her goblet.

Twenty-One

"I know how it feels to be in a cage, Baba," Christianne sighed, "And I feel you hate your imprisonment just as much as I hate mine, mmmm?"

The lemur regarded her curiously, its fox-like head cocked to one side, its brown saucer-shaped eyes shining with interest. The mask of black fur about those shining eyes ringed them like a highwayman's mask, Christianne thought with a smile.

As she moved away from the wicker cage, the furry animal clutched the bars with its amazingly human-looking fingers and uttered a mournful cry like that of a human child.

Isabella, across the stone-flagged adobe cookhouse, clucked in reproof and shooed Christianne away from her pet. "Aiee, see what you have done?" she scolded mildly. "You have made him unhappy again, reminding him of his lost freedom, and now he will try to escape. There, there, my poor little Baba," she crooned until the lemur calmed again.

"I'm sorry, Bella," Christianne said contritely, "but I know now what it is to be a prisoner, and it bothers me to see any creature caged."

Isabella nodded. "You are right, *amiga,*" she agreed as

she climbed onto a rough, wooden three-legged stool to cut an onion from the string that hung from the beams above, "but I cannot bear to set Baba free, though I know it would be kinder to do so. He is the only friend I have here, on St. Mary's Isle."

Christianne thought of Bones, left behind when she fled the *Fair Amanda,* and nodded sympathetically, feeling guilty for causing Isabella's pretty face to darken with unhappiness. In an effort to distract her from brooding, she nodded again at Baba. "He is a strange little fellow indeed!" she observed, "unlike any animal that I ever saw in England."

"This island is filled with such strange creatures," Isabella acknowledged. "I have even heard tales of a bird that once inhabited this place that was as tall as two men stood end to end, and whose eggs were as large as pumpkins!" She spread her arms wide to demonstrate just how large. "It is said that this bird could lift a man in its talons and would swoop down—" her hand swooped down—"like so, and carry him off to her nest like a fine, fat worm. It was called a 'roc,' I believe."

"You tease me, Bella!" Christianne laughed, her smile dimpling her cheeks. She pretended to pout. "I am no child to be wide-eyed at your tall stories," she grinned, "but go on, anyway!"

Isabella sniffed. "Believe it or not, as you wish, but it is true! I have seen enough strange creatures here to discount nothing so readily. One morning, Jonathan and I went to the shore. It was soon after I first came here and he had not yet tired of me. At first I could not believe my eyes, for the beach was covered with beautiful birds as tall as myself. They had beaks that were curved at the end, you know, like a parrot's but longer, much longer and more flat, yet the cruelty of those beaks was at odds with the long, graceful necks of these birds, which reminded me of a swan. Their feathers were white as snow for the most part, but their wings were striped with bands of pink. Others were this same brilliant pink all over, like the rosy pink of the dawn that was breaking all about us." She sighed, remembering. "As we drew near, the birds flapped their wings and rose into the sky, their beating causing the sand to rise in clouds from the beach. In seconds the air was filled with them, and I"—she blushed, embarrassed—"and I could not help but think of angels, come to Earth."

Christianne nodded, trying very hard not to smile at Bella's flights of fancy. "I wish I had been there to see it," she said earnestly.

Bella nodded. "That Baba, his name I took from the native word *babakoto*, which is how the Malagasy call these creatures. Not all *babakoto* are black and white like my handsome Baba; there are many, many different kinds. The natives believe that the white ones, the *sifáka*, incarnate the spirits of their dead ancestors and guard their final resting places, and so they are *fady*, taboo, to all men. You will see many such *babakoto* at night about the tombs of the Malagasy rulers." She rolled her eyes expressively.

Christianne, too, wrinkled her nose in distaste. "Then I shall forego any such sights," she vowed firmly, "and remain here, in the realm of the living!" She smiled. "You have learned much since you came here, Bella," she said admiringly.

"Si, for what good it has done me," the Spanish girl agreed ruefully. She paused in separating the head of a plump chicken from its freshly-plucked body to toss a handful of chopped onion into the bubbling soup pot suspended over the fire. As she did so, Christianne noticed that she swayed dizzily as she turned back to her chopping block, and that her olive complexion had paled.

"Are you unwell?" she asked anxiously, darting forward to steady her friend.

"No, *amiga,* it is only the child. Like I, he cares little for the heat! Soon he will begin to move inside me, and the sickness and the dizziness will pass as he grows," Isabella reassured her.

Christianne stared at Bella's gently rounded middle as if half-expecting to see the child that Bella spoke of with such confidence. "How—how does a woman know if she carries a child within her?" she asked very casually, reddening at her ignorance of such things. To her relief Bella did not laugh.

"Oh, in many ways. The monthly bleeding ceases until after the baby is born. Sometimes there is a feeling of sickness in the morning when you awaken, and a tenderness to your bosoms. Some women find that a certain food they have enjoyed before seems suddenly tasteless, while others they never liked before now taste like ambrosia from the gods!" She laughed. "And then," she said with a gentle smile curving her lips, "life is felt and the belly swells." She caressed her own belly tenderly.

Christianne shuddered and screwed up her face. "Then I have no wish to have children," she declared with feeling, "for it seems more a time of ill health and madness than the joy you seem to find it."

Isabella laughed. "Such feelings will change, *amiga mia,* when you find a man to love—si, do not shake your head, they will, I promise you!" She smiled and added chunks of chicken to the pot. "There! It is done! We shall have a fine stew for our supper, yes? Ox!" she shouted, going to the cookhouse doorway. She cupped her hands to her mouth and shouted again, "Ox!"

The bearded giant appeared as silently as a shadow at the window beside Christianne. He smiled shyly at her and thrust his beefy fist through the opening. In it was a bunch of vividly-colored wildflowers that bore a sweetly exotic perfume.

She took them from Ox, who was blushing furiously from beneath his shaggy beard and locks. "Why, my thanks, Ox!" she exclaimed with pleasure, "they are lovely!"

He looked away, embarrassed by her gratitude and her delighted smile, and suddenly grateful for Isabella's request for more wood for the cooking fire so that he could escape from her eyes. He lumbered off to fetch it.

Isabella smiled. "You have tamed him, Christianne, as in the fairy tale my *mamacita* used to tell me, of how great goodness and beauty won the heart of the beast. Before you came to Ile Ste. Marie, Ox was a man to fear, but he has come back changed. Why, before, even Jonathan thought twice before he goaded him too far! Once I saw him angered by the insults of one of Captain Wilhelm's men. The lout ached to prove himself against so big a fellow as Ox, to build himself a reputation, you understand? He cast the first blow. Ox picked him up and hugged him like a great bear!" She shuddered. "We all heard the crack of each bone in his body as it broke, like the snapping of brittle twigs. I do not believe Ox intended to kill him, yet when he released him, he was dead. He did not know the extent of his own strength, you see."

Sighing, Christianne nodded. "Poor Ox! I do not care what he has done, he has been gentleness itself to me. It is only that he cannot talk, and so all think him little more than a beast. Why, he has not even the dignity of a true name—does nobody know it?"

"Not that I have heard of. Jonathan told me once that he believed Ox was of a good family. He suspected that he could write, si, and read and cipher, too, unlike most men who become sailors. Well, I must get on, there is much to be done! There are linens to scrub, and for that I will need water from the lagoon." She hesitated, bucket in hand. "I know Jonathan has forbidden you to talk with me, but would you stay and talk some more when I come back—just for a little longer?" She smiled self-consciously. "It has been so long since I had a friend to talk to."

Christianne smiled. "I shall do better than that—I shall help you! It is not fair that you should have to do all the work when you are with child. Here, give me the bucket! I shall fetch the water while you rest awhile. Now, you sit down." She pushed Bella down into the three-legged stool.

"No! You must not! Jonathan will—"

"Jonathan can go to the devil, for all I care!" Christianne declared defiantly with a flick of her pale hair. She tugged the wooden bucket from Isabella's protesting hands and walked out into the dazzling sunshine of the courtyard.

She sped across the empty expanse and beneath the stone archway. Once outside the fortress walls, she breathed a little easier. Jonathan had said he intended to go down to the southernmost tip of the island today, to see how repairs were progressing on the *Red Scorpion* and the *Voyager*. Both vessels were having numerous timbers replaced that had been worm-eaten. He had seemed eager to have the repairs completed 'before the *Fair Amanda* appeared on the horizon,' still very much convinced that James Mallory would pursue them. He had left his right-hand man, Pierre Le Chat and Stephen Tancred, in charge during his absence. Le Chat, Christianne thought with a grim smile as she walked across the sparse grass swinging the bucket in one hand, was indeed well named, that one! The Frenchman could steal up on one with the light-footed grace of a cat, without being heard. Stephen she disliked too, though he was a handsome enough young man with silky fair hair and a baby face. There was the suggestion of a curl to his lips, a certain look in his eyes, that belied his gentle outward manner and hinted at a cruel nature beneath.

The lagoon was blue-green and gleaming in the strong light, overhung with many trees. Christianne quickly filled the wooden bucket, eying the water warily as she did so for those loathsome crocodiles. She still recalled very vividly the way the water had been churned to foamy white by just one whipping slap of its massive tail when they had poled across the lagoon that first day. She had no wish to encounter one of those awful creatures first-hand! She set the bucket down in the sandy earth and crouched gingerly over the lagoon banks to splash her perspiring face. Its wetness refreshed her somewhat, although the water itself was far too warm to be really refreshing. Straightening up, she looked about.

Across the lagoon, smoke rose from the Malagasy's little settlement, and the smell of cooking fish wafted on the silky breeze. Bushes hung low over the water all about her, their greenery broken by vibrant pink blossoms that made her think of enormous butterflies with frilled edges perched there. She picked one and tucked it into her hair, then picked another for Isabella, which she slipped into her bodice for safe keeping. Harsh laughter rang out as she stooped to pick up the bucket.

"Well, well, ain't you a pretty sight, gal! Ain't she pretty, Pierre, with her pretty li'l *flowers?*" Stephen Tancred jeered.

"*Oui, mon ami!*" Le Chat agreed. "It is fortunate we saw her depart and decided to follow her, yes? Who knows what terrible dangers might await such a pretty mademoiselle in such savage country as this!" He grinned evilly and bowed.

Christianne assessed the situation instantly. The glitter of lust in their eyes was unmistakable. With her back to the lagoon, she could not hope to evade them! Biting her lip, she hefted up the bucket and walked briskly across the sandy earth to one side of Pierre. But, as she had expected, he immediately sidestepped to block her path. Her eyes flashed.

"Let me pass, you rogues!" she demanded, sounding far bolder than she felt.

In answer, the Frenchman only laughed. He reached out and fingered a strand of her silvery hair. "It has been too long since I touched a white woman's pale flesh, too long since I felt silky hair such as this," he said hoarsely. "I am tired of these native sluts with their woolly hair," he rasped, knotting his other fist in the neck of Christianne's blouse and pulling.

She flailed the bucket at him by its handle. Its weight slammed into his belly and he doubled over, releasing her in that same instant. She sprang away from him in the direction of the fortress, but Stephen pounced on her and brought her to the ground. He gripped her slender wrists so tightly she feared they would snap. His handsome face was wreathed in a gentle smile as he clamped his teeth into the soft flesh of her shoulder. She screamed and jammed her knee upwards at his groin. Her kick missed and landed, instead, harmlessly against his thigh. She thrashed and writhed and wriggled to escape his grip as he bore her back down to the sand, but could not. As he leered triumphantly down at her, she saw that his eyes were aglitter with excitement, his lips cruelly twisted. He forced his lips on hers. They were wet and foul and she gagged and tried still harder to escape. His grasping hands covered her breasts and squeezed cruelly. She dimly realized that Le Chat crouched beside them, unbuckling his broad leather belt.

"Aye, Pierre," Stephen panted, "a taste o' your belt

across her bared back will tame her wildcat's blood!" He easily rolled her over onto her belly, and wrenched her wrists up over her head, forcing them down into the sand.

Desperate now, she twisted and turned furiously, eating sand as her mouth ground against the bank. "No!" she screamed. "Let me go! Your captain—he will kill you both if you harm me!"

Stephen spat. "Captain be buggered!" he jeered. "Flynn's captain only because it suits *us,* us, his loyal crew, my lovely doxy! By the saints, Pierre, see how she bucks and kicks?" He sniggered. " 'Tis a lively tumble we'll have off her, an' no mistake! Give the wench a taste o' yer belt, lad, that'll show her who's master here right enough—and it ain't your blasted Captain Flynn, gal! Nay! He may give hisself airs, but the men ain't fools, see, for when a pirate ship is captured, 'tis the captain who do be hung t' make an example, by the British—not the crew. The crew are all pardoned!" He laughed, well pleased at their cleverness.

Without warning, the belt sang through the air and cracked across her back. She jerked violently, a high shriek of pain torn from her. She bit her lip so fiercely she tasted her own blood on her tongue. She couldn't stand it again, no! She had no head for pain!

But suddenly a garbled roar of outrage sounded behind Pierre. She craned her head around as Stephen abruptly released her, in time to see the Frenchman lifted bodily and hurled through the air into the lagoon with a scream of utter terror. Across on the opposite banks, three "logs" immediately slithered down them and into the water. Tancred scrambled to his feet, his face ashen. He decided to bolt a second too late as Ox lifted him bodily by the shirt into a far from tender embrace. Tancred's legs scrabbled wildly as Ox's grip tightened about his ribs. Loud cracks were audible as they snapped. Tancred's fair complexion turned an unhealthy shade of mottled purple. His blue eyes began to bulge noticeably from his head. Christianne scrambled to standing, gathering her torn blouse over her breasts.

"Enough, Ox, enough!" she pleaded. "They have learned their lesson—let him go!"

Ox glanced at her, nodded once and simply spread his massive arms wide apart. Tancred crashed to the ground like an oat sack filled with rocks. Meanwhile Pierre, she saw, had staggered up the banks of the lagoon, breathing heavily and streaming water from his impromptu swim. The crocodiles, only their eyes and snouts visible above the green water, had obviously dined well already that morning. They made no attempt to follow the Frenchman up the bank but merely lay in wait, hoping perhaps that the entertaining fellow would join them later for supper.

Panting, Le Chat leaned against a tree trunk and shook his fist at Ox in a threatening gesture. "You will pay, *mon ami,*" he menaced, "both of you will pay!"

"Aye," Tancred agreed, wincing as he rubbed his bruised throat and cradling his broken ribs.

To Christianne's surprise, a rare broad smile split her shaggy-haired savior's face. He bent and picked up a fallen branch some four fingers in diameter. Without so much as a muscle bulging with the effort, he pointedly, easily and casually broke it in two, then drew his finger across his throat in a gesture that needed no words of explanation. He followed this with a step towards the two men, who backed away at first then took to their heels and fled.

Merry laughter tumbled from Christianne's lips as she

watched them tripping and stumbling as they ran. Her laughter ended in a wince of pain as the belt-stripe across her back began to smart. Ox noted her expression and stooped to lift her, but she shook her head.

"No, friend Ox, I can walk. My heartfelt thanks for your timely rescue! If you would fill the bucket for me again, we will go back to Isabella."

They walked companionably back to the fortress. Once Ox stopped and pointed beneath a Madagascan jessamine bush, its branches laden with pungent white blossoms. He pressed his finger against his lips to bid her be silent. Eyes narrowing, she spied a lizard, a little green dragon of some two spans in length. Ox's hand darted out with surprising speed and gentleness and he grasped the little fellow by the tail. Motioning for her to watch, he set the lizard upon a sandy patch of earth. Before her eyes, it changed in color from green to a sandy hue that perfectly matched its surroundings.

Christianne gasped. "What magic is this?" she exclaimed.

Ox shrugged, grinning at her amazement. Indeed, Bella had not exaggerated when she had said strange creatures inhabited these savage lands, she thought as they moved on!

They walked beneath the shadows of a massive baobab tree. Its trunk bulged hugely like the swollen belly of a woman with child. Bats hung like folded leather gauntlets in its topmost boughs. About its roots snuffled a hedgehog-like tenrec, which hurriedly scuttled off as they passed. From time to time a flash of brilliant wings caught her eye, and she would turn to spy an enormous, gaudy butterfly flitting over the bushes, or a pair of parrots squabbling on the wing. She sighed. Everything was so different here, strangely beautiful, but different. She felt a sudden ache of longing for the familiar sights and smells of dear, old England.

It would be springtime there now, she realized, and the meadows would be decked out with buttercups and scarlet poppies and cowslips. The woodland dells would be rich with the violet-blue of the harebells, bluebells, and the pristine whiteness of the snowdrops. Tears smarted in her eyes. She should have stayed aboard the *Fair Amanda*, she realized too late. She should have confided Flynn's plan to James, and let him decide what was to be done. On reaching New Orleans she could have paid a perfunctory visit to her aunt and turned about and found passage on the first ship back to London. A crystal tear slipped down her cheek and she averted her face so that Ox would not see her misery.

When Isabella learned of the attack on her friend she hurried to fetch ointment for her back, cursing the two lust-crazed sailors who had harmed her in torrents of rolling Spanish that needed no translation.

"You must tell Captain Flynn what has happened," she insisted. Her sloe-black eyes glowed. "He will have them flogged at the very least for what they did to you, *amiga*, his Christianne," she said gleefully.

"Nay!" Christianne exploded. "Nay, he must never know, don't you see? If he fears for my safety, he will demand that I stay in the bedchamber, and then I'll have no chance to escape."

"Ah, si," Isabella reconsidered, "you are right. Well, go and lay down for a little while, at least. I will bring you some chicken broth later, with healing herbs added to it. It will ease the pain."

Christianne agreed. She felt suddenly bone-weary after her narrow escape and the thought of sleep was an enticing one.

When she awoke several hours later it was to hear Ox hammering at her door. He mimed that Jonathan had returned and wished her to grace his supper table once again. She groaned and struggled from the bed, calling that she was coming, but giving the cool sheets a last lingering glance as she left them. She flung open the sea chest with little enthusiasm and selected an emerald-green satin gown with a quilted insert in the front panel of a paler shade of green. After brushing her hair with an ornate, ivory-handled brush, she hurried outside to the hallway where Ox waited to escort her to Flynn.

"Why can he not dine alone for once," she grumbled. "My back pains me sorely and I am sleepy yet." Ox shrugged, his eyes sympathetic. "What is that?" she asked, ears cocked, pausing at the foot of the staircase. A muted roaring sound reached her ears, a sound she could not identify.

Ox wiggled his fingers up and down.

"Rain?" she queried, her disbelief obvious. "No, that's impossible. Rain does not roar!" she said scathingly, her irritable mood making her snap.

In answer, Ox went across to the heavy arched door and swung it open. Christianne's eyes widened. Outside, a drumming sheet of rain poured down onto the flagstones of the courtyard. The rain gutters sang and burbled as they filled and raced to be emptied in the rain barrels at each corner of the fortress. The sun-heated flagstones steamed as the cooler water met the heat.

"But it's wonderful!" Christianne cried. "Oh, Ox, I love it!" she declared, her former crotchety mood vanished. "Come on," she urged the shaggy giant, pulling him to the doorway, "I want to feel it cascading down my skin!"

Ox pulled back, motioning to the dining room where Jonathan awaited her. He raised his eyebrows questioningly.

"Devil take him," she said recklessly, grinning like a naughtly elf. "Come on!"

Without further ado, she picked up her skirts and raced headlong out into the roaring rain, a whoop of delight pealing from her as the first warm deluge soaked her. She whirled about, reveling in the rain's freshness and the scent of the earth as it soaked it up like a dry sponge. She twirled and danced, her hair spraying about her like slick, wet whips, her eyes sparkling with sheer pleasure, her satin skirts limp as wet lettuce leaves and plastered about her body.

Ox laughed too, his fists on his stocky hips. Yet he did not venture from the doorway and his expression, though affectionate, said that he thought her quite mad! It was several minutes before he turned, feeling eyes boring into his back, and saw Jonathan Flynn watching him from the opened dining room door.

"What is this foolishness?" Flynn snapped. "Go bring your mistress inside, you great oaf!"

Feigning meekness, Ox nodded and lumbered head down across the courtyard, rain drenching him instantly. It took some time to persuade Christianne to come back inside, and even then he had to tug the reluctant girl after him by the hand.

"So," Jonathan said without a trace of amusement, "you are given to dancing in the rain, are you, like some wild creature who has lost her reason!"

Christianne tossed her hair over her shoulder and set her fists aggressively on her hips. "And what if I am?" she challenged him. "What harm does it do anyone if I choose to 'dance in the rain?" He would not rob those precious, carefree moments of their pleasure, she determined fiercely.

Jonathan's eyes raked her, their expression one of contempt mingled with lust. "What harm?" he echoed. "Look at you! Your garments cling to your flesh like a second skin, like the wanton garb of a harlot, for all to see your female form."

"I see no one here but you and Ox," she retorted hotly, "and since you are my future husband and Ox, as you have said, can 'never be a man,' what harm have I done, I ask again?" Her deep blue eyes sparked challenging fire into his obsidian-black ones, brazenly defiant. She laughed mockingly as he stood silent. "You see? Even you have no answer, Captain Flynn! Now, I will go to my chamber and dry myself, with your permission, sir?" She swept him a deep curtsy that mocked him further.

Jonathan's eyes darkened with fury. His lips curled cruelly below the thin line of his dashing moustache. "I think not," he said thoughtfully, his eyes resting greedily on the swell of her breasts, outlined by her plastered-down bodice. "No, I think not," he repeated. "You are dressed admirably as you are, me darlin'," he jeered as he offered her his arm. "As you said, soon I shall be your husband. I shall enjoy you as you are tonight, a little foretaste of our wedding night. Come!"

Christianne stood her ground stubbornly. "No. I will change first or else I will not dine with you. You may take your choice, sir."

"You forget who is master here," he reminded her in purring tones. "I am captain of my ship and lord of this island. You will do as I say, slut!"

"Never!" Christianne flung back, pacing furiously now. "Your men laugh at you behind your back, Jonathan," she taunted recklessly, "they only follow you because it is the safer course. When the British capture a pirate vessel, 'tis the captain who is hung, is it not, while his crew are

293

pardoned? They *use* you for their scapegoat, and if you are not careful, sir, your brother's fate will soon be your own! You are too puffed up with pride to see the truth beneath your nose!" She bit her lip the second the words left her mouth. Fool, she cursed herself inwardly, why did you have to goad him so?

His mouth tightened into thin, lipless lines. He strode forward and grasped her hair cruelly in his fist. "Who has told you this, who? Was it that fool?" he demanded roughly, jerking his head at Ox, who stood with his fists clenched in mute frustration off to one side. That he wanted to squeeze the lifeblood from Jonathan's body was patently obvious to Christianne, who shot him a warning look.

"No one had to tell me!" she spat back. "I have a mind and can reason as well as any man. Will you let me go to my room, or nay?"

A muscle twitched in Flynn's jaw. His grip slackened. "Go, then," he agreed, in gentler tones. "My apologies for my harshness. For a second, you reminded me of me darlin' mother—she too, loved the rain. I shall pour our wine and await you anxiously." So saying, he kissed her hand in a gallant fashion, and watched as she mounted the staircase.

Christianne was bewildered by his mercurial change of mood. She changed quickly into a sprigged muslin gown, dried her hair with a linen towel until it curled damply about her face, then forced her reluctant footsteps back in the direction of the dining room.

Stephen Tancred and Pierre Le Chat bent to their captain's ear she saw as she entered the oak-panelled room. Their sly smiles died on their lips as they turned to see her there in the doorway.

"Good evening, gentlemen," she said with a beguiling

smile, "I trust I do not disturb you?"

Tancred and Le Chat exchanged wary glances. Tancred, she observed, moved stiffly, no doubt favoring his cracked ribs.

"Of course not, me darlin'," Jonathan denied. "They were just leaving. I will speak with you again in the morning," he told the pair curtly. "Meanwhile, see that men are posted on the ramparts. At first sign of his ship, I want to know of it, understand?"

"We understand," Tancred said sourly, glancing sideways at Christianne. He moved carefully towards the door, Pierre Le Chat in his wake. "Good evenin', milady," Tancred sneered under his breath as he passed.

"And a good evening to you too, Master Tancred," she replied easily. "I trust you are not ill? If I am not mistaken, I thought I detected a certain stiffness to your gait?"

Her implication was obvious. *Guard your tongue,* it said, *or I shall loosen mine.* Tancred swallowed nervously. Despite his professed contempt for Flynn, he seemed ill at ease.

"My thanks for your concern, Mistress Alexander," he muttered. "But a touch of ague is all that ails me."

"Then see that you take care, good Master Tancred," she said silkily, "for I am knowledgeable in such things and I wager that without such caution as I advise, it will assuredly worsen."

Tancred glowered at her and he and the Frenchman beat a hasty exit, leaving Christianne and Jonathan alone.

"You need not concern yourself with my men and their ailments, lass," he said jealously, "they are my concern, not yours."

"On the contrary, Jonathan dear," she simpered, wide-eyed and innocent, "anything that concerns my future

295

husband must be my concern also." She smiled. "Is that not the proper way of it between husband and wife?"

Completely gulled, he nodded. "Indeed it is." He smiled fondly. "I was wrong when I compared you to my mother. You are not a whit alike. Now come, me darlin', sit here beside me."

Like a condemned Christian entering an arena full of starving lions, she crossed the room towards him.

Twenty-Two

"Four days—four *wasted* days!" Christianne fumed, "And we've come up with nothing, nothing at all, Bella!" Her expression was deeply troubled as she paced the marble floor of the bedchamber.

"Si," Bella agreed dolefully. "And the time, it is growing short." She bit the sewing thread and tossed the ivory-colored gown aside. "There!" she said contemptuously, glowering at the bridal dress, "at least the gown is altered as 'His Majesty' demanded!" She made a face.

"Ay, but I shall never wear it," Christianne vowed hotly, "ready or nay. There must be some way off this island, and St. Mary's both. Think, Isabella, think!"

"Think! Think! A pox on thinking!" Isabella cried furiously, her hands on her hips. "I have thought and thought until my head, she aches!" She shook that head resignedly. "No, Christianne, you will have to wed Jonathan, I believe, for I can see no way out. He expects the priest here this very evening. Why, his men are already bringing sides of beef and chickens and rice and wine across the lagoon for the wedding feast, and they have been hammering timbers for tables to set up in the courtyard since dawn!"

"I know," her friend replied, grimacing. "Their clamor

woke me long before the cock crowed this morn."

"Well," Isabella said, forcing a smile, "since what will be will be, why don't you try on the gown, yes?" she urged, a trifle wistfully, Christianne thought.

"No!" she refused fervently. "If you are so anxious to see the results of your handiwork, Bella, try it on yourself! I would as soon don my shroud as don that bride's garb." She flung herself sulkily across the bed.

With a grin, Bella shrugged. She had been itching to try on the sumptuous gown! She quickly peeled off her blouse and skirt and lifted the bridal gown's billowing folds over her head. The neckline was square, edged with ivory lace sewn with seed pearls. The sleeves were of a filmy white satinet, full but caught up in bands of white ribbon at the wrists and elbow, the ribbon sewn with still more pearls, to form dainty puffs. The bodice ended in a deep point that reached to midbelly, whereupon the full skirts billowed out like the petals of an upside down water lily above under-skirts of heavily embroidered brocade, to the floor.

"Well, *amiga,* how does Isabella Muñiz look?" she asked Christianne, sweeping her an elegant curtsy and fluttering her sooty lashes coyly.

Christianne grinned. The Spanish girl looked radiant, beautiful — and well she knew it!

'You are *muy — muy —* " she struggled to recall the newly-learned word, "*muy hermosa,* Senorita Muñiz, very, very beautiful."

"*Gracias,* Christianne," Bella simpered, prancing elegantly about the chamber in a grand-dame fashion that caused Christianne considerable merriment.

She sprang across the room and delved into the sea chest, triumphantly withdrawing an ivory-ribbed fan, ornately carved, and a mantilla of exquisite ivory Spanish lace.

"There, Doña Isabella," Christianne cried, draping the veil over the Spanish girl's blue-black hair in the manner of a lady's maid, "now you are ready for the ball!" She handed her the fan, and Bella flipped it open expertly and held it before her face, accenting her lovely, luminous dark eyes in the manner of a true coquette.

"Gracias, muchacha," she said aloofly, "do not wait up for me. I shall dance and dance until the moon gives way to the sun, and the stars fade in the heavens!" She fluttered her fan flirtatiously as Christianne bobbed her a sketchy curtsy.

"Right you are, mum," she mimicked.

Isabella's haughty expression crumpled. Her lips twitched. The two young women crumpled to the bed, giggling.

"On the streets of Barcelona I would never have recognized you, Bella!" Christianne exclaimed. "You are the very picture of a grand lady, a *doña.*"

Bella grinned. "I doubt that even my dear departed little *mamacita* would have recognized me," she said with a smile. The smile fled, to be replaced by a bitter expression. "It is said that fine feathers do not make a fine bird, yes? But, aiee, Christie, they help, no? For a moment, I felt very grand, very fine—not at all like the pirates' *puta* that I am!" Tears filled her dark eyes.

Christianne instantly sat up and put her arms about the girl. " 'Tis not so, Bella," she scolded. "What counts is what you are here, in your heart, not what others try to make you, or what names they may call you, don't you see?"

Isabella smiled wanly. "Yes, I suppose you are right, *inglesa.*" She laughed softly, seeming suddenly shy. "I hated you when I first saw you, Christianne, for your beauty and for stealing my child's father away from me, or so I thought. But in these few days, I feel as if we have been friends for many years. I like you very much, Christie, and I wish with all my heart that I could find a way to help you escape from Jonathan."

"I know," Christianne said, "and I feel the same way about you! Without you and Ox, I don't know what I would have done. If I find some way off this island, by some miracle, won't you come with me?"

Stubbornly, Bella shook her head. "No, *amiga*, I cannot," she said sadly. "My place is here, where my child can grow up knowing his father, even if that father refuses to acknowledge his own blood. Try to understand, please?"

Christianne nodded silently. Isabella scrambled off the bed.

"Now, I had best take off this lovely gown," she said regretfully, "or Jonathan will accuse me of playing the imposter, yes?"

Her eyes met Christianne's, and the sudden thought that leaped into her mind was mirrored in the sudden brightness flaring in the English girl's eyes. They both gasped.

"Are you thinking what I am thinking?" Christianne asked breathlessly.

Bella nodded vigorously. "Yes, I think so!" she agreed. "Do you think it would work?"

Christianne's jaw came up resolutely. "We will make it work!" she said determinedly. "You shall marry Jonathan in my stead. He will not suspect until he lifts the veil to claim his husband's kiss. By then, it will be too late! You will be his wife and your child will take his father's name!"

Isabella clapped her hands. "Si! Everyone will be at the feast, Jonathan will see to that. You must slip away with Ox, take the raft across the lagoon, before he discovers the truth. I will ready a sack of provisions for you both. If you headed for Fénérive, across the channel on Madagascar, you might be able to stay there until an honest captain puts into shore for provisions, yes?"

"Yes!" Christianne echoed. "It will work, I feel it in my bones!" Her face darkened. "But what of you? When Jonathan finds out he has been tricked, he will kill you!"

"He will be angry, but he will not kill me, I am sure of it. He has threatened to do so many times, but never has. I will be all right. Do not worry about me, *amiga.*"

"Christianne!" roared Jonathan's voice at the door. He hammered upon it. "Let me in, me darlin'! I bring good news!"

"One moment, Jonathan," she cried loudly, helping Isabella out of the gown. "I am fitting my wedding gown, and to see me in it before our wedding would bring grave ill-fortune upon us! Hurry, Bella," she hissed softly.

"An old wife's tale!" Jonathan declared from beyond the door, "yet I will wait upon you, my sweet love!"

Christianne stuck out her tongue at the door. In seconds Bella was dressed again in her blouse and colorful skirts. Christianne held her finger to her lips to silence Isabella's muffled laughter. "You may come in now, sir," she called sweetly. The door flew open at once.

"Be off with you, shrew," Jonathan said cruelly. "I have words for your mistress' ears alone."

Christianne hid her anger as Bella bit back a furious retort and bolted from the room like a frightened rabbit.

"You are too harsh with Bella, Jonathan," she chided. "She means well, and is fond of you."

Jonathan's black eyes flashed angrily. "The wench has the morals of an alley cat," he spat. He eyed Christianne speculatively, fingering his golden earring. "She told you why I cast her aside, gave her to my men? She fancied herself as my bride—my *bride*, Christianne, though she knew she was tarnished goods before ever my ship raided hers! Can you not see why I treat her as the doxy she is?"

Defiantly, Christianne shook her head. Bella was her friend, a dear friend. She could not let him speak so ill of her. "Nay, not so!" she challenged him. "As well you know, Jonathan Flynn, Isabella was savagely ravished by a drunken sailor when her colonists' ship was but miles out of Madrid. It was he who took her, and the captain of that vessel had him keelhauled on account of it. She is no doxy!" She glowered at him fiercely, tossing her creamy hair from her eyes.

He scowled. "Pah! 'Tis fabrication on her part, all of it!" He waggled his finger at her sternly. "And I'll thank you t' stay away from that Spanish witch and not t' listen to her lies!" He turned sourly towards the casement windows. "Here, come here, beside me. Forget about her! Did I not say I bring good news, for the both of us? Well, it is twofold, me darlin'! Look, out there upon the ocean. Do you see her canvas?"

Christianne shaded her eyes against the brilliant sunlight streaming into the chamber. A white speck edged with silver gleamed against the dark blue shimmer of the Indian Ocean.

"A ship?" she ventured.

"Aye," he confirmed, his excitement evident. "But not just any ship — 'tis the *Fair Amanda!* She has followed us, Christianne, just as I said she would! Her damned captain no doubt is lusting for revenge for his worthy Ben Wright, now long dead, and for you, me darlin'. I wager his jealousy consumes him! Soon, I am certain, he will send a party ashore, armed to the teeth — but we're ready for him, and 'tis a warm welcome he'll be after having from Jonathan Flynn! When he comes, as I know he *must* come, he and his men will be cut down like stalks of wheat where they stand, and his pretty ship ours for the taking!"

Christianne had paled, but she nodded uneasily. "And—and the second 'good fortune' you spoke of?" she asked, though regretfully she believed she already knew what it would be.

Jonathan kissed the crown of her fair head. "The second is that tonight we shall be man and wife. One of the native chiefs sent a runner up from the beach. The priest's dugout has been sighted in the channel. By dusk he will be here on Paradise to perform the nuptials. Now, come, where is your smile, me darlin' girl? It is not fitting for a bride to look so melancholy on her wedding day." He chucked her beneath the chin and she smiled a tight-lipped smile.

"A little nervousness is all it is, Jonathan," she lied. "I hope to be a good wife to you, but I am fraught with doubts."

"I ask only that ye be faithful to me always, bear me sons to carry my name and stay as lovely as you are, lass, naught more," he said fondly, kissing her full upon the lips. He turned away. "Now, I must leave you. There is much yet to be done," he nodded out of the window, "in both directions! Until tonight?"

"Tonight!" she agreed, smiling fixedly. She sank down upon the bed, trembling, after he had gone. Tonight! Perspiration broke out on her palms and her brow caused by fear, not the steaming Indian climate. Could she and Bella pull it off, their masquerade? She squeezed her eyes tightly shut, her fists clenched in the folds of her skirts. *Please God, let it work! Though I have been a thief and a scoundrel in my lifetime, I swear on my mother's grave I'll never pick another pocket as long as I live, if you just let our plan work!* Did God strike bargains with reformed cutpurses, she wondered? She hoped fervently that He would, this time.

The remainder of the morning alternately flew past or tarried. Apprehension built to fever pitch in her. She was as edgy as a cat on hot coals, leaping with alarm at any sudden sound, whirling about at every opened door, eyes wide with alarm, her heart seemingly in her mouth.

The fiery ball of the sun began its leisurely arced descent into the midnight-blue ocean shortly after midday, and with its descent went some small portion of the blistering heat of the day. The savory aroma of roasted beef, turned on a spit over an open fire, wafted up from the courtyard, and with it the yeasty odor of fresh-baked bread. Flies buzzed drowsily against the shutters, which she had closed halfway to keep the room cool and shaded. The sweet fragrance of Madagascan jessamine mingled with the aromas of the feast being prepared below. She slipped out of her clothes and lay down in her shift, trying to rest. If their escape proved successful, she would need all her wits and every second of sleep she could get to carry it through.

Late afternoon, Ox came to her bedchamber, bearing buckets of water for her to bathe. She drew him hurriedly inside the room and quickly explained her and Bella's plan. Half afraid of his response, she asked if he would flee with her. To her delight, he readily agreed, nodding eagerly.

He squatted down on the floor, the sooty taper he had used to light the candles brandished in his fist. His face set in concentration, he quickly sketched a map on the marble with his makeshift quill. Christianne squatted next to him.

"Ah, yes, 'tis Paradise, and here the lagoon and St. Mary's proper," she said, pointing.

Pleased, Ox nodded. He drew on the floor again, and mimed the two of them running through the jungle, shown by the trees he had drawn as sticks on the crude map.

"No, Ox, we could never escape that way," she disagreed. " 'Twould be better to head for the shore and steal a boat of some kind. We can make our way across the channel to the Red Island. I'm sure we could find some passage to a civilized land from there.

Ox shook his head vehemently, waving his hands in the air. His actions said that that was exactly what Flynn would expect them to do, and that they would be quickly overtaken and—he drew his finger along the line of his throat.

She nodded shakily. "Very well, I see your point," she agreed, "but then how are we to get clear of this damnable island?"

Ox's pale eyes lit up. He pointed to the cornelian bead necklace about her throat, and made signs of offering them to someone.

"Trade these?" she asked. "But I am sure they are worth very little. How about these?" She pointed to the sapphires strewn on the dressing table.

The shaggy-haired giant shook his head. He pointed to the vein in his wrist, then again to the beads and drew the shape of a star in the air. It was several minutes before she grasped his meaning.

"Because they are the color of blood, the Malagasy value them highly as amulets?" Ox nodded so violently she feared his head would tumble to the marble floor. "Ah, I see." She shivered. He seemed convinced that the natives would hide them in exchange for the beads until Jonathan had given up looking for them, but she was not so certain of that. The few natives she had seen since their arrival had been, for the most part, the *Scorpion*'s crew's women. And even the women had not seemed friendly towards her. "If you are so sure it will work, we will try it, friend Ox," she agreed at length, still doubtful. "When the priest arrives, Jonathan will send Bella upstairs to help me to dress. Instead, I will help her! When she goes downstairs for the ceremony, I will slip away and meet you at the landing. Agreed?" He grinned and gave her a jaunty thumbs-up sign as he left.

She scuffed the charcoal marks from the floor and made a hasty toilette with the water Ox had brought. Only God knew when next she would be able to bathe after tonight! Feeling calmer now that Ox had agreed to go with her, she lay down and tried again to rest.

Coarse voices carried from the ramparts outside. Flynn's men must be readying the cannon in preparation for the attack on the fortress he expected from James and his crew, she realized. James! Despite hating him with a fervor, in truth she hoped neither he nor any of his men would be killed! She could not bear to think of those laughing green eyes forever closed, that handsome face forever frozen in its deathmask. Aye, the passion he had stirred in her had engendered other feelings too, feelings of affection that warred with her fury at his taking her away from England, the lies he had told her, his taking of her innocence. Did all women feel this way for the first man who'd shown them the delights of love? She thought so. It was not that she cared for James at all that made her feel this way, simply that it had been he who had made her a woman. How he must loathe her now! She shivered though the room was close with the stored warmth of the day. She hoped fervently she and Ox would be long gone before James launched his attack — if he did indeed come — so that she would not have to see the contempt for her, the hatred, in his eyes!

She was almost asleep when frantic hammerings at her door sent her springing from the bed to answer it. Ox stood there, wild eyed, grunting incoherently and waving his arms about like a windmill. She glanced quickly left and right along the gallery, before pulling him inside.

"Calm yourself, Ox, else I shall never understand you!" she implored him. At length Ox calmed and began the gesticulations she had learned to interpret so well. Her face blanched as she grasped the reason for his distress.

"God in heaven, no!" she whispered, her spirits plummeting. "Isabella imprisoned? But why?"

It transpired that Isabella had lost control of her volatile temper under Flynn's sneers and insults, and flown at him like a wildcat. Flynn had had his men lock her in the treasure chamber below the fortress. *Oh, Bella,* she thought ruefully, *if only you could have borne it just a little longer!* Ox apparently feared Jonathan intended to make good his threat to sell her to the Arab slave-traders that raided the islands for slaves, for he had never seen Flynn so angry before.

"We must free her," Christianne said firmly, "and we will escape together. She can have no wish to stay here now." She pursed her lips thoughtfully. "Ox, do you think you could draw the men's attention away from the fortress to the courtyard? I believe I might be able to pick the lock to the storeroom, given a little time to do so."

He nodded.

"Go on then," she urged, "and make it worth our risk! Good luck and God be with you!" He rested his hand on her shoulder briefly. Their eyes met and the expression of concern, of caring, for her that she saw there needed no words. How dear he was, this silent friend, she thought with deep affection! He had proved himself a man among men, for all that Flynn had told her otherwise.

"Don't worry, I will be very careful," she reassured him.

He nodded and slipped through the door.

She rummaged through the sea chest until she found what she was looking for, a jewelled bodkin pinned to a fancy plumed hat. She fastened it in her bodice and hoisted her shift up about her thighs before going out onto the balcony of her chamber. She leaned over it and craned her head back to look up to the tiled roof above, and then down. She gulped. La! If she fell! She muttered a curse. What lily-livered cowardice was this?

Gritting her teeth, she climbed up onto the narrow wrought-iron railing, poised there, arms outstretched for balance, before reaching up and gingerly grasping the rain gutter with the tips of her fingers. She hung there briefly to catch her breath, then hauled herself up, inch by painful inch, onto the sloping roof. Her wrists and shoulders were screaming with pain by the time she made it. She scrabbled up the roof to the apex, realizing belatedly that the red tiles were blistering hot from the sun. She peered over into the courtyard below. A smile curved her lips. Dear Ox! Jonathan and his men were circled about the great bear of a man, laughing uproariously and nudging each other as Ox—feigning being very drunk—cavorted and whirled about in a comical dance. Not one of the pirate crews of either the *Red Scorpion* or the *Voyager* thought to look up to where Christianne perched, like a stork who has decided to build its nest against the chimney-breast of a house for warmth!

She scrabbled across the hot tiles until she was directly above the dining room. Off it ran the hallway and thence the stairs that would lead her directly down to the treasure room where Bella had been imprisoned. She frowned. Dropping down into the courtyard at this point meant certain discovery, for two of Captain Wilhelm's men squatted on the flagstones directly below, dicing and swilling wine from leather *botas*. It seemed an eternity that she waited until they tired of their wagering and ambled off drunkenly to the rest of the men. Grinning with triumph, she slithered down the roof and sprang, bent-kneed, to the ground.

Dust motes danced in the meager rays of sunlight that had fingered their way into the gloomy hall. She was temporarily blind after the bright light outside. Her eyes adjusted rapidly and she sprinted down the hallway to the last door. A quick glance to the left and right assured her that no one was about. She crouched down at the door.

The lock could have been picked by a suckling babe, she thought scornfully as she wiggled her makeshift bodkin key in the keyhole and heard it click open. She slipped through and closed it behind her before hurrying down the short flight of spiral stone steps. The air was cooler down here, but musty.

"Bella!" she hissed softly, rapping with her knuckles at the door. "Bella—are you there?"

A low laugh carried through the door. "Of course, *amiga mia*—where else would I be except here?" Isabella retorted softly.

Christianne grinned at her own stupidity. She inserted her pick into this second lock, wiggled the bodkin carefully and turned. Nothing. Though she yanked on the iron ring handle, the door remained solidly locked. Perspiration broke out on her brow and palms and slithered down her spine. "Stay calm," she murmured to herself, "stay calm and don't lose your nerve. There's time, plenty of time." But the lock still refused to give and panic welled up inside her.

"A hairpin, Bella," she whispered, "do you have a hairpin?"

"Si!" Isabella confirmed quickly. *"Momentito!"* Christianne saw a narrow hairpin appear under the door. She snatched it up and jiggled it expertly in the lock. After minutes that seemed like hours, there was a loud, miraculous click that was like music to her ears. She turned the ring and the door swung open.

Isabella stood in the opened doorway, festooned with row upon row of priceless necklaces, rings, bracelets and a mischievous smile twitching her lips.

"*Buenas notches*, Christianne," she said with a curtsy, welcome to my humble prison cell!" The treasure room glittered and winked with priceless booty, and Isabella was little less dazzling than it was.

Christianne glowered at her. "We have no time for this frippery, Bella," she said crossly, "take off the baubles and let's be gone from here."

Isabella sighed and did as she was told, except for the rings. "These," she said firmly, "I shall keep. For Jonathan's son!" She patted her stomach.

"As you wish," Christianne agreed. "Come on! Follow me!"

They slipped up the stairs, out into the corridor and through the gloomy dining room.

"I'm glad you'll be coming with Ox and myself," Christianne panted, leaning against the French doors to catch her breath. "We'll find a ship bound for England that will deliver you safely to Spain en route. You'll be able to—"

"I am not coming with you and Ox, *amiga*," Isabella said sadly, touching Christianne's hand. "I can never go back to Spain, not now, after all that has happened. I know this island and many of her people. I will hide in the jungle with them until my child is born or until I am certain Jonathan is no longer angry with me. Then I shall return here." The expression on her face was grim and determined.

Christianne's eyes widened. "No, you must not! Come with us, I beg you! I fear for your safety here, truly I do, my friend. If you will not leave, then I must also stay."

Isabella shook her head. "Don't be foolish! As long as you are still here, there can be no hope for me or my child, so long as he can still see you and want you. If you are truly my friend you will wish me Godspeed and good fortune, as I wish you—and go!"

"Very well," Christianne sighed. They hugged each other briefly. "Come on, let me give you a boost up onto the roof. Head for the wall closest to the archway. When you jump down, remember to bend your knees so that your legs will not break when you land. Wait until no one is looking, then slip out through the archway. Now, go!"

"I can't," Bella argued. "I have no head for heights or for climbing. There must be some other way!" Her dark eyes were imploring.

"There is—if you want to get caught," Christianne snapped. "Come on, climb up on my shoulders. You can do it, Bella, trust me!"

"But who will lift you after I am gone?" Isabella pointed out, "It is too high for you to reach up."

"Not for me," Christianne lied, forcing a grin. "I am as agile as a cat. I was a cutpurse before, in London, Bella. I am no stranger to rooftops!" She swaggered a little to add further weight to her boast, then held out her hands, cupped, for Isabella's foot. She boosted the Spanish girl up until she could grasp the gutters and gain a foothold.

"Godspeed and good luck!" she murmured.

"*Vaya con díos!*" came the shaky reply.

Isabella was gone.

Christianne looked about her. As Bella had observed, she could not climb back up unaided; the rain gutter was too far from the ground. Instead she slipped back inside the dining chamber, through it and back out into the stone-flagged passageway. Somehow she would have to try to skirt the merrymakers in the courtyard and slip out through the arch, praying they would not see her. She would be without cover all the way, but what choice did she have if she intended to escape? None, she acknowledged, none whatsoever!

The pirates, she saw as she crouched down behind a stone pillar, had tired of their sport of watching Ox play the buffoon, and had returned to their drinking and feasting. Some of their native women had accompanied them, and the dark-skinned beauties lolled on their men's laps and drank from their tankards and kissed and embraced them like the bawds of any seafaring port. The men were dressed in a garish assortment of garments, obviously booty stolen from merchant ships during one of their bloody raids. Some wore silk frockcoats in rainbow hues, embroidered lavishly with silver and gold threads. Beneath the coats they were bare-chested and wore their sailors' loose, white cotton drawers, which was a peculiar sight when contrasted with the satin coats. Huge, plumed hats were much in evidence, as were heavy, gold chains and weighty silver crucifixes. Some men had golden earrings in one ear, and their heads were bound with vivid kerchiefs.

For the greater part, they were a heavily-bearded, unkempt crew, with unevenly-cut, matted hair, scarred, deeply-tanned complexions and rough, foul-speaking manners. They reminded Christianne of a flock of squawking, gaudy parrots! The makeshift trestle tables that lined the courtyard were littered with food scraps and spilled wine, and most of the men were already reeling drunk.

Jonathan had seated himself off to one side, splendid in a fine satin coat of a deep burgundy shade, embroidered with silver, and a burgundy and black stripe waistcoat. He looked, she thought with a shudder, the very picture of the nervous groom on his wedding day. She ducked back into the shadowed archway and waited. Her heart seemed almost in her mouth, pounding louder than a tambour in her ears. She pressed her fingertips against her breast to silence it. A minute passed, then another and another. Come on, come on! The waiting was nerve-wracking. But just when she thought she would be pressed against the stone archway forever, she sensed a current of excitement ripple through the men and heard a few loud whoops as they all surged towards the fortress gates.

"Señor Capitán Flynn!" cried one young pirate. "The priest, señor, he is here!"

Jonathan rose eagerly to his feet and strode across the courtyard to greet the two men. Christianne rose curiously on tiptoe to see. The two priests wore the dark cowled robes of their order and seemed a pious pair, heads downcast, hands hidden in the full sleeves of their robes. She saw them decline Flynn's offer of refreshment with solemn shakes of their heads. Jonathan apparently approved this display of temperance and lifted the hand of the taller priest and kissed it reverently, much to Christianne's disgust. It was a wonder his lips were not seared in retribution for his sins as their foulness touched the holy father's flesh!

With the coming of the priests, Jonathan attempted to set some order to the gathering. He and Tancred and Le Chat bullied and chivvied the men to seat themselves in civilized fashion on either side of the long tables, a move which greatly enhanced the impression that this was a solemn occasion, but which made Christianne's escape through the courtyard and out of the gate impossible now! Without the men milling about, her intended route to freedom was completely without cover. What in heaven's name was she to do now?

A frightened squeak came from her as a hairy hand clamped over her mouth. "Dear God, Ox," she whispered hoarsely, "that hand near caused my death from fright!"

Ox pulled her back into the panelled hallway. Excitedly, he mimed that Flynn had sent him to her chamber to bid her dress and ready herself for the nuptials.

"I will not," she vowed desperately. "I will not marry him! He makes my flesh crawl with his talk of chastity and purity when he himself is like a rosy apple that hides a maggot at its heart! No!" She clenched her fists and squeezed her eyes shut to staunch her frustrated tears.

Ox's massive hand was gentle as he reached out and tilted her face to look at him. The expression in those pale gray eyes said more than words or gestures. Marry him now and escape will be possible later, they seemed to say. Despite the priest and the trappings, it will never be anything but a mockery in the eyes of God. Misery in her heart and in her deep blue eyes, Christianne nodded. She had little choice, not now, common sense argued. At least Isabella had escaped safely. That was something.

"Lead on then, friend," she consented dully, "I will do it."

Less than an hour later she stood ready in her bedchamber, a vision of angelic beauty and innocence in the shimmering ivory satin gown. A tall Spanish comb of ivory, studded with opals and pearls, fastened her upswept hair at the crown, while the remaining silvery tresses spilled loose down her back. With a defeated sigh, she lifted the ivory lace mantilla—with which she and Bella had planned so recently before to hide the Spanish girl's dark hair—over the comb. Perhaps, she thought miserably, it will hide my tears! With a brief moment of prayer for Bella's safety and Ox's and her own, she left the chamber.

Ox's eyes were misty as he took her arm to escort her to the curving staircase, and she was grateful for his silent strength and the affection of his support. Jonathan looked up, his handsome face wreathing in a possessive smile as he saw his Christianne, apparently ready and eager to become his bride. He strode swiftly to her side, motioning Ox away as he lifted her icy hand for his kiss.

"Come," he breathed in her ear as he led her across the courtyard, "all is ready. The priest is here and I am a most anxious bridegroom!"

Her legs felt stiff and alien as he led her toward the priests. A hysterical urge to burst into peals of nervous laughter assailed her. What a travesty this was, what a parody, she thought! Yet even that thought was swiftly banished as they halted before the narrow desk that had been dragged out of the fortress to serve as an altar, behind which the two Jesuit fathers loomed like great black ravens in their robes. All eyes were upon her as she lifted the lacy mantilla to reveal her lovely pale face. The men's sighs at her beauty were like a single note blown through a hollow reed.

The priest, his head bowed, nodded to his assistant and briefly raised his hand in benediction. He turned then to face the couple.

Christianne's eyes were downcast, the thick fringe of her dark gold lashes trembling on the creamy curve of her cheek, as she waited nervously for the service to begin. Seconds that seemed like hours passed on leaden wings.

Jonathan coughed. A brightly-feathered bird squawked rudely in the jessamine bushes. A fly buzzed overhead. The very air seemed to hold its sultry breath in anticipation of the priest's first words.

Impatient for the awful travesty of a wedding to begin, be over and done with, Christianne looked up. In that same instant, the priest threw back the cowl of his dark robe. But his face, she saw, all color draining from her lips, was that of no Portuguese priest.

It was James.

Twenty-Three

His eyes raked her with contempt. If she were an insect, he would have crushed her beneath his heel without second thought; a cur, he would have kicked her, so filled with loathing was the blazing green of his eyes, the curl of his lips.

"Aside, wench, while I deal with your master," he ordered, "And then, 'twill be your turn, dear heart!" he promised mockingly as he flung off his priest's robes and kicked the desk aside.

There was a swift grating of steel as he unsheathed his rapier, a grating that set Christianne's teeth on edge. She backed away, scared, casting desperately about her for Ox. Somehow she was more afraid of James than she had ever been of Flynn.

Jonathan had likewise drawn his weapon. A hush fell over the gathering, which minutes before had been a rowdy one. Benches scraped on flagstones as seats were hurriedly pushed back. Tankards clattered dully to the ground.

Jonathan grinned with triumph. It was the grin of a tiger. He poised on the balls of his elegant boots, his own rapier in his left hand, a slim dagger in the other. That he was confident in his skill as a swordsman was evident in his

317

cocksure stance. "So, me bucko, you've come at last," he said softly, "Captain Mallory with your fine talk of honor an' your gentlemanly ways! Do you have a mind to take the whip t' me again, eh, Captain, sir?" he purred with heavy sarcasm. "Well, James, lad, I'll have ye know *I'm* the lord o' these here parts, and I'll relinquish none o' what is mine to ye—and especially not my lady—so if ye would take her, you'll have to take me first!"

He lunged suddenly, but it was no more than a feint and his blade whipped harmlessly away.

A muscle in James' cheek twitched, but apart from that one involuntary reaction, he remained immobile. Jonathan Flynn laughed. His obsidian-black eyes danced with excitement, heightened by the certainty that he would kill this man who had made him a laughingstock, aye, and at his leisure! "I confess, Jim, I like your color. Aye, despite everything," he said with a slight inclining of his head, "I admit you're no coward, and that's a fact!" He lunged again, this thrust no feint.

James nimbly sidestepped. Steel rang against steel as he parried the thrust. "You talk too much, Flynn," he drawled. His eyes were deceptively lazy, heavy-lidded. "If you value your island and your murdering whore, cease your prattle and fight!"

Color drained from Flynn's face. With a snarl of rage he attacked clumsily, his fury—as James had anticipated—robbing him of caution. There was a tearing sound, loud in the deathly silence, as James' rapier slit the shoulder of Flynn's fine silk coat. With an oath, Flynn tore it off and hurled it aside.

"By St. Patrick and the Snakes," he spat, "you'll take back your words, aye, if I have to cut out your tongue and have you eat it. En garde!" He advanced lightly, gracefully, like a cat, in the manner of a man skilled at sword-play, his blade an extension of his arm and his whip-lean body. James stood his ground calmly.

"Nay, Flynn, you'll not have her; nor will I retract. Whore she is and whore she will ever be, and a murdering one at that! She lay with me and feigned her pleasure like a true harlot, plotting in her heart to plunge her dagger into my worthy Ben's chest!" His wrist flicked and his blade sang through the air. Flynn jumped backwards. Blade crashed against blade as they battled around the courtyard. When it seemed at one point that James had the upper hand, several of Flynn's men started forwards. Captain Wilhelm's bulk blocked them.

"*Nein,*" he growled, something akin to amusement in his fleshy features, "if Flynn would lead here, then let him show his mettle, *ja?*

Flynn's men fell back, and Mullens—now also devoid of his priest's skirts—heaved a sigh of relief. He cast about, looking for the girl. She's backed away, unnoticed in the hubbub, to the perimeter of the circle of men, and with her, the mute one, Ox. Mullens' single eye narrowed. So, the slippery vixen intended to flee, did she? The cap'n would take none too kindly to that, 'twas certain! He edged through the men, furtively headed after her.

James flicked runnels of sweat from his eyes. The stone staircase leading to the ramparts was at Flynn's back. He jabbed the point of his rapier at the other man. The sudden, darting thrust drew blood, a small, deep nick that welled red against the white silk of Flynn's shirt. Flynn cursed and retreated up the steps, parrying each of James' deadly thrusts with wicked skill. Below, the men surged forwards, gaping upwards as the two continued their ferocious fight, the whirr and metallic singing of their blades the only sound that broke the silence, like a furious battle 'twixt armored bees. A lucky slash caught James across the face, the tip of the rapier curving downwards from temple to jaw. Blood seeped in shiny rivulets down his cheek, unnoticed by him.

Mullens, too, gaped upwards, then his good eye flickered to a flurry of movement further along the ramparts. Pierre Le Chat and Tancred had taken the other stairs and were bent on aiding Flynn, 'twas clear! "Behind ye, sir," he cried. "The bloody sea wolves, they'll take ye·from behind! Scurvy, lily-livered scum!" He would have charged to his captain's rescue, but a meaty fist stayed him.

"And who be ye calling lily-livered?" demanded the querulous, grog-slurred voice that belonged to that meaty fist.

"You, you free-booting whoreson!" Mullens raged. He slammed his fist into the other man's face. Scarlet torrents poured from the man's shattered nose. The sight of blood and the excitement acted like a tinder spark amidst a rick of sundried hay. Tempers flared; old animosities between Wilhelm's crew and Flynn's burst into raging fire.

"He's right!" roared one. " 'Tis our captain's fight. Let 'em fight it alone!"

"Nay!" roared another, "Stay out of it, you! Come on, lads! Cap'n Flynn do be needing us!" The man flung himself forward, felled like a log by Wilhelm's billy club. Pandemonium ensued as the crews of the *Red Scorpion* and the *Voyager* settled their differences, using platters, tankards, fists, teeth, boots or daggers to do so. Blood ran as freely as the grog and wine had earlier. Groans and curses filled the sultry night air. Flaming torches fell in showers to the flagstones, toppled in the melee. The chickens that had survived the massacre for the wedding feast ran hither and thither and clucked and flapped in alarm, as if, like their relatives earlier, their heads had been axed and the nerves yet jangled.

His captain, Mullens saw as he disentangled himself from the struggling mass of bodies, was holding his own. He glanced quickly about. The girl and Ox were gone, swallowed up by the night that walled even the sturdy fortress with its impenetrable darkness. He stuck his fingers in his mouth and blew two strident whistles.

James' jaw hardened. The signal, though not prearranged, was obvious. It was time to go, by Mullens' reckoning! He suddenly flicked his wrist, using his rapier like a whip rather than a sword. His lash caught Flynn across the knuckles of his sword hand, neatly lifting the topmost slivers of flesh from the knucklebones. The numbing blow made Flynn drop his weapon with a howl of pain. James neatly kicked the fallen rapier over the edge of the rampart to the courtyard below, where a full-scale brawl was in process.

"My apologies, Flynn, but I regretfully must leave your gracious company," James said with a mocking flourish of his hand. "I have a rendezvous with a pale-haired witch and may not tarry! We will continue our sport some other time!" He smartly saluted and leaped for the top of the rampart's wall. A second's hesitation, and he had sprung down, leaving Flynn and Le Chat and Tancred, who had rushed to the Irishman's side too late, gaping after him.

James landed in the soft, loamy earth that was everywhere on the islet. He recovered his balance and sprinted for the lagoon, Flynn's cries of, "After him, you bungling swabs!" ringing in his ears as he went. Mullens was at the landing, but alone, he realized instantly.

"Where is she, damn her soul?" he growled.

"Gone, Cap'n! Her and the mute, Ox. They've taken the raft!"

321

"No matter," James said grimly, "we'll swim for it! I wager 'tis safer to brave the crocodiles than that mob back there!" He peeled off his leather jerkin and boots. "Come on, man!"

They dived into the silent, black water, striking out at once for the shore opposite. They made the swim without incident and hauled themselves out on the opposite banks. Breathing heavily, they straightway plunged into the dense jungle that backed the native village where Flynn's men and their women lived. The village, they saw as they passed, was nigh deserted, only one toothless old crone huddled by the fire to tend the half-breed children left behind while their mothers made merry at the fortress, no doubt.

The jungle possessed a steamy heat even at night, made still more oppressive by the choking vines and roots and bushes and trees that grew so closely together it was virtually impossible to force a path through it without a sturdy machete to hack the way clear. Disturbed birds hooted and chattered as they crashed on, both men breathing heavily. Gray moonlight filtered down through the treetops, distorting form and distance with its puny, ethereal light.

"Hold up, Mullens, hold up," James ordered roughly. " 'Tis madness to go on! We are like babes in the wood, with no idea of our direction in this cursed darkness." He slumped against a tree trunk, swatting a bloodthirsty mosquito away with an irritable curse. He had been convinced he would not leave the fortress without Christianne, that his plan would work. What he had not bargained for was that Flynn's men would rally about their captain. Could it be they believed his promise of a new republic, where all men would live in equality? Fools!

Mullens squatted on his haunches beside him, his raspy

breathing loud in the eerie silence. "They have the advantage, sir," he wheezed. "The hairy brute knows his path, no doubt."

James smiled grimly in the shadows. "Aye, man, you're right. But the girl will slow him down, as will her weighty skirts and this blasted jungle." He wiped his streaming face on his shirt sleeve. The heat seemed to rise from the ground like steam, he thought, and the swarms of mosquitoes that were attacking every portion of his flesh left uncovered were maddening. Nevertheless, there seemed little point in trying to carry on. "We'll rest here," he decided. "Chances are, if Flynn and his men try to follow us, the darkness and their drunkenness will steer them wrong."

"And how long do we wait, Cap'n?" Mullens asked, swatting his face.

" 'Til first light. Then we'll find her, and, by God she'll pay for her treachery!"

Christianne sobbed with exhaustion as she was half-dragged after Ox through the jungle. Every breath was an agony to her lungs, and further worsened and vicious cramp in her side. Her hair was a mare's nest of twigs and leaves and wringing wet with perspiration. The sumptuous ivory gown was now little better than a rag, ripped and torn and stained with mud and blood from the scratches on her arms, and it was hot, to boot.

" 'Tis no use, Ox! I cannot go on," she panted, pulling back.

Ox halted. He turned to face her, his massive shoulders a dark wall outlined against the jungle beyond and about them. Gesticulations were useless in the gloom, for she could not see them. With a grunt, he picked her up and slung her over his shoulder before continuing on.

He carried her for what seemed like hours and for several miles in this fashion, her upper torso flopping like a rag doll. At length, he set her down. She moaned as blood rushed into her feet, long since gone numb from his awkward carrying of her. He silenced her by placing a stubby finger across her lips, holding aside the foliage and pointing so that she could see why silence was necessary.

Between the parted bushes lay a welcome sight: the pale expanse of a crescent-shaped bay, and beyond, the Indian Ocean, black and unfathomable save for an occasional wave that broke the black-glass surface and was touched by silver. The faint glimmer of moonlight on furled sails, and the flicker of a ship's lantern far out revealed a vessel riding at anchor. She frowned. It was not the *Scorpion* or the *Voyager,* for they had been anchored off the southern-most point of St. Mary's. Was this, then, the *Fair Amanda* she had seen from her bedchamber window, awaiting her captain's safe return from his quest for revenge?

She made to go through the leafy aperture, but Ox grasped her by the arm and jerked her back. Even in the gloom, she made out the definite shaking of his shaggy head. He pointed further down the beach to where the red glow of a campfire illuminated the darkness and now and then the dark, flat-featured faces of the men who encircled it.

"Malagasy?" she whispered, her eyes widening in alarm.

Ox nodded. He crouched down and pulled her after him, apparently intending to rest and bide his time. Christianne turned about this way and that, seeking to get comfortable in the sticky, unwieldy gown, which was now sodden with her sweat. It was useless! She stood and lifted the voluminous tattered skirts over her head. Beneath it she wore only her lace-trimmed shift, with narrow bands of lace for shoulder straps and row upon row of lacy frills at the hem. It was a silly, frivolous garment, but more than adequate both for modesty's sake and this intolerable climate, she decided. Her arms were bare now, as was much of her bosom, yet she cared not a whit. Even the humid air felt cooler by comparison against her over-warm body now! She sank back down next to Ox, who pulled her against him, offering his chest for her to lean upon. She gratefully did so.

"You have proved a friend indeed, dear Ox," she whispered gratefully. "I will be forever in your debt. I shall not forget your kindness, I promise, you'll see. I shall find some way to repay you." She leaned back against him. A mosquito droned loudly by her ear, but the man swatted it away. She yawned hugely, exhaustion creeping over her. Her eyelids wavered, her head drooped forward on her chest. In seconds, she had fallen into a heavy sleep.

She awoke some hours later to find herself alone, her head pillowed on Ox's leather jerkin. She sat up, stiff from the dampness of the night air and her exertions, and looked about her. The sky was lightening in the east, she saw between the trees. Dawn was imminent. But where was Ox? She crawled forward and parted the bushes as Ox had done earlier. The Malagasy were still camped further down the beach, their fire now extinguished. It was possible to make out the prone silhouettes of several men, rolled in their woven sleeping mats about the dead fire. Another, their lookout, she surmised, was the only man sitting up, yet he, too, she judged to be sleeping by the way his head slumped forward on his chest. She sank back down to the moist earth.

Birds were stirring now in the vegetation all about her, warbling joyfully at the coming of day. Their warbles mingled with the harsher hoots and chatters of the parrots.

The sun suddenly leaped upon the horizon, flooding every-where with dazzling golden light. A rustle in the bushes behind her sent her whirling about, her mouth open with fright. Ox stood there, grinning broadly through his shaggy beard. He made signs of a boat floating on water and pointed behind him and then to himself.

"A boat? You've stolen a boat?"

Ox nodded and Christianne returned his grin. "From the pirates?"

He shook his head and pointed down the beach.

"Ah, from them," Christianne murmured in under-standing. "When do we make a run for it—now? They are still sleeping."

But Ox said no, indicating the Malagasy would soon awaken to retrieve the fishing nets they had spread the night before in the shallows.

Christianne sighed. This inactivity was more nerve-wracking than some definite action on their part. Her belly growled. Her arms were covered in itchy welts, the mosquitos' legacy despite Ox's attempts to drive them off. Her elfin face was daubed with mud, her hair a tangled, pale blond mane. There was little resemblance left to the angelically beautiful vision she had appeared less than twelve hours before in the bridal gown. She looked up, caught the twinkle in Ox's eyes and the rare twitch of his lips as he tried to hide his amusement and failed. Christianne grinned.

"Laugh at me, will you, you great brute! Well, you'd not laugh if you could see yourself! Like a bear, you are, a great shaggy bear!"

Ox's gray eyes brightened. He reached into his belt and withdrew a knife, its edge paper thin and wickedly sharp. He pointed it at his hair, and then, with a questioning expression, at Christianne.

"Aye, I'll trim your shaggy locks, friend, Ox," she agreed with a nod. "Let's see what manner of fellow lies beneath them!" Ox promptly squatted down and she deftly trimmed his beard and hair. She hummed as she worked, recalling the drawing room at the house on Darling Lane, when she had played barber to Coalie Joe and Lumpy Jack. That seemed years ago and as distant as the moon. Who would have guessed she would ever be here, trimming the shaggy locks of a pirate on the edge of a jungle, while in hiding from savage natives, Flynn, and a no-doubt-livid Capt. James Mallory! Life was indeed filled with surprises.

"There," she proclaimed at length, stepping back to admire her handiwork, " 'tis done! By the saints, Ox, you are a changed man!" I'faith, he appeared so, neatly shorn, she realized, a broad, admiring smile on her lips. Though nothing could disguise the huge stature of the man, her barbering had civilized his appearance considerably. She curtsied. "Good morrow, Master Ox," she said genteelly.

Ox's eyes glowed with adoration and gratitude. He fingered his new beard and hair with something akin to wonderment in his expression, then drew himself up to the full extent of his already considerable height and set his shoulders square and proud. He beckoned to her and took her hand. In the palm of it he drew the letters O and X.

"Aye, your name," she repeated to show that she understood. Isabella had been correct, she recalled. She had said she believed Ox was educated. But Ox vigorously shook his head. He wrote in her palm a second time. William. She smiled gently up into his face, "Ah, now I understand. I am honored to make your acquaintance, Master William," she said gravely, "and no more shall I call you Ox, but Will." He nodded solemnly, obviously well-pleased.

Soon after, the Malagasy awoke and retrieved their fishing nets, obviously disappointed to find them only half full. The fire was raked and the fish spitted on sharpened sticks and hung over the glowing embers. The savory aroma wafted on the silky breeze to where they were hidden. Her belly growled audibly and saliva gushed into her mouth.

"Lord, I'm starved," she muttered. Ox grunted. He tapped her arm and lumbered to his feet.

She frowned in puzzlement as he left her, weaving between the bushes that swallowed the massive man up as if he had never been. She shrugged and sank back down. No doubt he intended to make sure their stolen canoe was still safely hidden.

Several minutes passed before she remembered her complaint of being hungry. Surely Ox couldn't have thought—? She jumped to her feet, heart thudding anxiously, and peered through the bushes.

The Malagasy had finished their meal and were now tossing the remainder of their catch into woven panniers, laughing and talking as they did so. Their backs were to the jungle that rimmed the sandy bay, and to the remainder of their meal, still spitted over the fire. Even as Christianne watched, she caught a glimpse of Ox, hidden in that jungle behind them. She stifled a cry of warning and held her breath, praying fervently he would not be so foolhardy as to try to take the fish, that he would realize the odds against success were too great and wend his way back around the bay to her side. Why, oh, *why* had she muttered that she was hungry! Why hadn't she realized that Ox, in his fondness for her, would attempt to obtain whatsoever she asked for!

She ground her teeth against her bottom lip, her fists balled at her side, as she saw Ox slip from between the trees and lope down the beach towards the campfire. Nervous heat swept over her as he quickly snatched the wooden spit, turned and began to sprint back toward the jungle. Her heart was in her mouth. He might just make it! The Malagasy still faced the ocean. *Come on, Ox, come on!* she urged silently. But then one of the dark-skinned men turned, saw Ox and yelled an excited alarm.

The natives raced for their spears, strewn on the sand. A shower of the deadly *sagais* rained down all about Ox. He stumbled, recovered and ran on unharmed. The Malagasy raced after him, whooping and retrieving their fallen spears as they ran. They hurled them again. Involuntarily, Christianne screamed as Ox went down, sand churning beneath him.

Her feet, with a will of their own, carried her through the tangled vegetation and out onto the shore, flying towards the fallen man. The natives turned to face her as she raced towards them, screaming. They formed a living wall between her and her fallen friend, who lay motionless, a *sagai* protruding from his upper back that still quivered with the impact.

"No! Dear God, no!" she screamed, sinking to her knees in the powdery sand, an agonizing sob wrenched from her. "Damn you! Damn you!" she cursed the savages, hauled herself upright and flung her way through them to Ox's side.

He was still breathing, but barely. His eyes flickered open and he tried to smile. She smiled too, attempting to reassure him and trying not to look where her eyes bade her look, at the ghastly wound with the spearhead still embedded in it. "I'll take care of you," she whispered, "I won't let them hurt you again!" She swung around the faced the Malagasy. "Go away, do you hear me?" she screamed at them. "Go away!" Her dark blue eyes blazed.

They looked at each other in undisguised amusement and grinned, their teeth a brilliant white against their dark brown skins.

"No go. You, woman, you come!" ordered one man, who was obviously their leader. He was tall and muscular with a bush of woolly black hair, clad only in a loincloth. He took a step toward her.

Christianne whipped Ox's knife from his belt, the knife she had used so recently to shear his shaggy hair. "Nay, you scurvy heathens, I'll not go with you, I'll not!" she cried, brandishing the knife and shielding Ox's body with her own slender frame.

"You go, woman!" menaced the Malagasy leader again. "Go now!" He jerked his fist threateningly.

Her mind raced desperately. She could not hope to stave off all of them, a dozen savage natives to her one. Was there nothing she could do or use to buy Ox and herself their freedom? It was then that she recalled what Ox had mimed earlier at the fortress, about trading her necklace of cornelian beads for a boat from the natives, or for them to hide in one of their villages. She tore the necklace from her throat, beads spilling from the broken chain like droplets of fresh blood on the sand.

"Here," she cried, holding them clenched in her fist, "take these, in exchange for our lives." Please, God, let him understand me, she prayed silently. "Trade!" she repeated. Her arm shook as the woolly-haired Malagasy came towards her and crouched at her side. He picked up a bead and grunted in apparent approval as he examined it. He smelled of fish and palm oil, she noticed dully.

At length he stood up, nodded and grinned again. "Good trade," he pronounced. "We go. Woman stay." He held out his hand for the remainder of the beads. "Give!"

Christianne hesitated, certain he could not be trusted. Yet what choice did she have? She emptied the beads into the native's cupped hands. Despite the blistering heat, her hands were icy.

He took them from her almost reverently and motioned his men away with a jerk of his head while he tucked the cornelian beads into a pouch that hung from his loincloth. The other men hoisted their fish-filled panniers onto their shoulders and padded off across the sand. Their leader glanced at Christianne's ashen face curiously. He reached out to touch her pale hair, laughing as she jerked her head away. Instead he stood and looked down at Ox's still form and spat in the sand.

"He die," he decided cheerfully, and braced his bare foot against Ox's back. Ox's gurgling scream as the Malagasy pulled the spear from his back was inhuman, high and ululating on the silence. Christianne covered her ears, unable to stand the sound. To her relief, it abruptly stopped as Ox lost consciousness again. "*Sagai* much good," the native said, scouring Ox's life blood from the spear with handfuls of white sand. He strode off after his companions without a backwards glance.

The knife fell unnoticed from her fist. She covered her face with her hands and wept, then sniffed back her tears and turned to her friend. Her tears would not help him, she told herself firmly. Somehow, she must stop the bleeding. She ripped the hem of her shift and fashioned a bulky pad, which she pressed hard over the huge, ragged wound. In seconds it dripped red. She made another bandage and tossed the first aside. Blood still seeped steadily, but not so swiftly she noticed now, hope filling her.

How long she crouched there, her hands fiercely pressing the cloth pad to Ox's wound, she did not know. The sun rose higher in the azure heavens, beating down fiercely on her bared arms, face and neck until they tingled painfully. Ox remained still, sprawled on his bed of sand and pink shells.

At length a shadow fell across her and Ox. She looked up dazedly, squinting against the glare, expecting to see the treacherous Malagasy, spears in hand. Her relief was only marginal to see it was James and Silas Mullens who stood there. They exchanged glances.

"Stand aside," James ordered roughly, "let me look at him."

Christianne stubbornly shook her head. Her lower lip trembled. Tears swam in her eyes. "No!" she whispered.

James frowned and nodded at Mullens. The bosun lifted her into his arms as if she were a lost child. She struggled briefly then gave up, instead watching James as he knelt to examine Ox's wound with terrified eyes.

"He's dead," he said gruffly.

"No!" she sobbed, writhing from Mullens' wiry arms and flinging herself past James towards Ox. Her fists flailed at his head as he reached out and trapped her about the waist, holding her still. "Aye, he's dead, and there's nothing more you can do for him, wench. He would have suffered had he lived. 'Tis better this way."

"Let me go," she whispered brokenly, "please let me go! I—I must bury him, I have to, don't you see? He—he was my friend." Her voice and expression were pleading.

James released her with a heavy sigh and stood back. "As you wish," he said resignedly. "But hurry. It will not be long before Flynn's men find us."

Christianne scrabbled at the sand with her bare hands, scooping a long wide trough from it. After a few moments, James and Mullens kneeled and helped her. She held back her tears as they rolled Ox's body into the shallow grave, tore another square from her shift and gently placed it over his face. His expression showed none of his final agony but seemed merely in repose. "Goodbye, dear friend," she murmured as the two men shoved sand over the body. They had dug well and deep. Only a mound showed where he lay, and the wind and the tides would finish the job.

"Come on, Christianne," James urged, moved despite himself by her obvious grief, " 'tis done, and the *Fair Amanda* awaits. We must swim for it."

"There's a canoe back there, by the tallest palm," she told him woodenly, kneeling by the grave. "Go on and get it. I—I want to stay here, just for a moment or two longer, I swear. Then I'll come with you."

He eyed her doubtfully. Was this another of her ruses, he wondered, looking down into her tear-streaked face and her swollen eyes. He nodded at length. He and Mullens strode off in search of the native dugout canoe.

Christianne picked up handfuls of the pink shells that were strewn all about on the sand. "I'm sorry," she wept as she worked. "It was my fault, all of it," she whispered, a painful lump in her throat.

James and Mullens were coming down the beach, carrying the canoe on their shoulders.

"Come on, lass!" Mullens shouted.

She waved, brushing wind-blown strands of ash-blond hair from her eyes as she turned to take a last look at the grave.

"Not much of an epitaph, is it?" she murmured sadly, and turned to walk down to the shoreline.

The shells she had arranged at the head of the sandy mound read simply: WILL.

She had gone only a few paces when she saw James motion Mullens into the canoe with a hurried gesture and turn and race back up the beach towards her, churning sand under his feet as he came.

A volley of musket fire whistled over his head, ripping great columns of sand from the beach. She stopped dead in her tracks as the saw Jonathan Flynn leading his pirate crew from the jungle like a pack of howling wolves, brandishing cutlasses and muskets. With them swarmed hordes of Malagasy, their *sagais* raised aloft. She froze.

As he reached her, James grabbed her wrist and hauled her after him toward the jungle without pause.

"Run!" he roared, his fingers biting painfully into her flesh.

They thrashed their way through vines and bushes, stumbling over tree roots in their haste. The jungle closed behind them like a wall, thick and all but impenetrable.

Her heart pounding fiercely, her sides knotted with a stitch, Christianne was dragged after the captain through the vegetation. He showed no sign of slackening his pace or of caring that he dragged her so swiftly her feet scarcely touched the ground.

"Stop! Stop, I beg you!" she panted.

He halted abruptly and swung around to face her so suddenly she sprawled backwards to the grass.

"Why, my little she-cat? So you can barter my life for your own? Nay! Where I go, then so shall you. On your feet!" His voice brooked no refusal. She crawled to kneeling, then standing, her small breasts heaving, the pain in her side making her close to swooning. She opened her mouth to defend herself, but before she could do so, James was charging through the trees again, towing her in his wake.

Twilight was falling when they at last stopped to rest, falling with the sudden violet beauty she had grown to love. Between the curtain of vines that hung like sinuous snakes all about them, and the tamarind trees and huge, fan-shaped raphia palms, she glimpsed the distant twinkling of the stars. The jungle creatures rustled and twittered as they settled down to roost or hole for the night and Christianne deemed it eminently fitting to do likewise. She sprawled on her belly on the carpet of lush grass and dead leaves, utterly spent. James sprawled beside her, his own breathing labored. For several minutes he remained silent and she lay there, her limbs aquiver, her eyes closed, and waited for her heart to cease its wild gallop and settle to a more leisurely throb as the minutes stretched. The smell of decaying humus and dew-soaked vegetation was sharp in her nostrils. But it seemed no sooner had she caught her breath than James stood and dragged her to her feet again. She shrugged off his hands.

"If you think I can go on, you are badly mistaken!" she snapped, backing away from him and leaning against a tree as he reached for her again.

"Then stay here if you wish, damn you, wench," James flung angrily over his shoulder as he strode on, "but I doubt you'll be welcomed back to become queen of Paradise a second time—if you survive Flynn's men having their turn at you, and perhaps a Malagasy warrior or two with a taste for white women."

Christianne blanched. "Wait!" she pleaded. "I'm coming!" He was right, she realized miserably. Whatever vengeance he had planned for her would no doubt seem mild compared to the fate that would undoubtedly be hers at Jonathan's hands, now that she had fled him!

They travelled on for an hour more through dense jungle and swamplands, finally exiting the heavy vegetation onto another beach, this one littered with timbers. A deep harbor gleamed in the violet light, and the massive silhouettes of the *Scorpion*'s and the *Voyager*'s bulks were black before the indigo sky. They crouched down.

"Flynn's ships!" Christianne whispered. "This must be

the southern shore. He told me the vessels were being refitted and repaired here. He planned that the *Fair Amanda* would replace Captain Wilhelm's ship, which is worm-eaten and damaged yet from a cyclone."

James snorted in disgust. His eyes scanned the darkened beach. "They'll be no use to us," he said. "What we need is a small boat. With it we could cross the channel to the Red Island and attempt a rendezvous with my ship." He looked at her keenly, as if weighing whether he could trust her or nay. "Stay here," he ordered, "while I take a look around."

"Not without me, you don't!" she retorted, sprinting after him. She had no intention of waiting for him on the edges of the jungle alone!

Whatever crew had been employed to refit the two vessels appeared to have been summoned to the fortress for Captain Flynn's wedding. Though tools and fresh-hewn timbers, cauldrons of pitch and wooden nails were much in evidence, there was no sign of a watchman to guard them. They found the vessels' longboats drawn up on the shore in an untidy line.

"Your Captain Flynn is a careless fool," James remarked with a grim smile, "fortunately for us. Or should I say, for myself? We may have our pick of worthy boats."

He selected one and commenced shoving it down the beach toward the black-crystal sea. After a second's hesitation, Christianne bent to help him. Together they pushed and shoved and hauled the trim, white longboat into the shallows. She scrambled aboard, James following. He took up the oars.

The enormous mass of Madagascar reared dark against the lighter sky as James pulled strongly on the oars. The rhythmic splash and slight sucking sound as they dipped in and out of the dark water were the only sounds. The distance between the bobbing white longboat and that towering island of red laterite and forbidding escarpments, known as the Red Island to seamen for centuries past, was narrowing by the minute.

They were safe from Flynn and his men, for the time being, at least, Christianne thought with relief. But would that green-eyed devil at the oars prove her salvation—or her undoing? Had she yet again jumped from the boiling pot only to find herself in the coals? Her intuition said she had!

The Great Red Island loomed ever nearer as the longboat, naught but a ghostly white glimmer on the glistening, onyx-black ocean, sailed on . . . and on . . . and on.

Twenty-Four

She must have slipped exhausted into the waiting arms of sweet Morpheus soon after, for she awoke to the glory of a saffron-and-cerise-streaked dawn, the rosy clouds bordered with gold like fanciful calling cards.

With a groan she struggled to sitting. But the sight that met her sleep-drugged eyes shredded the last remnants of sleep from her, for James slept too! He sat straight up on the crosspiece, his head slumped on his chest, one oar still in its oarlock and clasped loosely in his slack hands. Of the second oar, there was no sign!

Christianne turned frantically about. There was no St. Mary's Island behind them now, only the Indian Ocean, touched with the sun's first tentative rays. In the opposite direction, the large mass of Madagascar was but a far-distant outline through the heat haze that danced on the water. Fear washed over her. Their craft had seemed small but sturdy in the narrow channel 'twixt St. Mary's and the Red Island. Now it seemed but a feather adrift on the rolling, endless, deep blue swells, a pitiful scrap of man-made flotsam at the mercy of the winds and tides and God.

She scrabbled over to James, heedless of the way the boat rocked in her panic. "James! Dear God, James, wake up! We're adrift!" she cried, shaking him by the shoulder. She recoiled in horror. Even through the cloth of his shirt, the harsh heat that rose from his body was unmistakable! Some fever racked him, that much was clear, though of what nature or origin she had no notion.

He stirred and moaned and slumped further forwards, and the single oar slipped dangerously far from his grasp. Shocked back to her senses, she grabbed wildly at it and laid it lengthwise in the bottom of the boat before turning back to the sea captain.

With great difficulty and many pauses to catch her breath, she managed to pull him down into the bottom of the boat. When she rolled him over onto his back, the boat rocked ominously and she held her breath, certain that at any second they would be pitched headlong into the shark-infested waters, there to drown at the very best, or at worst, be eaten alive. Yet her luck held and the longboat righted itself.

James, she saw, slept deeply in the fever's thrall, his eyes—long-lashed as any woman's—closed, his normally deeply-tanned complexion grayish, save for a high flush of color that stained his stubbled cheeks. His flesh seemed stretched too tightly over his bones. Her heart skipped a beat. Could any man survive such a sickness without a physician's aid? In all her eighteen years, she had never seen a fever rage so heatedly through anyone as that which raged through James. What would Granny Rags, that wily old queen of potions, with her powders and salves and blood-letting leeches, have done for him? She sighed. Whatever Gran would have done was of little import here, for she had no medicaments at her disposal, only endless quantities of water, and salt water, at that.

Pressing her already ragged shift into further use, she tore a strip from the tattered hem and dipped it over the longboat's side. Gently she bathed James' face, then lay the cloth aside and unfastened his shirt. Her hands were trembling as she bathed his chest, recalling another time when her hands had moved lingeringly across that oaken expanse with its light furring of red-gold. A hefty serving of guilt, well-laced with despair, welled up behind her eyelids and spilled forth as stinging tears. Fool! Dolt! she chided herself. Why had she fallen for the honeyed snare of Flynn's false tongue? Why could she not have stayed aboard the *Fair Amanda*, bided her time until they reached this Godforsaken New Orleans and then, when James had discharged his duty to her Aunt Nell and returned to his ship, made good her escape back to England?

As she squeezed out the cloth and swabbed his chest once more, she recalled in painful detail what had thrust her irrevocably over the last precipice of doubt to take the final step of slipping the draft into James' wine and of casting her lot with Flynn's. James had said, with complete honesty—and at her urging to tell her his thoughts—that of all the women he had bedded, he had found her the most pleasing. Her pride had been stung that, even at such an intimate moment, he had thought to compare her with others. Was she jealous, that such a comparison had wounded her so? Was not jealousy a sign that she cared for him in some small way? Nay! There was no caring in her for the sea captain, for all that she had found pleasure in his lustful love-making. It was only her wounded pride that had brought her to this pass, she was sure of it.

She leaned back in the bows, runnels of perspiration streaming down her face and making the lawn shift stick to her spine and the valley between her breasts. Lord, 'twas hot! She glanced up. The sun was already high in the heavens, a golden galleon adrift in a sea-blue sky, where the clouds were the foamy crests of the waves. Soon it would be midday and hot as Hades in the small, unprotected craft without means to shade themselves. She cradled James' head in her lap, shielding his face from the sun with her body.

"Aye gentle Ben, aye . . . due west, sail on . . ."

Christianne startled at the rasping voice that broke through her thoughts. She looked anxiously down at James, whose eyes were open now but glazed with fever.

"An angel?" he mumbled as he looked up into her face. "Then . . . perforce, I—I must be dead . . . and this, heaven!" His eyebrows drew together in a puzzled frown. A tremor ran through him and his expression contorted. "So cold . . . so cold! For God's sake, swim!"

He was raving, she realized, lost in the nightmarish realms of the fever and plagued by countless demons. His chills came and went, alternating with sweating spells that left his body drenched and trembling. She lost count of the number of times she bathed his burning brow or simply soothed him in a gentle, crooning voice when he cried out loud in the midst of his delusions. Once he began to thrash about, fighting some fiendish, invisible foe. Fearful he would capsize them, she pinned his arms to his side with the weight of her body until he calmed and murmured for water.

Water! she thought sardonically, what she would give for water, for both of them. Her own throat was parched, her arms, shoulders and face blistered with sunburn. She sorely regretted her impulsive decision to discard the bridal gown the night before. It would have afforded them some protection against the fiery sun, and the petticoats could have been put to good use to rig up an awning for shade. La! What use were if-onlys and might-have-beens? It was the here and now that mattered. Satisfied she could do no

341

more for James, she clumsily slid the remaining oar into its oarlock and attempted to row. She realized only belatedly that rowing with a single oar caused the boat to spin in circles like a wooden top. Bitterly disappointed, for she had harbored the hope she could somehow row them closer to land, she sank back, defeated by the shattering of her last hope.

She awoke from a restless sleep some time later, a sleep that had been frought with nightmares. She had dreamed they were swallowed whole by a whale like the biblical Jonah, and unable to find their way out of the leviathan's cavernous belly; then that the giant "roc" bird that Isabella had told her of had swooped down upon them from the sky like a Harpy bent on stealing a soul, and carried them off to her nest and her ravenous young, who, mysteriously, had been hatched from enormous pumpkins. She shuddered and opened her eyes.

It was late afternoon, she judged now, for the bright azure skies of morning had fled. The sky now held a dun-colored cast and the clouds looked bruised and swollen. She licked her salty, cracked lips, apprehension building within her. She did not have to be a sailor to recognize the signs. Foul weather was brewing! Jonathan Flynn's account of the *Voyager*'s damage by a cyclone while riding at anchor off St. Mary's came sharply back to mind. If the storms of this savage land could wreak such havoc on a mighty ship of sturdy English oak, what might it do to their fragile craft? They would be blown like a feather before some gigantic bellows! Yet what measures could she take to improve their chances for survival? None, none whatsoever, save to entrust their lives to God—and pray she had not sinned so terribly he would ignore her desperate pleas for salvation.

The sky broiled like a cauldron of pea soup as the hot

winds lifted, swirling masses of grey-yellow cloud. The scent of rain hung in the oppressively humid air and Christianne waited with pounding heart and bated breath for the onslaught to commence.

It came with slanting sheets of warm rain that stung like pinpricks on her burned flesh. The ocean grew choppy and the longboat rocked ominously, water slopping over the sides and filling the bottom. She tried bailing with cupped hands, but soon gave up for the water level rose as fast as she could bail it out. The wind began to blow in earnest, scudding the tiny craft before it with careless ease. She huddled in the bows, shielding James from the furious brunt of the storm with her body, while they pitched and plummetted up and down, up and down in a sickening fashion that made the gorge rise in her throat. The water in the bottom rose inch by inch in direct proportion to her desperation. They were doomed, she realized, short of a miracle! Waves towered over the longboat, threatening to engulf it in their awful embrace. She closed her eyes and prayed fervently.

The longboat heaved and pitched, rolled and righted itself countless times, and each time it seemed would be the last and tore a terrified scream from Christianne's throat. Hair hanging in streaming rat-tails about her face, she clung to James, her face buried in the angle of his shoulder and neck, deriving some little comfort from the mere fact of his presence in her terror. The wind howled like a banshee, whirled like a dervish, cracking the rain like stinging whips, screeching and howling and moaning until she thought she would go mad with the sound.

She toppled headlong from bow to stern as a massive wave slammed against the longboat. As if motion were slowed, she felt herself tumbling head over heels, over and over into the foaming sea. Her last conscious act was to claw wildly for James before blackness closed in like the swirling folds of a sodden cape.

Water lapping lazily at the soles of her feet revived her. She opened her eyes, the realization that she was alive dawning slowly. She struggled to sit up on the wet sand, her head pounding. She retched miserably, her belly ridding itself of swallowed salt water. Gingerly she reached up to touch the back of her head and there discovered the cause of her headache; a knot of no small proportions swelling there like a goose egg beneath her salt-stiff hair. With exquisite slowness, she managed to stand, swaying as a dizzy spell swept over her. As she stood, a great clamor arose and she gaped in disbelief as she surveyed the beach nigh covered with giant birds that were a glorious pink that matched the rosy dawn even now breaking above her. It was as Isabella had so fancifully described! As she took a faltering step toward the shattered remnants of the longboat—flung higher up on the beach—the magnificent flamingo flock rose as one into the heavens, filling the air with the frenzied whirring of their wings and appearing much like the pink-feathered angels Isabella had told her of.

Still awestruck, she staggered up the sand. The longboat was fragmented beyond repair, little more than a framework of timbers. Of James, there was no sign. She sank down to her knees, a sob catching in her throat, and covered her face with her hands. First Ox, dead because of her thoughtlessness, and now James, drowned, and his death, too, was her doing, however indirectly. She couldn't bear it!

"Enough tears, madam," said a croaking voice behind her. " 'Tis my belief we saw water aplenty last night, did we not?"

She looked behind her into James' haggard face. He leaned weakly against a palm tree, and even as she watched, open-mouthed with disbelief, he appeared pale of a sudden and slid limply to the white sand.

"You're alive!" she cried, her joy and relief boundless. She summoned her remaining strength and staggered towards him, flopping down beside him.

"Aye, I believe I am, for the time being, anyway," he agreed with the trace of a grin. "What happened to me? God's blood, woman, I am weak as a babe!" he groaned, struggling up onto his elbows and eyeing her warily. "Is this your doing? Answer me, vixen! Is this the result of another of your damned powders? I sensed no sickness in me when we left St. Mary's last night."

Her happy expression fled, to be replaced by a look that would have withered a lesser man. " 'Tis none of my doing, you ungrateful cur!" she denied, her deep blue eyes flashing. "I awoke the next day to find us adrift, one oar lost and yourself racked with fever. We were far from land even then. And it was two days hence, not last night," she corrected him waspishly. Lord, her head felt like a spike had been nailed into it!

"*Two days!*" He scowled. "A fine captain, am I not, to desert my little vessel in such a fashion! Nay, don't bother to agree with me, wench, I know full well your low opinions of me, and I am too tired to bandy words with you! Forgive me for accusing you," he apologized gruffly, "it was uncalled for."

"Aye, it was, Captain," she agreed, relishing his apology. "But then, a 'murdering whore' is capable of any act, however unlikely and foul, is she not?"

He recalled his words when he had thrown aside his priest's disguise at the fortress to face Flynn. "I spoke in anger and haste then, wench," he growled, a cruel half-smile on his lips, "Ben Wright yet clings to life." The mocking smile deepened. "To my knowledge, you are not yet a *murderer.*" He wearily closed his eyes.

Christianne's face flamed beneath its blisters. His implication was obvious. In his eyes she was no murderer as yet, but the other—aye, he thought her a whore! Well, sick or nay, he could go to the devil! More pity he had not drowned last night, she thought furiously, revitalized in some peculiar way by her anger. Despite it, she was immeasurably pleased to hear that Ben yet lived.

Jungle flanked the sandy cove they had been washed up upon, rimmed with groves of palm and tamarind trees and dense bamboo. Sea birds screamed and wheeled over the dark blue ocean in search of fish, and parrots chattered and scolded in the trees. Still seething, she got to her feet and stalked up the beach towards the jungle.

She brushed aside choking liana vines and springy, leaf-laden branches, searching for the fan-shaped raphia palms she remembered so well from St. Mary's, which Bella had called the traveller's trees. The palm did not come by its name undeservingly, she soon discovered, for within the fleshy center of its fronds was formed a cup that held ample fresh water with which to quench her raging thirst. Herself refreshed, her next thought was for James. She scowled. However intensely she hated him, she could not let him die, and without water he *would* die, and soon, in this heat. He was in no condition to seek water for himself. Muttering angrily under her breath, she cast about her for some means to carry the precious water back to the beach and James, and found it in unexpected fashion; the broken half of a fallen coconut shell, picked clean by the columns of ants that were everywhere about her feet to make a serviceable goblet.

Reluctant gratitude and grudging admiration were reflected in James' eyes when she returned bearing her precious water. She sensed that his pride was sorely pricked and that he would much have preferred to refuse it, but his thirst was victor over his pride. He sipped it sparingly, allowing the water to trickle down his parched throat.

"Nectar, by the gods, 'tis nectar!" he croaked, handing the drained cup back to her.

"Indeed," she agreed sourly, "Are you not afraid that I have poisoned it?"

"Beggers cannot be choosers, madam," he said pointedly, yet his tone was not as sharp as his words, and even as she watched him, a tremor ran through his body.

She smothered her indignant retort. Whatever his sickness was, it still held his body in thrall. The furrows in his tanned face were deeply etched about his cracked lips, and his weary green eyes were rimmed with dark shadows.

"Take off your shirt, sir," she snapped, all crisp efficiency. She dropped to her knees and mounded the sand beneath the shade of the palm tree where he sprawled for a pillow. It was powdery and soft and would serve well.

"Vixen!" he murmured, "What manner of man do you take me for that I would undress at your command?"

"Enough of your banter," she scolded. "Aboard your ship you are indeed master and in command, but here you are but a man, and a sick one at that. Take off your shirt, or else I shall be forced to take it from you." She smiled sweetly.

He did so, amused by her bossiness despite himself. She whipped the shirt from his hand, folded it and spread it over the sand mound. "There, sir, your pillow," she said. Standing again, she brushed the sand from her shift and legs.

James sank back down, cursing his weakened state under his breath. By God, a day or two more of this, and it would be the hen that ruled this roost and not the rooster! he thought. He watched her through slitted eyes as she padded barefoot across the sand, away from him, and began gathering the fallen palm fronds that were strewn all about after the storm. Whatever her sins, the lovely vixen had the power to cause his body to react in almost embarrassingly virile fashion, despite his illness. Had he truly pursued her to St. Mary's for the sake of vengeance alone, he wondered uncomfortably, or had the memory of her small, warm body pressed close to his, and the vision of that sweet elfin face alive with laughter, her thick-lashed eyes aflame with passion, been the real cause for the single-minded doggedness of his pursuit? He groaned inwardly as she labored to pile the heavy fronds neatly. The natural, unself-consciously sensual grace of her carriage and the lithe ripple of her slender figure beneath the thin lawn of her shift were torture to watch! As she bent to her task, her movements afforded him a maddening glimpse of her creamy breasts and the darker cleft between them. Desire hardened him. He wanted her, aye, he *wanted* her! And why not, he argued jealously with himself? She had not balked at leaving his warm bed for Flynn's, and for all he knew, the mute giant, Ox, had taken her, too. So why should he not have her, since she dispensed her favors so freely, he rationalized?

"It is a hard pillow you have made me, Christianne," he remarked idly. "I see another, softer place that I would rest my head upon." His boldness was rewarded by a frosty glare. "I tease you not," he lied, "there is a plaguesome lump beneath my head. A rock, mayhap? I would be forever in your debt if you would remove it."

She eyed him with more than a little mistrust. He

appeared so weak, stretched out there beneath the tree, yet there was a wicked gleam in his eyes now that had not been there minutes before. "Remove it yourself, you wretch," she flared. "I am no innocent maid—thanks to you—to fall for your tricks!" She tossed back her tangled mane of sun-kissed hair and resumed her labors.

"Tricks? What tricks?" he demanded in wounded tones, the very picture of bewildered male innocence.

"You know very well what tricks," she retorted, continuing to stack the palm fonds.

James said nothing. When she peered between the strands of pale hair that fell like a curtain all about her face as she worked, she saw him sigh heavily and wearily pull himself up to sitting. He leaned against the palm trunk briefly to catch his wind, then slowly began sifting through the sand mound for the "plaguesome lump." She watched him for several minutes, certain he had been trying to trick her. Yet when he continued at his search without calling on her for aid again, she began to doubt her suspicions. He had not asked for much. Would it have hurt her to do as he had asked? With a resigned sigh, she stalked over to him and dropped to her knees on the sand next to him.

"Very well, where is this ro—!"

Her question was rudely cut short as his arm snaked around her shoulders and hauled her down onto his chest. His lips slanted across hers, branding them fiercely with fiery kisses that drove the breath from her. She squirmed her hands up between their chests and rained blow after blow at his head and shoulders.

"You conniving rogue!" she panted furiously when he at length drew his lips from hers. "You lied!"

"Aye," he growled, his mouth parting over hers again. His eyes smoldered devil-green with desire. As he kissed

349

her, his hands stroked downwards over her writhing body, gliding across the sleek lines of her waist and hips to cup the impudent globes of her buttocks. She stiffened at this intimate caress and redoubled her furious efforts to free herself from his arms, yet she was held as securely by his arms as a poacher in the village stocks. With ease he rolled her to his side on the sand, throwing one muscled thigh across her hips to keep her there. He chuckled at her outraged expression as he trapped first one thrashing arm by the wrist and then the other, holding them above her head in just one of his fists. Grinning wickedly while she cursed him lustily, he torched a path of fiery kisses from her throat to her breasts, his maddening tongue inflaming the sensitive crests in ever-narrowing circles. Despite herself, quivers of treacherous passion spread insidiously through her veins, sending warm currents to her fingers and toes. Fury filled her. Damn his soul! Would he call her whore one minute and use her for his own the next? And would she, like a fool without an ounce of pride, permit him to do so? He must not take her again, must not see how dangerously she was weakened by his touch, how his kisses and caresses inflamed her, she thought desperately. Aye, it was best she fend off his advances, armor her heart and her body and her mind against him. James Mallory was a highwayman of hearts, plucking them as casually as those "gentlemen of the road" were wont to pluck a purse. And he hated her! To him, this was just another means of avenging her betrayal with Flynn, or, as he believed, her wounding of Ben Wright. She would not be just another of his women, would not let him sweep her reason and sensibility away on tides of meaningless passion, only to continue as before when his lust was sated. Nay! Armed with fresh determination, she knotted her fingers in his russet hair, prepared to tear it out by the roots if he still would not release her. Only belatedly, she realized such measures were unnecessary, for in the few moments she had spent in furious thought, James had fallen asleep, his head pillowed upon her breasts, his warm breath fanning her bare skin. She lay her palm against his cheek, concerned to find his face afire with fever once more, dry and burning to the touch. His body had been too filled yet with the sickness to fulfill the lustful whims of his mind. With a relieved smile, she gently lifted his head from her bosom and slid from beneath him. It was better this way, she told herself firmly, far better. But despite her sensible reasonings, her blood still ran swift and hot as she resumed her labors with the palm fronds.

Long before midday, she had constructed them a hut of sorts. Sapling branches, braced against the longboat at an angle and covered with palm fronds, formed a crude but serviceable lean-to. By the dint of her stubborn will, she managed to drag James inch by inch by his heels beneath its shade, mindful that as the sun climbed to its zenith, the place where he had lain before would lose its leafy shadow. Satisfied he was as comfortable as was humanly possible under such circumstances, she set the coconut shell, filled with water, within easy reach should he awaken, and set off in search of food.

Even in broad daylight, the jungle was an eerie place. As she ventured deeper within it, she was forced to duck and squirm her way between the liana vines that hung everywhere. Tall grasses, still sodden with morning dew, drenched her bare calves and ankles. Bright green tree ferns sprang up about the bases of the trees, their stems curled back on themselves like the handle of a fiddle, she noted fancifully. Between two of the ferns stretched a spider web, its delicate lattice-work ashimmer with dew drops in the green-gold light. Yet she did not tarry to wonder at its beauty overlong, for the spider that had spun that work of art was surely the empress of spiderdom, fat, black and furry, and large as a small crab! She shuddered and hurriedly pressed on.

What little light filtered down through the bushy tops of the swollen-bellied mothers of the forest, the ugly baobab trees, and the tamarinds and vines, was transformed to a peculiar green-gold by the lushness of the vegetation, and the shifting light created the sensation of being under-water. The rank, wet smell of decaying plants and humus and the moist odor of the burgeoning foliage all about her was stifling and seemed to clog rather than cleanse the nostrils. Chatters and hoots and squawks ricocheted in the treetops. She craned upwards, spying several gaudily-feathered parrots there, disturbed by her presence.

There were mushrooms everywhere underfoot, enormous and horribly misshapen, but not knowing whether they were safe to eat, she quickly discarded any notion of picking those for food. The ground was alive, too, with crawling things. Ants of giant proportions and irridescently-carapaced beetles moved busily about her feet. Butterflies with wing spans over four inches in breadth danced from tree to tree in the steamy air above her head. She dared not venture too far, afraid if she did so she might not be able to find her way back to the beach and James. Trying to keep her directions clear in her mind, she struck out now in the direction that she hoped would keep her parallel to the shore.

It was a plaguesome task to fight her way through the trees and bushes, but the hope that there might be banana trees growing here somewhere kept her going. The ripe fruit was a tasty delicacy she had enjoyed in St. Mary's, and they were filling to boot, a perfect repast for a growling belly such as hers and easy to digest for an ailing man such as James.

The undergrowth thinned of a sudden and all at once she found herself in a clearing. The thought struck her like a thunderbolt that she had stumbled upon a native graveyard, for what else could the strange poles, each with a carved wooden bullock or a sun or a moon atop it signify, unless these were the markers of the final resting places of the Malagasy dead? She shivered and hugged herself. A massive escarpment backed the taboo grove, and the eerie silence here, so remote from any other person, was palpable. The terrain was barren and stony in this place, too, as if even the rampant vegetation abhorred this place of the dead. Instead of grass beneath the poles, there were only rocks, obviously carried there from somewhere else by anxious relatives desiring that their loved ones' remains rest undisturbed by predatory *fossas*, the small carnivorous wild cats.

Christianne stifled the urge to turn and careen headlong back the way she had come, and instead steeled herself to cross the native cemetery and plunge into the jungle again beyond it.

Her courage was rewarded! Not many yards further she came across what she sought. Several split-leaved banana trees, some afire with crimson, heart-shaped blossoms, grew lushly in a sunny spot. Many trees were hung with giant bunches of the yellow fruit. She had not thought to bring James' knife, and an entire bunch would prove too heavy to carry very far, so she picked only the ripest ones and filled the skirt of her shift with them. Feeling enormously pleased with herself, she turned to retrace her path back to the beach, but some sixth sense halted her.

She crouched down in the nick of time as a band of Malagasy natives strode into the grove, scant yards from where she was hiding. They wore the same *salaka* loincloths and silk *lambas* or shawls, as the Merina tribe of St. Mary's, and were as dark-skinned and woolly-haired as they. Their women were bare-breasted with brightly patterned silk sarongs wrapped about their hips. One woman, obviously a chiefess or princess by the deference shown to her, pointed to one of the banana trees and spoke a few, imperious words to one of the warriors, who obliged by withdrawing a wicked-looking machete from his hip and cutting down the bunch she had indicated.

Her heart almost in her mouth with fear, Christianne waited motionless in her hiding place until long after the natives had moved on. After what they had done to poor Ox, she had no wish to come up against one of those savages ever again, let alone an entire party of them! When she was certain they had gone, she moved cautiously back the way she had come, using broken and trampled vegetation—made by her clumsy outwards journey—as her signposts. Twice she lost her way and almost succumbed to panic, the urge to cry with relief on finding her path again nigh overwhelming.

She judged almost three hours had passed by the time she plunged out of the jungle and found herself back in the dazzling sunlight on the sun-baked beach. It was late afternoon, she guessed by the sun's position halfway toward the horizon, and she said a hasty prayer of thanks that she had found her way back before dusk.

James still slept deeply in the palm-frond lean-to, but a quick glance showed that he had awakened at some point and drank the water she had left him. She pressed her palm to his forehead, consternation filling her. The fever was rising yet again. His skin was burning and the crimson flush against his pallid cheeks boded ill. It seemed another night of torture lay ahead for him. How many times could his body withstand the racking chills, the outpouring of his sweat, the consuming heat that devoured it, before relinquishing the fight?

She ate two of the bananas without tasting them, determined to maintain her own strength so that she could minister to James if need be. Afterwards she lobbed rocks up into the coconut trees, hoping to dislodge the green-husked nuts that hung there so that she might use the shells to collect more water from the traveller's trees, or at least give James their sweet, white milk to drink, to slake his raging thirst. Her efforts were futile. Though several of the husks crashed to the powdery sand at her feet, she was not strong enough to hack them open with James' knife to release the brittle, hairy nut within. She was forced to content herself with filling the single shell, drinking her own fill before returning to the lean-to.

That night was the longest, loneliest she had ever experienced. The least rustle of the wind in the palms, and she was certain hordes of screaming savages would leap out of the darkness to slay them both. In the shadows of the dancing palm fronds, she imagined all manner of horrible monsters or ferocious beasts. James' fever rose alarmingly that night, too, as she had expected. When he cried aloud for water, she moistened his cracked lips with fresh water from the coconut shell; when he moaned that he was being burned alive, she made trek after trek down the starlit beach to the shoreline, to wet yet another scrap of her shift to bathe the rivers of sweat from his body. When he shivered and his teeth chattered with cold, she warmed him with the heat of her body. As she lay there, looking up at the starlit sky through the slatted palm fronds, she wondered if the dawn would find him rid of his fever, or a stiffening corpse in her arms.

The fever broke in the wee hours, much to Christianne's relief. Torrents of perspiration poured in rivulets down his face and chest, and he thrashed and cursed and shouted, communing with his demons. As she had the night previous in the longboat, she soothed him with soft-spoken words and wiped his brow, until at last his breathing eased and became regular, as one who sleeps a normal sleep.

Exhausted to the point of numbness, Christianne fell down beside him and slept, too.

Twenty-Five

It was three days before James was strong enough to leave the lean-to. Beneath his new growth of beard, which was but a shade less fiery than his russet hair, he still appeared somewhat gaunt and pale but immeasurably better than he had at the height of the fever, and her fears that he would succumb to the sickness abated. Whatever its cause, he had weathered it.

The morning after her foray into the jungle for bananas and her abortive attempt to break open the coconuts, she availed herself of James' knife. For the past two days she had laboriously dehusked several of them, both for the tasty nutmeats and the milk, and for use as cups. Her hands showed the toll the arduous task had exacted. Blisters had formed but long since been broken, and angry, raw flesh showed red over the entire palms of both hands. She rocked back on her heels and wiped the perspiration from her brow with her knuckles, wincing as its salt bit into her wounds. Though it was not yet midday, it was already fiercely hot in the cove. Her hair was damp and curled about her sunburned, peeling face in limp tendrils. The ragged shift clung to her body like a second skin. 'Twas hotter than Hades, she thought, wearily, inspecting her sore hands.

James, clad only in his tattered breeches, his dripping shirt slung over his shoulder, noticed her pained expression as he came striding up the beach, refreshed by his swim. He spread the wet shirt across the palm-thatch roof of the lean-to and dropped to his knees beside her on the sand.

"Come, give me the knife, Christie," he said. " 'Tis my turn now."

Stubbornly, Christianne shook her head. "No, I can manage," she insisted. "You must rest until you regain your strength."

"I have rested long enough while you labored," James said, his tanned hands closing over hers. He turned them over, palm up, an unfathomable expression in his eyes. "Look at your hands!" So saying, he drew her bloodied palms to his lips and kissed them gently. "I would prefer a healing balm to soothe your hurt," he murmured huskily, "but, alas, my kisses will have to suffice. I owe you my life, Christie! Forgive me for my churlishness before?"

"I did nothing that anyone else would not have done, under similar circumstances," she insisted, her heart behaving most erratically as she looked up into his eyes. In the dazzling sunlight, she saw that the irises were not green alone, as she had thought, but flecked with hazel and amber. The thin cut down his cheek where Jonathan's sword had nicked him had healed well. The paler scar was but a thin, pink line against his tan. She looked hurriedly away, suddenly aware that she had been staring at him over-long. "You have no need to feel beholden to me," she continued, "I but repaid my debt to you. If you had not made me run with you into the jungle, I, too, would be dead by now at Flynn's hands, or at the Malagasy's. So you see, sir, we are even," she pointed out with an uncertain smile, "Your life for mine. A fair trade."

James shook his head grimly, unable to look her in the

face himself now. "Nay, lass, not so. You see, it was with no such noble motive of saving your life that I came back up the beach for you. I had sworn to recapture you from Flynn and to have revenge for Ben's wounding at all costs!" She had paled a little at his frank confession, but her jaw came up defiantly, he saw.

"I see," she said levelly, trying to appear unmoved by what he had said. "Well, whatever your reasons, you did save my life—unless you intend to now kill me yourself?" Her voice quavered as she said the latter, for at the fortress he had seemed quite capable of doing so in his anger. She watched him from beneath lowered lashes. Who was he really this man beside her? Was he James Mallory the avenger, hurling aside his priest's skirts, green eyes blazing emerald fire, to challenge Jonathan Flynn to a duel to the death and spitting contemptuously that she was a "murdering whore"? Or was he James Mallory the lover, he whose caresses could cause her to tremble, whose kisses could sear her lips with flaming passion and reduce her token protests to sighs of sweet surrender? She suspected the real man lay somewhere between the two extremes, a combination of fierce loyalty to those he held dear, and bitter, merciless hatred towards his enemies. He was a man who loved life and lived each day to the fullest, drinking deeply of the cup of experience that life poured him, be it bitter or sweet to the palate.

"If you had been near at hand when I found Ben, I would have killed you with my bare hands," James said, eyes narrowing. "But now—no. You need not fear me."

She laughed shakily. "I am glad! Your—your honesty is a little disconcerting, sir. I confess, it has shaken me. Now may I be as honest with you?"

He nodded, his handsome face grave, and paused in his husking of the coconuts, knife in hand.

"Whatever you may choose to believe," she began uncertainly, "the dagger that wounded Ben was thrown by Flynn, not me. Surely you could not think that I would harm Ben? He was my friend! I would a thousand times have wished the blade had struck my belly than his! Ben Wright was kindness itself to me," she averted her eyes, "especially at times when you, sir, were . . . not kind. I—I was gulled by Jonathan's silver tongue, I admit it. I hated you for taking me against my will, for forcing me to leave England, for comparing me to your past women even as I lay in your arms! My only thought was to run away from you, to somehow find my way back to England. I agreed to jump ship with Jonathan, thinking he would help me to do so. He promised there would be no bloodshed, but I know now that his promises count for naught. He asked for my dagger, in case we were attacked by sharks when we leaped into the water, he said. But when Ben came running across the decks towards us, I believe his hatred of him surfaced. Ben was unarmed, and could have done nothing to prevent us from fleeing the ship, yet Jonathan hurled the dagger at him before we jumped over the side. I knew then that I had made a grave error in trusting him, but by then it was too late." She shivered. "I think now that Jonathan blamed Ben for his flogging. He *wanted* him dead!"

"And yet if I had in truth been the priest, you would have married such a man!" James remarked, his tone scornful.

Christianne sighed heavily. How could he, a man, understand? "I could see no other alternative, can't you see? If I balked at agreeing to wed him, he would have ravished me! I had hoped to buy myself some time by agreeing to become his bride, by going along with his madman's notions, but my time had run out."

"Madman?"

She shrugged. "Aye, at times he seemed a madman. At others, he had charm enough to lure the very birds from the trees! He is obsessed with the notion, you see, that all women are but harlots at heart, as was his mother. It was only by convincing him that I was not like her, that I was as unsullied and chaste as he wanted me to be, that I was able to protect myself. I was so afraid he would learn the truth! Ox — Ox was fond of me. He appointed himself my guardian. He and I planned to escape, with Bella's help. Isabella is Jonathan's former mistress, you see. We planned that she would take my place and marry him, but everything went wrong and we were forced·to abandon the masquerade. I believed I had no choice but to go ahead with the ceremony."

James frowned. Her story seemed far-fetched, though much of it, he had to admit, tallied with what Nicholas Drew at the trading post at Fénérive had told him of Flynn's peculiar attitude towards women. Could he believe her? The Christianne he had known would never have permitted any man to take her weapon from her, save by force, as he had.

Christianne read the doubt and disbelief in his expression and her hopes that he would understand, would believe her, died a miserable death. She jumped to her feet. " 'Tis as I expected!" she cried. "You will never believe me! I should have known better than to try and explain it all to you. Well, Sir Captain, think what you will, I care not! For all that I have been a cutpurse and a pickpocket in my life, I still have my honor. Everything that I have told you is true. I can say no more to convince you. The rest is up to you!" She turned and would have run from him, tears already springing into her deep blue eyes, but before she could flee his hand snaked out and his steely fingers fastened about her wrist.

"Where was your 'honor' the night you cried out your passion in my arms and but minutes after slipped poison into my wine?" he demanded cruelly, green eyes scorching her.

" 'Twas no poison," she retorted, "but a harmless sleeping draught!" She did not add that she had drugged him for his own safety, that it was to have been his watch that night and she had feared he would try to prevent Flynn and herself from jumping ship and be harmed, perhaps killed, in the process. If he did not believe the rest of her story, he would hardly be likely to believe that! Let him think what he would, she thought dully.

"We shall never know if 'twas poison or nay, will we," he said darkly, "since I drank none of it?" His hold on her wrist tightened, his gentleness of just minutes before fled with the resurgence of his bitterness over her betrayal.

"You may ask Matthew Locke when you rejoin your ship!" she shouted. "It was him I got the powder from! Now, let me go!" She wrenched her wrist free and ran from him down the beach, blinded by her tears.

James took a single step after her, then thought better of it. What could he say if he followed her? That he believed her, trusted her? Nay, she would know he lied. As much as he wanted to believe her, he could not. He muttered an oath and wearily rubbed the itchy stubble sprouting along his jaw and chin. Lord! The sickness had left him weaker than he cared to admit! Was it the miasma, or malaria, as some called it, or some other sickness? He fancied it was malaria, for he had seen other men, sea faring men who sailed the warmer climes, similarly afflicted. If it was the same, there was more to come. The disease was said to be caused by the vapors that rose from the steaming swamps found in tropic lands, or from the bite of the plaguesome mosquito. Once affected, the sickness lay dormant in the body for weeks, perhaps months, only to rise up and strike the victim as virulently as the first time when he was weakened by fatigue. Even should they find their way back to civilization, his future was bleak. How could he ever again captain a ship when the miasma could lay him low at any time—perhaps a time when his vessel and his crew needed his captaincy desperately? Aye, he might as well face up to the worst now: his sailing days were done. In the meantime, he must plan for their survival. He looked about him.

Whatever else Christianne might be guilty of, he could not fault her on courage, nor on ingenuity. The lean-to she had made had shaded them from the sun during the hottest part of the day, a sun that burned down so fiercely it appeared like a spinning, white-hot ball of fire. Without the lean-to's shade, he could not have survived, he knew. She had amazed him, too, with her collecting of fresh water from those enormous, fan-shaped palms—what had she called them? Ah, yes, travellers' trees! Liar she might be, and perhaps more, but she was no weakling and no coward despite her fragile appearance and dainty beauty. Beneath them lay a core of steel! He glanced down the beach at her small figure, wading listlessly along the waterline, white-foam ruffles licking up the sand to ripple over her feet. Her slender shoulders were bowed as if she carried all the woes of the world upon them, and he knew instinctively that within that creamy curtain of hair that shielded her face from him she would be crying. God in heaven, why could he not reconcile his warring feelings for her? Part of him wanted desperately to go after her, to take her in his arms and kiss away her tears, to tell her he believed in her, would protect her, care for her. The other part of him wanted only to hurt her, exact vengeance for

Ben's stabbing, to be well rid of her. He shook his head, confused, and retrieved his knife from where he had dropped it earlier. Given a sturdy handle, the knife would serve well as a fishing spear, he decided. He strode towards the jungle in search of wood to fashion one.

The harsh heat of noon was soon upon them. The sun danced on the glittering, dark blue water and turned the white sand hot as coals beyond the shade of the palms. Christianne returned eventually to seek that shadow. Only silence lay between she and James since their impassioned exchange earlier.

He sat cross-legged on the sand, whittling away at several sturdy lengths of bamboo he had found at the edge of the jungle. There were massive stands of the elegant plant everywhere. By the morrow, he promised himself, they would have a hut for their shelter and fish for their board.

"Christianne," he began with unaccustomed hesitance, "we are cast here, unwilling companions thrown together by the hand of Fate. For our survival, we must combine forces, think you not, and put aside our animosity for the time being?" He grinned. "If we cannot be friends, can we at least be as we were before—cordial enemies? We have hardships enough to face without being constantly at each other's throats!" He waited hopefully for her answer.

At length, she sighed heavily. "Very well," she agreed, "but on one condition only—you will treat me as an equal, not as a child."

He nodded. "Agreed. I, too, have a condition. That we both agree to venture nowhere alone, beyond this cove, forthwith. If one goes, then so must the other. Does that strike you fair?"

She saw the sense in what he suggested and nodded assent. "Indeed it does, sir."

"Good!" James declared, smiling. The tension between them had thinned considerably now. "The bargain struck, we must seal it, must we not?" he suggested roguishly.

"How?" she asked innocently. "We have no parchment nor quill with which to set it down."

"There are other ways to strike a bargain, my sweet," he said solemnly, "much as you paid your debt to me aboard the *Fair Amanda!* We could seal it with a kiss, mayhap?"

"I think not!" she exploded. That crafty fox! That honey-tongued rogue! So that was his little game! She was not good enough to be trusted to tell the truth, yet worthy enough yet to warm his bed when the fancy struck him. "A simple clasping of hands will more than suffice, sir," she said coldly.

He inclined his head, eyes twinkling. "As you wish," he agreed.

Christianne extended her hand with a frosty smile. His warm, dry hand enfolded it. She made to withdraw hers but his fingers tightened about it. With a swift jerk, he hauled her across the short distance that separated them and over his muscled thighs. Wasting no time, he gathered her up into his arms and staunched her scream of outrage with a lengthy kiss that drove the breath from her lungs.

When he released her, she scrambled from his lap, her eyes hurling shards of sapphire glass into his grinning face.

" 'Twas as I expected, lass," he drawled, rolling away as she raised her hand to slap his face, "a kiss is ever the most satisfying means to seal a bargain!" He sprang lightly to his feet.

"Traitor!" Christianne gritted under her breath as she watched him return to his whittling. She spoke to her heart.

"Tomorrow I'll scout around and try to discover where we are," he said casually as if the kiss had never been. "If

I'm not mistaken, we're on the eastern coast of Madagascar."

"Madagascar!" she exclaimed, her anger forgotten. "But I thought this was an island, a small island, I mean?"

James grunted noncommittally as he tore strips of his shirt to lash his knife to the handle he'd made. "Could be, but I doubt it. There aren't many islands in these waters, and judging by the way everything was flattened by the storm, we must have been blown in a northeasterly direction. Madagascar is enormous—thrice the size of England, to be exact. I would wager my life that's where we are! We'll rest up for a week or so, then make our way along the coast. Sooner or later, we'll strike civilization again."

"Whatever you think is best," Christianne agreed with a marked lack of enthusiasm. "But we'll have to be careful. There's a Malagasy village not far from here."

James' head snapped up. "How do you know that?" he asked sharply.

"When I went into the jungle that first day to look for bananas I saw them, a whole party of them, with their chiefess. There was a cemetery or a burial ground of sorts, too. It was very strange," she finished, wrinkling her nose.

"You went off on your own?" James shook his head in exasperation. "You little idiot! Did it not enter your pretty little head that you could have been lost—perhaps even killed?"

She shrugged. "Of course it did, I am not entirely stupid! But we would have died without food and water. As I saw it, I had very little option left to me."

James reluctantly had to admit she was right.

He knotted the cloth strips firmly about the handle of his knife and thrust the makeshift spear hard into the sand.

"Well," he said with a grin, "it's finished. Our days of

feasting on bananas alone will shortly be over! With this little beauty we will soon have fish aplenty for our board. Why don't you gather some wood while I give it a try—but stay out of the sun, you're burned to a crisp already."

She nodded, unable to resist a smile. "I'll gather it, but only as a *token* of my good faith in your talents as a fisherman!"

Fists on hips, he feigned a wounded expression as he towered over her. "Good faith? You saucy baggage! Madam, I will have you know that I am no novice fisherman! Why, when I last fished the river near my family home in Salem, the fish stood upon their tails in the water and implored me to catch them! Aye, laugh if you will, vixen, but 'tis true!" he vowed indignantly. "Those I could not fit into my basket leaped over the banks and followed me home through the grass like pups."

"A tall tale, and told without embellishment, as befits a true fisherman!" she laughed. "Lead on then, King Neptune! I would see you charm the fish of these waters to that trident in your hand! And after you have, oh, perhaps a baker's dozen or so to prove yourself, *then* I will gather the kindling," she promised with an impish smile.

James grinned. "You have another bargain, lass! Shall we seal it as we did before?"

She shook her head. What a rogue he was!

His green eyes twinkled merrily. "Spread my shirt over you, then, and let's go."

He spent the greater part of the afternoon waist-deep in water along the coral reef that encircled the cove, the crude spear brandished aloft over his shoulder. From time to time his arm would plunge downwards and he would yell with excitement, only to curse lustily on finding his spear empty on bringing it back up. His patience was further strained to hear Christianne's merry laughter tinkling over the shallows each time he missed his slippery quarry.

"Silence, wench," he growled good-naturedly over his shoulder, "your laughter frightens the damnable fish away!"

"Do not blame me for your lack of skill, sir!" she retorted. "Mayhap the fish of these waters are not so well-mannered as those of Salem, or speak a different tongue and understand not your charm!" She smiled sweetly. "Why not admit it—you are bested! We will make do with *my* bananas and coconuts."

"Never!" he gritted, setting his jaw stubbornly and scanning the crystal-clear, blue water about him. "I shall perservere until I succeed. We will have fish for supper, by God, or nothing at all!" He glanced over his shoulder at Christianne, who sat on the sand hugging her knees, his shirt spread over her shoulders. "Gather the firewood, lass. It will convince these plaguesome fish that I mean business."

She laughed and scrambled to her feet. "Aye, aye, sir!"

She had a fair-sized stack of kindling gathered when a triumphant whoop carried from James. She shaded her eyes against the dazzling light to see him holding his bamboo spear aloft, impaled on which was a wriggling silverfish. The set of his bare, muscled chest and shoulders and his arrogant swagger as he carried his catch to a flat rock at the water's edge said it all, without need for words! That first catch of the day also bespoke a change of his fortunes. Soon three other fish lay bright-eyed and scaly next to the first. At length he waded from the water, picked them up by their tails and sprinted up the beach to their camp. He flipped the fish into her lap.

"Supper, milady!" he declared as she jumped in surprise.

"So I see!" she agreed, grimacing. Her deep blue eyes

challenged him. "Would you eat them raw?"

"Why not?" James answered unabashed, sprawling on the sand beside her. "In many parts o' the world, 'tis sacrilege to cook such fine, fresh fish as these." He grinned.

She made a face and tossed them at his head one by one, but he caught them easily. "Ugh!" she said with a shudder, "then I shall eat only bananas this even', sacrilege or nay!"

James laughed. "For a woman marooned and half-starved, you are a fickle wench. However, I shall bend to those fickle tastes and cook a feast for you the like of which you have never tasted before," he promised

"Without tinder or flint to light the fire?" she challenged.

He smiled unfathomably but said nothing as he gathered a small pile of dried leaves and sere grass, of which there was plenty about the jungle's edge. Her puzzlement turned to frank amazement as he knelt and vigorously set about rubbing a pair of dry twigs together. Soon a spark ignited the dried foliage and started it smoldering, then burning. In minutes he had a crackling driftwood fire ablaze and had gutted the fish and spitted them lengthwise on shafts of bamboo. Sea birds swooped down to carry off the innards as the appetizing aroma of cooking fish wafted into the sultry late-afternoon heat, making her mouth water. Christianne watched the fire and the fish with almost unbearable anticipation and impatience.

They feasted in grand fashion that evening, filling their bellies with crisp fish, bananas and coconuts. Afterwards they sat in amicable silence and watched the fiery, crimson orb of the sun sink over the horizon, washing the violet ocean with blood-red momentarily before it vanished. A milky crescent moon rose through the hot dusk to govern the night. The silence between them lengthened and expanded to fill the velvet darkness, through which myriad pin-pricks of starlight glittered hotly far above them. James heaped more driftwood on the fire. The crackle of burning branches, the restless splash of the ocean, the sigh of the warm night breezes in the trees and the reedy chirrup of the cicadas were the only sounds.

James glanced across at Christianne. Her face was illumined by firelight, the alternating light and shadow of the flickering flames of their campfire lending an aura of mystery to the elfin loveliness of her face.

She chanced to look up at him at that moment and caught his silent appraisal of her. She quickly looked away, warmth flooding her face. But before she had done so, he had seen that her wide, long-lashed eyes had held an inner radiance, as if he had caught a glimpse into her soul and seen her desire for him shining there more brightly than the flames, the amber glow of which touched the slim curves of her shoulders and danced in her silvery hair.

Her blush deepened as she felt his eyes upon her still. A tingling warmth flooded through her under his grave scrutiny. Did his thoughts in any way parallel her own, she wondered breathlessly, acutely aware of the sudden racing of her heart and the trembling in her limbs. It was madness, she knew, but a single green-eyed glance from the man who sprawled across the fire from her could inflame her desire for him as surely as the most intimate caress. She had thought in her naiveté that perhaps any man could have that effect, that wonderful, wonderful effect, on her senses, but now she knew better. Jonathan had also kissed her, touched her, held her in his arms, but she had felt only revulsion from his kisses and embraces, while in James' arms she felt—what? Whole, complete, as if she belonged there.

I love you. The words sounded crystal-clear in her mind, like the sweet pure notes of a silver bell, and she startled half-afraid for a moment that she had said them aloud, that he had heard. But no, he was still gazing dreamily into the fire, its amber flames reflected in his green eyes.

She clenched her fists in her lap, then unconsciously unfurled them very slowly, like flower buds unfurling, until they were flat. She pressed them against her belly, as if cradling the mystery within. *Not yet!* a voice said inside her head, *not a word, not yet!* Now was not the time to tell him. Perhaps there never would be a right time. A tear slipped down her cheek, a teardrop of topaz, colored by the fire. She carried his child, yet he felt nothing but hatred for her! If they found their way back to civilization and thence, somehow, to New Orleans, he would discharge his obligation to her aunt and quit her life without a backward glance. She would become just a memory to him, if he remembered her at all, tucked at random into the storeroom of his mind along with all the other pleasant memories of women he had taken to his bed and made love to. Another woman, one with less pride, perhaps, than she possessed, would have used the fact that she carried his child to bind him to her, but not Christianne. Hers was a fierce pride. She would rather he left her than stayed with her out of pity or for the child's sake alone. More tears sparkled on her lashes. She looked at him across the fire. Since he had kissed her teasingly that morn, her fingers had itched to touch him, to trace the outline of his chiselled lips, his strong, square jaw, to feel the rippling sinews of his arms and back flex beneath her fingertips. And, oh, how she ached to feel his touch upon her, too! Sudden, sweet warmth encompassed her, and under her sweeping lashes her gaze became transfixed upon his mouth, dreamily imagining, half-hoping he

371

would make some move to kiss her again. *Devil take my pride!* she thought, mesmerized by his lips, she wanted him, hungered for him with every part of her, ached to feel those lips upon her body as if he had bewitched her in some way! Seen through the rainbow-colored flames which leaped and writhed in a pagan ballet against the black backdrop of the jungle, she could well believe he was a wizard with powers of ensorcelment, capable of casting spells with those mysterious green eyes. Those eyes were hooded now and withheld his thoughts and feelings from her. Did he desire her, too, she wondered?

"Christianne?"

The huskily-spoken word roused her from her reverie.

"I—I!" She began and faltered, not knowing what she had intended to say, if anything.

Somehow he knelt behind her now. He reached out and parted the silken swathes of her hair and hungrily pressed his lips to the nape of her neck. His lips were warm, his breath hot, and delicious dancing shivers of pleasure eddied up and down her spine, making her moan softly with delight.

"Don't! Don't!" she cried in anguish, while her body cried, "Yes!" with every fiber of its being. "I will not!" With her erotic imagings just minutes before, her resolution to refuse him slipped dangerously away from her, like smoke in the wind or water through her fingers.

"Why?" he whispered, nuzzling her throat, his warm breath inflaming her beyond reason or thought, "Tell me why not, my beautiful Christianne!"

She shook her head helplessly. What reason could she give? Normal morals had no place here, under such abnormal circumstances! "I—I don't want you to make love to me!" she whispered, spiralling inch by inch into the whirlpool of pleasure he was creating with his lips.

"Liar!" he challenged with a low, husky laugh, "you want me as much as I want you, my sweet, my wild, sweet Christie! I feel it here—and here—and here!" So saying, he kissed her throat, her slender shoulders, the narrow ridge of her spine.

She gasped and arched backwards against his broad chest, feeling the heat that radiated from him as fiery as a brazier, and wanting to warm herself at the source of that heat. His powerful arms encircled her, drawing her fiercely backwards against his chest. He filled his hands with the soft weight of her breasts and buried his lips in the angle of her throat and shoulders, kissing hungrily along her neck to the curve of her cheek and then to her ear. A soft, pleasure-filled sigh escaped her as he outlined its delicate shape with the tip of his tongue. Her breasts tautened beneath the lawn shift. The crests, so soft just seconds before, surged and became tumescent beneath his touch. His breathing grew husky and rapid against her ear.

"I want you," he whispered urgently, drawing her down to the sand beside him, "I want you more than words can tell! Aye, my love, and I will have you!" He kissed her brow, her nose, her flaming cheeks, butterfly-fragile kisses that made her hunger for more.

She would have cried out recklessly that she wanted him, too, but his lips parted over hers, inflaming, masterful lips as she had remembered. He gathered her into his arms as if he could not hold her close enough nor tightly enough, could not bear that a hairsbreadth should separate her body from his. Her total surrender to his embraces ignited the smoldering embers of his desire as surely as if she were a torch. And so she seemed, to him! Her body beneath his caresses was fire and heat, glowing and vibrant; her flesh was silken to his touch, her taste as nectar to his lips!

She returned his caresses with a wild, reckless abandon

he had never known before, her hands stroking hungrily across his furred chest, wonderment filling her as his masculinely flat nipples hardened as had hers under his touch. She stroked downwards, brushing the red-gold pelt there with her lips and fingertips, her breath catching in her throat as she touched his hard belly and his flanks and realized the measure of his desire for her. With trembling hands, she unbuckled his belt and his breeches, a shuddering sob wrest from her as his manhood surged under her faltering caresses. The man that lay unclad on the sand before her now was a wonder of creation, she thought, dizzy with desire, every part of him lean, well-muscled and wholly, masculinely beautiful, from his broad shoulders to his golden-tanned torso and thence to his strong, virile legs. There was no shame in his nakedness. Rather, the shame was to cover such glorious, animal beauty with garments, she thought as she gazed shamelessly upon him, the firelight shifting and dancing over his body like a jealous mistress. He lay there, a half-smile on his face, watching her through eyes that were dark, a sensual forest green, and heavy-lidded with desire.

Overwhelmed by passion, she moaned softly, resting her flaming cheek against his hard belly momentarily before leaning up and lifting the ragged hem of her shift. She wanted to be as naked and natural as he; to feel the delightful sensation of her aching flesh pressed tightly to his; to clasp him deep within her and move with him upon the sand in ancient rhythms as old as humankind itself.

He stayed her hands with his own. "Nay, my heart, let that pleasure be mine!" he whispered, raising himself to kneeling. The leaping flames lit his russet hair from behind, and made of it a fiery halo as he reached out to raise her shift. Inch by glorious, unbearable inch, he lifted the tattered garment from her. As each new portion of her pearly flesh lay bared before him, he kissed it with branding lips, claimed it as his own, until her breathing grew throaty and quickened unbearably, and her fingers knotted and unknotted in his hair with her passion.

When she finally knelt unclad before him, he hungrily devoured her loveliness with his eyes for endless moments that were an eternity to her. Her deep blue eyes were blatantly pleading, shamelessly wanting when at last he bore her down to the sand beneath him.

His emotions as he moved deeply against her were overwhelming. Never had he known such intensity of feeling before, never! It was madness; he was nothing to her, she meant nothing to him! Yet he wanted her with a fiery passion that consumed him, tore at his body and racked him. He mistrusted her, believed her capable of any trickery, yet beside her all other women paled, ceased to exist, became nothing! He could not, would not let her go, nay, not even for Ben's sake, gentle Ben who lay still and fevered in the *Fair Amanda*'s great-cabin, her knife wound in his belly! Sweat poured from his brow, his chest. A moan of anguish tore from his lips. He thrust deeper, faster within her, hoping in desperation to purge himself of his soul-consuming, mindless desire for her that possessed him like a demon. Her cries of pleasure, her whispered endearments, were more erotic than any eastern aphrodisiac to his careening senses. She was a she-devil, a temptress, a vixen, an angel—his life!

"Christianne!" he cried, and thrust one last time against her, pressing his lips against her throat as a shuddering spasm of ecstasy released him from his sweet torment.

"Yes! Oh, yes!" she cried brokenly as she arched upwards to receive him, feeling a flaming whirlwind of rapture lift and soar her upwards, as if borne on fiery wings, to the very zenith of the heavens.

A dawn of pearl-pink and saffron-yellow found them still entangled in the afterglow of their passion, beside the dying fire. A chorus of noisy seabirds and squawking parrots sang raucous matins in the palm trees, and the sun yawned and stretched and leaped over the horizon, extending golden arms to embrace the rising world.

Many miles north of that isolated sunlit cove, the storm-tossed *Fair Amanda* limped into a safe harbor, too crippled to continue on to the Caribbees as her captain had ordered.

Twenty-Six

Conversely, instead of their passionate love-making bringing them closer together after that night, it had the reverse effect and acted as a wedge to drive them apart.

Long after Christianne had fallen asleep in his arms, James lay awake, scowling up at the moon and the star-lit sky as if angry at them for mocking his confusion. Try as he might, he could not reconcile the warring emotions inside him for Christianne! She had willfully betrayed him, endangered his life and those of all aboard the *Fair Amanda,* and that betrayal had caused the grave, perhaps mortal, wounding of his dearest friend and first officer, and the death of Luke Hardcastle, who had been guarding the brig. He should have felt only contempt for her, hatred and mistrust. Yet what he felt instead was a growing depth of affection for her, a desire to cherish and protect her that sat uneasily with his conscience. The pleasure that had sung through him when he had made love to her was now tainted by guilt in his memory. And, so, unable to reconcile his desire for Christianne with his fury at her, he rationalized the former as being nothing more than a purely physical obsession and sternly denied his more tender feelings.

Aye, he told himself as he strode the damp, dark sand,

she was his, the spoils of his vengeful quest to recapture her from Flynn, to be used as he, the victor, saw fit. Women, he told himself, had always been chattel, used by men, traded like other possessions by men. Why should he feel guilt or remorse for using her to slake his lust as any other man would have done, under similar circumstances? He cursed and angrily kicked the unblemished sand, leaving an ugly, dark wound in its smoothness. He was lying to himself, now! Aye, he lied, he thought with a heavy sigh. He had always been unlike his peers in that he had never thought of women in those terms. He had always considered them delightful equals, in intelligence and in talents and in the sight of God, lacking only in physical strength from being all that men were, and making up that difference by being much, much more pleasing to look upon and softer-curved in one's arms! True, he had taken more than his fair share of women to bed, but with the exception of Amanda, and then Christianne, they had all been warm, willing and eager to partake in his lustful forays. Even Amanda's ravishment by him had been more a misunderstanding than anything, and he had not forced himself on her a second time—as he had with the creamy-haired minx. He had used his greater experience against her, he knew full well, aware that she was too naive, too innocent to resist his knowing lips and his caresses. Aye, he had used her very innocence against her as a weapon, wielded his considerable skills in the arts of love to overcome her resistance and her protests. Though he had used no physical strength, was he not guilty of a form of ravishment? Perhaps the depth of his feelings for her, that will o' the wisp, faerie creature, was his punishment for that seduction? Never had he admitted it before, but he had wanted her since the first night he had seen her as a woman, with the candlelight and the firelight bathing her in their amber glow in the room at the Golden Goose tavern in London, then again when she had looked up at him in the house on Darling Lane, her face framed perfectly by a halo of silver fox fur and the folds of her cloak red as blood about her slender form.

He sighed heavily, recalling how he had disentangled himself from her arms that night, seeking an answer to his troubled thoughts in the solitude of the deserted white beach and the rhythm of the ocean and the yawning vastness of the night.

Christianne had awakened the next morning to find him again at her side, though she knew he had left her briefly during the night to walk to beach, for she had missed the warmth of his body beside her on the sand and wakened to see his tense frame silhouetted against the moon-washed ocean.

There had been a marked reserve between them that next morning, as if they both were stunned by the heights of passion they had scaled together the night before. Christianne had moved about their camp with shyly downcast eyes, afraid to look James full in the face for fear she would not see reflected in his eyes the same emotion she knew must be revealed in hers. When finally she had dared to look at him, she felt as if her heart would wither up and die in her breast, for she saw only anger and distance in James' eyes, nothing more.

Tears rolled in torrents down her suddenly-pale cheeks. She had cast aside the coconut she carried and fled to the perimeter of the jungle, there to sob out her grief in private. Last night had changed nothing between them, she realized bitterly, nothing! He had only been using her again to satisfy his lust. When he is hungry, he eats; when he is thirsty, he drinks; when he has need of a woman to ease his body, he takes me, she thought, hating him and loving him simultaneously. Could he not see how he had wounded her with his eyes? Was he blind where she was concerned? Or—was he merely indifferent? She sobbed, her shoulders heaving. Even the lowliest strumpet deserved better than indifference, the remoteness and anger she had read in his expression! She could deal with his hatred, and his contempt, for both showed true emotion, however negative. But his indifference? Never!

That morning had been nigh two weeks ago, she recalled, and things between them had changed little. They still labored together for their survival, but it was as if they were strangers, too polite, too considerate of each other. He had made no attempt to kiss her or to touch her in any way. She felt akin to a leper. All I need is a bell and a sign that reads, "Unclean!" for all to see and know, she thought miserably, feeling little better now than she had back then.

James noted her listlessness as he strode up the beach and his eyes narrowed. She had grown thinner over the past two weeks and looked weary and fragile. Guilt pricked him. He had done this to her by shunning her, he realized, and the knowledge wrenched at his heart. He wanted her still, had never stopped wanting her, but since that night he had made love to her beside their campfire, he could not be certain if he wanted her for herself or simply to still the cravings of his body, or for a perverted need for satisfaction of his revenge for her stabbing of Ben. He had determined that until he could take her in love, without the doubts that plagued him, he would not take her again. He scowled and tossed the fish he'd caught down on the sand before her.

"Here!" he ordered, brusque with anger at himself, "clean them."

Angry color flooded her pale face. How dare he talk to

her in such a fashion! "Clean them yourself!" she retorted. "We are not master and servant, nor husband and wife, that you may tell me so rudely what to do!"

His jaw tightened. "Aye, thank the gods, indeed we're not," he acknowledged with feeling. "But nevertheless, since I have caught them, you *will* clean them. Remember, you asked that I treat you as an equal, not as a child?" She nodded. "Then do it, and cease this sulky pouting like a spoilt child!"

"Sulky pouting indeed!" she flared, tossing her pale hair over her shoulder. "At least I do not growl and curse from morn to even' like a bear with a thorn in its paw!" Her deep blue eyes flashed angry sparks, and with her hands on her hips she appeared like a beautiful warrior from some ancient tribe of Anglo-Saxons. "As for the fish, I am tired of cleaning them and more tired of eating them! Can you find us nothing else? I swear, the smell makes me retch! 'Tis like Billingsgate Market of a Friday morning!"

"So it would appear," he agreed sourly, "But since we already have a fish market, you do not seem out of place when you act like a shrewish fishwife!"

The wind firmly deflated from her sails, Christianne found herself without the caustic retort she would dearly have loved to make. Muttering curses, she snatched up the fish and the knife he held out to her and stormed down the beach to a flat-topped rock. As she severed the fish heads and tore out their guts before flinging them to the screaming gulls that wheeled overhead, she imagined each one was James, and derived enormous pleasure from the messy task that she normally hated!

Finished, she waded into the shallows and tried to rinse the spatters of fish blood from the tattered hem of her ragged shift. It only reached mid way down her thighs now, and left a great quantity of pale golden-tanned flesh bare. Her tangled, fair mane gave her a wanton, savage beauty, bleached almost white by the blazing sun. She grimaced as she scrubbed at the spatters. It was doubtful if Granny Rags or Lumpy Jack or Coalie Joe would ever have recognized her now, she thought ruefully. James, that arrogant, scurvy rogue, looked little better than she. He had cut his breeches off at the knees and used the sturdy cloth to cut strips with which to bind the framework of bamboo poles of their hut together, which had replaced the lean-to she had made but was also walled with fallen palm-fronds. Reluctant as she was to admit it, it served much better for shade and for shelter from the rain. In these climes, he had explained, it was winter now, not summer, and the weather would grow wet and very windy. There might come a time when they would be glad of a sturdier abode than the lean-to. If only he were not so cold, so distant, she thought, lifting her head and peering through her hair to look up the beach towards him. With his new beard and his bare chest and limbs deeply tanned, he looked more a buccaneer than a gentleman captain, aye, and a very attractive one, too, she admitted, squeezing out the hem of her wet shift.

She turned to wade back up to the water line, her feet squelching and sinking into the sandy bottom. Suddenly, a hot, searing pain knifed through her calf! She cried out at its sharpness, then screamed again as another, then another, red hot pain pierced her tender flesh.

James' head jerked up at her pained cry. He saw her bowed over in the water and flung aside his knife and raced down the beach towards her.

There were transparent blobs of jelly everywhere in the shallows, each with a long, brilliant tentacle trailing behind it. There were jellyfish everywhere, he realized, splashing toward her. The little fool had stumbled into a whole damned school of them! He swept her up into his arms and carried her from the water and up the beach to their hut. She was bravely trying not to cry out, but her eyes were brimming with tears he saw as he lay her down inside it.

"It burns! It burns like fire!" she sobbed as he bent to look at her legs and feet.

She had not one but many stings, he saw, the long welts livid against her golden skin like vicious whip lashes.

"Portuguese men o' war, lass," he told her as he reached for water, "aye, and rightly named! It feels like red-hot shot does it not?"

She nodded weakly then bit down on her lower lip so she would not cry out as he poured water over the weals and rubbed them mercilessly with his palms. "Oh, it hurts, Lord, it hurts!" she cried, unable to stay silent. "I have no stomach for pain!"

"Aye, it hurts, but it will take the poison away," James told her grimly, still rubbing. He dare not let her see the anxiety in his eyes. He had encountered jellyfish once before, while taking a dip over the side of the *Fair Amanda* off Spain a year or so past. The pain had been excruciating from even that single sting, and he was a man and well able to withstand pain. She was but a dainty creature, and had been stung not once but many times.

"Lie still!" he commanded her sternly, brushing his hand down her cheek in a gentle gesture that was at odds with his tone of voice.

She nodded, her expression fearful. This was beyond her range of experience. "Will—will I die of it? she asked tremulously, her lip quivering like a hurt child.

"Nay, sweet," he reassured her, "you will not. But there will be more pain. You must be brave, love! Here, take my hand." The vicious cramps that followed hot on the heels

383

of a sting from a man o' war would not be long coming, he feared, for already her brow was beaded with sweat.

"Aah!" she cried, clutching frantically for his hand, "Holy Madonna, I cannot stand it!" Her nails gouged his arms, drawing blood, and she writhed on the bed of coconut fiber and grasses, drawing her knees up to her belly.

He held her tightly against his chest as wave after wave of cramping pain racked her from head to feet. She was rigid in his arms, her perspiration soaking them both. Her teeth chattered when she spoke.

"D-Don't let me d-die! Hold me, please, hold me!" she begged, clinging desperately to him.

"I won't, never fear! I'm here, Christie, I have you! I won't let you die, I swear it!" he murmured, kissing her face, her cheeks, her hair. "Hush, my love, my dear heart, hush!"

She started to retch, as he had expected, and he helped her outside, holding her poor head until she had finished. Then he gently bathed her face and hands and helped her back into the hut once more. The long welts on her legs and feet were swelling rapidly. He pressed her down and withdrew his knife. Her deep blue eyes widened with fear, and what little color there was left in her face drained away, but she said nothing, instead turning her face away.

"I'm not going to cut you, never fear," he assured her. "Traces of the poison still cling to your skin. I must scrape it away, that is all." She nodded and lay very still until it was done, yet her lip was bleeding again where her teeth had bitten it. He washed the stings vigorously again, wishing fervently that he had medicines for her cramps. As he recalled, the pain was like an iron band about the chest, squeezing the breath from one, or alternately like a knife twisted in the belly, unrelenting pain that lasted an hour, sometimes two. Why had she been the one to be stung, he wondered angrily, she who was so fragile and unable to withstand it? Why could it have not been him!

Through a red haze of pain, Christianne saw the expression on his face. He is angry with me, she thought miserably, fighting the cramps, angry with me and my foolishness and weakness.

"I didn't see them!" she sobbed. "I didn't know what they were. Don't be angry, please, not now!"

"I'm not," he insisted in an attempt to convince her, but she saw the thin-lipped, dark scowl on his face and believed that he lied. He hated her! He probably wished she would die and that he'd be free of her once and for all, she thought, rolling onto her side away from him and clutching her belly as another wave of cramps knotted her muscles.

James tried to put his arms about her, wanting to comfort her, but she refused to let him, shrugging his hands away, and in the end he gave up and only watched her with deeply troubled eyes.

Her reaction to the stings was a bad one, as he had expected, both from their number and on account of her fragility.

The heat of noonday had cooled to the more bearable warmth of late afternoon before the pain ceased and Christianne was able to fall into an exhausted sleep.

James left her then to her rest and cooked the fish she had gutted earlier and laid on the rock. It had almost cooked itself in the sun, he thought as he bit into its dry flesh with a grimace. The wild yams he had set to bake in the coals had long since blackened beyond recognition. He let Christianne sleep for several hours, knowing she dearly needed the rest. He was surprised at his loneliness without her. He had always enjoyed being alone before, on the deck of his ship of a night or in a quiet, moonlit wood about his home in Salem. But tonight—tonight the loneliness was unbearable, for it was more than a physical thing; it was a loneliness of the spirit! He could not go on this way, he realized, able to be near her and yet not touch her, hold her. He must decide once and for all his feelings for Christianne, or go mad! Gloom descended upon him like a pall.

He fell asleep by the fire, awakened by torrents of warm rain that fell in sheets from a dun-colored sky. The fire sizzled and extinguished itself. He hastily set out the coconut cups to catch the water, grabbed up the remaining fish, some bananas and an already-filled coconut goblet, and quickly ducked under the hut's low doorway.

She was still asleep, he saw in the gloom. Her hair streamed across the grassy pallet, a glorious mane of sun-kissed silver and gold. Her lashes were tawny crescents against the pale gold of her cheeks, in which the delicate pink bloomed like roses beneath a veil of gold. Her skin held the texture of a rose petal, too, he remembered, gazing silently down at her. Beneath his fingertips her pale, creamy flesh that was still untouched by the sun had been silken-smooth and vibrantly alive. His green-eyed gaze dropped to the slender column of her throat where he could discern the even throb of her pulse as she slept, then down to her breasts which peeped out shyly above the torn shift, breasts of swan's down softness and shell-pink aureolas that were fashioned, it seemed, to perfectly fill the cup of his hand. The lush curve of her hips and the sweeping line from her thighs to her knees and thence to her pretty ankles were covered by the remnants of his shirt, but he did not need to remove that covering to recall that that which was now hidden from his eyes was as perfect as

386

that now revealed. He scowled. Had she gone to Flynn's bed? Had that black-hearted rogue made love to her, or had she told the truth when she had said he had not? She was his, not any other man's!

She stirred. Her eyelids fluttered open. Her brows drew together in a frown. What was that muted roaring sound, she wondered?

" 'Tis the rain," he supplied, guessing the reason for her puzzled expression. He crouched down beside her. "How are you feeling?"

"Better, much better, thank you. I'm just a little tired still," she murmured.

He pulled aside the shirt that he had·covered her with. He was pleased to see that the welts were fading, much of their angry redness gone.

"Good," he pronounced. "Here, I have brought you your victuals abed, milady."

She ventured a smile and sat up. The angry look he had worn so fiercely the day before and again when he had entered the hut had gone. He looked gentle, almost, now. She murmured her thanks and took the food from him, surprised at how hungry she felt. His hand brushed hers as he handed her the water, and she trembled all over.

"Cold?" he asked, draping the shirt about her shoulders now.

She shook her head.

"Then why are you trembling?" he asked softly.

She shrugged and pretended to eat, though her mouth was suddenly dry as sawdust. She set the bowl of fish pieces aside, acutely aware of James' nearness. She could even feel the heat that rose from his body, smell his warm, masculine scent, a mixture of fresh surf and the wood smoke from the campfire.

"Are you afraid of me?" he pressed.

"No—not anymore," she said so softly it was almost a whisper.

He looked away. "I'm sorry for the way I spoke to you this morning. It was unforgivable," he said gruffly.

"No," she disagreed, "what you said, about me behaving like a spoilt child—it was true, I see it now." She sighed. "I suppose I've been behaving like a child all along. If I hadn't been so impulsive and gone off with Jonathan to nurse my wounded pride, we wouldn't be here now. Ben would never have been wounded, Ox would still be alive and you would not be here, without your ship. I've been wrong, I admit it, terribly wrong! And—and I'm sorry, sorry I have ruined your life!" She scrambled to her feet and lunged for the low doorway.

James reached for her a second too late. "Come back! he bellowed, "It's raining out there, you little idiot!"

"I want to be alone!" she cried over her shoulder. "I need time—to think! Oh!" she squealed as the first warm deluge soaked her. "Oh!" She gasped, the rain stealing her breath away momentarily.

"Christie!" James called after her. "Wait! I've done some thinking, too! I love you, Christie!" he roared as he raced after her. "I love you, you crazy, wonderful vixen!"

She took to her heels and ran. "No, don't say it!" she cried, racing away from him across the sand, her hands pressed over her ears. "You don't mean it! I don't want you to say it!"

He caught up with her and spun her around to face him, holding her prisoner in the circle of his arms. The rain streamed down her glowing face, drops poised on her spiky lashes. "I *mean* it, believe me!" he said huskily, before he pulled her hungrily against his chest and kissed her breathless.

He was breathing heavily himself when he at last broke

the kiss. Her lips were stained crimson from his ardent assault, her expression was unguarded, vulnerable as her eyes searched his face. "Oh, James!" she whispered, trembling.

Instinctively they moved together, she finding his arms perfectly about her, his lips sweet and urgent on her own. He kissed her tenderly, deeply, while the rain teemed about them, tasting its freshness mingled with her kisses on his lips, revelling in the slippery sleekness of her slender body as she pressed ardently against him. She felt the hardness of him against her belly and moaned raggedly against his mouth. Wordlessly, he lowered her to the sand.

They made love without speaking, without preliminaries or foreplay. Their need for each other was too urgent for delay. They made love with a fierce, savage joy upon the pale, wet sand, as sleek and pale and giving as was she, bare now, beneath her golden-tanned beloved. His hair clung to his fine head like a helmet of copper. The rain bounced off his broad shoulders to shower her face. The elements raged about them and cascaded down their bodies as they moved together, joined by a force as vital and electric as the blue-white lightning that scarred the dun-colored afternoon sky with brilliant jagged arrows, and lit the treetops and the foaming sea. Thunder crackled and boomed in the distance and the palms bent low in the rising wind to catch its angry mutterings. But the pair heard none of it, heard only the sighs of the other as they found release and cried out their rapture in the midst of their own passionate storm.

Christianne's eyes were like radiant stars in her glowing rain-wet face when James stood and tugged her gently to her feet. He looked at her for a long moment and she saw in his eyes what she had hungered to see! Then he drew her against his side and they walked together back to the hut, along the sand, as if the storm did not exist in their world.

The hut's palm-thatch was leaking and the walls groaned and shifted in the fierce-blown rain, but to Christianne it was a palace. James moved the coconut-fiber pallets to a drier corner and pulled her onto his lap. She quickly fell asleep curled in his arms, his hand cupping her cheek. His lips were pressed against her damp hair in an endless kiss.

Twenty-Seven

The weeks that followed that night were a beautiful dream for Christianne. She felt more content and happier than she had ever been before, and as the golden days drifted by, she began to hope that they would never be found, or find their way out of the little cove that had become, in her heart, their home.

For her safety, James had taught Christianne to swim, warning her to do so only within the boundaries of the reef and to be on her guard for shark and for jellyfish. To his pride and delight, city-born and bred Christianne—who before boarding the *Fair Amanda* had seen the sea only twice in her entire life—learned quickly. Soon they swam together in the deep blue Indian Ocean, or floated face-down to peer at the wonders of the deep through the crystalline water.

Christianne was entranced by the loveliness she saw there, and astonished that such beauty could exist unseen from the surface. Fascinated, she saw an enchanted garden, an undersea kingdom of coral, white and pink and black, each one different, all like lovely, surrealistic trees. She watched as schools of rainbow-colored fish swam idly beneath her or alternately darted past as if in a frenzy; yellow and black striped, orange spotted, brown, red and white, their colors and varieties were endless!

There were turtles, too, swimming leisurely along like enormous birds through the watery sky of their garden of Eden. James' thoughtful comment that turtle meat was a tasty treat he might enjoy drew such outraged protests from her that he hurriedly withdrew his statement and vowed that he was only teasing. There were crabs there, too, and huge, red starfish, clams with giant shells and squid, and since every garden of Eden must have its serpent, more than one sea snake. Swimming soon become a favorite pastime, though not her most favored, for nothing could compare with the delight she found in James' arms each night under the starlit sky, the indigo-velvet heavens a yawning canopy above them. The silvery moon was their lantern, the rustle of the palm-fronds and the lulling, rhythmic washing of the ocean their music. And each night it seemed too soon that the stars faded from the heavens, that the sun set and rose again in the merest blink of an eye, and the dawn sky, ablaze with glorious saffron and pink, replaced too soon the intimate darkness.

By day, they sought the palm-thatched hut and made love there, the fiery sun blistering through the fronds and the furious din of the sea birds screaming and wheeling on the shore outside.

Mornings were spent in performing the tasks necessary for their survival: fishing and gathering fruits, or water from the small spring she had discovered the day after the storm. Yams, and kelp, gathered at low tide, bread fruit, coconuts, bananas as well as fish and other sea creatures, provided them with a varied diet. Christianne, at James' suggestion, had attempted to weave baskets from stripped palm fronds, as he had seen sennit baskets woven by the Malagasy natives in Fénérive at Nicholas Drew's trading post. After several clumsy first efforts, her skill grew and the baskets she had woven made food gathering a simpler task. James had fashioned a crude lantern using yet another coconut shell and palm oil, and some nights they would wade out to the reef, their bamboo spear held aloft, to spear the squid which came like moths to the flickering light. But, try as she might, Christianne could not acquire a taste for the rubbery, chewy flesh of the squid, though James seemed to enjoy it and laughed at the faces she made.

The afternoons were long and leisurely. They swam or waged sand ball fights or chased each other along the beach with seaweed whips, all child-like games as natural and carefree as the rest of their existence, and even the vanquished soon found that defeat could sometimes taste as sweet as triumph, for the spoils of their seaweed wars were always the same!

The only thing that marred their perfect existence was Christianne's concern over James' health. Twice since the afternoon he had declared his love for her, he had fallen victim to the fever again. She had nursed him through each bout of violent sweats, racking chills and tortured sleep with a depth of anxiety that was terrifying to her. All the people she loved were taken from her. Why should her James be any different? Oh, the pain of loving, she thought with anguish one night as she stretched beside him, warming his body with the heat of her own, why must the joy of love always be tainted with that pain, that fear of losing one's beloved? Love was indeed a bitter sweet thing, a double-edged sword of unbearable keenness!

She had not told him of the child she carried. Some small part of her doubted that he truly loved her, feared that in telling she would force him to a commitment he was unwilling to make. She had no such doubts of her love for him! She lived for his touch, his smile, trembled when he said her name, surrendered herself to his love-making completely when he took her in his arms with a fierce, passionate giving of her body, heart and soul that drained her wholly for that moment.

James came up behind where she sat daydreaming against a rock, her face uplifted to the sun, and covered her eyes with his hands. "Who goes, wench?" he growled in a voice quite unlike his own.

She smiled, playing the game. " 'Tis not King George, for his voice is mellower than your voice is wont to be, sir," she teased. "Is it then Lumpy Jack, or mayhap Coalie Joe? Aye, I fancy it is one of that pair, by the roughness of your hands, sir!"

Grinning, James uncovered her eyes and dropped a kiss to her sunburned nose, where a spattering of freckles could now be seen. " 'Tis best you answer, 'James, my own true-love!' wench," he cautioned with mock severity, "lest I beat you for being unfaithful to me!"

She laughed and pulled him down to the sand beside her, running her fingertips lightly across the red-gold fur of his tanned torso. "How could I be unfaithful, when there are but the two of us in this whole, wide world, sir?" she asked, her voice a husky, seductive purr that did strange things to James' breathing.

He caught her to him and kissed her, then stretched out beside her on the sand. Leaning up on one elbow, he idly spilled her creamy hair through his fingers.

"You grow more beautiful with every passing day, my sweet," he said tenderly, outlining the pretty curve of her cheek and jaw now.

"As do you!" she quipped back, ruffling his russet hair as she smiled impishly up into his handsome face. His eyes seemed even greener, his teeth even whiter, with the darkening of his tan these past weeks, she thought.

He leaned over and pressed his lips to the valley of her breasts, tugging aside the bodice of her tattered shift to expose both rosy-tipped treasures to his mouth as he continued his explorations. He smiled at her sudden, sharp intake of breath as he drew the sensitive flesh between his lips and teased it with the tip of his tongue to stand firm. The maddening, encircling caresses sent heat flooding through her. Her breathing quickened and grew husky, her heartbeat beneath his ear accelerated to a racing gallop. Her fingers, before drifting lazily through his hair, tightened painfully.

"Have a care, madam," he warned her, stroking the impudent curves of her delightful derrière, "lest you leave me bald-pated before my time!"

She giggled and wriggled appreciatively as he continued his inflaming kisses and caresses across her abdomen, which rose and fell rapidly now with her quickened breathing.

"I would love you anyway," she responded dreamily, "but — with my eyes closed."

He snorted at her cheeky response and playfully bit her shoulder. " 'Tis well, then," he teased, "for I shall do likewise when you have lost your lissome curves and are a portly dame!" He patted her belly playfully. "It will not be long now, I fear. Already you are beginning to thicken a little."

Her heart skipped a beat. She held her breath. Had he noticed? She laughed shakily. "Consider yourself fortunate, sir," she tossed back at him. "If I grow stout with the passing years, you will have that much more of me to love, will you not?"

He chuckled. "Aye, I will indeed," he agreed. "Stout or slender, old or young, I will love you always!" His expression was grave, she saw, his merry eyes unusually solemn.

He caressed her golden belly, loving its sleek, velvety texture beneath his palm. He darted quick, light kisses against the warm flesh, and as always when he kissed her there, she giggled—for it was a ticklish sensation—and tried to pull his head away. But he refused to be parted from his pleasure.

"Stop, oh, stop, you rogue!" she wailed, a mixture of passion and torment in her eyes. " 'Tis torture!"

He laughed and unbuckled his breeches before lifting himself onto her and parting her thighs with his knees. "Torture, mmm, sweeting?" he asked huskily against her ear. Goosebumps rose all along her arms, he noticed as he entered her and gathered her up into his arms. "Is this, then, torture, too?"

She tangled her arms about his neck and drew his lips to hers. "Aye, my captain," she agreed, sighing blissfully as he began to thrust powerfully against her, "the sweetest torture imaginable!"

They made love languorously, prolonging their pleasure, delaying their final ecstasy until such delay proved impossible and they were caught up in the throbbing crescendo of desire that could end only in tumultuous waves of rapture.

Afterwards, they swam together in the deep blue Indian Ocean, exchanging the kisses and gentle caresses that follow in the afterglow of making love. The cove grew hushed and the birds winged their way to their roosts. The cicades chirrupped. The shadows lengthened on the bleached-white sands with the coming of evening.

James built their fire while Christianne cooked the fish he had caught earlier. When he had a merry fire ablaze, he went to the palm tree outside their hut and withdrew his knife. He scored the ridged trunk deeply beneath several rows of similar deep cuts. The scoring had become a nightly ritual for him, as a means of keeping track of the days, something Christianne cared nothing about.

"Two-and-a-half months!" he exclaimed, thrusting the knife back into his belt as he came to sit beside her. "The days fly past!"

She reached out and took his hand, pressed it to her lips, the first fluttering of fear beginning in her belly. "Has it been so terrible here, just the two of us?" she asked lightly, uncertain of where his present train of thought might lead. "We have been happy here, have we not, James?"

He nodded and kissed her cheek. "Aye, my sweet, happy beyond reason! But we cannot stay here forever." He waited, wondering if she would now confirm his suspicions that she was with child. Instead her tawny brows drew together in a frown.

"But why not?" she asked. "If you are happy and I am happy, why can't we stay?"

"Because I have responsibilities—my ship, my men, your Aunt Nell—that must be taken care of. And because I have family that I love who would grieve to think me lost to them. And because this life is not real, Christianne, however carefree and beautiful it is! Pleasure and lack of purpose will pall if we stay here, for pleasure is sharpened by sharing all that life has to offer, including striving together for a living, hardships, sorrow. We cannot hide from the real world forever. Sooner or later, we must go back," he explained gently.

"Let it be later, then," she insisted crossly, turning her back on him. "I want to stay here, just the two of us. Please, James?" she implored him, her voice breaking.

She was crying, he knew. He sighed. Did she fear his love for her would vanish if they left the magical cove where it had blossomed? He thought so. But—if she was with child, they must somehow find their way back to some civilized place, where there would be physicians and midwives to attend her in her childbirth. She was a fragile English rose, unsuited to the harsh, unrelenting heat of these climes. She would wilt and perish here, with the new life inside her growing daily and robbing her of her strength. Furthermore, she was slender of hip, overly so for an easy labor, he fancied. Nay, he had no choice but to insist that they leave. He would not have her, his love, his life, his heart, and the child they had made, die here needlessly! Pain clutched at his heart. Life without her would not be life at all, but mere existence! Why did she not tell him of the child? Did she fear that in doing, his love for her would lessen? Or did she mayhap not believe that he truly loved her? He went to her and brushed a wind-tousled, fair curl from her cheek. In the firelight, he saw that her face was wet with tears.

"Nay, we must leave," he said gently. "Have no fear, my dearest, nothing between us will change, I swear it! I will love you always, whether we be in New Orleans, or aboard my ship, or in some other country. The place may change, but my love will not!"

The fluttering fear that had begun in her belly became a roaring monster. Despite his words, she knew what he had been before; a ladies' man, a rake. Here it had been easy for him to swear undying love to her, having no other women about to catch his fancy. But out there—! Aye, she would lose him, she thought desperately. She glanced sideways at him. His expression was stern, unbending. With a sinking heart, she realized there would be no changing his mind. He had already decided. But she had to try!

"What of your fevers?" she pressed. "It would be

dangerous to leave here! If you were stricken, how would I care for you? There may not be water nearby, and what of food? Who knows how many savages await us? Nay, 'twould be madness to leave!"

He saw the fear and pain in her deep blue eyes and took her in his arms. "Hush, now. All will be well. The fevers have lessened. And besides, 'tis not too early to begin to adjust my life around the damnable miasma. I have lost a day or two before, while in my cups!" he jested, trying to put a smile on her woebegone face.

"Adjust your life? Explain yourself, sir. You have lost me," she queried.

"I will have to quit my seafaring life," James said heavily. "I cannot master a ship when I know not when this damned sickness will strike."

"What! But the sea is your life!" she exclaimed, pulling from his arms.

"There are walks of life other than that of a sea captain, lass," he said softly. "Perhaps that plantation in the Caribbees? With you beside me, I fancy I would not miss the sea."

She nodded, unconvinced. "When?" she asked tremulously, looking up into his eyes.

"When what?" he asked absently, his mind still on her and the question of whether she carried his child or nay.

"When must we leave?" she said, her voice husky with unshed tears. The beauty of the evening seemed to have dulled. The vivid crimson and orange of the sunset seemed washed out and colorless now.

"Oh, three days from now," he said levelly. "We'll need those days to dry some fish and gather provisions for the journey. Sooner or later we will find a trading post or a village where the natives are not hostile to white men. We'll go east, along the coast."

True to his word, they set off at dawn three days later. James carried bananas and yams and dried fish-strips in one of the baskets she had woven, slung over his shoulder.

They passed the ruins of two wooden settlements on their journey, ramshackle cabins of obviously European design now broken down and overgrown by the rampant jungle, the scars of failed attempts at colonization of this savage land by the white man.

One day, as dusk was falling, Christianne took herself off into the bushes at the edge of the jungle to relieve herself. On her way back to join James, she happened to look up, and screamed at what she saw above her, caught between the bushy topmost branches of a baobab tree: a yellowed, grinning skull, gleaming horribly in the amethyst light!

Immediately James came crashing through the undergrowth to her side, spear at the ready.

"Holy Madonna! What is it?" he cried, gathering her into his arms.

"Up there! Look!" she whispered, burying her face against his chest. She was trembling.

James looked where she pointed and laughed with relief. "You have nothing to fear from that poor devil, my sweet," he reassured her. "His days as a fierce warrior are long past! Only his skeleton remains."

She hesitantly lifted her head from his chest and looked again. "It's horrible!" she said with a shudder. "How did it get way up there?"

James shrugged. "I fancy they must have put his body in the hollow tree trunk for a grave. The tree grew as the years passed until he became as you see him now, lord of the jungle, looking down on his kingdom from that great height."

Despite James' reassurance, she remained jumpy that night, flinching at every sound. She fancied the jungle was a dragon, not the glorious, flamboyant dragon of St. George, all fiery breath and smoking nostrils, but a green, serpent-like beast that curled about them, waiting, waiting, to devour them in its slimy jaws. It was not until James took her into his arms and made her sweetly exhausted with his loving that she was able to sleep.

Another day they climbed to the crest of a tall, heavily forested hill, in an attempt to see if there were any villages or trading posts ahead of them along the coast.

They found themselves looking down into a broad, lush valley, the far walls of which were terraced with light green rice paddies. On the valley floor lay an enormous Malagasy village of several hundred rectangular huts, surrounded by thickets of bamboo and tamarind and breadfruit trees. Herds of grazing cattle made a huge, moving, dark blot on the ground outside the wooden palisades of the village. By the banks of the green river that cut through the vista, they could barely discern the curling horns of the zebu as they lowered their heads to drink. Further downstream the vivid silk sarongs and fringed *lambas* of the Malagasy women made bright splashes of color as they drew water or bathed by the riverbanks. There were no sign of any Western influence on that isolated, self-contained little civilization below, and when Christianne asked if James intended they should go down there, he shook his head.

"No, I think not. We've travelled quite far inland. There's a good chance those people have never seen white men. Nay, lass, our best chance is to press on, and hope to find a coastal village, like Fénérive. The natives there will have likely traded for provisions with passing ships. Come on, lass!"

Christianne let out the breath she had been holding. Thank God, he intended to continue! Tears of relief filled her eyes. It had been over two months since poor Ox had been killed, but she would never forget the casual way the Malagasy leader had hauled the spear from his awful wound—not to help the injured man but to retrieve his prized weapon! Nay, if they were to find another village, please, oh, please, let it be a colony of Europeans!

They made their fire and ate a hasty meal of fruits and coconut meats, their fish long since having been eaten. Their trek up the hillside had left James no daylight time in which to spear more. The squawk of the parrots and the jays' raucous laughter faded and was replaced by the cicadas' trill and the muted roar of the surf against the shore.

James sat cross-legged opposite her, his handsome face thoughtful as he poked idly at the fire with a branch. A now-familiar aching gripped Christianne as she watched him. Was it wicked to pray that they would never find their way back to civilization, when James wanted it so badly? Wicked or nay, she had done so daily since they had left the cove! Despite James' reassurances to the contrary, she knew he would cast her aside for another once they reached New Orleans. Had he not said himself many times that he was weak-willed where the fair sex were concerned? Aye, he would be gentle, regretful, but when faced with other women, lovelier and more worldly-wise and experienced in how to please a man than she, he would choose them! And besides, they had never betrayed him, caused the injuring of his friend. For all that he had said he believed her, did he, did he truly in his heart, hold her blameless? She fell asleep pressed closely to him, her hand enfolded by his large hand, her other clasping the cloth of his shirt tightly, as if she sought even in sleep to bind him to her.

Another night, as they slept on the beach beneath the starlight, she was roused from the cradle of James' arms by a strange cry, like that of a human child. She sat up and quickly woke James. He rubbed his eyes, uncertain as to whether what he was seeing posed them any threat or nay.

Almost surrounding them on the star-washed, silent beach was a troupe of bushy tailed, monkey-like gray and white animals, with huge, shiny round eyes that peered at them curiously in the firelight. One of the lemurs had found a piece of discarded banana left over from their supper. He held it in his long fingers and ate it with great delicacy, seeming not to care that the pair watched him.

"What the devil are they?" James whispered. "I've seen no creatures like them before."

"*Babakoto,*" Christianne whispered back. "Isabella had one for a pet on St. Mary's. They are curious but harmless. The Malagasy eat them, some of them! Others, the pure white *sifáka,* she told me, they believe are the spirits of their dead rulers, come back to Earth in animal form, and so they are sacred."

Relieved, James nodded and replaced his knife at his side. His movements startled the lemur troupe, who leaped back up into the trees so swiftly it was as if they had never been.

The lemurs part in Malagasy religion and Christianne's knowledge of it proved invaluable a few days later.

They had walked the better part of the day, resting only briefly during the midday heat, but James seemed driven by some demon to press on well into the afternoon. At first Christianne was irritated by his single-mindedness. Did he not care if her feet were worn to the bone? she wondered crossly. But then she saw the fevered emerald glitter of his eyes and knew the reason for his behavior. She reached up, pretending to wipe the perspiration from his brow, and found that her suspicions were correct. His brow had felt burning to her touch.

"Enough!" she cried, flopping down and feigning exhaustion. "I can go no further without rest."

Concern flared in James' face. "I have pressed you too far," he muttered, angry at himself. "Yet I would rather we passed the night on open beach than here, in this cursed jungle. Come, I shall carry you." He bent to scoop her into his arms but instead sagged wearily to the ground. "A pox on this damned sickness!" he cursed. He groaned and hung his head, his exhaustion obvious.

"You are as stubborn as a donkey, my lord captain," she scolded, straightening his legs for him so that he lay comfortably. "I am not yet blind, sir! Any fool could see that you are ill, and I am no fool! Be still, I say!"

He shot her a lopsided grin. "Aye, 'tis true. The miasma has returned, as I feared. I had hoped you would not notice. Lay here beside me, sweet. It comforts me to know you are nearby." He shivered suddenly, though the jungle's heat was steaming all about them. She noticed he was forced to clench his jaw to keep his teeth from chattering. "Cold . . . 'tis so cold!" He shuddered.

She lay beside him, her arms wrapped around him, holding him close until he drifted into an uneasy sleep, the fevered, tortured sleep she had come to recognize during his past bouts of the sickness. When she was certain he slept, she slipped from his side and cocked her head to one side, listening intently. Two months of living off this savage land had heightened her senses acutely. As she had thought, the gurgle of a stream sounded nearby. She would need fresh water desperately once the drenching sweats of James' fever began in earnest. She could, she hoped fervently, find the stream and fill several coconut shells with water before nightfall. She bent down and gently kissed his brow in farewell, before slipping between the trees.

Twenty-Eight

She moved as silently as a shadow under the trees, stopping from time to time to listen intently for the sound of rushing water.

The jungle lay suspended halfway between day and night, and the peculiar demi-light made distorted monsters of the baobabs and other trees all about her. In their contorted boughs she heard shrill squeaks and sounds like the creaks of leather harness and the flap and whirr of leathery wings as the bats that hung by day and slept stirred for their nocturnal travels. Hidden birds twittered nervous vespers before uneasily settling to roost. An eerie, almost deathlike hush descended over the jungle like a pall. A faint mist steamed from the earth and wreathed about the bases of the trees. Yet above the eerie hush, the stream gurgled and trilled its promise of fresh water, and so she chased her fears firmly into the recesses of her mind and forged on, careful to mark her path with broken branches and knotted grass all the way.

She found the stream bubbling down from a miniature spring deep within the jungel's bowels. Dropping to her knees, she filled her hollow coconut shell in its flow, then waited impatiently until the second was also full. James had improved on her coconut goblets somewhat. He had taken whole nuts and simply cut a small piece from them, then he had left the nuts upon the ground for the ravenous ants to finish the cleaning. The result had been several hollow, gourd-like vessels capable of holding over twice as much water as the broken half-shells had held. Carrying them carefully against her bosom, she started back the way she had come.

But in the gathering gloom, she missed her marked path. She tried first one way, then another, but there was no trace of her broken branches nor her knotted grass clumps. Panic filled her. To pass the night in the jungle with Ox or James for companionship was one thing; to spend it alone was entirely another! Her fear sent her flying to left and right, back and forth, but all paths looked the same in the dusk. At length she leaned against a tree trunk and closed her eyes, taking deep breaths to calm herself before trying once more. This time she forged confidently between the bushes, upbraiding herself for behaving like a ninny, to find herself in the midst of yet another native burial ground! The startled cry that was born in her throat was stillborn on her lips, for the sacred clearing was not deserted. A group of Malagasy warriors stood gaping at her in open-mouthed horror as she stopped short at the base of one of the ancestor poles, this one bearing a mighty pair of zebu horns. She was so shocked that her wits fled her. Still clutching her precious coconuts to her breast, she simply stood stock still, too paralyzed with fear to run, trying desperately to gain some measure of control over her quaking limbs.

"*Fady! Fady!*" cried one native, gesticulating wildly in her direction.

"*Sifáka!*" wailed another.

And Christianne realized that although she was terrified of them, they were equally terrified of her, for the words one had cried meant "taboo," and the *sifáka* was the sacred white lemur, who was believed to incarnate the spirits of their dead rulers! Was it possible that, with her long, ash-blond hair and very fair complexion, coupled with the tattered white shift that might, with imagination, pass for moldering burial robes, maybe she appeared in the half light to the superstitious natives as some wandering spirit of one of their ancestors?

Hysteria swept through her at the insanity of the realization, and she had to fight to smother a nervous giggle that might have well proved her undoing. To turn and run was what she dearly wanted to do! But such an action was so blatantly human it would destroy the supernatural illusion she had unwittingly created. The savages would come to their senses and hound her through the jungle until they caught her. There was no telling what brutal tortures they inflicted on their captives before killing them!

So, instead of running, she did the unexpected and took a faltering step towards them, then a second and a third.

The party of four stalwart Malagasy warriors and one royal astrologer shrank away from her as one man, their eyes rolling whitely in abject terror in their ebony faces. Unintelligible moans that she took to be Malagasy prayers against the evil eye poured in garbled torrents from their wobbling, thick-lipped mouths.

Their rank terror armed her with fresh courage! She glided—not walked!—lightly around one burial pole, then wove sylph-like between two more, praying that they would think her dancing among their tombstones in true ghostly fashion. Yet her movements were, in truth, far from aimless! Little by little, she was edging back to the spot where she had exited the jungle just minutes before! Just as she was about to stage a hasty disappearing act between the bushes, the terrified natives' last shreds of courage deserted them. They took to their heels and fled, tumbling and tripping over each other as they went. If they heard the triumphant peal of feminine, very human, laughter that rang through the jungle in their wake, they never returned to discover its source! No doubt they believed the laughter not of their world but of the nether regions beyond the tomb!

Reaction set in as Christianne sought once again for her path. Her knees shook alarmingly and she felt decidedly queasy as the narrowness of her escape hit her fully. She leaned against a malevolently twisted baobab to steady herself, and almost shouted in joy instead when she heard the leathery rustle of wings above her. Looking eagerly about, she discovered the broken branches that marked her path. Never, in my entire life, she thought, will I be as glad to see anything as I am to see this tree filled with horrid bats!

By the time she had found her way back to James, night had fallen like a sweltering woollen cloak all about her.

He lay as he had when she had left him, perspiring copiously or shivering with cold by turns. She forced as much water as she could between his cracked lips, mindful that his body would be dangerously weakened if he should lose more of its fluids than could be replaced. He cursed in his delirium and fought her soothing hands when she tried to wipe away the rivulets of sweat that poured down his face and neck. He tossed his head from side to side, mumbling incoherent gibberish for the greater part, interspersed with snatches of conversation.

"Get away, Flint, damn your soul! Get away!" he raved, flailing wildly. "Nay . . . not so, not so! Oh, sweet Jesus, the ship! Swim for it, lads . . . swim for it! Amanda! Amanda, where are you? Dear God, I can't find you! Amanda! *Amanda!* I love you! Forgive me . . . forgive . . ."

He thrashed again at his unseen foe, but there were no comforting words from Christianne to lull him back to restful sleep. She sat beside him woodenly, her hands like wilted flowers in her lap, staring blindly into the darkness. Her heart felt rent in two by his words, and her hurt and her jealousy swept through her like a cold, icy wind. She had worried these past few days that he would find someone else to love when they reached civilization again, but she need not have done so, she thought bitterly, for there had always been someone else, even when James had held her in his arms and sworn he loved her and her alone. Amanda de Villarin. A sob caught in her throat, threatening to choke her. When he had made love to her, was it the lovely, glowing Amanda's body he had ached to possess? Was it her kisses, her lips, he had desired? Had she been nothing but a substitute for the woman he truly loved? Damn your soul, James Mallory! she screamed silently. Love me, not her! Want me, not her! Second best, that's all she would ever be to James. She could just see it now, the three of them; James and herself in some mockery of a marriage, over which the image of his "fair Amanda" would float, always tantalizingly out of his reach since her marriage to the handsome Don Miguel. The aching lump in her breast became unbearable, crushing. Had he turned to her merely out of pity, sensing that she loved him? Or was it for some darker reason, some perverse need to revenge Ben's death, that he had sworn his love, perhaps intending to laugh in her face at some later date. Dear God, no! I cannot bear it! she cried silently, could not bear that he stay with her out of pity or out of a sense of obligation for taking her maidenhead, or out of hatred. Aye, whatever it might be called, it would not be love, never love. Never love. . .

Nothing had changed, not really, she realized suddenly, except for the child she carried, and he knew nothing of that. She could still leave him at the first opportunity that presented itself, and make her way back to England and home. Somehow, she'd find some honest employ to support herself and the babe. She laughed bitterly. She was no stranger to hard work, and there were always scullery maids needed, or street sellers, or if the worse came to the worst, there was always the sporting house. Aye, even that, if it came to it, she decided, to feed her child. After all, was it not the family tradition? Nay, nothing had really changed

. . . except that it felt as if her heart were broken.

James' fever lasted for five days. Whether its lengthy duration was due to fatigue after their gruelling trek along the coast, or to the withdrawal of Christianne's tender nursing, only God knew. She did not neglect him in his suffering, and in effect did all for him and more than she had before, but the quality of her ministrations had changed. She touched him only when she could not avoid doing so, as when she wiped his burning brow. She spoke to him just as rarely. Though she sensed that he missed her soothing voice and the light, gentle touch of her hands, it now hurt too much to be near him, to touch him as before, knowing he loved another. Consequently, she kept her distance and wondered if the numbness would ever pass, if the icy wall about her heart would ever melt away.

He awoke at midday on the sixth day, his green eyes clear and his thoughts rational. The unhealthy flush had left his cheeks, but he was still ashen beneath his ruddy beard.

"Come here, love," he rasped weakly, reaching out for her, "I have missed you sorely. Have you not missed me, my sweet?"

"I must fetch more water," she murmured without looking at him, and turned quickly away.

James fell back on his grassy bed, too weak still to question her avoidance of him. He slept the day through, and it was the next morning before he again awoke, feeling far stronger.

"Good morning, sweet," he greeted her tenderly. "Come, kiss me!"

"You must eat, to regain your strength," she told him curtly, "and there is no food. I will be back before long."

Despite his weakness, his hand snaked out as she attempted to hurry past him, his tanned fingers curling about her wrist before she had a chance to sidestep him. He chuckled and pulled her into his lap, locking his arms about her. "Do not play reluctant with me, Christie Alexander. I know better!" he growled, nibbling at her ear. To his confusion, she stayed stiff and unyielding in his embrace and when he forced her to turn her head that he might kiss her, she was as cold and remote and stony as a marble statue. His dark russet brows came together in a frown.

"The food," she began again, trying to rise from his lap.

"Devil take the food," he growled. "What's wrong, Christie?" He shook her by the shoulder. "Why do you draw away from me?" he demanded.

"Nothing's wrong," she lied, refusing to meet his eyes. There was an edge of bitterness to her voice. "I am weary, 'tis all."

"You lie," he accused. "Tell me the truth! Has someone hurt you? Are you unwell?" he asked, towering over her now. "Tell me and tell me quickly, lass, before I lose my patience with you. What has changed you?"

"Nothing happened and nothing has changed!" she flared. "Everything is just as it was before. Everything!" She shrugged off his hands and ran from him into the forest, but not before he had seen the pain in her deep blue eyes, the tremulous quivering of her lower lip.

Puzzled, he stared after her. Could it be that carrying the child had made her subject to this strange mood? He had heard that some women were prone to fits of melancholy and strange tempers when they were breeding. Was this why she had shunned him so coldly? He shrugged. If she would not tell him, she would not. He had no choice but to bide his time until she was ready to do so. Meanwhile, he decided, he would behave as if there were nothing amiss. In time she would come about, he was sure of it.

But as they continued along the coast, he realized the gulf between the two of them was widening. It was as if they were no more than strangers, united only for the duration of the journey. His gently probing questions could uncover no cause for her change of heart, neither could his angry, heated demands that she tell him what had made her that way. At night she sought the opposite side of the campfire from him and slept alone.

Ten days more brought them to a rise above a thriving village, set at the head of a beautiful bay. Smoke curled up from the cooking fires outside the log-hewn cabins, which were laid out in rows, European fashion. James let out a whoop and hurled the basket into the air. He caught Christie about the waist and kissed her soundly.

"We made it, Christie, my angel, we made it!" he roared. "Look at that harbor—'tis a natural wonder! And look at the number of vessels! Come on, lass, we're homeward bound!"

He started slipping and sliding down the rough trail toward the village. In his excitement, his green eyes danced merrily, his stride was swift and easy, all traces of the miasma vanished.

Christianne hung back. "I cannot go down there like this," she insisted, gesturing at her ragged shift which now scarcely covered her thighs.

"To Hades with appearances," James laughed. "There's no woman could match you for beauty, my lovely, not on the face of this Earth! If you wore but a flour sack, you would be just as beautiful!"

"Aye—and a deal more decently covered," she observed dryly.

He frowned. Her scanty attire had not seemed remarkable at their beach encampment, nor in the steaming jungle, when clothes had entered his mind at all. But when he looked at her with an eye to what the perhaps woman-hungry colonists would see, he understood what she meant. The shift, with its fraying, deeply-scooped neckline and slender shreds of lacy shoulder straps, revealed a delicious quantity of pale golden flesh and thrusting,

413

proud breasts. The tattered hem hung raggedly to only inches below her hips, exposing strong, slender thighs and shapely calves and a neatly-turned pair of ankles. Her hair was a long, tangled, sun-kissed mane, and her lovely face, now deeply golden from the sun, was at odds with the vivid sapphire-blue of her eyes. She radiated vitality and a sort of savage beauty as she stood there, one hand on her hip, the other holding the bamboo-handled spear, like an Amazon warrior of petite proportions.

"In truth, you are right!" he breathed, aware that desire was coursing through him. "Will you wait here for me? I'll be back with some garments for you in a thrice."

She nodded.

"Promise, me Christie. Swear to me on—"

"—On my mother's grave I will not leave this place," she finished for him, smiling a little now despite herself at his obvious excitement. "Go on with you, now!"

She sat down and watched him sprinting down the hillside, misery in her eyes.

He returned shortly with some plain but sturdy homespun clothes: a dress, a shift and a bonnet, of all things. They felt stifling and uncomfortable after her skimpy attire of the past few months but she donned them anyway, with the exception of the bonnet.

"The port below," he told her excitedly as he fastened her buttons, "is Diégo Suarez. I should have guessed it! It has the best, the deepest natural harbor hereabouts. And," he said with a twinkle in his eyes, "an old friend awaits us there, herself a casualty of the same storm that tossed us up onto land!"

"The *Fair Amanda?*" she asked incredulously. Her hands were unwieldy paws as she finished dressing. She wanted very badly to ask if he knew how Ben Wright had fared, but dared not.

"None other!" James declared. "She was forced to put into port to effect substantial repairs. My crew have been

414

billeted amongst the villagers. Diégo Suarez is a French port, but we will be received without hostility there. The clothes were loaned by Madame Muette, the village gossip, I fancy!" He chuckled. "She seemed nigh dying with curiosity to meet you!" He kissed her brow and tilted her chin. "Tonight you will bathe in fresh water, dine off the finest platters Diégo Suarez has to offer, upon the finest victuals I am able to find, and sleep in a bed with a goose down pallet if I have to scour the port for one. Ah, lass, I have all a man could wish for! My woman, and my worthy ship! Come on!" he ordered, hauling her after him down the slope.

The villagers had turned out to meet them in force, she saw. Even now, women, men and a few children were heading up the hill toward them, waving and chattering excitedly.

Fine victuals! Fine pallets! A bath! What did she care for any of them? She would barter them all, aye, and her soul with them, to be back at their deserted cove, eating fish he had speared for them, sleeping on coconut fiber pallets, bathing in the blue waters of the Indian Ocean, and spending the sultry, starlit nights in his arms!

With leaden feet, she let him lead her down to the village.

Twenty-Nine

It was in Diégo Suarez that Christianne realized the potent effect of her appearance on mere males for the first time. Her delight in this new discovery grew in direct proportion to the amount of jealousy James displayed over it. Although such games were infinitely cruel and petty, to boot, this did not in any way diminish their delightfulness for her! She had discovered, in completing her hasty transition from girl to woman, that she was capable of the entire spectrum of human emotions and moods, from the more pleasant ones of self-sacrifice, tenderness and caring, to the less endearing qualities of jealousy and the over-whelming urge to hurt the man she loved and whom she felt had lied when he vowed he loved her! When, on brief occasions, she permitted herself a long, hard look at this side of her character, she was alarmed at what she saw. Nevertheless, she hurriedly turned a blind eye to it and rationalized that since James had lied when he had sworn he loved her, she was no worse than he, and that all was fair in love and war, anyway.

James, for his part, was like a terrier with a broomstick tied to its tail, snapping and snarling at any man who crossed him, and even at those who went out of their way to be amicable. He had thought he had learned the true misery of unreturned love, for the first time in his life, when they had travelled up the coast and Christianne had been so cold and distant. But now he truly knew what it was to suffer, for to that coldness that cut him to the quick he must now add the pain of jealousy. Aye, he was jealous of the men that flocked about her like bees to a honeycomb, and she—that damned, beautiful witch—seemed to go out of her way to keep him so!

The news of their deliverance from the jungle had spread like wildfire throughout the village port. Indeed, with the odds so heavily stacked against them in that land, where the bloody flux, dysentery, pox and murdering savages claimed hundreds every year in the area of the comparatively civilized French colony of Diégo Suarez, that they had survived in the wilds alone and done so virtually unscathed, was little short of a miracle. That one of the survivors was a fragile woman—and one possessing considerable beauty, furthermore—added further fuel to the raging fire of gossip that swept through the port, fanned by the incendiary tongue of Madame Muette.

Accounts of their entry into Diégo Suarez varied. Some had it that La Belle Sauvage, the Beautiful Savage, as Christianne had been dubbed, had strode into town bearing a spear like an Amazon queen, naked save for her mantle of astonishingly fair tresses. Others bruited it about that the pair had been captured by Malagasy and that La Belle Sauvage had thrown herself at the feet of their king and tearfully offered him her virtue in exchange for the handsome sea captain's life, whereupon the native king, swearing undying love for her after their single night of rapture, had sent her regretfully on her way astride an enormous zebu bull, his gift for her courage and her beauty! Whatever rendering of the story one accepted, Christianne acquired status bordering on angelic, though of necessity one with a somewhat tarnished halo. Her virtue—or rather, her lack of same—mattered not a whit to the Frenchmen, all natives of a country renown for its citizenry's delight in the pursuit of fleshy delights and *l'amour*. To them, she was a veritable goddess of love, and they were drawn to her like moths to a flame. Their womenfolk, though decidedly less enamored of her, were doubly curious to meet a bona fide "scarlet woman" and become moths in their own right, though for different reasons. Yet others flocked to her merely to maintain surveillance on their wandering husbands!

The governor of Diégo Suarez, one Antoine Truffaut, welcomed them to his colony with effusive greetings in flowery, French-accented, terrible English, interspersed with many kisses to either side of James' face, a custom the irritable captain found highly distasteful. He would have seriously questioned the portly, foppishly-dressed Governor Truffaut's sexual preferences, were it not that the governor also devoted equal energy to the repeated kissing of La Belle Sauvage's—alias Christianne's—hand, and in trying to peer down the front of the bodice of her borrowed gown. This latter habit in particular incensed the captain, who ached to lodge his knuckles against the governor's powdered face!

Antoine Truffaut reminded Christianne of a modiste's mannequin. His pale and pox-marked face with its velvet beauty patches and his powdered half-wig and the heavily embroidered canary-yellow silk frockcoat he sported, from the collar and cuffs of which spilled inordinate quantities of fussy lace, bespoke a style now outmoded but markedly reminiscent of the French court. He had an irritating habit of posturing with his amber-knobbed cane extended and making a leg to exhibit his flabby calves, encased in white silk hose, that would have reduced Christianne to giggles had she been of a lighter frame of mind. As it was, she merely found him annoying. However, since he was their host, in effect, they were forced to be polite and put up with their host's peculiarities.

The citizens of Diégo Suarez opened their hearts and their meager storehouses to feast their hero and heroine in grand style, by arranging an open air gathering to which all were invited, including the crew of the *Fair Amanda*, who had been lodged amongst them.

Flaming torches lit the earthen village square. Trestle tables sagged with the weight of piled trenchers of beef, chicken, sweet potatoes and other tasty fare. Madeira, canary, porter and rum flowed as freely as water. The residents of Diégo Suarez donned their Sunday best and came to feast and to dance to the merry music of the fiddle, flute and drum, and more than one of them felt the effects of the liquor before many hours had passed!

The reunion between James and his crew, who had all feared him dead, was a touching sight, accompanied by much back-slapping, hand-shaking and good-natured banter. Greetings dispensed with, James' eyes darkened and he drew Silas Mullens away from the throng.

"And my worthy Ben—how does he fare, Mullens?" he asked the bosun gravely.

Mullens' single eye rolled alarmingly. His discomfort was intense, it was obvious. "Mister Wright, sir, it saddens me to tell you, is dead. Mistress Lucy did all that was possible, sir, but his wound had festered, yer see. We—we buried him at sea, sir, the mornin' after the storm, with a gun salute and all, as was fittin'. Matt Locke read from the Good Book and Mistress Lucy sewed his shroud. It were all done proper, sir, as we knowed you would ha' wanted it yerself, if'n you were there."

James nodded and lifted his gaze to Christianne, who hovered nervously a few feet away. She had caught James' question and without consciously realizing she did so, stayed to hear his answer. The blood drained from her face at the coldness, the accusation in James' eyes. They were a penetrating emerald that seemed to bore into her soul! Grief over Ben's death and fury reborn at her part in his mortal wounding burned hotly in their depths. A sob choked her. Part of her wanted desperately to comfort James and to restate her own innocence, to make him

419

believe in her. Yet the other part damned him for that accusatory look, cursed him for his doubt! For over two months they had lived together, strived together, aye, and slept together. Despite knowing her better than anyone else on the face of the Earth, he could still believe her guilty of harming someone she had called friend! Her own guilt, long buried, resurfaced and nibbled at the edges of her indignation like a peckish mouse. If she had not chosen to believe Flynn's threats and go with him, would not Ben yet live? If Ox had not loved her in his own way, and wanted to please her, would he not be alive, too? The nibbling mouse of guilt grew to a roaring lion. Poor Ben! Poor, poor Ox! Scalding tears burned her eyes as the choking sob dissolved.

She turned sharply about and pushed her way between the wine-swilling, belly-stuffing merrymakers to the shadow of the tamarind trees, and there gave vent to her pent-up emotions. It was all happening as the gypsy in Barcelona had foretold! She was destined never to become James' bride, despite her deep love for him. And her pride, as the gypsy had warned her, had indirectly caused the deaths of two fine men, and almost proved her own undoing. Aye, the carrion bird of death had indeed sat upon her shoulder all the way!

She sobbed against the tree trunk until her eyes felt as if they had been pickled in brine and her face was ravaged by her tears. She had no desire to return to the torchlit village square, or to listen further to the pleas of Diégo Suarez' motely menfolk begging her to grant them the next dance, while their womenfolk murdered her with their eyes. She wanted to be alone. Picking up her skirts, she circumnavigated the gathering and made her way back to their lodgings, Governor Truffaut's two-story timber dwelling, the only one of such pompous and peculiar dimensions in the entire village. Everyone jestingly referred to it as the governor's "mansion." Governor's Folly would have been more apt, she thought wryly as she let herself

420

inside the house. Perhaps in sleep she could blot out the memory of those accusing, blazing-green eyes.

She scuttled through the darkened hallway and hurriedly mounted the stairs. The air here still smelled of the fresh-hewn logs used to build the house and of the governor's heady cologne. Not halfway up, a gleeful chuckle froze her in midstep.

"Ah, c'est bien! La Belle Petite Sauvage has returned! Good evening, my lovely mademoiselle!"

She turned about to see Antoine Truffaut at the foot of the stairs. He held a lighted candle in one hand, the flame of which he shielded from the cooling draft with his other. He sported a ridiculous tasselled nightcap and a voluminous white nightgown that reminded her of Wee Willie Winkie in her nursery rhymes. Beneath the night-gown, his pale feet protruded like a pair of pasty flippers! She wavered, torn between replying and pretending she had not heard him. But if she did the latter, there was a chance he might follow her upstairs to repeat his salutation!

"Good evening, Governor Truffaut," she said politely. "Was the celebration not to your liking?"

"I left early," Truffaut said as he set the candlestick on a table. "I suffer from time to time with the gout, you see, mademoiselle. To my regret, I was so afflicted this evening. Won't you join me for a brandy—purely for medicinal purposes, *naturellement?*" He wetted his fleshy lips as he awaited her reply. His somewhat protruding eyes roved over her body, greedily savoring its beauty.

Christianne could almost read the fantasies that flitted beneath his night cap as if they were scratched upon a child's slate. The old goat was feeling his horns, i'faith! Her wisest course now, she decided quickly, would be to return to the square posthaste. She started back down the stairs accordingly.

"Your invitation is most kind, sir," she said as she went. "But I believe I should go back to the feast, don't you, since

421

I am one of the guests of honor?" She made to step past him, but he sprang to block her path with an agility that belied his gout.

"Before you go, *ma petite,* tell me, was it true that you gave yourself to a Malagasy king to save your Capitaine Mallory's life?" he asked eagerly, plundering her bodice with his greedy eyes and moistening his lips.

Her deep blue eyes flashed in the candlelight. "That, sir, is none of your business! Now, let me pass, you old goat!" she demanded, dispensing with all pretenses at civility.

"Mais cherie," he simpered in wounded, silky tones, "why are you so cruel? Come, come to Antoine! Remember, it was I who took you in, gave you comfort after those gruelling months in the wilds. And you will find, *cherie,* if you but give me the chance, that an older man, a man well-versed in the arts of pleasure, can be a more than satisfying—and most generous—paramour, after your younger and perhaps somewhat *gauche capitaine!"* He sniffed distastefully. "And certainly as much a man as any black savage, reeking of fish and palm oil! Ugh!" He reached confidently for her bosom, squealing like a pig with its throat cut as a high-heeled slipper, well-aimed, came forcefully down upon the arch of his gouty foot. *"Mon dieu!"* he gasped, hopping about on his uninjured foot, "you have lamed me!"

"My favors are *not* for sale, sir!" Christianne snapped, flouncing past him. "I would thank you to remember that."

"Indeed?" Truffaut sneered through tears of pain, "then we in Diégo Suarez have been badly misinformed! You see, your reputation has preceded you to our fair port, *cherie!* All here know that you are a common doxy, that you were the pirate captain, Jonathan Flynn's woman, and that you left him to warm your Captain Mallory's bed after you had fleeced Flynn of a considerable fortune!" Truffaut chuckled. "It would be better for you to accommodate me *non?* If not, I might be forced to send word to the good captain of your whereabouts—and believe me, he is most anxious to find you!"

Christianne gaped. "Really?" she asked softly, controlling her outrage as she sidled back toward him. "Well, Governor, that casts an entirely different light on our little situation here, does it not?" Her voice was a silken purr that would have warned him had he known her better, but he did not and he preened visibly as she came closer and closer, believing she had capitulated.

"Ah, *bien!* I knew you would see it my way, my dear," he said, his voice gravy-thick with lust.

"And you were correct, sir," Christianne simpered. "May I call you Antoine?"

"But of course. I insist!" he sighed.

"Good. Now, Antoine, *cheri,* won't you give me your cane? You will not be needing it tonight, after all, will you?" she wheedled seductively.

His eyes fairly bulged from their sockets at what he took to be the blatant hunger in her eyes. *La Belle Sauvage* was hotter for him that the pit of Hades itself! He tossed the cane to her in a pitiful attempt at carefree, boyish enthusiasm.

"*Non, non,* I have never truly needed it. It is but an affectation of style, that is all. I am as vigorous and as lusty as a schoolboy!" He giggled. "And most agreeably virile!"

"That is good, sir," Christianne said, smothering a shudder of revulsion, "for you will need manly attributes aplenty when I am done! Blackmailer! Lecher!" she cried, and so saying, she brought the cane around full force across the back of his knees.

With a howl of pain, he bent over. In a thrice, she raised the cane again and whacked him across his plump buttocks with a wicked "thwack!" before she raced to the door.

She ran full-tilt into James as she burst from the door of the governor's house.

"Whoa!" he cried. "What's your hurry, madam?" He

peered over her shoulder. "And what have you done to our good governor, minx? He appears demented!"

"Demented? Pah! He is a lecherous old goat!" Christianne fumed. "But I fancy I have cooled his ardor some! Enough of him. Come with me!" She drew him into the shadows. "Listen to this. Flynn is searching for us! He has spread the tale that I was his doxy, and that I fled with you after we robbed him of his treasure. According to Truffaut, Jonathan is scouring the coast for us with murder on his mind!" she exclaimed.

"Is he now?" James said thoughtfully. "I should dearly like to encounter Captain Flynn once more, and to settle our accounts!" A heated luster had come into his green eyes.

"Be that as it may," Christianne said hurriedly, "I believe we would be wise to bid a hasty farewell to this port. Flynn is in favor here and we are not . . . especially now, after what I just did to him!"

"He did not harm you?" James asked sharply.

"Nay, sir, he did not!" she reassured him. "Is the *Fair Amanda* yet ready to sail?"

"Almost. Two days more should be adequate, from what Mullens tells me."

"Two days! But anything could happen in that time, and we would be trapped here like rats in a—"

"We have no other alternative, Christie," James cut in, "until our vessel is readied. It is best that we return to the square and try to convince the residents of Diégo Suarez that we are most anxious to be their friends. In the event that there is trouble before we are ready to depart, the more friends we have the better, think you not?"

She nodded. "Yes. James—I am truly sorry about Ben."

He nodded noncommittally and offered her his arm. With a heavy sigh, she slipped her arm through his, and together they returned to the torchlit square.

Within a half hour of their return to the square, one of

Governor Truffaut's manservants returned to the timber mansion to see if his master required anything further of him that night. Minutes later he left again, this time bearing a hastily-penned missive, on which the ink had not yet dried. He returned to the gathering to seek out one Capitaine Gabrielle amongst the revellers, and to draw him secretly into the shadows and exchange urgently whispered words.

Less than one hour after Christianne had soundly thwacked the governor's derrière, a swift vessel skimmed across the harbor of Diégo Suarez, headed for the Bay of Antogil further down the eastern coast of Madagascar, where, Capt. Francois Gabrielle had been informed by the governor, the *Red Scorpion* lay at anchor. Gabrielle's ship was named the *Jezebel,* and, like her Biblical counterpart, her purpose was betrayal!

Meanwhile, James and Christianne danced and conversed with vivacious grace or with dashing charm, determined to utilize their time well in the making of allies, unaware that they had overestimated the time left them. Even now, the *Red Scorpion* was nearing Diégo Suarez Bay. They had not seventy-two hours left in which to ready the *Fair Amanda,* but less than twelve.

Thirty

Among the French colonists gathered to celebrate the safe deliverance of James and Christianne from the wilds of Madagascar was a chubby, mustachioed little man from the Basque regions of *la belle* France, whose name, he told them, was Papa Fouchet.

He had kept a fine old posting inn in the old country, an inn renown for its excellent food, fine, ancient wines and comfortable lodgings. But, alas, the inn had been gutted by fire during a long, hot summer, and he had been left without a sous to his name. With little else but his unflagging optimism, he had decided to start a new life elsewhere. Consequently he had signed on as a passenger aboard one of the colonizing ships bound for Madagascar, where rumor had it fortunes were to be made in the gems and the precious ores the island was supposedly littered with! Papa Fouchet had reasoned that where there were people, there was a need for food, lodgings and stores, and his keen head for business and industrious and likable personality had stood him in good stead. He was now the proprietor of Diégo Suarez' only inn-cum-chandler's store, a position of which he was justifiably proud. It was to his inn that Papa Fouchet invited Christianne and James to retire after the gathering, on hearing of the liberties the governor had attempted to take with the lovely Mademoiselle Alexander.

"Poof! He is a man much inflated with his own importance, our Governor Truffaut," Papa Fouchet declared, "though everyone here knows that Antoine was given this position because he had become an embarrassment to King Louis." He chuckled. "Who else would want such a position? To be governor here is more a trial than an honor, *oui?* Truffaut believes that because he is governor he may take any liberties he chooses with the ladies. You are not the first, *mademoiselle,* I regret to say. Our Antoine has made enemies amongst more of the husbands of Diégo Suarez than I can count, and their wives are equally disenchanted with *cher* Antoine! Certainly you will not return to his house, *non, non,* I will not permit it! Until your ship is repaired, you will be my guests." He spread his hands in an expansive, generous gesture, beaming.

"My thanks, Papa Fouchet," James accepted gratefully, and Christianne warmly echoed his thanks.

So it was that James and Christianne found themselves comfortably lodged that night.

Papa Fouchet, Christianne thought warmly, had uttered not a chortle or a snigger when she had insisted on separate chambers for herself and James. He had treated her with deference and respect and a fatherly concern that was charming and a refreshing change from the village's other menfolk, who had exchanged sly, knowing glances when she passed by them and murmured about *la belle sauvage's* supposed lustful exploits in a lewd fashion that had made her blush hotly on hearing them.

She had almost dropped off to sleep that night when she heard what sounded like someone knocking softly upon the log walls of the chamber. She raised her head from the goose down bolster and listened. Nothing. She could hear only the night breeze soughing in the tamarinds and the lazy, rhythmic slap of the tide against the hulls of the vessels in the harbor. Certain she had been mistaken, she plumped her pillows and wriggled about to get comfortable again, snuggling into the plump, feather-filled pallet with a blissful sigh. Governor Truffaut might boast of his monstrously ugly house, but his beds had been sorely lacking in comfort, unlike Papa Fouchet's luxurious accommodations.

She stretched languorously, feeling the dreamy sensation that precedes sleep envelop her inch by inch. But then the rapping at her walls came again, this time accompanied by a voice.

"Christianne!" hissed the urgent whisper. "Christianne Alexander! Over here, by the window!"

Irritated, Christianne swung out of bed and padded to the aperture. It must be James, she thought, made lustful by the wine he had drunk and determined to woo his way into her bed. Well, he would find out soon enough that she had no intention of resuming that portion of their relationship! She lifted the crude curtain that covered the window.

"What brings you here at this late hour, my lustful cap—oh!" she managed before a meaty hand covered her mouth.

In the moonlight she glimpsed a bearded giant of a man before he swung himself over the sill and into the chamber, his hand still clamped firmly over her mouth. Frightened, she jabbed her elbows backwards into the man's ribs. He gasped and cursed.

"Be still, wench! We are friends!" he growled.

Another, shorter cloaked figure scrambled through the window after him.

"Promse you won't scream, and I'll let ye go?" the first man whispered hoarsely.

Christianne nodded and he released her.

"It is alright, *amiga mia,*" whispered the second figure, "It is I, Isabella."

"Isabella!" Christianne exclaimed, incredulous, then added in a lower tone, "But what are you doing here? And who is he?" she queried, jerking her head at the bearded blond giant who towered over her, grinning broadly.

"He is Nicholas Drew," Isabella announced, adding

proudly, "my husband of almost a whole month now! He kept the trading post at Fénérive, to where I fled after I escaped St. Mary's."

"But—what are the two of you doing here?" Christianne asked again, striking the tinderbox to light the candle. Amber light washed the chamber. "And why do you come here at dead of night, like brigands?"

"To warn you of danger, Christianne!" Isabella whispered urgently, stepping forwards and grasping Christianne by the upper arms. Beneath the concealing cloak, Christianne glimpsed her belly, now swollen hugely with child. "We arrived here an hour ago, and went straightway to Governor Truffaut's house. It was from him we learned of your and the captain's arrival in Diégo Suarez a few days ago. It was very obvious," Isabella smiled ruefully, "that Truffaut has no fondness for either of you! Nick has had some dealings with him in the past, and says he is not to be trusted, *si*, Nick?"

"Aye," Nick confirmed with a nod.

"I could not believe my ears when I heard you were here, but I realized that what we know would be of vital importance to you, and to your captain. We slipped away while the household slept to find you and to warn you."

"Warn me of what?" Christianne asked with bated breath.

"Of Jonathan Flynn, and the *Red Scorpion* and the *Voyager!* For two months now he has scoured the coast, searching for the two of you! You see, at some point during the fight at the fortress and afterwards, when you fled across the island from him, someone robbed Flynn of his treasure! I believe it was that Stephen Tancred and Pierre Le Chat—remember, that pair who attacked you by the lagoon that day?"

Christianne nodded. How could she forget?

"Well, it is my feeling that they stole it and have hidden it until later, when they can carry it off, but meanwhile they have convinced Flynn that somehow the two of you doubled back and had the treasure taken to the *Fair Amanda!* Jonathan has sworn to kill you both!" She shuddered. "His hatred of you is like a rat, gnawing at his vitals. He believed that Nick helped Captain Mallory in his masquerade as a priest. He sailed to Fénérive and destroyed the trading post and butchered all but a handful of Nick's men. We were fortunate to escape with out lives! If it were not for his friendship with the Malagasy, we would even now be dead," she finished breathlessly, reaching for her husband's hand.

"Aye," Nicholas Drew agreed solemnly. "We made our escape along the coast but a step ahead of Flynn all the way. I spoke with a native chief shortly before dusk yesterday, and he said that he had seen the two vessels—the *Scorpion* and the *Voyager*—earlier that morning, headed north. They'll be here by the morning tide, I'd wager, for Truffaut sent his own ship to tell them you are here!"

Christianne blanched. "No! The *Fair Amanda* is not seaworthy—she suffered heavily from a storm two months past, and is still undergoing repairs! I must tell James!" she decided. "Stay here while I go and wake him."

James' consternation was much apparent in his troubled green eyes and the tightness of his jaw. He paced back and forth the length of her chamber like a caged panther, slamming his balled fist repeatedly into his other palm. "We must plan on having only until dawn to prepare a warm reception for Captain Flynn," he said thoughtfully. "Papa Fouchet will aid us, I am certain. Wake the good innkeeper, Christianne. He knows where my crew are billeted in the village. Have him round them up and bring them here, and swiftly!"

Less than a half hour later, the crew of the *Amanda* was crowded into the taproom of Papa Fouchet's inn, the walls of which were festooned with kettles, pots, buckets and other chandler's goods. In a decisive, calm voice that belied any need for haste, James outlined the situation to his crew.

"And so you see, men, we have only until first light to ready our ship for sailing. By dawn, I want us out of this harbor and on the high seas—else we risk being bottled up in the bay, at the mercy of Flynn and Wilhelm's cannon! If we must meet with them, I would prefer we did so on a more equal footing than we have at present. What say you, men? Do we do our damnedest?" he challenged them.

"Aye!" the men all murmured fiercely.

In small groups they left the inn, headed for longboats that would carry them out to the *Fair Amanda*. The ship's carpenters went first, then the riggers and sailmakers, then the remainder who would turn their varied talents to any task required of them. With them went every lantern Papa Fouchet could find amongst his stores.

"It is a race against time, Christie, my sweet," James told her, cupping her face and kissing her pert nose briefly before springing into the last longboat. "With fortune on our side, I will return for you long before dawn! Farewell, my love!"

"Godspeed!" she murmured numbly, and watched him go, suddenly overwhelmed by the awful premonition that she would never see him again. Isabella noticed the anxiety in her face and slipped her arm about her comfortingly.

"Do not be afraid, *pequeña*," she said, "he is a clever one, your *capitán*, even my Nick says so. He will not be bested by the likes of Flynn." Isabella smiled. "And besides, Lady Luck, she is a woman, yes? And no woman would let such a handsome *caballero* die!"

Christianne forced a smile at her friend's attempt at humor, but remained unconvinced. Never had her love for James been so sharply brought home to her as it was now, when the serious possibility of losing him knotted her heart. If they survived, could she play out this pretense of not caring for him to the last act? Or should she follow him to the ends of the Earth, if need be, her pride and his secret love of Amanda be damned? Even knowing he still loved *her*, wouldn't a little of his love be better than none at all? Perhaps in time she could make him forget her; in time, perhaps, he would come to love her as deeply as she loved him, and their child would at least know its father. Tears smarted in her eyes as they walked slowly back to the inn beneath the tamarinds. *James, my beloved, take care!* she prayed silently, *Come back safely to me!*

All through that night the muffled sounds of hammering carried across the bay to the little port, yet the villagers never awoke to hear them. They had feasted and drank too well the night before, and lay in sotted stupors for the greater part. Even the governor, the fop, Truffaut, smiled as he snored the night away on his lumpy cot, his cognac-laden breath fanning the tassle of his nightcap. He dreamed of a Dresden shepherdess with a savage temper and wanton, wild beauty that belied her fragile porcelain appearance, and who flitted away from him through the corridors of his mind, laughing at him . . . mocking him . . . taunting him.

Christianne passed the next few hours nervously awaiting James' return. The least sound made her rise expectantly from the wooden settle where she and Isabella sat, only to sit back down each time with a heavy sigh when Papa Fouchet shook his balding head regretfully.

"Here, *ma petite,* drink this, it will steady your nerves," the mustachioed innkeeper advised Christianne, setting a pewter tankard of foaming ale before her.

Christianne shuddered and pushed it away with an apologetic smile. Her deep blue eyes were large and liquid in the candlelight, her delicately-boned face pinched with strain. "Forgive me, sir, but I cannot drink it!" she whispered. "My belly is of a rebellious nature tonight, I fear."

Papa Fouchet nodded understandingly and squeezed her slender shoulder to reassure her before he went back outside.

"You love him, yes?" Isabella remarked solemnly after the innkeeper had left him. "The *capitán*, I mean?"

Christianne nodded, hesitating before answering. "Yes," she confirmed miserably.

"And does he not return your love?" Isabella pressed.

"He says that he does," Christianne said, "but I know better. His heart belongs to another, one who is the wife of another man. I can never be first in his affections." She briefly explained to Isabella what she had heard James say at the height of his fever.

Isabella snorted in disgust. "And that is why you cannot believe that he loves you? *Diós,* I am ashamed of you, Christianne! It was but the fever talking then, believe me. It is what he says when the sickness has passed that counts, for it is then he says what is truly in his heart. Self-pity does not become you, *amiga mia!* Where is your spirit, your fire, that I saw on St. Mary's? For shame! The Christianne that I knew then would have fought tooth and nail for the man she loved. She would have scoffed at the thought that he could *ever* love another woman, and vowed to bewitch *el Capitán* until his heart was bound in the silken bonds of her love, and he could not even remember the name of this "other woman"! That Christianne would *never* have accepted defeat so easily." Isabella reached across the table and clasped Christianne's hand. "Fight for him, *muchacha,* if you love him. Fight!"

Christianne blinked away her tears and nodded. Perhaps Isabella was right. "I will try, I promise," she said with a wan smile. "You see, I have not only myself to fight for, Bella. Like you, I am with child." She straightened a little and set her shoulders resolutely. "And you—what is all this about Nicholas Drew?"

"Ah, Nicholas!" Isabella said with a grin. "Si, he is my husband, and more importantly, my friend. When Jonathan discovered his treasure gone, I realized that this time I could not return to the fortress. With the help of some of his crew's native women, I made my way to Fénérive. Nick took me in and befriended me. He treated me with respect, Christianne, as if I were not the sullied *puta* of the pirates but a woman again. When he asked me to marry him, I said that I would—but only if he gave up his Bety and Rahena, his native women," she grinned again and her dark eyes flashed, "for I was jealous of their place in his affections even then! The next day, I learned that they had returned to their villages, and Nicholas and I were married by Father Luis." Isabella giggled. "That priest, I believe he holds your James in as much hatred as Jonathan! Nick found he and Father Pedro wandering, dazed and quite naked, outside the stockade the morning after James and the other man stole their priests' robes. According to Nick, their language would have shamed a sailor—and they men of the cloth!" She tutted reprovingly.

She and Christianne's laughter was abruptly cut short by Papa Fouchet's explosive entry into the inn, Nicholas Drew hard on his heels.

"The repairs are complete!" the innkeeper announced, his excitement evident. *"Oui,* and with very little time to spare! The lookout has sighted canvas to the east, a vessel bearing steadily for Diégo Suarez. Capitaine Mallory is even now returning for you, mademoiselle! *Vite, vite!* We have not a second to lose! Down to ze beach with you, *ma petite!"*

Christianne needed no further urging. With hurried thanks to Papa Fouchet and brief hugs to Isabella and her husband, she sped from the inn and into James' arms as he raced up the beach toward her.

The first flamboyant pennants of pink were streaming across the sky to herald the new day.

Thirty-One

Bosun Silas Mullens was at the oars of the longboat when Christianne and James raced down the sand. James splashed knee-deep into the shallows, his arm outstretched to help Christianne into the bobbing craft. As she reached gratefully for his hand, explosions sounded from behind them. She felt a searing, hot pain as a musket ball whined past her cheek and lost her balance and pitched forwards into the water. More musket fire ripped up fountains of white water all about the boat, and scored a narrow trough from the wood of its bows.

"That fool, Truffaut, damn his soul!" James cursed as he hauled Christianne into the boat, before leaping in after her, "Keep low and row like Lucifer himself were after us!"

Mullens acknowledged his order with a grin and ducked low as another volley of musket balls fell like giant hailstones all about them. Certain Christianne was only grazed, James risked a glance over his shoulder. Antoine Truffaut was egging his men on from a vantage point higher up the beach. He still wore his ridiculous tasselled nightcap and voluminous night gown, while some of his men were still in their small-clothes, no doubt having received the summons to take up arms while yet abed! Even from this distance, the governor's face was a mottled purple with outrage, James saw with a wicked smile.

Mullens hauled strongly on the oars and in minutes their bows bumped against the towering sides of the *Amanda*. A rope ladder snaked down immediately, and the three quickly shinned up it. In seconds of them reaching the decks, the sails were unfurled, snapping and crackling with the God-sent breeze. The decks were alive with sailors, laboring like demons at their various duties. Far above, still more sailors crawled amongst the spars and hung from rat-lines, like enormous busy spiders spinning some fantastic web.

James began barking orders from left to right, and for a few moments Christianne was forgotten except by Bones, who greeted her with nigh uncontrollable joy after so long an absence. The musket ball had traced a stinging scratch across her cheek but had already stopped bleeding. She watched, fascinated, as James strode back and forth. His shirt was sodden with his sweat and grimy, to boot. His men had not labored alone last night, it was clear. Isabella's words came suddenly back to her full force. Aye, she thought, her eyes fastened upon James, he was indeed a man worth fighting for! I will *not* give him up, she vowed silently, nay, not to any woman, let alone his "fair Amanda"! I will make him believe in me! A wild, sweet gladness swept through her. She longed to run to him, kiss him, to tell him she loved him with every fiber of her being, with everything she was now and ever would be, body and soul, mind and heart!

As if he sensed her eyes upon him, he swung around.

"Mullens, take Mistress Christie below," he ordered, his green eyes tender as they caressed her face. "The decks are no place for my lady."

"Aye, aye, sir!" Mullens responded, grinning, for he had seen the look that had leaped like forked lightning betwixt the two of them. He took her elbow and hustled and chivvied her belowdecks to join Lucy Waller, immune to her protests.

The *Fair Amanda* scudded across the deep natural harbor, headed for the open sea between the two land spits that embraced the harbor mouth with protective arms. Far above the rolling decks in the crow's nest, Mark, the cabin boy, shielded his eyes against the first brilliant rays of morning sunlight and scanned the cobalt-blue ocean for signs of the vessels that had been sighted earlier from Diégo Suarez.

"Loose the topsails!" James roared to the men who clung in the ratlines, barefooted, their legs wrapped about the rigging for safety. They responded swiftly to their captain's command. More bleached-white canvas billowed in the breeze as the ropes sang through the blocks and loosened the sails. "Master Mullens, the helm! Take us out of this damnable harbor, if you please! Gunners, stand by your cannon until I give the order to fire."

Immediately, the gun captains leaped to their posts, their crews but a second behind them. "Ready, sir!" they sang out in unison. Stripped down to their white, loose cotton drawers, scarlet kerchiefs knotted about their foreheads to catch their sweat, they were a fearsome bunch, indeed. The black barrels of their cannon poked out ominously from the gundecks of the *Amanda* like squat, black snouts, ready to blaze fire.

James looked about him critically. All appeared in order. They were fast approaching the enormous harbor mouth, but there was still no cry of, "Sail-ho!" from aloft. If their luck held, they could be clear of Diégo Suarez before running up against Flynn. He frowned, suddenly wary. Drew had told him the *Red Scorpion* and the *Voyager*'s arrival was imminent. Then where the devil were they?

"My glass, Andrew," he rasped, his suspicions growing by the minute. The sailor leaped back up the foredeck with the spyglass as agilely as a young monkey. James raised the glass to his eye and scanned both heavily-forested spits of land that projected across the harbor mouth, first to east, then west, then east again. He chuckled softly. He had been right! Their apparently clear passage through the harbor mouth was naught but a trick! He was certain he had glimpsed the blinding white of a sail shimmering beyond the foliage. That silver-tongued Flynn was as sly a fox as ever walked this Earth!

"Ahoy aloft!" he bellowed, cupping his hands to his mouth.

"Aye, Cap'n?" came the drawn-out response from the crow's nest way above.

"Look to the east, lad, to the harbor mouth!" James ordered. "Do you spy a sail?"

Mark Duggan's yelp of surprise carried even to the foredeck.

"Aye, sir! Sail-ho!" the cabin boy sang out. "Twin sets o' mast, carrying all the sail they can handle, sir!" he cried eagerly.

"Where away, lad?" James barked.

"Due east, sir, beyond the spit!"

James grunted with satisfaction. An ambush, as he had expected! Should he lay low here in the harbor until nightfall, he wondered, and pray that Flynn would not grow impatient and blockade them in? Then he could send a boarding party overland by cover of darkness to the two hidden ships, with the intent of firing their powder magazines. Nay, Flynn would not bide his time so long. There was but one other option open to him: to quit the harbor at speed, cannons blazing, and meet the *Scorpion* and the *Voyager* head on! He frowned again. That would be a risky business. Another ploy presented itself. He smiled grimly. There was more than one wily fox at sea this day!

"Andrew, bring up rags, lad, as many as you are able to lay hands on! Pile them here, by the firebox, then dampen them a little."

Andrew opened his mouth to question the strange order, then shrugged. This was his first sea battle. Who was he to question his captain's orders?

James grinned and strode to the rail. He stood there, the

wind ruffling his russet hair and flapping his full shirt about him, his green eyes aglitter like shattered emeralds with excitement. Soon he would see if that rogue, Jonathan Flynn, could be bested at his own game!

As they drew level with the land spits that concealed Flynn's miniature armada, the *Amanda*'s gunners lit their tapers at the firebox in readiness.

"Open the port-covers on all sides!" James ordered. "Shot and powder ready?"

"Ready, sir!" responded the gun-captains.

"Check breeching ropes."

"All checked, sir," came the swift reply.

James nodded curtly, feeling the tension inside him build to fever pitch as their prow nosed out of the harbor mouth. Soon, he knew full well, that tension would be replaced by the glorious surge of elation that always accompanied danger.

God's Blood, there they were, the pair of them, both the *Scorpion* and the *Voyager!*

"*Fire!*" James roared.

The twenty-six pounders blazed and bucked against the breeching ropes restraint as lit tapers were applied to their touchholes. Eight cannonballs, black as the devil's hooves, whistled and whined through the air. Almost simultaneously, there was answering yellow-orange spurts of fire from their enemies' port-covers and the scream of their cannonballs as they arced through the air towards the *Amanda*. But each ball fell short or whistled harmlessly into the water yards from their side. As James had judged, they were out of range of both Flynn and Wilhelm's guns as yet!

"Light the rags!" James snapped to Andrew, who stood by with a flaming torch.

"But, sir—!" the youth protested.

"Light them, and sharpish!" his captain barked, slamming his fist down on the rail.

Confused, Andrew torched the rags. In seconds, clouds of thick black smoke belched from the smoldering pile, wreathing about the decks and enveloping the *Amanda*. A faint cheer of triumph carried clearly across the water from the enemy ships to the watery-eyed, coughing crew of the *Amanda*. As James had intended, they believed they had scored a hit!

James would have given his eye teeth to see the look on Flynn's and Wilhelm's faces when they exited that smoke cloud undamaged and with their guns blazing! One of their cannonballs ripped through the *Voyager*'s decks. Another fired her magazine and the vessel exploded in a blaze of colorful pyrotechnics, orange and yellow and crimson, before beginning to sink.

"Hoorah!" whooped one of the *Amanda*'s gun-captain. "A hit, Cap'n, and a bloody good one, at that!"

James grinned. "Well done, lads!" he shouted. "Fire again when ready!"

The *Scorpion* was taking a wide tack about, no doubt intending to flee. "After her, Master Mullens!" James ordered. "Nip at her heels!"

The smokescreen had gained them precious seconds and also given them the element of surprise. No doubt Flynn had anticipated an easy victory over the outnumbered and unsuspecting *Amanda* and was now sorely chagrined to find their numbers more evenly matched, he thought!

The *Scorpion* had lost her sting. She fled before their barrage of fire like a graceful swan fleeing the hunter's arrow. Her canvas was white as the driven snow against the glittering cobalt of the Indian Ocean, and edged with gold in the morning sunlight. The ruffled white foam of her trough was cleanly cut and marked her speedy flight.

Ruthlessly, James urged his ship on, until the *Scorpion* was once more in range of his cannon. "Fire!" he roared, and the graceful swan plunged and listed as a ball gouged her broadside, mortally wounded. The distance between the two vessels closed irrevocably, and the crew of the *Amanda* could see the frenzied racing of the *Scorpion*'s crew to take up arms even as they broke ranks and scattered to take up their own.

Seconds later, grappling irons were hurled over the *Scorpion*'s rail and the *Amanda*'s crew were swarming over her sides to take on Flynn's men in hand to hand combat, their captain, his sword in hand, with them. Other men swung to the *Scorpion*'s decks from the ratlines.

Steel crashed against steel as the bloody battle commenced, interspersed with cries and screams as men fell beneath the daggers and cutlasses, swords and billy clubs that swathed a path through their numbers as a sickle through a field of wheat.

James flung one man away from him and spun to take on another, his rapier red with blood. He felt no joy as he vanquished man after man with his deadly blade, for he had no quarrel with Flynn's men; it was their captain he sought! Where was he, the rogue? He heard a cry behind him, and whirled to see Andrew Prior pinned to the slippery decks, a dagger impaling the flesh of his upper arm. The youth's eyes were clouded with pain and horror as he lay in a pool of his own blood. Ruthlessly James gripped the dagger's handle and wrenched it free, hauling the ashen-faced lad to his feet in almost the same move.

"Get back to the *Amanda,* you young fool!" he growled. "And stay there!"

"Captain! Look out!" Prior gasped, his eyes widening as he looked over James' shoulder.

James flung around in the nick of time to find Pierre Le Chat at his back, a slender blade in his fist. The sly Frenchman's eyes shone fiercely as he lunged forwards, executing the classic fencing thrush of the passado. James parried it with an easy flick of his wrist, moving in with the short, thrusting cut, the riposte, forging forwards with wickedly skillful, lightning-fast moves until the astonished

441

Frenchman suddenly found he could retreat no further, for the rail was at his back. Le Chat's eyes were afraid now, James saw. He slammed the man's blade from his hand and knotted his fist in Le Chat's collar.

"Where is he?" James growled, eyes blazing. "Where's Flynn?"

Despite James' obvious fury and the chance that his own death was imminent, the shifty-eyed Frenchman laughed. "Capitaine Flynn? He is not aboard the *Scorpion, m'sieu!*" he jeered.

James cursed and knotted his fist even tighter in the Frenchman's collar, forcing his knuckles against Le Chat's windpipe. "Then where the blazes is he? Tell me, and swiftly, friend, before I slit your blasted throat!"

Le Chat's face was mottled now, his breathing labored. James forced him backwards over the rail and raised his rapier. Le Chat's eyes flickered fearfully to the shining blade scant inches from his face and back to the captain, whose expression was murderous.

"The *mademoiselle!*" he gasped, clawing to tear James' vice-like fist from his throat. "When you boarded the *Scorpion,* he said he was going to get the girl!"

James drew back, lifted Le Chat by the heels and toppled him overboard before whirling about. That devil, Flynn, was aboard the *Fair Amanda!* And Christianne was unarmed and unprotected. The realization clawed at his gut as he sprinted across the *Scorpion*'s decks.

Christianne paced back and forth in the great-cabin, wringing her hands, while Lucy Waller tended to Andrew Prior's ugly wound. The youth, whey-faced from lack of blood, sat in the captain's chair, his arm bound with strips of sheeting.

"Dear God, what's happening up there!" Christianne wondered aloud. "I cannot stand this not knowing!" Faint cries and crashes reached them here, in the bowels of the ship, but little else.

"Be patient, mistress," Andrew advised weakly, appearing close to swooning and falling from the chair, "the cap'n knows what he's about, never fear! He were fightin' like a demon, last I saw him!" he finished proudly.

Christianne appeared unconvinced. Her features were set stubbornly, her deep blue eyes alight with resolve. She recalled all too vividly her fears for James' safety last night when he had left her at Papa Fouchet's, and her sudden premonition that she would never see him again. Was he even now dead, she wondered, a dagger plunged into his breast? Dear God, no! She loved him so, loved him with all her heart! Life without him would not be life at all, but mere existence, so what had she to lose—?

"I'm going abovedecks," she announced, hurrying to the door. Before Lucy or Andrew could stop her, she had flung it open and hurried down the passageway, Master Bones following eagerly at her heels.

The acrid smell of burnt cloth and gunpowder was sharp in her nostrils, and smoke wafted down the stairway as she sped up it. A deep snarl came from Bones as she clambered onto the deck. She gasped, for Jonathan Flynn stood there, smiling his charming smile. He appeared unhurried and as cocksure as ever as he came toward her.

"Well, if it ain't me darlin' girl!" he sneered. "And where do ye think you're off to, lass?"

Christianne sprang forwards, bent on slipping past him. Flynn's arm snaked out, catching her about the waist. "Nay, mavourneen, not so fast!" he chuckled.

"Let me go!" she panted, writhing in his arms, clawing for his face.

"I'll not let ye go," Flynn growled, hefting her over his shoulder. " 'Twill be as before, lass! I've a longboat waiting below, for the two o' us. We'll find a ship to carry us back to Paradise."

"I won't go with you!" she cried, " 'tis James I love, James Mallory, captain of this vessel and master of my heart! I *never* loved you, Flynn, it was all a lie!"

He snarled a curse as he carried her, wriggling and scratching across the decks to the rail. From the decks of the *Scorpion* carried the sounds of the ferocious battle still being waged aboard her.

"I was wrong, Christie," Flynn panted, "you're a harlot at heart, like my own blessed mother, the lovely Maureen! Aye, and 'tis my harlot you'll be, instead of my queen!"

"Let her go, Flynn!" roared a voice at their backs.

Looking over his shoulder, Jonathan Flynn saw James standing there. His head jerked about at a footfall on the decks before him, and he saw Mullens, pistol cocked, blocking his retreat. He slid his dagger from his belt and lay the blade across Christianne's throat. Her lovely eyes widened in fear. Her elfin face paled. She ceased her flailing at Flynn's face and stayed quite still in his arms.

"I've nothing to lose, Mallory," Flynn jeered. "My treasure is gone, along with my lady's love. One move from either of ye, and the lass dies! Put down your sword, my fine captain. Bosun, drop that pistol to the decks—and carefully, mind. You'd not have time to stop me before the deed was done!"

Dragging Christianne before him, the wicked blade still tight against her throat, he backed away towards the rail. Both James and Mullens watched helplessly as Flynn prepared to lift her over the rail. An involuntary whimper escaped her as she felt the cold steel against her flesh. At the sound, Bones growled deep in his throat. His hackles rose. With a snarl, he hurtled past James and leaped on Flynn, a streak of gray and white fur atop him as he lost his balance and fell. Bones' small, sharp teeth sank painfully into the flesh of the Irishman's thigh. He cursed and lost his grip on Christianne, who quickly rolled away from him as he raised his dagger to the little dog. There was a yelp, then silence. Flynn sprang lightly to his feet. Grinning with triumph, he leaped for the rail. The grin changed to an expression of disbelief as yellow flame spurted from the pistol, now again in Mullens' hand. He clutched at his chest, the fast-spreading stain of crimson at his heart escaping his fingers, before he toppled backwards into the ocean below. There was a splash seconds later as his body hit water.

With a cry, Christianne dropped to her knees at Bones' side. He lay very still, his chocolate-brown eyes closed, his joyful tail quite motionless. She gathered him up into her arms and held him, tears flooding down her grazed cheeks and spilling onto his shaggy fur.

"Bones, oh, Bones!" she sobbed, her shoulders heaving. "He was e-ever my f-faithful hound, e-ever my friend!" She buried her face in his fur.

"Come, let me look at him," James urged gently, plucking the limp little dog from her arms. He felt along the dog's body and found the knife wound, high on the shoulder. It was bleeding and severe, but not, he thought, enough to have killed the little beast. "Rum, Mister Mullens!" he asked, holding out his hand. A flask appeared from the bosun's jersey. James spread Bones' teeth and forced a few drops of the potent grog between them. There was a sneeze, then what sounded like a cough, and then suddenly a long, pink tongue swiped wetly down James' face. He let out a great bellow of laughter. Bones might be wounded, but he was far from dead!

"Faithless hound!" Christianne scolded him happily. "You would not reassure *me* that you yet lived, and yet you do so for the captain!"

James grinned. "Aye, 'tis clear we've made a seafaring hound out of him. He follows only the captain's orders, as a good sailor should—unlike his mistress, disobedient baggage! Take the little beast down below and tend to his wounds. A bone will serve as his meal of valor this night, for if not for him, you would be gone with Flynn by now! I'll join you when all is done here. Make haste, my sweet, and mark you take care. I would not wish either my future wife or my son harmed, you understand?"

She had only time enough to gasp and stare open-mouthed after him as he and Mullens hurried to rejoin the battle on the *Scorpion*.

"God bring you safely back to me!" she breathed fervently as she watched him go. Then she turned and carried Bones below.

Thirty-Two

Crooked, narrow streets, lined with galleried, three-storied houses of lime-washed stone and red-tile roofs, led up from the sparkling harbor of St. Pierre, the prettiest port town of the West Indian isle of Martinique. Lush mountains dominated the island, their summits rising from banks of creamy cloud like magical kingdoms of blue-green glass. Plantations of banana, cane and tobacco clothed the lower mountain slopes, and above, valleys and gorges, meadows and lakes, thick with ferns and tall grasses, guava and bamboo, collided with each other in strange and wonderful confusion.

Christianne noticed that a plantation drum was throbbing in the distance, an insistent summons to the fields that matched the throb of her heart. The Caribees were as exotic and exciting as James had promised, she thought as he lifted her onto the horse!

"Ready?" he asked, his hand resting lightly on her leg as he grinned up at her, perched precariously astride the great beast.

"Aye," she said with a grimace. She had never ridden before, and was alarmed at how far from the ground the back of a horse seemed once astride it. "I'm ready as I will ever be! Where are we going?"

"You'll see," he promised, and kneed his own horse forwards, leading her ancient, docile nag behind it while she clung grimly to its mane.

They clattered out of St. Pierre and into the countryside,

where the brilliant tropical sunshine was diffused by the leafy shade of the trees to golden and green sovereigns that patterned her fair complexion like a veil. The sultry tradewinds ruffled her hair about her shoulders like silken silver pennants streaming from the ramparts of a castle. Her cheeks were rosy with excitement and warmth, and her deep blue eyes alive with happiness, James noticed as they rode. A warm glow of pleasure infused him. How lovely she was, his woman, Christianne! His woman . . . he liked the way it sounded. A feeling of contentment had replaced his former restless nature since they had left Diégo Suarez behind nigh three months ago. Ben's murder had been avenged. Christianne had ceased her coldness toward him and now came to him joyfully, her love for him as bright and warm as flame. Aye, he was a happy man!

The crew of the *Red Scorpion* had relinquished the fight after their captain's death, and dived overboard to swim for shore. The victorious crew of the *Fair Amanda* had plundered the sinking *Scorpion*'s holds, and her extra water barrels had yielded a surprising secret—Jonathan Flynn's glittering treasure trove, hidden there beneath his very nose by Pierre Le Chat and Stephen Tancred! Without hesitation, James had ordered the booty divided equally amongst his men. They had earned it, by God, in taking on Flynn's crew like demons at his command! Aye, he would bid farewell to his men in New Orleans without regret, leaving them all wealthy men in their own right, to begin a new life with his Christianne, and in time, their child.

What was he smiling at now, she wondered, glancing at him from under the broad brim of her beribboned straw hat? Her body tautened beneath the flimsy, cool cloth of her muslin gown as he felt her eyes upon him and shifted that sensual green-eyed gaze to her face. A now-familiar stirring began in her loins, darting, delicious currents of tingling warmth throughout her. How handsome he is, she thought, with his hair the color of cinnamon sticks in the sunlight, and his eyes like emeralds against the bronze of his skin! Memories of rapturous nights spent in the bed of the great-cabin, while the silver moon danced on the ebony sea outside the cabin windows, washed over her. She trembled and all but toppled from the steadily plodding horse as it picked its way between the baby ferns and the luminous moonflowers that carpeted the ground like fallen stars.

The track wound upwards, and the air grew cool and sweet as the climbed higher, as sweet as the mountain water that tumbled down through the lowland forests in sparkling torrents. They spied sapphire-capped hummingbirds and lavender and white doves, scarlet butterflies and the metallic blue-green glint of the dragonflies as they rode on, sometimes between avenues of towering green cane rustling with the perfumed breeze like a whispering sea, or through banana groves, the trees burgeoning with sun-ripened, golden fruit like enormous candleabras in their fronds. The heartbeat of plantation drums was even louder here, a frenzied, pagan beat like the heartbeat of the land itself. Black-skinned men and *filles de couleur* bent to their labor in time with its beat, singing the chants of the Congo from where they had been plucked like ebony flowers to till the soil of the white man in far off lands.

At length James turned in the saddle and shoved back the hat that had shadowed his upper face.

"Up there!" he cried. "Look!"

She looked, and her heart skipped a beat. La Reine du Ciel, the Queen of the Sky, rose from the lush green of her plantation like a diadem of white from a cushion of green velvet. Her white columns were like arms uplifted to the mother-of-pearl clouds and the blue-smoke mountains above. Between two of the misty summits stretched a perfect West Indian rainbow, ashimmer with translucent bands of grape, lemon, orange sherbet and guava pink. She was struck speechless, her expression registering awe and delight.

"La Reine du Ciel, Christianne!" James breathed, kneeing his horse to her side and taking her hand in his. "Our home!" he added, kissing her fingertips in turn.

"Ours?" she whispered, her eyes as wide and blue as the mountain lakes they had passed earlier.

He nodded. "Aye, my sweet, ours." He withdrew a key from his belt. "As of yesterday, when I outbid all others at the auction!"

She smiled impishly. "It appears you always get what you want, do you not, sir?"

"Always!" he agreed. He leaned across and lifted her from her saddle to his own. "It is fitting that we ride home together, my love," he murmured, brushing his lips against her hair.

Not long after, they were standing in the portico of La Reine, and James was turning the key in the heavy balata-wood door. Before she could protest, he swung her up into his arms and carried her over the threshold like a bride.

Sunlight fell through the slats in the shutters and patterned the golden wood floors with bars of light and shade like tiger stripes. Millions of dust motes eddied and swirled in those bars. Beyond in the shadow, she saw snowy banks of dust-sheeted furniture, glimpsed the sparkle of crystal chandeliers, imprisoned rainbows in their glass, before James took her hand and led her up a curving staircase to the chamber of the master of La Reine.

It was a long, airy room, with French windows that opened out onto a veranda and shutters, closed now, on all sides. James flung open these shutters and the room was suddenly filled with golden light, perfumed breeze and the sweet chorus of birdsong.

The view was breathtaking. Half the island of Martinique dropped away from their doorstep to the pale blue shimmer of the distant sea, where yet another West Indian island, only a misty amethyst shadow against the blue, was barely discernible. The thundering surf was only a frothy white ruffle against the white-gold ribbon of sand from this distance, and St. Pierre but a red and white mosaic that broke that perfect ribbon briefly before it continued on. Every shade of green imaginable mantled the valleys and meadows below, ranging from dark olive to almost yellow lime-green.

Nearer, the gardens of La Reine were a riot of tropical color; the deep crimson of the hedges of *roses d'Inde,* and the magenta, cerise and purple of the bougainvillaea, the canary-yellow and parrot-red of the flamboyant hibiscus, and the soft, luminous yellow-white of the moonflowers. The silk cotton, or kapok trees, shaded fern-floored bowers where balata-wood benches had been set, and a small, sparkling fountain splashed merrily in a secluded corner.

James slipped his arm about Christianne's waist and drew her against him. "Moonflowers," he whispered, "remind me of you, my sweet. There were times during my fevers on Madagascar when I dreamed of the moonflowers at La Reine, gleaming in the hot dusk, and when I opened my eyes it seemed I had dreamed of you in the shadows, with your moonflower hair and your moonflower skin." He caressed her uplifted face with a hesitant fingertip, and she moved her cheek against his touch like a kitten, to return the caress.

A sweet, wild yearning swept through her, causing her to tremble as she had earlier when they had first set out that morning. She offered her lips joyfully to his kiss, coming into his arms like a traveller who has journeyed many miles and at last come home.

"I love you," she said for the first, very first time, aloud. "I love you!"

"And I love you, Christianne," he said huskily, rubbing a curl of her pale hair between his tanned fingers. Wordlessly he lifted her and carried her to the bed.

As his strong arms engulfed her, as his lips worked their magic on her senses, she knew that he was right. She had come home, for the last time.

Epilogue

Christianne waited with barely containable excitement for James outside some shipping offices. He had gone to see to the unloading off his vessel and the signing over of her cargoes, leaving her and Lucy Waller to enjoy their first sight of New Orleans alone. Lucy, however, had left long ago, strutting happily on the arm of Andrew Prior, to explore the city. When the young sailor had shyly asked Lucy if she would accompany him, Lucy had at first declined, but Christianne had guessed accurately that her only reason for declining was her reluctance to leave Christianne alone.

"Oh, go along, Lucy, do!" Christianne had laughed, "I shall be quite all right here until James comes."

"Well—if you're certain?" Lucy had said doubtfully, giving her Andy a hopeful smile.

"Quite certain!" Christianne said firmly. "Now, go! I shall just stay here and watch everyone passing by."

And so it was that Lucy had left. Indeed, she had not been bored in the past hour. There was so much to see, so many diverse people and things to watch that she had not had time to be bored!

The Mississippi River was like a river of chocolate, though possessed of an odor that was not near so sweet as its appearance promised, but despite this minor point, New Orleans promised to be an exciting place. She saw huge bales of cotton, almost bursting with fluffy white bolls, being loaded onto one ship. Casks of sugar and coffee beans were stacked on another side. By standing on tiptoe, she could see that a wide boulevard led away from the wharves into the city proper, and that it was lined with trees boasting heavy, waxy clusters of white blossoms, and hedges of some flamboyant bright pink and lavender flowers. She stepped out into the sunlight to attempt to see further, and in so doing collided with a petite, smartly-dressed woman in green.

"Your pardon, ma'am!" she gasped.

The woman laughed merrily, tilted her plumed hat back into place and patted her arm. "No harm done, ducks! Think nothing of it!" she declared, stepping past Christianne to scan the shipping lists posted outside the shipping office. Her eyes lit up. "Well, glory be!" she cried. "An' about bloody time, too!"

Christianne smiled at her obvious pleasure. "Good news, I trust," she remarked conversationally. "Congratulations!"

The woman nodded, her red ringlets bouncing on her shoulders. "Aye," she confirmed, "news I'd just about gone an' given up on getting, too!"

"You're English," Christianne said, walking alongside the woman back into the sunny levee.

"Aye, love. As English as bloody London fog, that's me," she agreed with a grin. "An' you, too, by the sounds o' it?"

Christianne nodded. "Yes. I just arrived here in New Orleans this morning."

"All alone, are ye?"

Christianne shook her head. "No, I was waiting for someone. He had some business to attend to, but it's taking him far longer than I thought."

"Ah, I see," the woman nodded sympathetically. The girl was a right beauty, if ever she'd seen one, and very obviously in the latter months of carrying a child. Men! she thought indignantly. What sort of a husband had the girl, who'd leave her alone in the hot sun in her condition? Bloody fool! A treasure like her would be snapped up, expecting or nay, in this wicked city. She sniffed. It would serve him right, whoever he was, to come back and find her gone! Maybe a few minutes of anxiety would do him a power of good, and make him realize his luck. She lifted the tiny gold fob watch pinned to her green satin bosom. "I've time fer a spot o' coffee, if ye'd like?" she offered. " 'Twill pass the time fer ye, while ye wait." The girl looked doubtful, and despite her expensive scarlet gown—which was somewhat tight about the middle—seemed curiously ill at ease and forlorn. "My treat!" she added. "I'll have ye back here in a shake. The coffeehouse is but one street down from here."

"Very well!" Christianne agreed, a dazzling smile lighting her lovely face. "My thanks for your kindness, ma'am. I would be honored to join you."

The woman laughed and the dark green plumes in her broad-brimmed hat danced jauntily. "Ye would, would ye?" she said with a grin. Stray cats or stray dogs or stray lasses, she thought ruefully, I never could turn 'em away! "Come along with me, then. I've a carriage waitin'."

They wove their way out of the clutter at wharfside to where a shiny black carriage waited, a fine pair of matched chestnut horses in the traces. A white-and-gold-liveried groom jumped nimbly down to assist the ladies.

"Maison Robineau, Harry," the woman ordered, "an' step on it, ducks!"

Harry grinned and nodded as he clicked to the horses. Christianne's eyebrows rose at the familiar tone the woman had used to her mulatto coachman, but then settled back comfortably on the gleaming leather seat, shaded by the woman's green-fringed parasol. An avenue of live oaks, with their spreading olive-green branches, lined the boulevard, and the scent of cape jasmine and magnolias, oranges and spices mingled with the less pleasant tang of the river as they were carried smartly along.

"Come a fair ways, our little city has," the woman

remarked, "in the two years I've been 'ere. Weren't no more than a blooming village when I got off the boat, it weren't, and now look at it! As pretty and civilized a place as ye'd ever want ter see. Here we are, love. Wait a bit and Harry'll hand ye down."

The coffeehouse was crowded and many of the patrons hailed her petite, vivacious companion with warm greetings that she returned with equal warmth and obvious pleasure.

"Why, Tom, you young sod!" she cried to one. "Where've you been? And you, Jacques—why, I ain't seen feather nor bone o' your ugly mug since last winter, I ain't!" she exclaimed in mock disgust.

The two massive men, dressed in fringed buckskins, rose sheepishly and hugged the woman in turn. "Aye, it's been too long," the smaller man, Tom, agreed, "but it were a good season for pelts. Made a pretty penny we did, Jacques an' me!"

The woman tweaked his leathery, bearded cheek fondly as if he were a smooth-faced, callow boy. "I'll bet ye did, boys," she declared, her blue eyes twinkling saucily, "and ye knows where ye can go t' spend it, right?" She winked and nudged them.

"Right!" they said in unison, grinning.

"Come, love, sit ye down," the woman told Christianne, gesturing to a nearby empty table of spotless scrubbed wood. "Henri will be out just as soon as he gets word I'm here, bless 'im."

Christianne sat, looking avidly about her. The coffeehouse was a cozy place, filled with the aroma of fresh-brewed coffee, fried *beignets* and some sort of savory soup. The furnishings were simple, rough-hewn wooden pieces, the ceiling beamed and hung with serviceable wooden chandeliers. The patrons were far more colorful than their surroundings, ranging from elegantly-dressed gentlemen in satin frockcoats and breeches, their exotic, beautiful quadroon mistresses dangling on their arms, to heavy-jowled, beefy farmers, pimple-faced clerks and a few seamen. It was a noisy crowd they made, and a merry one, and Christianne found herself warming to her surroundings. Perhaps New Orleans would not be so different from home after all?

Henri Robineau, the cafe's proprietor, proved to be a bald, rotund little Frenchman who reminded Christianne of Papa Fouchet in Diégo Suarez. He had the same sort of kindly face and twinkling eyes, but without the moustache. He greeted the woman in green with a gallant kiss to both her rouged cheeks and her heavily beringed hand, and bustled off to fetch their order of coffee and *croissants*, whatever they were, from the kitchen.

"Loverly lad, that Henri," the woman remarked. "A widower, yer know—aye, an' lucky fer him!" Christianne's eyes widened over the rim of her sturdy coffee cup, and the woman laughed. "His wife, Solange, 'er name was, was a bleedin' old harridan, built like a bloomin' carthorse! Made poor little Henri's life hell on earth, she did, until he got lucky one night and she tripped on the stairs and broke her neck. Luckiest day o' his life, it were!" the woman said with relish.

Christianne attempted to appear shocked, but failed. Instead, she giggled. Her companion was not only flamboyant but outrageously frank. She liked her enormously!

"Got a loverly smile ye have, ducks," the woman noted with a grin. "It fair lights up the room. What's yer name, sweetheart?"

"Christianne," she mumbled through a mouthful of flaky, delicious *croissant*. "Christianne Alexander."

"Now there's a coincidence!" the woman exclaimed. "That were me sister's name, sort of," she added evasively, eyes twinkling.

Christianne's head jerked up. "Your—your sister's?" she echoed, hanging on to the coffee cup for dear life. "And—and what is your name, ma'am?" she asked haltingly, feeling faint of a sudden.

The woman chuckled. "Why, ducks, *everyone* knows *my* name! I'm Nellie Flagg!"

She gaped as Christianne slithered silently to the floor.

James waited with drawn breath in the crackling silence, for the storm that was about to erupt. Nell's face was nigh purple with rage since his words!

"You wot?" she shrieked, advancing on him furiously, red ringlets bouncing.

James sighed heavily. "I said," he repeated in a doom-filled voice, "that the child Christianne carries is mine."

"Well, is it now!" Nell said, quivering from head to toe. "An' how did that happen, I'd like ter know? I send ye ter London t' find me nephew, and when ye learn 'tis not a nephew but a niece, ye right away take her t' bed! 'Tis fortunate I've a soft spot in me heart for ye, James Mallory, ye black-hearted scoundrel, else I'd take a knife to ye an' put an end to yer tomcatting ways—once and fer all time!"

James winced. "We are to be wed, Nell, never fear. I told you that in the coffeehouse, did I—?"

"You can bet yer bloomin' breeches you're to be wed, aye, an' sharpish!" Nell cut in hotly. "Look at the poor little love in this bed!" she clucked, throwing her arm about Christianne's shoulders and squeezing her fiercely, "if'n ye don't get a move on, I'd wager the babe'll be here afore any priest can give ye His blessing!" Nell smiled fondly at her niece. "Rest, lovely," she urged, "ye look fair drawn again. Ah, I can see our Jenny in ye, though she was never so comely as you. Aunt Nellie will see ye decently wed, never fear. Then if his lecherous lordship here decides to run off after, he can leave, an' good riddance! You and the babe will always have a home with yer Aunt Nell, never fear." She patted Christianne's cheek.

James glowered and reached inside his coat, withdrawing

457

an official-looking rolled parchment. "Christianne will be mistress of her own home when we are wed, Nell," he said, endeavoring to sound stern. "We put in to the Caribees en route to New Orleans, and I have a bill of sale here for a fine plantation, on Martinique, *Le Reine du Ciel*, it is named. She and the child will be well provided for, never fear." God's blood, Nell Flagg was an infuriating baggage, he thought angrily. From her tone of voice, one would have thought he was some sort of monster, a woman-beater, or worse!

"Aye, happen she will," Nell agreed, though appearing unconvinced, *"if* that do be what she wants. Well, lovey, what say ye? Will ye marry this lustful rogue and go with him t' the Caribees, or nay?"

Two pairs of eyes fastened on her keenly. Christianne hid a smile. For once, James' usual confidence seemed to be foundering on the rocks of doubt! It would not hurt to play with him a little longer, she thought mischievously. He would learn how it felt to be teased, rather than the teaser!

"Well," she said thoughtfully, "I believe I should ponder this matter a while yet. You see, Aunt Nell, I am not at all certain that I can marry a man who believes me capable of harming a friend, nor one who swears undying love to me and then vows he loves another when he is rambling with fever!" She side-eyed him.

"What other?" James exploded, striding across the room to her bedside, where she was cozily tucked into Nell Flagg's own massive four-poster. "Name her!" he challenged.

"Amanda de Villarin," Christianne supplied immediately. "Your fevered mutterings made for interesing listening, sir, believe me! I had oft wondered why it was you had named your vessel the *Fair Amanda*. Well, I found out during our trek along the Madagascan coast, in no uncertain fashion!"

"So that was the cause of your sudden coldness towards me!" James exclaimed. "And in all these months you said nothing, never thought to ask me about Amanda?"

"Oh, I thought of it often enough, sir!" she retorted. "But I hoped that in time you would tell me yourself, without my prompting."

"I am no mind reader, madam, that I can guess the questions that fill your pretty head!" James growled. "And besides, that question would never have occurred to me, for what was between Amanda and I happened years ago, and was over and done with before she even met her Don Miguel. If I spoke of my love for her, 'twas but my mind reliving the past on account of the fever. 'Tis you that I love, Christianne, only you," he vowed, taking her in his arms, "now and for all time."

"Mmmm," she murmured ambiguously, "be that as it may, what of your certainty that 'twas I who harmed Ben? Can you explain that so smoothly, you rogue?"

"Aye, I doubted you," he admitted, "I doubted you for several weeks. I never questioned that you were not guilty until we were cast ashore in the cove. Our solitude there gave me opportunity to reassess what I knew of your character. It dawned gradually," he said, a smile tugging at his lips, "that despite your *many* faults, you had always proved very loyal to your friends—that trio of ragtag thieves; the mute, Ox; your shaggy hound; even Flynn, before you learned his true character! . . . 'Could such a loyal wench have cold-heartedly flung a dagger into gentle Ben, who was her friend?' I asked myself. The answer was, 'Nay, never!' " He gently grasped her chin and tilted her head up so that she looked him full in the face. "Does that satisfy you, minx?" he asked, his green eyes caressing her.

She smiled. "Aye, sir. For the time being, anyway!"

He bent his head to kiss her but as their lips touched, she thrust her hands up between their chests and gently pushed him away. "Nay, not now!" she whispered, "My Aunt Nell!"

James chuckled and hauled her into his arms. The statue of Aphrodite, still draped with the red-feather boa, seemed to wink at him encouragingly. "Your aunt, my sweet, has gone, long since. Did I not tell you that, though a madam, she is every inch a lady? She may mot know whem it is correct to enter a room, but by the gods, she knows, when to leave one!"

James and Christianne walked arm in arm down Royal Street towards the Vieux Carré. The market was filled with people: somber-dressed Spanish and French matrons, quadroons of exotic and dark-eyed beauty with vivid *tignons* on their heads, gentlemen and ladies in pretty silks and satins, as well as ordinary folk in scratchy homespun and serviceable *cord du roi*. The air was warm and rich with the strange, exciting aroma of chickory-flavored coffee, jambalaya, the tang of citrus fruits and the perfume of the cape jasmine and magnolias. Christianne inhaled deeply, glad they had chosen to walk to the priest's home, rather than taking a carriage.

"You were right, I do love it here!" she exclaimed, a happy smile lighting her face. "And I adore my Aunt Nell, and I love you, too, James," she added, almost, it seemed, as an afterthought.

"I'm glad to hear it," he said dryly. "I would hate to think we'd finally settled it that you did, only to hear you'd changed your mind, you fickle wench."

"Aunt Nell says that my fickleness, as you put it, is but a part of my condition," Christianne replied pertly. "I'm afraid you'll just have to put up with it for a little longer." She patted her belly, beautifully rounded with child. "La! He kicked again!" she exclaimed, her elfin face radiant, her eyes deep blue pools that shimmered with happiness.

"Aye, and if we're to make an 'honest woman' of you as your aunt wishes, before the babe makes its appearance, we'd best be on our way to have the banns read," James said with a grin.

Christianne nodded, but it was apparent she had not really heard him, for she stopped in her tracks and stared openly at an old black woman who was making a beeline across the cobbles toward them. She wore an old, calico dress and a vivid tartan *tignon*.

"*Gris-gris!* You wish to buy *gris-gris, madame?*" she wheedled hopefully, sidling up to Christianne. Smiling a crafty, gap-toothed smile, she jiggled what looked like a cloth sachet in Christianne's face. "It will rid you of any rivals for your husband's affection *madame!*"

"We want no *gris-gris*, Lilah," James said sternly, leading Christianne away. "Be off with you, and find someone else who believes in your voodoo nonsense!"

The black woman scowled, muttered darkly under her breath and turned to pounce on yet another passerby.

Christianne craned her neck to watch her as James strode on across the cobbles, towing her in his wake. "Wait," she cried, "I wanted to see what she was selling!"

"No, you don't," James insisted cheerfully, "Lilah's just an addled old woman who believes she's a voodoo doctor, a priestess of voodoo, black magic! These women fancy they can make spells, tell fortunes or have other special powers."

Christianne smiled eagerly and grasped him by the elbow.

"Fortunes? Oh, please, let's go back! Mayhap this Lilah can tell me if the babe will be boy or girl, and if we'll be happy together," she grimaced, "at long last. The gypsy in Barcelona told me—"

"Fortune tellers!" James cut in scornfully. "You have no need of fortune tellers!" He grinned. "Indeed, mistress, *I* will tell you your future with such accuracy it will astound you!"

"You? But you have no such powers!" she scoffed.

"Oh, but I have, my love," he insisted, "I have powers such as you have never dreamed of!"

She eyed him warily, well-used to his teasing. His hand-

461

some face was serious, yet there was a suspicion of a twinkle in his green eyes.

"I don't believe you," she accused at length.

"Many have not, but they have come to believe 'ere long," James said mysteriously, drawing her into the shadowed doorway of a galleried, Spanish-style house. "My predictions will make your *gitana* in Spain seem but a charlatan," he promised. "Now, let me see."

He lifted her hand, inspecting the palm intently. "Aha!" he exclaimed, " 'tis all here, my lass, for all who know to read. I see a happy life ahead for you, and a handsome, russet-haired husband, and a fine red-headed boy-child to dandle on his lap."

"Red-headed?" Christianne giggled. "La! I hope not!"

"Silence, wench, I am not yet done," he chided sternly. "Ah, there are more children here, five, mayhap six, in all, all fine, lusty lads like the first-born—"

"No girls?" Christianne interrupted.

"Not a one! But 'tis for the best, since their mother was ever a plaguesome hellion!" he said with a grin.

She snorted. "And what of my husband? Will he be faithful to me as the day is long—or will his eyes follow each twitching skirt that passes?" Christianne questioned, holding back her laugher.

"Nay, minx, he will have eyes for only you, like a wagon-horse with blinkers on! He will love you, honor you, cherish and keep you, always," he said softly, all teasing done with as he drew her into his embrace. He kissed her softly-parted lips, then his mouth travelled along the curve of her cheek to her ear. "Always," he repeated huskily, his breath warm and exciting.

Christianne melted into his arms with a sigh of pleasure, snuggling against his broad chest with a deep sigh of contentment.

"Aye," she murmured dreamily, "just as I will love and honor and cherish him always."